P9-BAU-077

"BEHOLD,
HE COMETH
WITH CLOUDS;
AND EVERY EYE
SHALL SEE HIM."

–REVELATION 1:7

Praise for the Novels
of Raymond Khoury

The Sign

"There's a fine line between science and religion. Too often that border becomes blurred, or confused, usually through either ignorance or fanaticism, which nearly always leads to conflict. *The Sign* expertly explores this ever-shifting line of myth and reality. But this book is not a religious thriller. Nobody is trying to destroy the Catholic Church; Christ is not being cloned; and there are no ancient theological secrets that could change the course of history. Instead, Raymond Khoury explores the concept of religion by posing the ever-present question *What If?* in a unique and appealing way. Protagonists Matt Sherwood, a former car thief (which is interesting in and of itself), and news reporter Gracie Logan are whom Khoury calls upon to determine if God has finally decided to reveal himself, or is something more sinister afoot? I like that in a Khoury book the title actually means something. That was true in *The Last Templar* and *The Sanctuary,* and it is equally true here. The sign is important. This story captivates with plausibility and imagination. It's fiercely intelligent and equally curious. Khoury casts his fictional world in a dark pall—a fitting atmosphere for his protagonists as they race both time and shadowy instincts toward a scintillating conclusion. *The Sign* is a rapid-paced adventure that delivers equal quantities of story and lesson, neither one suffering in the process. Khoury's background as a screenwriter shows. He is especially adept at action scenes. His expertly chosen verbs cause the scenes to leap from the page. You can literally feel the blows as they're landed, wince as the bullets find their marks. He has an intense brand of storytelling all his own. *The Sign* is a prize to be savored."

—Steve Berry, *New York Times* bestselling author of
The Charlemagne Pursuit

"[A] solid thriller . . . unrelenting action and a suitably twisted ending." —*Publishers Weekly*

"*The Last Templar* made [Khoury] a bestseller, and he's now one of the top writers of intelligent thrillers, and *The Sign* is a real humdinger that taps into some of our deepest fears over the state of the planet." —*Evening Telegraph* (Peterborough)

continued . . .

"Khoury pitches an eloquent argument for the value of personal responsibility toward one another while maintaining careful stewardship of the earth. This is a thoughtful book with a powerful message and yet also a thrilling read with compelling, well-developed characters. Highly recommended."
                                                    —*Library Journal*

"Khoury's thrillers engage the reader's mind, even as they move at a breakneck pace. His first two novels were first-rate adventure yarns, and so is this one. . . . Readers who like their thrillers to have a solid intellectual component will enjoy Khoury's books very much. Given the high quality of each of his novels, it seems fair to say that he may be around for a while."
                                                    —*Booklist*

"It weaves elements of religion, the military, and science together to create a well-written and descriptive story. . . . *The Sign* is an exciting and entertaining adventure that will not disappoint."
                                                    —Armchair Interviews

"A pulse-pounding thriller that spans continents in pursuit of an audacious . . . high-tech conspiracy to reshape the global balance of power, told in eight-five punchy chapters, which cries out Hollywood blockbuster."
                                                    —*The Daily Telegraph* (UK)

The Sanctuary

"[Khoury] follows up the thrills of *The Last Templar* with . . . more thrills."
                                                    —*The Tampa Tribune*

"A high-octane roller-coaster ride of thrills and spills. . . . Khoury is a screenwriter and the novel's tight construction and hyperfast pacing owe an obvious debt to that discipline."
                                                    —*Irish Mail on Sunday*

"Ancient, mysterious clues mingle with the latest scientific advances in this cinematic thriller. The pace is fast, the dialogue sharp, the characters plausible. Khoury knows what he is doing."
                                                    —*Evening Times* (Glasgow)

"Fresh and exciting. . . . Khoury makes the conspiracy feel utterly believable and imbues his characters with infectious passion for finding the truth. A surefire hit with fans of conspiracy-based historical thrillers."
                                                    —*Booklist*

THE
SIGN

RAYMOND
KHOURY

A SIGNET BOOK

SIGNET
Published by New American Library, a division of
Penguin Group (USA) Inc., 375 Hudson Street,
New York, New York 10014, USA
Penguin Group (Canada), 90 Eglinton Avenue East, Suite 700, Toronto,
Ontario M4P 2Y3, Canada (a division of Pearson Penguin Canada Inc.)
Penguin Books Ltd., 80 Strand, London WC2R 0RL, England
Penguin Ireland, 25 St. Stephen's Green, Dublin 2,
Ireland (a division of Penguin Books Ltd.)
Penguin Group (Australia), 250 Camberwell Road, Camberwell, Victoria
3124, Australia (a division of Pearson Australia Group Pty. Ltd.)
Penguin Books India Pvt. Ltd., 11 Community Centre, Panchsheel Park,
New Delhi - 110 017, India
Penguin Group (NZ), 67 Apollo Drive, Rosedale, North Shore 0632,
New Zealand (a division of Pearson New Zealand Ltd.)
Penguin Books (South Africa) (Pty.) Ltd., 24 Sturdee Avenue,
Rosebank, Johannesburg 2196, South Africa

Penguin Books Ltd., Registered Offices:
80 Strand, London WC2R 0RL, England

Published by Signet, an imprint of New American Library, a division of Penguin
Group (USA) Inc. Previously published in a Dutton edition.

First Signet Edition, April 2010
10 9 8 7 6 5 4 3 2 1

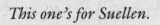

This one's for Suellen.

The idea that religion and politics don't mix was invented by the Devil to keep Christians from running their own country.
—Jerry Falwell

My kingdom is not of this world.
—Jesus Christ (John 18:36)

Prologue

I.

Skeleton Coast, Namibia—Two years ago

As the bottom of the ravine rushed up to meet him, the dry, rocky landscape hurtling past Danny Sherwood miraculously slowed right down to a crawl. Not that the extra time was welcome. All it did was allow the realization to play itself out, over and over, in his harrowed mind. The gut-wrenching, agonizing realization that, without a shadow of a doubt, he would be dead in a matter of seconds.

And yet the day had started off with so much promise.

After almost three years, his work—his and the rest of the team's—was finally done. And, he thought with an inward grin, the rewards would soon be his to enjoy.

It had been a hard slog. The project itself had been daunting enough, from a scientific point of view. The work conditions—the tight deadline, the even tighter security, the virtual exile from family and friends for all those intense and lonely months—were even more of a challenge. But today, as he had looked up at the pure blue sky and breathed in the dry, dusty air of this godforsaken corner of the planet, it all seemed worthwhile.

There would be no IPO; that much had been made

clear from the start. Neither Microsoft nor Google would be paying big bucks to acquire the technology. The project, he'd been told, was being developed for the military. Still, a significant on-success bonus had been promised to every member of the team. In his case, it would be enough to provide financial security for him, his parents back home, and for any not-too-overly profligate wife he might end up with along with as many kids as he could possibly envisage having—if he ever got around to it. Which he conceivably would, years from now, after he'd had his fun and enjoyed the spoils of his work. For the moment, though, it wasn't on his radar. He was only twenty-nine years old.

Yes, the cushy future that was materializing before him was a far cry from the more austere days of his childhood in Worcester, Massachusetts. As he made his way across the parched desert soil, past the mess tent and the landing pad where the chopper was being loaded for their departure, and over to the project director's tent, he thought back on the experience—from the lab work to the various field tests, culminating with this one, out here in this lost netherworld.

Danny wished he'd be allowed to share the excitement of it all with a few people outside the project. His parents, firstly. He could just imagine how stunned, and proud, they would be. Danny was making good on all the promise, all the lofty expectations they'd heaped on him since, well, birth. His thoughts migrated to his older brother, Matt. He'd get a huge kick out of this. Probably try to get Danny to back him in some dodgy, hare-brained, borderline-legal scheme, but what the hell, there'd be plenty to go around. There were also a few big-headed jerks in the business that he would have loved to gloat to about all this, given the chance. But he knew that any disclosure outside the team was strictly—

strictly—not allowed. That much had also been made clear from the start. The project was covert. The nation's defense was at stake. The word *treason* was mentioned. And so he'd kept his mouth shut, which wasn't too hard. He was used to it. The highly competitive industry he was in had a deeply ingrained subterranean culture. Hundreds of millions of dollars were often at stake. And when it came down to it, the choice between an eight-figure bank account and a dingy cell in a supermax federal penitentiary was a no-brainer.

He was about to knock on the door of the tent—it was a huge, air-conditioned, semirigid wall tent, with a solid door and glass windows—when something made him pull his hand back.

Raised voices. Not just raised, but angry.

Seriously angry.

He leaned closer to the door.

"You should have told me. It's my project, goddammit," a man's voice erupted. "You should have told me right from the start."

Danny knew that voice well: Dominic Reece, his mentor and the project's lead scientist—its PI, short for principal investigator. A professor of electrical engineering and computer science at MIT, Reece occupied hallowed ground in Danny's world. He'd taught Danny in several of his formative classes and had kept a close eye on Danny's work throughout his PhD before inviting him to join his team for the project all those months ago. It was an opportunity—and an honor—Danny couldn't possibly pass up. And while Danny knew that the professor had a habit of expressing his opinions more forcefully and vociferously than most, he detected something else in his voice now. There was a hurt, an indignation that he hadn't heard before.

"What would your reaction have been?" The second

man's voice, which wasn't familiar to Danny, was equally inflamed.

"The same," Reece replied emphatically.

"Come on, just think about it for a second. Think about what we can do together. What we can achieve."

Reece's fury was unabated. "I can't help you do this. I can't be a party to it."

"Dom, please—"

"No."

"Think about what we can—"

"No," Reece interrupted. "Forget it. There's no way." The words had an unmistakable finality to them.

A leaden quiet skulked behind the door for a few tense moments; then Danny heard the second man say, "I wish you hadn't said that."

"What the hell does that mean?" Reece shot back.

There was no reply.

Then Reece's voice came back, tinged with a sudden unease. "What about the others? You haven't told any of them, have you." An assertion, not a question.

"No."

"When were you planning on letting them in on your revised mission statement?"

"I wasn't sure. I had to get your answer first. I was hoping you'd help me win them over. Convince them to be part of this."

"Well, that's not going to happen," Reece retorted angrily. "As a matter of fact, I'd like to get them all the hell away from here as soon as possible."

"I can't let you do that, Dom."

The words seemed to freeze Reece in his tracks. "What do you mean, you can't let me do that?" he said defiantly.

A pregnant silence greeted his question. Danny could just visualize Reece processing it.

"So what are you saying? You're not going to . . ." Reece's voice trailed off for a beat, then came back, with the added urgency of a sudden, horrible realization. "Jesus. Have you completely lost your mind?"

The outrage in the old man's tone froze Danny's spine.

He heard Reece say, "You son of a bitch," heard thudding footfalls striding toward him, toward the door, heard the second man call out to Reece, "Dom, don't," then heard a third voice say, "Don't do that, Reece," a voice Danny knew, a harsh voice, the voice of a man who'd creeped Danny out from the moment he'd first met him: Maddox, the project's shaven-headed, stone-faced head of security, the one with the missing ear and the star-shaped burn around it, the man he knew was nicknamed "The Bullet" by his equally creepy men. Then he heard Reece say, "Go to hell," and the door swung open, and Reece was suddenly there, standing before Danny, a surprised look in his eyes. Danny heard a distinctive, metallic double-click, a sound he'd heard in a hundred movies but never in real life, the all-too-familiar sound of a gun slide, and the second man, the man who'd been arguing with Reece all along and whom Danny now recognized, turned to the Bullet and yelled, "No—"

—just as a muffled, high-pitched cough echoed from behind Reece, then another, before the scientist jerked forward, his face crunched with pain, his legs giving way as he tumbled onto Danny.

Danny faltered back, the suddenness of it all overwhelming his senses as he struggled to keep Reece from falling to the ground. A warm, sticky feeling seeped down his hands as he struggled to support the stricken man, a thick, dark red liquid gushing out of Reece and soaking Danny's arms and clothes.

He couldn't hold him. Reece thudded heavily onto the ground, exposing the inside of the tent, the second man standing there, horrified, frozen in shock, next to the Bullet, who had a gun in his hand. Its muzzle was now leveled straight at Danny.

Danny dived to one side as a couple of shots cleaved through the air he'd been occupying; then he just tore off, running away from the tent and the fallen professor as fast as he could.

He was a dozen yards or so away when he dared glance back and saw Maddox emerging from the tent, radio in one hand, the gun in the other, his eyes locking onto the receding Danny like lasers as he bolted after him. With his heart in his throat, Danny sprinted through the temporary campsite—there were a few smaller tents, for the handful of other scientists who, like him, had been recruited for the project. He almost slammed into two of them, top minds from the country's best universities, who were emerging from one of the tents just as he was nearing it.

"They killed Reece," he yelled to them, pausing momentarily and waving frantically back toward the main tent. "They killed him." He looked back and saw Maddox closing in inexorably, seemingly carried forward on winged feet, and took off again, glancing back to see his friends turn to the onrushing man with confused looks, crimson sprouts erupting from their chests as Maddox gunned them down without even slowing.

Danny had ducked sideways, behind the mess tent, out of breath, his leg muscles burning, his mind churning desperately for escape options, when the project's two ageing Jeeps appeared before him, parked under their makeshift shelter. He flung the first car's door open, spurred the engine to life, threw the car into gear, and floored the accelerator, storming off in a spray of sand and dust just as Maddox rounded the tent.

Danny kept an eye on the rearview mirror as his Jeep charged across the harsh gravel plain. He clenched the steering wheel through bloodless knuckles, confused thoughts assaulting his senses from all directions, his heart feeling like it was jackhammering its way out of his chest, and did the only thing he could think of, which was to keep the car aimed straight ahead, across the deserted terrain, away from the camp, away from that crazed, insane maniac who'd killed his mentor and his friends, all while fighting for a way around the horrifying truth of his predicament, which was that there was nowhere to run. They were in the middle of nowhere, with no villages or habitations anywhere near, not for hundreds of miles.

That was the whole point of being there.

That fear didn't have much time to torment him as a loud, throaty buzz soon burst through his frazzled thoughts. He looked back and saw the camp's chopper coming straight at him, reeling him in effortlessly. He pegged the gas pedal to the floor, hard, sending the Jeep bounding over the small rocks and undulations of the outback, slamming his head against the inside of the car's canvas roof with each jarring leap, avoiding the occasional boulder and the lonely bunches of dried-up quiver trees that dotted the deathly landscape.

The chopper was now on his tail, its engine noise deafening, its rotor wash drowning the Jeep in a swirling sandstorm. Danny strained to see ahead through the tornado of dust, not that it made much difference since there was no road to follow, as the chopper dropped down heavily on the car's roof, crushing the thin struts holding up the roof and almost tearing Danny's head off.

He veered left, then right, fishtailing the car as he fought to avoid the flying predator's claws, sweat seeping down his face, the car careening wildly over rocks and cactus bushes. The chopper was never more than mere feet from the Jeep, connecting with it in thunderous blows, slapping it from side to side like it was toying with a hockey puck. The thought of stopping didn't occur to Danny: He was running on pure adrenaline, his survival instincts choking him in their grasp, an irrational hope of escape propelling him forward. And just then, in that maelstrom of panic and fear, something shifted, something changed, and he sensed the chopper pulling up slightly, felt a spike of hope that maybe, just maybe, he might make it out of that nightmare alive, and the twisting cloud of sand around his Jeep lifted—

—and that was when he saw the canyon, cutting across the terrain dead ahead of him with sadistic inevitability, a vast limestone trench snaking across the landscape like something from the Wild West, the one he'd seen in countless cowboy films and had hoped to visit someday but hadn't yet, the one he now knew, with a savage certainty, that he'd never get a chance to see, as the Jeep flew off the canyon's edge and into the dry desert air.

II.

Wadi Natrun, Egypt

Sitting cross-legged in his usual spot high up on the mountain, with the barren valley and the endless desert spread out below him, the old priest felt a rising unease. During his last few visits to that desolate place, he'd sensed a more ominous ring to the words that were re-verberating inside his head. And today, there was something distinctly portentous about them.

And then it came. A question that sent a straightening spasm shooting up his spine.

"Are you ready to serve?"

His eyes fluttered open, blinking against the soft dawn light. He glanced around instinctively, as he'd done many times before, but it was pointless, as it had been each time before. He was alone up there. There was no one around. Not a soul, human or animal. Nothing at all, as far as the eye could see.

Despite the early-morning chill, sweat droplets sprouted across his bald pate. He swallowed hard, and concentrated again.

And then it came again.

The voice, the whisper, coming from inside his own head.

"The time of our Lord will soon be upon you. Are you prepared to serve?"

Hesitantly, with a tremor in his voice, Father Jerome opened his mouth and stammered, "Yes, of course. Whatever you ask of me. I am your servant."

There was no reply at first. The old priest could feel the individual droplets of sweat sliding down the rugged skin on his forehead, one after another, skating across the ridge of his brow before dropping onto his cheek. He could almost hear them trickling down, a slow, tortuous progress across his tightened, weather-beaten face.

Then the voice inside his head came back.

"Are you ready to lead your people to salvation? Are you prepared to fight for them? To show them the errors of their ways, even though they may not want to listen?"

"Yes," Father Jerome cried out, his voice cracking with equal doses of passion and fear. "Yes, of course. But how? When?"

A suffocating silence gripped the mountain; then the voice returned, and simply told him, "Soon."

Chapter 1

Amundsen Sea, Antarctica—Present day

The static that hissed through the tiny, noise-isolating earpiece disappeared, replaced by the authoritative-yet-soothing voice of the show's anchorman.

"Talk us through why this is happening, Grace?"

Just then, another wall of ice crumbled behind her and collapsed on itself, crackling like distant thunder. Grace Logan—Gracie, to her friends—turned away from the camera and watched as the entire cliff plummeted into the gray-blue water and disappeared in an angry eruption of spray.

Perfect timing, she thought with a glimmer of satisfaction, a brief respite from the solemnity she'd been feeling since she'd arrived on the ship the day before.

Under normal circumstances, this could well have been a pleasant, sunny, late-December day, December being the height of summer in the Southern Hemisphere.

Today was different.

Today, nature was in turmoil.

It felt as if the very fabric of the earth was being ripped apart. Which it was. The slab of ice that was tearing itself off the rest of the continent was the size of Texas.

Not exactly the kind of Christmas present the planet needed.

The breakup of the ice shelf was now in its third day, and it was only getting started. The cataclysm had kicked up a ghostly mist that thinned out the sun's warming rays, and the cold was starting to get to Gracie, even with the adrenaline coursing through her. She could see that the rest of her team—Dalton Kwan, the young, breezy Hawaiian cameraman she'd worked with regularly over the past three years, and Howard "Finch" Fincher, their older, über-fastidious and annoyingly stoic veteran producer—were also far from comfortable, but the footage they were airing was well worth it, especially since, as far as she could tell, they were the only news crew around.

She'd been out there for over an hour, standing on the starboard observation deck of the RRS *James Clark Ross,* and despite the thermals and the gloves, her fingers and toes were shivering. The royal research ship, a beefy three-hundred-foot floating oceanographic and geo-physical laboratory operated by the British Antarctic Survey project, was currently less than half a mile off the coast of Western Antarctica, its distinctive deep red hull the only blip of color in an otherwise bleak palette of whites, blues, and grays. Gracie, Dalton, and Finch had been on the continent for a couple of weeks, shooting footage in the Terra Firma Islands for her big global-warming documentary. They had been ready to pack up and head home for Christmas, which was only days away, when the call from the news desk back in D.C. had come in, informing them that the shelf's breakup had started. The news hadn't been widely circulated at that point; a contact of the network inside the NSIDC—the National Snow and Ice Data Center, whose scientists used satellite data to track changes in the spread and thickness of the polar ice caps—had given them the heads-up on the sly. With the competition snoozing and the *James Clark Ross* a day's sail away from the action and already heading toward it, Gracie and her crew had jumped on the opportunity for an exclusive scoop. The BAS had graciously agreed to have them on board to cover the event, going so far as to arrange for a Royal Navy chopper to ferry them in from the island.

Several of the ship's onboard scientists were also on deck, watching the walls of ice disintegrate. A couple of them were filming, using handheld video cameras. Most of the crew were also out there, staring in resigned and awed silence.

Gracie turned back to face the camera and pulled her microphone closer. In between the irregular, thunderous collapses of the cliff face, the air reverberated with the distant, muffled retorts of the ice's tortured movement farther inland.

"This breakup was probably caused by a number of factors, Jack, but the main suspect in this very complicated investigation is just plain old meltwater."

She heard more hissing as the signal bounced off a couple of satellites and traveled ten thousand miles to the network's climate-controlled newsroom in D.C. and back; then Roxberry's voice returned, slightly confused. "Meltwater?"

"That's right, Jack," she explained. "Pools of water that build up on the surface of the ice as it melts. This meltwater is heavier than the ice it's sitting on, so—basic law of gravity—it finds its way down into cracks, and as more and more water pushes through, it acts like a wedge and these cracks grow into rifts that grow into canyons, and if there's enough meltwater to keep pushing through, the ice shelf eventually just snaps off."

The physics of it was simple. The highest, coldest, and windiest continent on the planet, an area one and a half times as big as the United States, was almost entirely covered by a dome of ice over two miles thick at its center. Heavy snowfalls blanket it in winter, then spread downward by gravity, flowing like ice-cold lava to the coast. And when this ice floe runs out of land, it keeps going, beyond the edge of land, but it doesn't sink: It floats, cantilevering over the sea in what we refer to as ice shelves. They can be over a mile thick at the point where they start floating, tapering to a no-less-staggering quarter mile at the water's edge, where they end in cliffs of a hundred feet or more above the waterline.

There had been a handful of major breakups in the last decade, but none this big. Also, they were rarely captured live on camera. They were usually only detected long after the event, after scrutinizing and comparing satellite images. And even though what Gracie was witnessing was only a localized portion of the overall upheaval—the collapse of towering cliffs of ice at the shelf's seaward edge—it was still an astounding and deeply troubling sight. In twelve years in television news, a career she'd dived into straight after getting her BA in political science from Cornell, Gracie had witnessed a lot of tragedies, and this one ranked right up there with the worst of them.

She was watching the planet fall apart—literally. "So the big question then is," Roxberry asked, "why is it happening now? I mean, as I understand it, this ice shelf has been around since the end of the last ice age, and that was, what, twelve thousand years ago?"

"It's happening because of us, Jack. Because of the greenhouse gases we're generating. We're seeing it at both poles, here, up in the Arctic, in Greenland. And it isn't just part of a natural cycle. Almost every expert I've talked to is now convinced that the melting is accelerating and telling me we're close to some kind of tipping point, a point of no return—because of man-made global warming."

Another block of ice disintegrated and crashed into the sea.

"And the concern here is that this ice shelf breaking off and melting will contribute to rising sea levels?" Roxberry asked.

"Well, not directly. Most of this ice shelf is already floating on water, so it doesn't affect sea levels in itself. Think of it as an ice cube floating in a glass of water. When it melts, it doesn't raise the level of water in the glass."

"Doesn't it?"

"I guess I'm not the only one who's forgotten their sixth-grade physics." She grinned.

"But you said there's an indirect effect on global sea levels." Roxberry's voice exuded expertise, as if he were generously allowing her a chance to display her knowledge.

"Well, this area, the West Antarctic ice sheet, is the one place on the planet that scientists have been worried about most, in terms of ice melts. More specifically, they're worried about the massive glaciers sitting on land, behind this ice shelf. They're not floating."

"So if they melted," Roxberry added, "sea levels would rise."

"Exactly. Up until now, ice shelves like this one have been keeping back the glaciers, sort of like a cork that's holding in the contents of a bottle. Once the ice shelf breaks off, the cork's gone. There's nothing left to stop the glaciers from sliding into the sea—and if they do, the global sea levels rise. And this melting is happening much faster than forecasts had predicted. Even the data we have from last year is now considered too optimistic. In terms of disaster scenarios due to climate change, Antarctica was considered a sleeping giant. Well, the giant's now awake. And, by the looks of it, he's really grumpy."

Roxberry quipped, "I'm trying real hard to avoid saying this could just be the tip of the iceberg—"

"A wise choice, Jack," she interjected. She could just picture the smug, self-satisfied grin lighting up his perma-tanned face and groaned inwardly at the thought. "A grateful audience salutes you."

"But that's what we're talking about here, isn't it?"

"Absolutely. Once these glaciers slide into the sea, it'll be too late to do anything about it, and . . ."

Her voice suddenly trailed off and dried up, as something distracted her: a ripple of sudden commotion, shrieks and gasps of shock and outstretched arms pointing out at the ice shelf. The words still caught in her throat as she saw Dalton's head rise from behind the viewfinder of the camera and look beyond her. Gracie spun around, facing away from the camera. And that was when she saw it.

In the sky. A couple of hundred feet above the collapsing ice shelf.

A bright, shimmering sphere of light.

It just appeared there, and wasn't moving.

Gracie concentrated her gaze on it and inched over to the railing. She didn't understand what she was looking at, but whatever it was, she couldn't take her eyes off it.

The object—no, she wasn't even sure it was an object. It had a spherical shape, but somehow, it didn't seem . . . *physical*. It had an ethereal lightness to it, as if the air itself was glowing. And its brightness wasn't uniform. It was more subtle, graded, intense at its core, then gradually thinning out, as in a close-up of an eye. It had an unstable, fragile quality to it. Like melting ice, or, rather, just water, suspended in midair and lit up, if that were possible, only Gracie knew it wasn't.

She darted a look at Dalton, who was angling the camera toward the sighting. "Are you getting this?" she blurted.

"Yeah, but," he shot back, looking over at her, his face scrunched up in sheer confusion, "what the hell is it?"

Chapter 2

Gracie's eyes were locked onto it. It was just there, suspended in the pallid sky over the edge of the ice shelf. Mesmerizing in an otherworldly, surreal way.

"What *is* that?" Finch asked. His hands went up to his glasses, fidgeting slightly with their position, as if it would help clarify things.

"I don't know." A surge of adrenaline spiked through her as she struggled to process what she was seeing. A quick, almost instinctive trawl through the possibilities of what it could be didn't get any hits.

This was unlike anything she was even vaguely familiar with.

She glanced across at the knot of scientists crowding the railings. They were talking and gesticulating excitedly, trying to make sense of it too.

"Gracie? What is that behind you?" Roxberry's voice came booming back through her earpiece.

For a second, she'd forgotten this was going out live. "You're seeing this?"

A couple of seconds for her question and his reply to bounce off a satellite or two, then he came back. "It's not perfectly clear, but yeah, we're getting it—what is it?"

She composed herself and faced the camera squarely, trying to keep any quiver out of her voice. "I don't know, Jack. It just suddenly appeared. It seems to be some kind of corona, a halo of some sort . . . Hang on."

She looked around, scanning the sky, checking to see if anything else was around, noting the sun's veiled position, unconsciously logging her surroundings. Nothing had changed. Nothing else was out there apart from their ship and the . . . *What was it?* She couldn't even think of an appropriate name for it. It was still shimmering brightly, half-transparent, its texture reminding her of a gargantuan, deep-sea jellyfish, floating in midair. And it seemed to be rotating, ever so slowly, giving it a real sense of depth.

And, oddly, she thought, a sense of being somehow . . . *alive.*

She stared at it, resisting all kinds of competing, outlandish thoughts, and focused her mind on getting a handle on its size. As big as a large hot-air balloon, she first thought, then adjusted her thinking upward. Bigger. Maybe as big as a fireball in a fireworks display. It was huge. It was hard to judge without a point of reference for scale. She ran a visual comparison to the height of the cliff face below, which she knew to be roughly a hundred and fifty feet tall. It seemed to be around the same size, maybe a hundred and fifty feet in diameter, maybe more.

Dalton looked up from behind the camera and asked, "You think it's some freaky aurora borealis thing?"

She'd been thinking the same thing, wondering if it was a trick of the light, an illusion caused by a reflection off the ice. In Antarctica, the sun never set during the austral summer. It just circled around at the horizon, a little higher during the "day," a little lower—almost a sunset—during the "night." It had taken some getting used to and it played tricks on you, but somehow Gracie didn't think it explained what she was seeing. The sighting seemed more substantial than that.

"Maybe," she replied, almost to herself, lost in her thoughts, "but I don't think it's the time of year for them . . . and I'm pretty sure they only appear when it's dark."

"Gracie?" Roxberry again, waiting for an answer. Reminding her that she was going out live.

To a world audience.

Christ Almighty.

She tried to relax and put on a genial smile for the camera, despite the tiny alarms buzzing through her. "This is just . . . It's pretty amazing, Jack. I've never seen anything like it. Maybe someone else on this ship knows what it is. We've got quite a few experts on board."

Dalton lifted his tripod and tracked along with Gracie as she edged over to the scientists and crew members on deck with her, keeping the apparition in frame.

The others were discussing it in excited, heated tones, but something about their body language worried Gracie. If it was a rare, but natural, phenomenon, they'd be reacting differently. Somehow, she got the impression that they weren't comfortable with what they were seeing. Not just uncomfortable, but . . . rattled.

They don't know what it is.

One of them, who'd been watching it through binoculars, turned and met her gaze. He was an older man, a paleoclimatologist she'd met on arrival named Jeb Simmons. She read the same confusion, the same unease, on his face that had to be radiating from hers. It only confirmed her feeling.

She was about to speak up when another wave of gasps broke out across the deck. She turned in time to see the shimmering shape suddenly pulse, brightening up to a blazing radiance for a heartbeat before dimming back to its original pearlescent glare.

Gracie glanced at Simmons as Roxberry's excited voice crackled back. "Did it just flare up?"

She knew the image on the screen he was looking at would be grainy, maybe even a bit jumpy. The live video uplink back to the studio was always compromised, nowhere near as clear as the original, high-definition footage on Dalton's cameras.

"Jack, I don't know how clearly it's coming through to you, but from out here, I can tell you, it's not like anything I've seen before." She tried hard to hang on to her unflustered expression, but her heart was racing now. This didn't feel right.

She suddenly remembered something, and turned to Finch and Dalton. "How quickly can you get the bird up?"

Finch nodded and turned to Dalton. "Let's do it."

"We're sending the skycam up for a closer look," Gracie confirmed into her mike, then turned to Simmons, breathless, and clicked her mike off. "Tell me you know what this is," she said with a tense smile.

Simmons shook his head. "I wish I could. I've never seen anything like it."

"You've been here before, right?"

"Oh yes. This is my fourth winter out here."

"And your specialty's paleoclimatology, right?"

"I'm flattered." He smiled. "Yes."

"And yet . . ."

He shook his head again. "I'm stumped."

Gracie frowned, her mind spinning, and pointed at his binoculars. "May I?"

"Sure." He handed them over.

She looked through them. It didn't add anything to what she'd already observed. The shimmer was more pronounced. It appeared hazy, slightly more mirage-like . . . but it was definitely there. It was real.

She gave the binoculars back to Simmons as a few of the others congregated around them. They seemed as bewildered as he was. She darted a look behind them. Finch had the skycam's arms clicked into place while Dalton was double-checking the second camera's harness and settings, both of them keeping an eye on the sighting. She noticed the captain coming out on deck. Two crew members hurried to join him. Gracie turned to the others. "None of you have any idea what we're looking at here?"

"I first thought it might be a flare," one of the other crew members said, "but it's too big and too bright, and it's just there, you know? I mean, it's not moving, is it?"

The sleek noise of air being whipped around startled them just momentarily. It was a sound they'd heard earlier that day, when Gracie and Dalton had used the small, unmanned remote-controlled helicopter to get some panoramic establishing shots of the ice shelf.

Dalton shouted, "We've got liftoff," over the whirr of the skycam's rotor blades.

They turned to watch it rise. The Draganflyer X6 was an odd-looking but brilliant piece of engineering. It didn't look anything like a normal helicopter. It was more like a matte-black alien insect, something you'd expect to see in a Terminator movie. It consisted of a small central pod that was the size of a large mango and housed the electronics, gyroscopes, and battery. Three small collapsible arms extended out from it horizontally, at twelve, four, and eight o'clock positions. At the end of each arm was a whisper-quiet, brushless motor, each one driving two parallel sets of molded rotor blades, one above it and another underneath. Any type of camera could be fitted to the rig under its belly. It was all powered by rechargeable lithium batteries, and the whole thing was made of black carbon fiber that was incredibly strong and yet superlight—the Draganflyer, weighing less than five pounds, was a high-definition video camera with a helicopter-to-ground link included. It gave great aerial shots with minimal fuss, and Dalton never traveled anywhere without it.

Gracie was watching the black contraption rise above the deck and glide away slowly, heading toward the ice shelf, when a female voice yelled out, "Oh my God," and Gracie saw it too.

The sighting was changing again.

It flared up again, then dimmed down from its outward rim inward, shrinking until it was barely a tenth of its original size. It held there for a couple of tantalizing seconds, then slowly flared back to the way it was. And then its surface seemed to ripple, as if it were morphing into something else.

At first, Gracie wasn't sure what it was doing, but the second it started changing, something deep within her knotted. The sighting had clearly come alive. It was shapeshifting, twisting into itself, but always within the confines of its original envelope. It was taking on different compositions with alarming speed, all while keeping up its barely noticeable rotation, and they were all perfectly symmetrical, almost as if it were a kaleidoscope, but less angular, more rounded and organic. The patterns it took on melted from one to another continuously at an increasing, dazzling rate, and Gracie wasn't sure of what they were, but they reminded her of cellular structures. And in that very moment, she felt a deeply unsettling sensation, as if she were staring at the very fabric of life itself.

The small gathering froze, equally dumbstruck. Gracie glanced over at them. A whole range of emotion was etched across their faces, from awe and wonder to confusion—and fear. None of them was debating what it could be, not anymore. They just stood there, rooted to the deck, eyes fixated on it, their only words brief expressions of their amazement. Two of them—an older man and woman—crossed themselves.

Gracie saw Dalton check on the fixed camera, making sure it was still capturing the event. He held the skycam's remote control unit, which was suspended from a neck strap, at waist level, his fingers expertly controlling both joysticks.

She caught his gaze and moved her mike down. "This is . . . Jesus, Dalton. What's going on?"

He looked up at the sighting. "I don't know, but . . . Either Prince has a new concert tour coming up, or someone's spiked our coffee with some serious shit." Dalton could usually see the humor in anything, but right now, he sounded different to Gracie. His tone was drained of all light.

She heard a few gasps, and someone said, "It's slowing down." All eyes strained in nervous unison as the sighting moved to take on a final shape.

For a second, it felt to Gracie as if her heart had stopped beating. Every pore of her body was crackling with fearful tension as she stared dead ahead at it. Without daring to take her eyes off it, she said, almost to herself, "Jesus."

The brighter zones of the sphere were being consumed by a spreading darkness, and it kept going until the sphere's entire surface looked blackened and coarse, as if it had been carved from a lump of coal.

Chapter 3

A ripple of terror spread among the crowd. The apparition had lost all of its splendor. In the blink of an eye, it had gone from being strangely wonderful to sinister and lifeless.

Finch moved close to Gracie, both of them riveted by the ominous sight.

"This isn't good," he said.

Gracie didn't reply. She glanced down at the skycam's control box. The image on its small, five-inch LCD monitor was very clear, despite the light mist. Dalton had guided it in a wide, slight arc, in order for it not to come between them and the sighting. With the Draganflyer now more than halfway to the shelf, Gracie was able to get more of a sense of scale. The apparition dwarfed the approaching flying camera, like an elephant looming over an ant. It held the dark, lifeless skin it had assumed for a minute or so, bearing down on them with what seemed like a malevolent intent; then it flared up again, burning brightly, only this time, it took on a more distinct shape, defined by the light that was radiating with different strengths. It now looked unquestionably like a three-dimensional sphere, and at its core was a bright ball of light. Around it were four equal rings, running along the sphere's outer face, evenly spaced. As they weren't facing the ship head-on but were at a slight angle, they appeared like elongated ovals. The outer shell itself was brightly illuminated too, and rays of light were projecting outward from the core, between the rings, petering out slightly beyond the edge of the sphere. The whole display was hypnotic, especially as it blazed away against the dull, gray backdrop.

The sight was beyond breathtaking. It electrified the crowd and brought some of them to tears. The couple who had crossed themselves were holding each other close. Gracie could see their lips trembling in silent prayer. Her own body stiffened, and her legs went numb. She felt a confusing surge of euphoria and fear, which seemed echoed in the faces around her.

"Whoa." Dalton recoiled.

Finch was also motionless, gaping at it. "Tell me I'm not really seeing this," Finch said. "Tell me it's not really there."

"It is," Gracie confirmed as she just stood there, enthralled. "It absolutely is."

She held the mike up and struggled for words as everything around her faded to oblivion, a complete sensorial disconnect from her surroundings, her every thought consumed by the apparition. It was beyond understanding, beyond definition. After a moment, she emerged momentarily from her trance, and faced the camera again.

"I hope you're still getting this, Jack, 'cause everyone here is just stunned by this . . . I can't even begin to describe the sensation out here right now." Her eyes dropped away for a passing glance at Dalton's monitor. He was using the joysticks to zoom in on the apparition, which filled the screen with its radiance before he pulled back out.

She looked out at it again. The skycam was closing in on it. "How far from it do you think it is?" she asked Dalton.

"A hundred yards. Maybe less." His voice had a slight quiver in it as his eyes darted from the monitor to the apparition and back.

Gracie couldn't take her eyes off of it. "It's just magnificent, isn't it?"

"It's a sign," someone said. It was the woman Gracie had noticed crossing herself. Gracie looked over, and Dalton panned over to her.

"A sign? Of what?" another answered.

"I don't know, but . . . she's right. Look at it. It's a sign of . . . something." It was the older man who was with her. Gracie remembered being introduced to them on her arrival. He was an American named Greg Musgrave, a glaciologist if she remembered correctly. The woman was his wife.

Musgrave turned to Gracie, waving toward the skycam, jabbing a nervous finger at it. "Don't send that"—he stammered, struggling with what to call the Draganflyer—"*thing* any farther. Stop it before it gets too close."

"Why?" Dalton sounded incredulous.

Musgrave raised his voice. "Pull it back. We don't know what it is."

Dalton didn't take his eyes off his controls. "Exactly," he shot back. "It can help us figure out what the hell it is."

Gracie looked out. The skycam was very close to the apparition. She glanced at Finch, then at Dalton, who seemed determined to see it through.

"I'm telling you, pull it back," Musgrave said, moving toward Dalton now, reaching out to grab the remote control console. Dalton's fingers jerked against the joysticks, making the Draganflyer yaw and pitch wildly, its gyroscopes kicking in to keep it airborne.

"Hey," Gracie yelled at him, just as Finch and the captain stepped in to restrain Musgrave.

"Grace, what the hell's going on?" Roxberry again, in her ear.

"Hang on, Jack," she interjected quickly.

"Calm down," the captain snapped at Musgrave. "He's gonna pull it back before it reaches it," then, to Dalton, pointedly, "aren't you?"

"Absolutely," Dalton replied flatly. "You know how much that thing cost me?" He checked out the monitor, as did Gracie. The apparition filled the screen. It was grainy, but there was a subtle, undulating shimmer within the image that really gave the impression that it was bubbling with life. Gracie caught the worry in Dalton's eyes, then looked over at the skycam. The tiny black dot was almost on it.

"Maybe it's close enough," she told Dalton, under her breath.

Dalton frowned with concentration. "A little closer."

"You shouldn't be messing with it before we know what we're dealing with," Musgrave blurted out sharply.

Dalton ignored him and kept the joystick pressed forward. The skycam glided on, inching its way nearer to the blazing apparition.

"Dalton," Finch said, low and discreet. It was getting uncomfortably close for him.

"I hear you," he replied. "Just a little bit more."

Gracie's pulse quickened, thumping away in her ears as the skycam sailed ever closer to the apparition. It seemed tantalizingly close now, perhaps fifty feet or less—it was hard to judge the relative distance—when the sign suddenly dimmed right down and disappeared.

The crowd heaved a collective gasp.

"You see that? I told you," Musgrave rasped.

"You kidding me?" Dalton fired back angrily. "What, you think I scared it?"

"We don't know. But it was there for a reason, and now it's gone." The scientist put an arm around his wife, and they both turned and stared out into the distance, as if willing it to reappear, dismay clouding their faces.

"Get real, man." Dalton shrugged, turning away.

Over the shelf, the Draganflyer continued on its trajectory unbothered. Nothing showed on its monitor as it buzzed through the air that the apparition had occupied. Dalton slid a glance at Gracie. He looked thoroughly spooked. She'd never seen him react that way, not to anything, and they'd been through some pretty gut-wrenching times together.

Gracie was just as shaken. She peered out into the grim sky.

There was no trace of the sign.

It was as if it had never happened.

And then, all of a sudden, Gracie felt the world around her darken, felt a momentous weight above her, and looked up to see the apparition right above her, hovering over the ship itself, a massive ball of shimmering light squatting above them, dwarfing the vessel. She flinched as the crowd gasped and recoiled in horror and Dalton pounced on the main camera to try to get it on film. Gracie just stood there, staring up at it in complete bewilderment, her knees trembling, her feet riveted to the wooden planks of the ship's deck, fear and wonderment battling it out inside her, every hair on her body standing rigid for a brief moment that felt like an eternity—

—and then all of a sudden, the sign just faded out again, vanishing just as startlingly and as inexplicably as it had appeared.

Chapter 4

Bir Hooker, Egypt

Yusuf Zacharia puffed ruminatively on his *sheesha* as he watched his opponent pull his hand back from the weathered backgammon board. Nodding wearily to himself, the wiry old taxi driver palmed the dice. Anything less than a double-six meant he would lose the game. He didn't have high hopes for the toss. The dice weren't doing him any favors tonight.

He shook the small ivory cubes vigorously before flinging them across the board, and watched them skitter across its elaborately inlaid surface before they settled into a six and a one. He frowned, turning the fissures that lined his grizzled, leathery face into canyons, and rubbed his mostly bald pate, cursing his luck. To add to his misery, he became aware of a bitter, fruity bite gnawing at the back of his throat. The coals of his water pipe had cooled down. He'd been so taken by the game and by his miserable run of rolls that he hadn't noticed. Fresh, red-hot replacements would rekindle the soothing, honey-mint taste that helped lull him into a tranquil sleep every night, but he sensed he might have to forgo that little luxury tonight. It was late.

He glanced at his watch. It was time to head home. The other customers of the small café—two young tourists, an American couple, he thought, judging by their familiar guidebooks and newspapers—were also getting up to leave. *Baseeta*, He shrugged to himself. Never mind. There was always tomorrow. He'd be back for a fresh *sheesha* and another game, God willing.

He was pushing himself to his feet when something caught his eye, a fleeting image on the TV set that loomed down from a rickety old shelf behind the counter. It was way past the ever-popular soaps' bedtime. At this hour, here, at the sleepy edge of the Egyptian desert, in the small village of Bir Hooker—haplessly misnamed after a British manager of the Egyptian Salt and Soda Company—and across the entire troubled region, for that matter, TVs would inevitably be tuned to some news program, feeding the endless debates and laments about the sorry state of the Arab world. Mahmood, the café's jovial owner, tended to favor Al Arabiya over Al Jazeera until, aiming to put forward a more tourist-friendly face, he invested in a satellite dish with a pirated decoder box. Ever since, the screen was locked onto an American news network. Mahmood thought the foreign infusion gave his café more class; Yusuf, on the other hand, didn't particularly care for the Americans' never-ending coverage of the recent presidential election there, even though it had been, unusually, keenly watched across the region, a region whose fortunes seemed more and more entwined with the vagaries of that distant country's leadership. But Yusuf's resistance to the channel was counterweighed by an unspoken appreciation for its occasional coverage of pouting Hollywood starlets and scantily clad catwalk models.

Right now, however, his attention was consumed by something entirely different. The screen showed a woman in heavy winter gear reporting from what seemed like one of the poles. In the image behind her, something shone in the sky. Something bizarre and otherworldly, the likes of which he'd never seen before. It was just floating there, blazing over a collapsing cliff of ice, and had—oddly, though it was unmistakable—the distinct, manifest shape of a symbol.

A sign.

The others also took note of the events on the screen and drew in closer to the counter, excitedly urging Mahmood to turn the sound up. The scene it showed was surreal, unimaginable, only that wasn't what disturbed Yusuf most. What really troubled him was that he'd seen that sign before.

His face pinched together with disbelief as he stared at the screen.

It can't be.

He inched forward for a closer look. His mouth dropped by an inch, his skin tingled with trepidation. The camera cut to another angle, and this time, the illuminated symbol took over the whole screen.

It was the same sign.

There was no doubt in his mind.

Unconsciously, his hand rose discreetly to his forehead, and he quietly crossed himself.

His friends noticed his sudden pallor, but he ignored their questions and, without offering an explanation or a farewell, rushed out of the café. He clambered into his trusted old Toyota Previa and churned its engine to life. The people carrier kicked up a small cloud as it fishtailed onto the dusty, unlit road and disappeared into the night, Yusuf riding the pedal hard, rushing back to the monastery as quickly as he could, muttering the same phrase to himself, over and over and over.

It can't be.

Chapter 5

Cambridge, Massachusetts

The crowd caught Vince Bellinger's eye as he ambled across the mall. They were massed outside the Best Buy, bubbling noisily with excitement, seemingly about something in the shop's huge window display. Bellinger was more than familiar with the window—it usually housed the latest plasmas and LCDs, including the mammoth sixty-five-incher he'd been fantasizing about for Christmas this year. Covetable, to be sure, but nothing that merited this much attention. Unless it wasn't the screens themselves, but rather what was on them, that had drawn the crowd.

Against the backdrop of piped-in seasonal Muzak and gaudy tinsel decorations, some people were talking animatedly on their cell phones, others waving friends over to join them. Despite being heavily laden with a pile of dry cleaning and his gym bag, Bellinger veered toward the store, wondering what all the fuss was about. Instinctively, he flinched at the possibility of another horror, another 9/11-like catastrophe, images of that terrible day still seared into his mind—although, he quickly thought, today's crowd didn't have that vibe to it. They weren't horrified. They seemed enthralled.

He got as close as he could and peered over the heads

and shoulders of the gathered people. As per usual, the screens were all tuned to the same channel, in this case a news network. The image they showed drew his eye immediately, and he didn't quite understand what he was looking at—a spherical light, hovering over what seemed like one of the polar regions, confirmed by the banner underneath. He was watching it with piqued curiosity, in a detached trance, catching snippets of the animated comments bouncing around him, when his cell phone trilled. He groaned and juggled his bag and laundry around to fish it out of his pocket. Groaned doubly when he saw who was calling.

"Dude, where are you? I just tried your landline." Csaba—pronounced *Tchaba,* nicknamed "Jabba," for not-too-subtle reasons—sounded overly excited. Which wasn't unusual. The big guy had a hearty appetite for life—and pretty much everything else.

"I'm at the mall," Bellinger replied, still angling for a clearer view of the screens.

"Go home and put the news on, quick. You're not gonna believe this."

Jabba, excited about something on TV. Not exactly breaking news. Although this time—just this once, Bellinger thought—his exuberance seemed justified.

A brilliant chemical engineer of Hungarian extraction who worked with Bellinger at the Rowland Materials Research Laboratory, Csaba Komlosy had a passion for all things televisual. Well-made, high-concept shows were normally his turf, the kind of show where a gutsy and intense government agent repeatedly managed to save the nation from mass destruction or where a gutsy and intense architect repeatedly managed to break out of the most escape-proof prisons. Lately, though, Csaba had veered into seedier territory. He'd embraced the netherworld of unscripted television—reality TV, so-called despite the fact that it had little to do with reality, or with being unscripted, for that matter—and, much to Bellinger's chagrin, he really liked to share the more singularly sublime moments of his viewing.

In this case, though, Bellinger was ready to give him a free pass. Still, he couldn't resist a little dig. "Since when do you watch the news?"

"Would you stop with the inquisition and put the damn thing on?" Jabba protested.

"I'm looking at it right now. I'm at the mall, outside Best Buy." Bellinger's voice trailed off as some heads in front of him shifted and the image on the screen snared his attention again. He caught sight of a banner at the bottom of screen, which read, "Unexplained phenomenon over Antarctica." There was also a small "Live" box in the upper right corner. He just stood there, transfixed, his eyes curiously processing what they were seeing. He recognized the reporter. He'd caught some of her specials over the years and remembered her reports from Thailand after the tsunami a few years back, when he'd first noticed her. Shallow as it sounded, the relative hotness of a TV newscaster was directly proportional to how much attention guys paid to the screen—especially if the news in question didn't concern armed conflict, a sports result, or a celebrity meltdown. For most guys, Grace Logan—with the unforgiving green eyes, the tiny, mischievous mole poised just above the edge of her lips, the unsettlingly breathy yet earnest voice, the blond curls that always seemed to have a slightly unkempt tousle to them, and the Vargas Girl body that owed its curves to burgers and milkshakes, not silicone—ticked the hot box with ease.

This time, though, Bellinger's eyes weren't on her.

The camera zoomed in on the phenomenon again, sending an audible shiver through the crowd.

"Dude, it's unreal," Jabba exclaimed. "I can't take my eyes off the screen."

Bellinger couldn't make sense of it. "Is this a joke?"

"Not according to them."

"Where is this exactly?"

"West Antarctic ice sheet. They're on some research ship off the coast. At first, I thought it's got to be a stunt for a new movie, maybe Cameron or Emmerich or even Shyamalan, but none of them have a live project that fits."

Jabba—film geek extraordinaire—would know.

"How long has it been up?" Bellinger asked.

"About ten minutes. It came on out of the blue while la Logan was yapping about the breakup of the ice shelf. First it was like this ball of light; then it morphed to a dark sphere—like that black planet in *The Fifth Element*. Remember? Totally creeped me out."

"Then it turned into this?"

"Yep." The crunching sound coming through the receiver spurred Bellinger's mind to picture the likely setting for his friend's call: sunken deep in his couch, a bottle of Samuel Adams in one hand—not his first, Bellinger guessed, since they'd both left the lab over an hour ago—and a half-empty pack of sizzlin' picante chips in the other. Which was why he was on speakerphone.

Bellinger's brow wrinkled with concentration as he rubbed his bald pate. He'd never seen anything like it. More people were gathering around now, crowding around him, jostling for position.

Jabba crunched noisily into another chip, then asked, "So what do you think?"

"I don't know," he answered, as if in a daze. The crowd oohed as an airborne camera gave a closer look at the unexplained apparition. "How are they doing this?" he asked, cupping the phone's mike area to cut out the noise around him. As a technology researcher and a scientist, his mind was instinctively skeptical and was immediately trying to figure out ways this could be done.

Jabba was obviously thinking along the same lines. "Must be some kind of laser effect. Remember those floating beads of light those guys were working on at Keio—"

"Laser-induced plasma emissions?" Bellinger interjected. They'd both seen press coverage of the recent invention at the Japanese university, where focused bursts from a laser projector heated up the air at specific points above the bulky device, causing tiny bursts of plasma emissions that "drew" small, three-dimensional shapes of white light in midair.

"Yeah, remember? The guy with the weird goggles and the white gloves—"

"No way," Bellinger countered. "You'd need a generator the size of an aircraft carrier sitting right under it for something this big. Plus it wouldn't explain the sustained brilliance or the way it's so clearly defined."

"All right, forget that. What about other kinds of projections? Spectral imagery?"

Bellinger stared closely at the screen. "You know something I don't? 'Cause except for the droid in—which one's the white one that looks like a fire hydrant?"

"R2-D2." The roll of the eyes came through in his mocking tone as clearly as if they'd been using high-def webcams.

"Except for R2-D2, I don't think 3-D projectors actually exist."

Which was true. Something that could achieve a free-floating, uncontained, three-dimensional moving image, like in Princess Leia's seminal "Help us, Obi-Wan" moment—of any size, let alone something this big—still eluded the best brains in the business.

"Besides, you're forgetting one pesky little detail," Bellinger added, feeling slightly more uncomfortable now.

"I know, dude. It's daylight." Jabba sounded spooked at having that realization reaffirmed.

"Not exactly projector-friendly, is it?"

"Nope."

Bellinger felt uncomfortable having that discussion out there, surrounded by people, his gym bag and laundry inches from getting trampled. But he just couldn't tear himself away.

"Okay, so we can forget about lasers and projectors," he told Jabba. "I mean, look at it. It's not contained within any kind of framework. It's not boxed in. There's no dark backdrop behind it, no glass panes around it. It's just there, free-floating. In daylight."

"Unless there are a couple of monster mirrors on either side of it they're not showing us," Jabba mused. "Hey, maybe it's generated from space."

"Nice idea, but how exactly?"

Jabba bit noisily into another chip. "I don't know, dude. I mean, this thing doesn't compute, does it?"

"No. Hang on," Bellinger told him, as he jammed the phone between his ear and his shoulder, grabbed his belongings, and inched back a few steps, out of the ever-growing crowd.

He and Jabba bounced around several other ideas, throwing everything they could think of at it, trying to pin some sensible, plausible explanation on it, but nothing stuck. Bellinger's excitement, though, soon gave way to a sense of unease. Something else was bothering him. An uncomfortable feeling that something buried deep within him was clawing for attention.

Suddenly, the fixed camera got jarred as an altercation took place on the ship's deck. Jabba lapped it up, as did the crowd at the mall, whooping and joking as the people on the ship filming the sighting scuffled; then the aerial camera came back. It closed in on the apparition, which then faded away, only to then suddenly reappear directly over the ship. The crowd around Bellinger shrieked and recoiled in shock as the shaky upward shot from the handheld camera on deck sent a shock wave crackling through them.

"Son of a bitch," Jabba blurted. "Is it turning?"

Bellinger focused on the apparition, now aware of a growing lump in his throat. "It's spherical," he marveled. "It's not some kind of projection. It's actually physical, isn't it?"

On the screen, Grace Logan was having trouble keeping calm, clearly rattled by the apparition that was just hovering there, directly over the ship. The crowd in the mall was echoing her reaction, visibly stiffening and going quiet.

Jabba's crunching had also stopped. "I think you're right. But how . . . ? It's not an object, and yet . . . It's almost like the air itself is burning up, but . . . that's not possible, is it? I mean, you can't light air up, can you?"

Bellinger felt a sudden rush of blood to his temples. Something clicked. It just rushed in on him, unannounced, out of nowhere. Long-forgotten, dormant neurons buried deep within his brain had somehow managed to reach out and find one another and make a connection.

An unhappy one.

Oh, shit.

He went silent, his mind racing to process that link and take it to its natural conclusion, lost in the dread of the possibility just as the sign faded from view and the sky above the ship went back to normal.

"Dude, you there?"

Bellinger heard his voice go distant, as if he were on the outside watching himself answer. "Yeah."

"What? What're you thinking?"

He felt his skin crawl. "I've got to go. I'll call you when I get home. Let me know if you come up with anything."

"Dude, hang on, don't just—"

Bellinger hung up.

He stood there, his feet nailed to the cool tiled floor, the commotion around him fading as he turned his thoughts inward. Only minutes earlier, picking up the colorful linen shirts, all folded up and ready for packing, he had conjured up a pleasant, warm feeling inside him. With the Christmas holiday days away, the sea, the sun, and the wide blue skies of the Dominican Republic beckoned—his annual pilgrimage, a welcome respite from the claustrophobic, windowless life he led at the research lab. Any feeling of warmth was now gone. A cold, crippling unease had taken its place and, Bellinger knew, wasn't about to let go.

He just stood there for a few long minutes, contemplating the disturbing—and, he hoped, surely unlikely—idea that had clawed its way out from the darkest recesses of his mind.

No way, he thought. *Be serious.*

But he couldn't shake the thought.

He stayed there as the TVs replayed the whole thing, lost in his thoughts as the crowd dissipated. He finally tore himself away from the screens, gathered his things, and drove home in silence.

No way.

He dumped his bags in his front hallway, decided to try to let it go and move onto other things, and headed for his fridge. He got himself a beer and went back to the hall and riffled through his mail, but it was no use.

He couldn't shake it away.

He switched on his TV. The images it threw back at him were spine-tingling. Snarled traffic in Times Square, where a crowd of people had just frozen in place, mesmerized by the images of the sighting on the Sony Jumbo-Tron; people in bars and stadiums, on their feet, their eyes peeled on the screens; and similar chaotic images from around the world. He moved to his desk and fired up his laptop and spent a couple of hours scouring Internet chat rooms while flicking around various news reports, trying to get a clearer picture of what was going on, hoping to come across some ammo to dismiss his theory.

It was insane, outlandish . . . but it fit.

It just fit.

Which brought up an even bigger problem.

What to do about it.

His primal instinct told him to forget about it and leave it alone. Well alone. If what he was imagining was really happening, then he'd be far better off expunging any trace of the thought from his mind and never mentioning it to anyone. Which was the sensible thing to do, the rational thing to do, and Bellinger prided himself, above any other qualities he might have, on his rationality. But there was something else.

A friend had died. Not just a friend.

His best friend.

And that was something that his rationality was finding hard to ignore.

Visions of the tragic accident in the Skeleton Coast sparked in his mind's eye, horrific images his imagination had conjured up long ago, after he'd been told about how Danny Sherwood had died.

He couldn't ignore it.

He had to find out. Make sure. Get the whole picture.

He got himself another beer and sat alone in the dark living room, staring into nothing, his mind alternating between what he'd just seen and what had happened two years ago. A few bottles later, he retrieved his phone and scrolled down his contacts list until he found the entry he was looking for. It was a number he'd been given a couple of years ago, one he hadn't called for almost that long.

He hesitated, then hit the CALL button.

He heard it ring through three, four times; then a man picked up.

"Who's this?" The man's tone had a detached, no-nonsense ring to it.

The sound of Matt Sherwood's voice brought Bellinger a modicum of solace. A palpable connection, however fleeting, to his long-dead friend.

"It's Vince. Vince Bellinger," he answered, a slight hesitation in his voice. He paused for a beat, then added, "Where are you, Matt?"

"At my place. Why?"

"I need to see you, man," Bellinger told him. "Like, now."

Chapter 6

Boston, Massachusetts

No one in the crowded arena could tear their eyes away from the huge video scoreboards. Not the fans. Not the players. And certainly not anyone in Larry Rydell's perfectly positioned luxury suite at the Garden.

His guests, the design team working on the ground-breaking electric car he hoped to launch within a couple of years, had been enjoying the treat. They'd spent the whole day in the project's nerve center over in Waltham, bringing him up to speed on the car's status, going over the problems they'd managed to solve and the new ones they'd unearthed. As with everything Rydell did, the project had world-beating ambitions. His friend Elon Musk—another Internet sensation, courtesy of a little online business he'd cofounded by the name of PayPal—had already launched his electric car, the Tesla, but that was a sports car. Rydell was after a different kind of driver: the legions driving around in Camrys, Impalas, and Accords. And so he'd recruited the best and the brightest designers and engineers, given them everything they needed to make it happen, and let them do their thing. It was just one of several pet projects he had running at the same time. He had teams working on more efficient wind farms, solar cells, and better wiring to ferry the resulting power around. Renewable energy and clean power were going to be the next great industrial revolution, and Larry Rydell was nothing if not visionary.

The only resource his projects fought over was his own time. Money certainly wasn't an issue, even with the recent turmoil in the markets. He was well aware of the fact that he had more of it than he'd ever need. Every computer and cell phone user on the planet had contributed his or her share to his fortune, and the stratospheric share price his company had enjoyed had done the rest. And although Rydell enjoyed the good life, he'd found better things to do with his money than build himself five-hundred-foot yachts.

They'd had a long, productive day, overcoming a big hurdle they'd been trying to solve for weeks, and so he'd decided to reward the team by sending them off on their end-of-year break in style. He'd treated them to a great dinner, all the drinks they could handle, and the best seats in the house. They'd just watched Paul Pierce slip past Kobe Bryant and slam home a two-handed dunk, and heard the first-period buzzer go, when the suspended cube of screens had flicked over to a live news feed and all noise had drained out of the arena.

As he stood there, mesmerized by the surreal display before him, he felt his BlackBerry vibrate in his pocket. The alert was one of three that never went comatose, even when his privacy settings were on, which was most of the time. One was entrusted to Mona, his PA—or, more accurately, the senior PA among the four who controlled the drawbridge to his office. Another was allocated to his ex-wife, Ashley, although she usually found it easier to call Mona and get him to call her back. The third, the one that was now clamoring for his attention, told him his nineteen-year-old daughter, Rebecca, was calling.

Something she rarely did when she was on a distant

beach, which was currently—and often—the case. The family villa in Mexico, he thought, though he wasn't sure. It could have been the chalet in Vail or the yacht in Antigua. Between her appetite for partying and his scant appetite for anything that didn't concern the projects he lived and breathed, that tidbit of information had some pretty large cracks to slip through.

He pressed the phone to his ear without taking his eyes off the screen.

"Dad, are you watching this?"

"Yeah," he replied, somewhat dazed. "We're all standing here at the Garden watching it like zombies."

"Same here," his daughter laughed, somewhat nervously. "We were about to go out when a friend of mine in L.A. called to tell us about it."

"Where are you anyway?"

"Mexico, Dad," she half-groaned, with an undisguised you-should-know-this tone.

Just then, the initial shock veered to cheers and claps as the already charged fans let their emotions rip. The noise reverberated through the arena. "Wow," Rebecca echoed, "it sounds wild."

"It is," he said with a curious smile. "How long have they been showing it?"

"I'm not sure. We just switched it on a few minutes ago." She paused for a moment, then said, "Dad . . . what do you think it is?"

And, in what was probably a first for a man who was rightly feted around the world as nothing less than a genius, Larry Rydell had no answer for his daughter. At least, not one that he could share with her.

Not now.

Not ever.

Chapter 7

Washington, D.C.

A light rain peppered the nation's capital as a black chauffeur-driven Lexus slipped out of the underground garage and slunk onto Connecticut Avenue and into the sparse late-evening traffic. In the cosseted comfort of its heated backseat, Keenan Drucker stared out in silence, lost in a streaming light show of passing cars, contemplating the events of the momentous day.

The phone calls had begun about an hour ago, and in the days to come, there would be plenty more; of that, he was certain.

They were only getting started.

He shut his eyes and leaned back against the richly padded headrest. His mind chewed over his plan, once again dissecting every layer of it, looking for the fatal flaw that he might have somehow missed. As with every previous run-through, he couldn't find anything to worry about. There were a lot of unknowns, of course—there had to be, by definition. But that didn't trouble him. Oversights and miscalculations—now those were different. Those he wouldn't tolerate. A lot of effort had gone into making sure there wouldn't be any. But unknowns were, well, unknowable. A lifetime of making questionable deals in smoke-filled rooms had taught him that unknowns weren't worth worrying about until they materialized. If and when they did, his thoroughness, his focus, and his level of commitment would ensure that, if it pleased the Lord—he smiled inwardly at his little joke—they wouldn't prove too hard to deal with.

His BlackBerry nudged him out of his reverie. The ring tone told him who it was, and a quick glance at the screen before picking up the call confirmed it.

The Bullet got straight to the point, as was his norm. They'd already spoken twice that evening.

"I got a call from our friend at Meade."

"And?"

"He got a hit. A phone call, between two of the peripherals on the watch list."

Drucker mulled the news for a beat. The Bullet, aka Brad Maddox, had initially suggested using one of his contacts inside the National Security Agency to—quietly—monitor for unexpected trouble. Although Drucker had thought the risk of exposure outweighed the unlikely benefits, it now looked like Maddox had made the right call. Which was why Maddox was in charge of the project's security.

"You've heard the recording?" Drucker asked.

"Yes."

"Is it anything to worry about?"

"I think it might be. The call itself was too brief to read either way, but its timing raises some concerns."

Drucker winced. "Who are the peripherals?"

"One of them's a techie, an engineer here in Boston. Vince Bellinger. He was Danny Sherwood's college roommate. They were tight. Best buddies. The other's Sherwood's brother, Matt."

A flash of concern flitted across Drucker's eyes. "And there's no history there?"

"Last communication we have between them goes back almost two years."

Drucker thought about it for a moment. Two years ago, they had a natural reason to chat. The timing of this new call, though, was indeed troublesome. "I take it you've got it under control."

Maddox couldn't have sounded more detached if he'd been sedated. "Just bringing you up to speed."

"Good. Let's hope it's a coincidence."

"Not something I believe in," Maddox affirmed.

"Me neither, sadly," Drucker replied. Then, almost as an afterthought, he asked, "And the girl?"

"Just waiting to be plucked."

"You're going to need to handle that one with even more discretion," Drucker cautioned. "She's key."

"She won't be a problem," the Bullet assured him. "My boys are ready. Just say the word."

"It's imminent. Keep me posted on the roommate," Drucker added before hanging up.

He stared at his phone for a moment, then shrugged and tucked it back into his suit's inside breast pocket. He looked out at the streaks of red and white light gliding past his wet window, and played out the next moves in his mind.

It was a good start, no question.

But the hardest part was yet to come.

Chapter 8

Amundsen Sea, Antarctica

Gracie watched the screen fade to a fuzzy gray and shook her head. The adrenaline rush was petering out, and she now felt exhausted, battered by a hurricane of exuberance, confusion, and unease. Yet another cup of the ship's surprisingly decent coffee beckoned.

"Let's see it again," one of the scientists told Dalton.

Dalton glanced over at Gracie, who shrugged, got up, and headed over to the corner bar for her caffeine fix. Her throat felt dry and hoarse, and she'd lost all sense of time. The continuous, seemingly never-ending daylight didn't help.

They'd stayed out on deck, scanning the skies, for about an hour after the apparition had vanished before heading inside for some warmth. Some crew members stayed out on watch, in case it reappeared, while Gracie and the others had crowded into the officers' and scientists' lounge—which sounded a lot more grand than it was—and watched the footage from both of Dalton's cameras on a big plasma screen. Several viewings and countless cups of coffee later, they still weren't anywhere remotely close to explaining what they'd witnessed.

The comfort zone of ascribing it to some spectacular weather phenomenon was quickly dispelled. The obvious candidates—aurora australis (southern lights), fogbows, and green flashes—didn't fit the bill. One possibility that did generate a brief debate was something called "diamond dust." Gracie had never heard of it. Simmons had explained that it was a phenomenon that involved ice crystals that formed from the condensation of atmospheric water vapor. When these crystals caught the sunlight at a particular angle as they drifted down to earth, they generated a brilliant, sparkling effect, sometimes in the form of a halo. Which might have explained the first part of the apparition, at a stretch, and a pretty big one at that. But it didn't even begin to explain the dazzling symbol that it had turned into.

Looking around the lounge, Gracie could see that the discussion was purely academic. Despite the heated debates and arguments, they were just grasping at straws, skirting the obvious. From the strained faces around her, from the wavering voices and the nervy eyes, it was clear that not one of those assembled really believed that this was a natural weather phenomenon. And this wasn't a simple group of layfolk prone to flights of imagination. They were all highly qualified scientists, experts in their fields, and more than familiar with the unique conditions out there. And they'd all been seriously shaken up by what they'd seen. All of which meant one of two things: If it wasn't natural, it was either man-made—or supernatural.

The first was easier to deal with.

Dalton frowned as he turned away from the footage. "Well, if it isn't a freak of nature, then maybe it's some goofballs messing with us."

"You think it could be a prank?" Gracie asked.

"Well, yeah. Remember those UFO sightings in New York a few years back?" Dalton continued. "They had half the city convinced. Turns out it was a bunch of guys flying some ultralights in formation."

"On the other hand, no one's been able to explain the lights over Phoenix back in 1997," another scientist, a geophysicist with a thick goatee by the name of Theo Dinnick, countered. The sighting in question, a major event witnessed by hundreds of independent and highly credible people, remained unexplained to this day.

"You're forgetting this was in broad daylight," Gracie remarked.

Simmons, the paleoclimatologist with the binoculars, nodded dubiously. "If it's a prank, I want to meet the guys behind it and find out how the hell they pulled it off, 'cause it sure isn't something I can explain."

Gracie glanced around the room. Her eyes settled on Musgrave, the glaciologist who'd become testy on deck, and his wife. They were both sitting back, not participating. They were clearly discomfited by the conversation, giving each other the occasional glance. Musgrave seemed really irritated, and finally stood up.

"For God's sake, people. Let's be serious here," he announced. "You saw it. We all saw it. You really think something that magnificent, something that . . . *sublime* . . . You really believe it could just be a vulgar prank?"

"What do you think it is?" Simmons asked.

"Isn't it obvious? It's a sign."

"A sign?"

"A sign," he repeated. "From God."

A leaden silence greeted his words.

"Why God? Why not aliens?" Dalton finally asked.

Musgrave flashed him an icy scowl.

Dalton didn't flinch. "Seriously. 'Cause that's the first thing that popped into my mind when I saw it."

"Don't be ridiculous." Musgrave wasn't making any effort to mask his contempt.

"Why is that ridiculous?" Dalton insisted. "You're

saying it's supernatural, aren't you? You're happy to entertain the notion that it's 'God'"—Dalton made some air quotes with his fingers—"whatever that means, but not that it's extraterrestrial, that it's coming from some intelligent life-form from beyond our planet? Why is that any more ridiculous than what you're suggesting?"

"Maybe it's a warning," Musgrave's wife suggested.

"What?" Simmons sounded incredulous.

"Maybe it's a warning. It appeared here, now, over this ice shelf. During the breakup. It can't be random. There's got to be a reason for it. Maybe it's trying to tell us something."

"I'll tell you what it's telling me. It's telling me we should get the hell out of here before it shows up again. It's bad news." Dalton again.

"Goddammit," Musgrave blurted, "either take this seriously or—"

"All right, calm down." Gracie cut off Musgrave before turning to Dalton and flashing him a castigating glance. "We're all on edge here."

Dalton nodded and leaned back, taking in a deep breath.

"I've got to say, I agree with him," Simmons added, gesturing at Dalton. "I mean, we're all scientists—and even if lasers or holograms or whatever the hell it could have been aren't within our areas of expertise, I'm guessing we're all pretty convinced that what we saw out there is, as far as any of us can tell, *way* beyond any technological capability we know of. Now, the fact that I can't explain it excites me and scares me in equal measure. 'Cause if it's not some kind of laser show, if it didn't come from DARPA or some Japanese lab or from Silicon Valley—*if it didn't originate on this planet* . . . then it's either, as Greg says, God—or, as our friend here was saying, extraterrestrial. And frankly, either one would be just extraordinary, and I don't see that the difference really matters right now."

"You don't see the difference?" Musgrave was incensed.

"I don't want to get into a big theological debate with you, Greg, but—"

"—but you obviously don't believe in God, even if you're presented with a miracle, so any debate is pointless."

"No, that's not what I'm saying," Simmons insisted calmly. "Look, you're saying this is God. You're saying our Maker has, for some reason, chosen this day, this location, this event—and this method—to appear to us, here, today—"

Gracie interrupted, saying, "Do we know if anything like this has happened elsewhere? Has anyone checked the news?"

Finch said, "I just got off the phone with the news desk. There are no other reports of any other sightings."

"Okay, so if He's chosen to show up here and now," Simmons continued, "then I've got to think He must have a damn good reason."

"Half the West Antarctic ice shelf is slipping into the sea. You need more of a reason?" Musgrave's wife said, irritably.

"Why do you think we're here?" Musgrave added. "Why are we all here?" His eyes darted around the room feverishly before settling on the British scientist. "Justin," he asked him, "why are you here?"

"England's at the same latitude as Alaska," the man replied. "The only thing that makes it livable is the Gulf Stream. Take that away—which is what happens if the ice melts—and that movie, the one with Manhattan swamped with ice and snow? That'll be London. Along with most of Europe, for that matter."

"Exactly," Musgrave insisted. "We're all here because we're worried. All the signs are telling us that we've got one hell of a problem, and maybe this—this *miracle* is telling us we've got to do something about it."

Gracie and Finch exchanged dubious glances.

"Okay, well," Simmons conceded, "all I'm saying is, if that's the reason, if it's a warning, then . . . why couldn't it be coming from a more advanced intelligence?"

"I agree with that young man," Dinnick said with a slight, disarming grin, pointing at Dalton. "It's just as ludicrous."

Musgrave's wife was clearly roiled. "It's pointless to discuss this with either of you. You're not open to the possibility."

"On the contrary, I'm open to *all* possibilities," Dinnick countered. "And if we're talking about some entity making contact with us"—nodding toward Simmons—"maybe to warn us, which, granted, could justify the here and now of it . . . Well, if you accept the notion of a creator, of creationism, of intelligent design . . . why couldn't that intelligent designer be from a more advanced race?"

Musgrave was incensed. "God isn't something you find in a science fiction book," he retorted. "You don't even have a basic understanding of what faith means, do you?"

"There's no difference. It's all unknowable as far as our current capabilities are concerned, isn't it?" Dinnick pressed.

"Believe what you will. I'm out of here." He stormed off.

Musgrave's wife got up. She looked at the faces around her with a mixture of anger, scorn, and pity. "I think we all know what we saw out there," she said, before following her husband out.

An uncomfortable silence smothered the room.

"Man. That guy's clearly never heard of Scientology," Dalton quipped, raising a few nervous chuckles.

"I've got to say," the British scientist finally offered, "while I was out there, looking at it . . . there was something rather . . . *divine* about it."

He looked around for endorsement. A couple of other scientists nodded.

The honesty of his simple words suddenly struck Gracie, their simple, brutal significance sinking in and chilling her more fiercely than any wind she'd felt out on the ice. Listening to the arguments flying around the room, she'd been swept up by the semantics and all but lost track of the fundamental enormity of what they'd all been arguing about. What had happened, what they'd witnessed out there . . . it was beyond explanation. It was beyond reason. It would have been beyond belief if she hadn't seen it with her own eyes.

But she had.

Her mind drifted away with the possibilities. *Could it be?* she wondered. Had they just witnessed a watershed moment in the history of mankind, something for which "before" and "after" attributes might be used from here on?

Her innate skepticism, the skepticism of a hardened realist, dragged her back from the swirl of dreamy conjecture with a resounding *No.*

Impossible.

And yet . . . she couldn't ignore the feeling that she'd been in the presence of something transcendent. She'd never felt that way before.

She suppressed a shiver and glanced uncertainly at Finch. "What did they say?" she asked, away from the others.

Finch said, "They're getting everyone they can think

of to check it out. But they're getting calls from broad-casters all over the world wanting to know what's going on. Ogilvy wants us to send him a high-res clip pronto," he added pointedly, referring to Hal Ogilvy, the net-work's global news director and a board member of the parent firm.

"Okay." She nodded. "We need to make some calls. You wanna see if we can grab the conference room?"

Finch nodded. "Yeah. Let's get out of here."

"Amen to that," Dalton added.

A barrage of clearly unamused looks greeted his words.

Dalton half-smiled, sheepishly. "Sorry," he offered apologetically, and left the room.

They walked down the hall in silence, the sheer mag-nitude of the discussion sinking in. As they reached the stairwell, Gracie noticed Dalton looking particularly adrift.

"What?" she asked.

He stopped, hesitated, then said, "What if that Bible-thumping nut back there is right?"

She shook her head. "There's got to be a better expla-nation for it."

"What if there isn't?"

Gracie mulled the question for a moment. "Well, if that's the case, if it's really God," she said somberly, "then for someone who had me totally convinced He didn't exist, He sure picked one hell of a moment to show Himself."

Chapter 9

Wadi Natrun, Egypt

Labored breaths and sluggish footfalls tarnished the stillness of the mountain as the three men trudged up the steep slope. Every step, every scattered rock and rolling pebble echoed, the small sounds amplified by the harsh, lifeless dryness of the hills around them. The moon had been conspicuously absent that night, and despite the fading array of stars overhead, the early dawn light and the chilling solitude weighed heavily on them.

Yusuf had driven straight to the monastery from the café. Like many other devout Coptic Christians, the taxi driver donated as much as he could afford to the monastery, delivering free fruit and vegetables from his brother's stall at the market and helping out with various odd jobs. He'd been doing that for as long as he could remember, and knew the monastery like the back of his hand. Which was why he'd been to the cave, delivering supplies every few weeks to the recluse who was its sole inhabitant, and why he'd seen what was inside it.

Muttering the most profuse of apologies, he'd startled the monk he knew best, a young man with alert gray-green eyes and a gregarious demeanor by the name of Brother Ameen, out of a deep sleep with his startling news. Ameen knew Yusuf well enough to take him at his word and, driven by the old taxi driver's urgent tone, he'd then led him to the cell of the monastery's abbot, Father Kyrillos. The abbot listened, and reluctantly agreed to accompany them back to the café at that ungodly hour.

The monastery's amenities, unsurprisingly, didn't include a media room, and so they'd all watched the footage on the TV at the café. It had thoroughly shocked the monks. And although they were both certain that Yusuf was right, they had to be absolutely sure.

And that couldn't wait.

Yusuf had driven them straight back to the monastery, where they'd counted down the hours anxiously. Then at dawn, he drove them six miles out, to the edge of the desert, where the barren, desolate crags rose out of the sand. From there, the three men had climbed for over an hour, pausing once for a sip of water from a leather gourd that the young monk had brought along.

.The trek up wasn't exactly a cakewalk. The steep, uneven slope of the mountain—a barren moonscape of loose, crumbling rocks—was treacherous and hard enough to navigate by daylight, let alone like this, in near-darkness, with nothing more than the anemic beams of cheap flashlights to guide them up the slope that was still bathed in shadow. It also wasn't a path they knew well at all. Visits to the caves were a rare event. Access to the desolate area was, as a matter of principle, fiercely discouraged out of respect for the occasional, driven soul who elected to retreat into its harsh seclusion. They reached the small doorway that led into the cave. A simple wooden door guarded its entrance, held shut by an old, rusted latch. A small timber window, fashioned from a natural opening in the rock, sat beside it. The abbot, a surprisingly fit man with penetrating yet kind eyes, dark, weathered skin, and a salt-and-pepper, square-cut beard that jutted out from the embroidered hood of his black cassock, shone his flashlight briefly into the window and peered in, then retreated a step, hesitating for a moment. He turned to Ameen, unsure of whether or not to proceed. The younger monk shrugged. He wasn't sure either.

The abbot's expression darkened with resigned determination. His hand shaking more from nerves than from the cold, he gave the door a soft, hesitant knock. A moment passed, with no answer. He glanced at his companions again and gave the door another rap. Again, there was no reply.

"Wait here," he told them. "Maybe he can't hear us."

"You're going in?" Ameen asked.

"Yes. Just keep quiet. I don't want to cause him any distress."

Ameen and Yusuf nodded.

The abbot steeled himself, gently lifted the latch, and pushed the door open.

The interior of the cave was oppressively dark and bone-chillingly cold. It was a natural cavern shaped out of limestone, and the chamber the abbot now stood in— the first of three—was surprisingly large. It was empty, save for a few pieces of simple, handcrafted furnishings: a rudimentary armchair, a low table facing it, and a couple of stools. Beside the window was a writing table and a chair. The abbot aimed his flashlight toward it. The table had a lined notebook on it, a fountain pen lying across its open pages. A small stack of similar notebooks, looking well thumbed, sat on a ledge by the window.

His mind flashed to the notebooks. To the frenzied, dense writing that filled their pages, pages he'd only glimpsed, pages he'd never been offered to read. To how it had all started, several months earlier, unexpectedly.

To how they'd found him.

And to the *miraculous*—the word suddenly took on a wholly different ring—way he'd come to them.

The abbot shook the thoughts away and turned. That could all wait.

He lowered the beam toward the ground and stood motionless for a moment, listening intently. He heard nothing. He took slow, hesitant steps deeper into the cave until he reached a small nook that housed a narrow bed.

It was empty.

The abbot spun around, shining his flashlight across the cave walls, his pulse rocketing ahead.

"Father Jerome?" he called out, his voice tremulous, the words echoing emptily through the chamber.

No answer.

Perplexed, he retreated back into the main chamber, and turned to face the wall.

His hand shook with a slight tremble as he raised the flashlight, lighting up the wall that curved gently into the cavern's domelike roof. With his heart pounding in his ears, he surveyed its surface, the flashlight's beam lighting it up from the cave's entrance all the way back to its deepest recess.

The markings were just as he remembered them.

One symbol, painstakingly painted onto the smooth rock face using some kind of white paint, repeated over and over and over, covering every available inch inside the cave.

A clearly recognizable symbol.

The same symbol he had just seen on television, in the skies over Antarctica.

Yusuf was right.

And he'd been right to come to them.

Without taking his eyes off the markings, the abbot slowly dropped to his knees and, making no sound, began to pray.

Chapter 10

Perched on the crest of the barren mountain, high above the caves, Father Jerome contemplated the majestic landscape spread out before him. The sun was crawling out from behind the mountains, backlighting their undulating crowns and tinting the sky with a soft golden pink hue.

The thin, old man with the wire-rimmed glasses, the white, buzz-cut hair, and the dishdasha robe spent most of his mornings and evenings up here. Although the climb up the rocky, crumbling terrain had been harsh on his frail body, he needed the escape from the crushing solitude and the oppressive confines of the cave. And once he was up there, he discovered, the mountain presented him with a reward he hadn't anticipated, a reward far beyond the awe-inspiring magnificence of God's creation.

He still didn't know what had brought him there, what had drawn him to this place. He wasn't the first to come to this valley to serve his faith and to glorify his God. Many before him had done the same, over hundreds of years. Other men like him, men of deep religious faith, who had felt the same divine presence when confronted with the purity and the power of the vast, empty wilderness that stretched up and down the valley. But much as he thought about it, in those endless nights in the cave, he still couldn't explain the calling that had led him to walk away from the orphanage—an orphanage he had only just opened, several hundred miles south, just over the border with Sudan—and wander into the desert, unprepared and alone. Perhaps there was no explanation. Perhaps it was just that, a calling, one from a higher power, one that he couldn't not heed.

And yet, somehow . . . it scared him.

When he thought about it, he knew it shouldn't. It was a grace from God, a blessing. He had been shown a route, a journey, and even if he didn't understand it or know where it would lead, it was still a great honor for him to be the recipient of that grace. And yet . . .

The nights scared him most. The loneliness in the cave was, at times, crippling. He sometimes arose in a cold sweat, woken up by the howl of the wind, or by the yelps of wild dogs roaming the barren hills. It was in those moments that he was most acutely aware of his extreme isolation. The mountain was a fearsome place. Few could survive it. The early ascetics, the hermit monks who retreated from humanity and lived in the caves long before him, went there to get closer to God, believing that the only path to enlightenment, the only way to get to know God, was through such isolation. Up on the craggy, bare mountain, they could avoid temptation; they could free themselves from all vestiges of earthly desire, and concentrate on the one thing that could bring them closer to God: prayer. But for those who had lived on it, the mountain was also a battleground. They were there to pray for us, believing that we were all constantly under assault by demons, no one more so than the hermits themselves, who also believed that the more they prayed, the more they were threatened by the forces of evil they were battling on our behalf.

If he'd been asked about it before coming to this mountain, Father Jerome would have said he disagreed with that rather bleak view of the world. But now, after living in the confines of the cave for months, after going through the hell and torment of solitary reflection, he wasn't so sure anymore.

Still, he had to forge ahead. He had to embrace the challenges before him and not resist them.

It was his calling.

The days were better. When he wasn't up on the mountain, he spent them either in quiet contemplation, in prayer, or writing. And that was something else he didn't understand, something else that troubled him.

The writing.

There seemed to be no end to the words, to the thoughts and ideas and images—*that* image, in par-ticular—that flooded his mind. And when the inspiration came—the divine inspiration, he realized, both exhilarat-ing and scary at the same time—he couldn't write down the words fast enough. And yet, somehow, he wasn't sure where they were coming from. His mind was think-ing them, his hand was writing them down, and yet it was as if they were originating elsewhere and flowing through him, as if he were a vessel, a conduit for a higher being or a greater intellect. Which, again, was a grace. For the words were, undeniably, beautiful, even if they didn't necessarily concord with his own personal experi-ence within the Church.

He drank in the view and its sea of haloed crests be-fore closing his eyes and tilting his head slightly upward, clearing his mind and preparing himself for what he knew was coming. And moments later, as it did unfailingly, it began. A torrent of words that flowed into his ears, as clearly as if someone were kneeling right beside him and whispering to him.

He beamed inwardly, locked in concentration, the warmth of the rising sun caressing his face, and drank in the words that were, as with each previous moment of revelation, simply wondrous.

Chapter 11

Boston, Massachusetts

Snowflakes dusted the dimly lit sidewalk as Bellinger climbed out of the cab outside the small bar on Emerson, a quiet, narrow street in South Boston.

It was late, and the chill bit into him fiercely. The run-up to Christmas was usually cold, but this was shaping up to be a particularly harsh winter. As he turned to duck into the bar, he slammed into a woman who emerged from the shadows. She pulled back, all flustered, holding up her hands, which had come up defensively, and apologized, her clipped words explaining that she was trying to grab the cab before it drove off. She hurriedly sidestepped around him and called out to the driver, and Bellinger managed a fleeting glimpse of her face, soft and attractive, nestling between a bounce of shoulder-length auburn hair and the upturned collar of her coat. It was an awkward moment. Beyond the thin veil of snow and the darkness, he was in a fog of his own, and before he could spew out any clumsy words, she'd hopped into the cab and it was pulling away.

He stood there for a moment, watching it recede and disappear around a corner, then snapped away from the distraction and headed into the bar.

Matt Sherwood had chosen the place. It was a typical,

low-key Southie bar. Cheap beer, dim lighting, twenty-five-cent wings, and darts. Some token Christmas decorations scattered around, cheap stuff made in China using paper-thin plastic and colored foil. The place was busy, but not mobbed, which was good. The conversation Bellinger needed to have was one he'd prefer to keep as private as possible.

He paused by the door, taking stock of the place, and realized—oddly—that he was subconsciously scanning for some unseen threat, which surprised him. He wasn't the paranoid type. He chided himself and tried to quash his unease, but as he made his way deeper into the bar, looking for Matt, the paranoid feeling was stubbornly clinging on.

The place had a mismatched cast of topers. Cliques of young, well-dressed professionals were toasting the night away in small, loud circles, in sharp contrast to the lone, sullen mopes who sat perched on their barstools like narcoleptic vultures, staring into their tumblers through vapid eyes. The music—eighties rock, a bit tinny, coming out of a jukebox in a far corner of the bar—was just the right side of loud, which was good. They'd be able to talk without worrying about being overheard. Which, again, Bellinger realized, wasn't something he normally thought about.

He also didn't normally have sweat droplets popping up on his forehead when he visited bars. Especially not in Boston. In December. With snow falling outside.

He spotted Matt sitting in a corner booth. As he wove his way through the pockets of drinkers to join him, his cell phone rang. He paused long enough to pull it out of his pocket and check it. It was Jabba. He decided to ignore the call, stuffed the phone back into his pocket, and joined Matt.

Even hunched over his drink, Matt Sherwood's hulking stature was hard to miss. The man was six-foot-four, a full head taller than Bellinger. He hadn't changed much in the two years since Bellinger had last seen him. He still had the same brooding presence, the same angular face, the same close-cropped dark hair, the same quietly intense eyes that surveyed and took note without giving much away. If anything, any changes Bellinger thought he detected, minor though they were, were for the better. Which was inevitable, given the circumstances. He'd last seen him around the time of Danny's funeral. Matt and his kid brother had been close, Danny's death sudden and unexpected, the family rocked by an even bigger—and far worse—tragedy to befall its sons this time.

Which made dredging it up all the more difficult.

As Bellinger slipped onto the bench without bothering to take his coat off, Matt acknowledged him with a nod. "What's going on?"

Bellinger remembered that about him. Laconic, to-the-point. A man who didn't pussyfoot around, which was understandable. Time was something Matt Sherwood appreciated deeply. He'd had enough of it taken away from him already.

Bellinger found a half smile. "It's good to see you. How are you?"

"Just terrific. I've got orders coming out of my ears, what with all this bonus money floating around." He cocked his head to one side and gave Bellinger a knowing, sardonic look. "What's going on, Vince? It's way past both our bedtimes, isn't it? You said we needed to talk."

"I know, and I'm glad you could make it. It's just that . . ." Bellinger hesitated. It was a tough subject to broach. "I was thinking about Danny."

Matt's eyes stayed on Bellinger for a moment; then he

looked away, across the bar, before turning back. "What about Danny?"

"Well, last time I saw you, after the funeral . . . it was all so sudden, and we never really got a chance to talk about it. About what happened to him."

Matt seemed to study Bellinger. "He died in a helicopter crash. You know that. Not much more to tell."

"I know, but . . . what else do you know about it? What did they tell you?"

From Matt's dubious look, it was obvious he could see through Bellinger's tangential, circumspect approach. "Why are you asking me this, Vince? Why now?"

"Just . . . look, just bear with me a little here. What did they tell you? How did it happen?"

Matt shrugged. "The chopper came down off the coast of Namibia. Mechanical failure. They said it was probably due to a sandstorm they'd had out there, but they couldn't be sure. The wreck was never recovered."

"Why not?"

"There was no point. It was a private charter, and what was left of it was scattered all over the ocean floor. Not very deep there, I'm told. But the currents are tough. There's a reason they call the area 'the gates of hell.'"

Bellinger looked confused. "What about the bodies?"

Matt winced slightly. The memory was clearly a painful one. "They were never recovered."

"Why not?"

His voice rose a notch. "The area's swarming with sharks, and if they don't get you, the riptides will. It's the goddamn Skeleton Coast. There was nothing to recover."

"So you—"

"That's right. There was nothing to bury," Matt flared. He was angry now, his patience depleted. "The casket was empty, Vince. I know. It was ridiculous. We cremated an empty box and wasted some decent wood, but we had to do it that way. It helped give my dad some closure. Now are you gonna tell me why we're really here?"

Bellinger looked away, studying the faces around the bar. He felt a cold sweat rising through him, and his head throbbed with the strain of his confused, unsettling thoughts. "Did you watch the news today?"

"No. Why?"

Bellinger nodded to himself, wondering how to go on.

"Vince, what's going on?"

Just then, Bellinger's BlackBerry beeped, alerting him to the receipt of a text message. Bellinger kept his hands on the table, ignoring it. He didn't have the patience to deal with Jabba now.

He fixed on Matt and leaned in. "I think Danny may have been murdered." He paused, letting the words sink in, then added, "Or worse."

Matt's expression curdled, and he looked like he'd been winded. "Murdered or worse? What could be worse?"

"Maybe he's being held somewhere. Maybe they all are."

"What?" His face was twisted with utter disbelief. "What the hell are you talking about?"

Bellinger motioned with his hand to keep it down and leaned in closer. "Maybe they killed Danny and the others and faked the chopper crash. Then again, maybe they've still got them locked up somewhere, working on it against their will." His eyes were twitching left and right, scanning the bar. "I mean, think about it. If you got a bunch of geniuses to design something secret for you, wouldn't you want to keep them around long enough to make sure nothing went wrong when you finally used it?"

His phone beeped again.

"To design what? You're not making sense."

Bellinger leaned in even closer and his voice dropped down almost to a whisper. "Something happened today, Matt. In Antarctica. There was this thing, in the sky. It's all over the news. I think Danny had something to do with it."

"Why would you think that?"

Bellinger was shaking visibly now, the words tumbling out of him nervously. His phone beeped again, but he ignored it. "Danny was working on something. He was playing around with distributed processing and he showed me some of his stuff and we talked about it and the possibilities were just mind-blowing, you know? I mean, he was brilliant—you know that. But then Reece showed up and whisked him away to work with him on that project of his, the biosensors, and—"

"Reece?"

"Dominic Reece. He taught him. He was his guru at MIT." Bellinger shook his head, as if trying to block an unwelcome thought. "He was also in that chopper. With Danny." He looked at Matt, as if to apologize for bringing it up. After a quiet beat, he added, "Anyway, it was a great project. The sensors would have saved thousands, tens of thousands of lives, and—"

His phone beeped for the fourth time.

Bellinger lost his train of thought and frowned. He ripped his concentration away from Matt and irritably fished out his phone. He grimaced as he fumbled to get to his in-box, and saw that three messages had come in from the same number.

Not Jabba's. The messages were all from a number he didn't recognize.

He punched up the last of the messages.

The words on the small screen hit him like a sledge-hammer.

They simply read, "If you want to live, shut the fuck up and leave the bar now."

Chapter 12

Boston, Massachusetts

"I think Danny may have been murdered."

The penny-sized mike tucked away under the lapel of Bellinger's coat sucked in the words and rocketed them over to the earpieces of the three operatives who sat in the van that was parked outside the bar on Emerson.

The two other operatives—the ones inside the bar with the barely noticeable, clear earpieces—heard them too.

In the van, the operative leading the surveillance team looked up pointedly at his auburn-haired colleague. She had done well. Her hands had been lightning quick, the move fluidly executed, the tag unnoticed. It had also helped that her beguiling eyes and teasing smile had distracted Bellinger. He hadn't been the first to fall under her spell.

But he now needed to be contained.

The voice of one of the men in the bar shot through their earpieces. "He's not going for it."

The lead operative scowled and brought up his wrist mike. "I'm giving him another prod. Get ready to move in if he still doesn't take the hint."

The harsh voice came back with, "Standing by."

He hit the SEND button on his cell phone again.

◄◦►

THE WORDS on the screen seared Bellinger's eyes. He glanced up, his alarmed gaze raking the bar, a tourniquet of dread choking the life out of his heart. Everyone around him suddenly looked suspicious, threatening, dangerous.

Matt noticed.

"What is it?" he asked.

Bellinger blinked repeatedly. He was having trouble focusing. For a confused moment, the faces in the bar all seemed to be staring at him with unbridled malevolence.

Matt's voice broke through again. "Vince. What is it?"

Bellinger turned to him, his words catching in his throat. "This was a mistake. Forget I said anything."

"What?"

Bellinger stumbled to his feet. He looked squarely at Matt, his eyes bristling with fear. "Forget I said anything, all right? I've got to go."

Matt shot up to his feet from behind the table and reached out, just managing to grab hold of Bellinger's arm. "Cut the crap, Vince. What's going on?"

Bellinger spun around, yanking his arm free with rabid ferocity before pushing Matt back with both hands. His frenzied reaction surprised Matt, who fell back and landed heavily, jarring his head against the booth's wooden edge and triggering a ripple of commotion that startled the drinkers closest to him and pushed them back a step.

Matt straightened up, his head throbbing from the knock, and staggered to his feet in time to glimpse Bellinger disappearing into the crowd, rushing for the door.

He bolted after him, ducking into his wake, into the

clear path that snaked through the drinkers all the way to the bar's entrance.

He burst out onto the pavement and stopped in his tracks at the sight of Bellinger being manhandled by two bulky men and getting dragged into the back of a van.

Matt shouted, "Hey," and charged at them, only his feet had barely left the ground when he felt something heavy slam into him from behind, catching him at the base of the neck and across his back, pounding the breath out of him and sending him flying face-first onto the snow-speckled pavement.

He landed badly, his right elbow taking the brunt of his weight and lighting up with pain, and before he could push himself back onto his feet, two sets of strong arms grabbed him, pinned his arms behind his back, and shoved him toward the van before throwing him in through its open doors.

He landed—hard—on the van's ribbed, bare-metal floor, heard the van's doors slam shut somewhere behind him, and felt his weight slide back as the van took off. Jarring images and sensations were coming at him thick and fast and assaulting him from all angles. Still face-down, one eye squashed against the floor, he heard muffled shouts and angled his head up to glimpse Bellinger, the two bulky men over him, and the vague outline of—that couldn't be right—a woman with a shoulder-length bob, seemingly attractive, looking back from the driver's seat, her head silhouetted against the van's windshield, backlit by the streaming lights from beyond. One of the men was sitting on Bellinger's back, pinning him down, one hand covering Bellinger's mouth and blocking his screams of protest. The other was bent down beside them and loomed over Bellinger. He held something that looked like an oversized electric shaver in his hand.

A vaguely familiar high-pitched whine, something powering up, pricked the edge of Matt's hearing, but in his frazzled state, he couldn't quite place it. He turned, trying to shift himself over and onto his back, but one of the men who had grabbed him stomped down heavily on his back and sent him splattering against the van's floor again. A jolt of nausea rushed through Matt as the whine reached a fevered pitch, and his muscles seized up as he realized what it was.

Straining to raise his head an inch, he caught sight of the second man bringing his hand down onto Bellinger and branding him with what Matt now realized was a pocket Taser. Bellinger screamed out in agony as a faint blue light flickered inside the van. A two-second burst was usually enough to bring a fit man down with major muscle spasms; three seconds were enough to turn most men into the sobbing equivalent of a fish flopping around on a dry dock. Bellinger's hit lasted well over five seconds, and Matt knew what the effect on the scientist would be. He'd been at the receiving end of those prods. It wasn't a pleasant sensation, especially not when they were wielded by neolithic prison guards. His skin bristled at the memory, the buzzing noise dredging up the pain of what felt like thousands of needles being shoved simultaneously into every pore of his body.

The van made a left turn, the shift in momentum allowing Matt a brief respite from the weight pinning him down, and he spotted Bellinger's tormentor finally putting down the Taser and bringing out something much smaller, something that glinted at him in the jagged lights cutting in and out of the van, a syringe, which he swiftly plunged into the stricken man's back, just below the neck.

Bellinger's flopping stopped.

"He's done," the man announced without a hint of exertion or discomfort in his voice, as if what he'd just accomplished was no more than a routine chore.

The bulldozer sitting on Matt asked, "What about this one?"

The man who'd dealt with Bellinger mulled the question for a moment. "Same deal," he decided.

Not the answer Matt was hoping for. Then again, none of the likely answers held much appeal.

One thing he knew: He wasn't about to sit back and let a million volts fry him inside out.

He glimpsed the man moving off Bellinger and making his way over to the back of the van, the pocket Taser in hand, the ominous whine cranking up again.

Just then, the van made another turn, a right one this time.

Time to be a killjoy.

The weight of the bulldozer sitting on top of him shifted slightly from the turn, lightening momentarily. Matt summoned up the furious energy in every corpuscle of his body and suddenly heaved back, as hard as he could. The move caught his captor by surprise, making him lose his balance and sending him flying against the wall of the van. Matt quickly managed to get both hands under him to increase his leverage, then followed through with a full twist, weaving his fingers together and locking them just as he swung around and used his extended arms as a baseball bat.

He caught the bulldozer flat across the nose, a loud, bone-crushing splat erupting in the van. The man's head ricocheted against the van's wall before he curled over, writhing with pain.

Matt didn't pause to watch. There were three other thugs to deal with. The two who'd been busy with Bellinger could wait. The bulldozer's partner, also at the back of the van, was the more immediate threat, and he was already leaping at Matt. Matt steadied himself on his elbow and bent down as he followed through with his roll, the move adding momentum to his leg, which lashed out and hammered the incoming attacker across the neck. As the man's head bounced heavily off the van's rear doors, Matt pounced up, grabbed his head with both hands, and pulled it down, connecting it with his knee. Something in the man's face cracked audibly and he went reeling backward, toward the front of the van, falling over the immobile body of Bellinger and interrupting the other two men's advance.

Matt saw them clambering over Bellinger and knew he only had a second or two of clear air. He also knew he wasn't likely to take them out as easily.

There was only one option, really, and he didn't hesitate.

He grabbed the rear door handle, yanked it open and, despite the microglimpse of a car trailing not too far back, flung himself out of the moving van.

He didn't have far to free-fall before hitting the asphalt. It was beyond brutal. His left shoulder and hip took the brunt of it, a lightning bolt of pain shooting through him as he landed. He rolled on himself several times, a cascade of confusing, alternating glimpses of streetlights and tarmac flooding his senses, every inch of his body getting its share of beating. A sudden, ear-piercing shriek hounded him, bearing down on him alarmingly fast, the sound of rubber scraping deliriously across asphalt, the hard-braking car's front bumper only a few feet behind him and gaining fast.

They finally came to a rest together, as if in a synchronized performance, Matt inches away from the car that had fishtailed slightly and was now at a slight angle to the road. Through his dazed whiteout from the pain and the headlights, Matt could feel the heat radiating out from the car's grille, and the air was thick with the smell of burned rubber and brake pads. His shoulder was alight with pain. He steeled himself and straightened up, and glanced down the road. The van was quickly receding, one of the men—it was already too far for anything more specific—looking back before reaching out and slamming the door shut.

Matt pushed himself to his feet. His left leg almost gave way, but he steadied himself against the car's fender. He staggered over to the driver's window. The driver—a man, old, sixties plus—was staring at Matt with a combination of trepidation and disbelief. Matt bent down to look in on him. The old man's window was still closed. Matt gestured for him to open it, but the man just sat there, riven with fear.

Matt rapped his knuckles against the window. "Open the window, goddammit," he shouted, gesturing frantically. "Open it."

The man hesitated, then shook his head, his brow furrowed with confusion.

Matt jangled the door handle brusquely, but the doors were locked. He slammed the flat of his hand against the window again, scowling at the old man and yelling, "Open the goddamn door."

The man did nervous little minishakes with his head again, darted an anxious glance into his rearview mirror, glanced over at Matt again, then turned to face ahead and just hit the gas. Matt reeled back and just watched, dumbstruck, as the car tore off and disappeared into the darkness.

Chapter 13

Deir Al-Suryan Monastery, Wadi Natrun, Egypt

Ablossoming glint of golden light rose from behind the distant horizon as the three men climbed down the mountain.

They'd waited for close to an hour for Father Jerome to show up, and when he still hadn't appeared, they'd finally given up and made their way back. They didn't speak at all during the hike down or on the drive back. The abbot had simply nodded when asked by the younger monk if he'd been right about what they'd seen, and left it at that.

He needed to think.

Yusuf pulled up outside the monastery and offered to stick around should he be needed. The abbot told him he wasn't, and thanked him; then his expression and his voice darkened.

"Yusuf," he said gravely, "I need you to keep what you know about all this to yourself. No one else must be told. For now. Things could get out of hand very quickly if news of this came out. We need to handle this with great care. Do you understand?"

Yusuf nodded somberly, and kissed the abbot's hand. *"Bi amrak, abouna."* As you wish, Father.

The abbot studied him fervently for a beat, making

sure his admonishment sank in, then nodded, giving him permission to leave. He and the monk watched as Yusuf climbed back into the Previa and drove away.

"What are we going to do?" Brother Ameen asked.

The abbot's gaze followed the disappearing minivan. "First, I need to pray. This is all too . . . unsettling. Will you join me?"

"Of course."

They entered the monastery through the small gate in the thick, forty-foot wall that surrounded it. Just inside the enclosure, to their right, the large *qasr*—the keep—a four-storied white cube punctured by tiny, irregular rectangular openings, squatted proudly in the dawn light, its timber drawbridge now permanently lowered and welcoming.

It hadn't always been the case. The sixth-century monastery had been rebuilt several times during its turbulent history.

The valley of Wadi Natrun, which owed its name to the abundant natron in its soil, the sodium carbonate that was a key ingredient in mummification, was the birthplace of Christian monasticism. The tradition had started in the third and fourth centuries, when thousands of followers of Christ had fled there to escape from Roman persecution. Hundreds of years later, still more went there, this time to escape persecution at the hands of the Muslims. The valley held a special resonance for the faithful: It was there that Mary, Joseph, and their infant son had rested while escaping from King Herod's men, before continuing on to Cairo.

At first, the small communities of early Christians had lived in the caves that dotted the low ridges overlooking the desert, surviving off the meager offerings of its scattered oases. Soon, they began to build monasteries where they hoped to worship in relative peace and safety, but the threats never went away, not for centuries. Desert tribes picked up the Romans' baton of aggression and proved even more ruthless. The most vicious of those attacks, at the hands of Berbers in 817, decimated the monastery. When men didn't threaten it, nature itself proved a willing understudy, with only one of the monastery's monks surviving an outbreak of plague in the fourteenth century. And yet, time after time, the persistence and dedication of holy men kept on resurrecting it, and today, the monastery was home to over two hundred monks who followed in the footsteps of the desert fathers of the Old Testament and came here to escape from the distractions of daily life and the temptations of earthly desire to battle their own demons and pray for the salvation of mankind.

The valley had been an oasis of Christianity from the very first days of the movement. The monastic tradition was born there, long before it was eventually adopted by the Christians of Europe. For centuries, profoundly religious men had been drawn to its desolate wilderness. And on the dawn of this portentous day, the abbot thought, it seemed eminently possible that the valley hadn't yet exhausted its relevance to the faithful.

And yet . . . the very thought scared him.

The world was a very different place.

More technologically advanced, undoubtedly. More civilized, perhaps—in certain respects, in certain pockets. But, at its core, it remained as vicious and predatory as it had ever been. Perhaps even more so.

The monk followed the abbot past the keep, through the courtyard that forked off into the Chapel of the Forty-Nine Martyrs—a single, domed chamber that was dedicated to the monks killed during a Berber raid in the year 444—and into the Church of the Holy Virgin, the monastery's main place of worship. Mercifully, none of the other monks was there yet, but the abbot knew the solitude wouldn't last too long.

He led the monk past the nave and into the *khurus*—the choir. As he passed the grand wooden portal that separated the two areas, his eyes drifted up to a wall painting adorning a half cupola overhead, a thousand-year-old depiction of the Annunciation that he'd seen countless times. In it, four prophets were gathered around the Holy Virgin and the archangel Gabriel. The abbot found his gaze drawn to the first prophet to the right of the Virgin, Ezekiel, and a chill crawled down his neck at the sight. And for the next hour, as he desperately prayed for guidance, he couldn't shake the thought of the prophet's celestial vision from his weary mind: the heavens opening up to a whirlwind of amber fire folding on itself, the wheels of fire in a sky "the color of a terrible crystal," all of it heralding the voice of God.

They prayed, side by side, for close to an hour, facing the black, stone altar, prostrating themselves against the cold floor of the chapel in the praying tradition of the early Christians, a posture that was later adopted by Islam.

"Shouldn't we have waited longer for him?" Ameen asked. With the sun comfortably ensconced in the eastern sky, they were now—alone—in the monastery's small, newly restored museum. "What if something's happened to him?"

The abbot had been concerned about that himself, and not for the first time. Still, he shrugged stoically. "He's been up there for months. I should think he knows how to handle the mountain by now. He seems to be coping well."

After a quiet beat, the younger monk cleared his throat and asked, "What are we going to do, Father?"

"I'm not sure what we should do," the abbot replied. "I don't understand what's happening."

Ameen's eyebrows shot up with incredulity. "A miracle. That's what's happening."

The abbot frowned. "Something we don't understand is happening, yes. But from there to say it's a miracle . . ."

"What other explanation is there?"

The abbot shook his head, lost for words.

"You said it yourself," the younger monk persisted. "The sign you described, what you saw on the news."

A confused tangle of images clouded the abbot's mind. He thought back to that day in the desert. When their guest had been found, before he took to the caves. The terrible state he was in. His recovery.

The word *miraculous* glided into his thoughts again.

"It doesn't fit any of the prophecies of our holy book," he finally said.

"Why does it need to?"

The comment took the abbot by surprise. "Come, Brother. Surely you don't mean to negate the truth in those writings?"

"We're living a miracle, Father," Ameen exclaimed, his voice flushed with excitement. "Not reading about it hundreds of years after the fact, knowing full well it's been translated and embellished and corrupted by countless hands. Living it. Now. In this modern day and age." He paused, then added, pointedly, "With all the power of modern communication at our disposal."

The abbot's face contracted with unease. "You want people to know about this?"

"They already know about the sign. You saw the woman on the news service. Her images and words will have reached millions."

"Yes, but . . . until we understand what exactly is happening, we can't allow this to come out."

Ameen spread out his hands questioningly. "Isn't it evident, Father?"

The abbot felt cowed by his colleague's fervent gaze, and nodded thoughtfully. He understood the younger man's exuberance, but it needed to be reined in. There was no running away from what was happening; of that, he had no doubt. He had to face it. He'd been thrust into this unwittingly, and now he needed to do what needed to be done. But with care, and caution.

"We need to study the scriptures more closely," he concluded. "Consult with our superiors." He paused, weighing the hardest part of the task ahead. "Most important, we need to go back up to the caves and talk to him. Tell him what's happened. Perhaps he will know what to make of it."

Ameen stepped closer. "Everything you say is reasonable, but it doesn't detract from the fact that we can't keep this to ourselves," he pleaded. "We've received a grace from God. We owe it to Him to share it with the world. People need to know, Father. The world needs to know."

"Not yet," the abbot insisted, firmly. "It's not up to us to decide."

The younger monk's voice rose with concern. "Forgive me, Father, but I believe you're making a mistake. Others, many others, will undoubtedly try to claim the sign as their own. And in doing so, they will cheapen and corrupt this most sublime of messages. We live in cynical, amoral times. These charlatans will make it harder for the true voice to be heard. Our message could easily be drowned out by impostors and opportunists, irreversibly so. We can't wait. We have to move quickly before the chaos turns this divine event into a circus."

The abbot sat down and sighed wearily, massaging his brow with his calloused hands, feeling the room tightening in around him. The young monk's words rang true, but he couldn't bring himself to take that step. The consequences were too frightening to contemplate. He sat there, tongue-tied with uncertainty, staring at the stone floor while the monk hovered nearby, his steps heavy with frustration, waiting. The painting in the chapel crept back into his mind's eye, and he thought again of Ezekiel's vision:

Wheels of fire in a sky the color of a terrible crystal, all of it heralding the voice of God.

After a moment, the abbot looked up, a frown darkening his face. "It's not up to us," he repeated. "We need to consult with the councils and bring the matter to His Holiness. They will decide."

◄○►

AN HOUR LATER, Brother Ameen stood in the shadows and watched from the sanctity of a dark hallway as the library's curator stepped out of his office.

He'd failed to convince the abbot. The old man was visibly overwhelmed by what he'd seen and seemed incapable of grasping the enormity of what was happening. But the younger man wasn't about to let that stop him.

He needed to take matters into his own hands.

He waited patiently, his eyes tracking the priest as he ventured across the courtyard and entered the refectory. Moments later, the young monk sneaked into the priest's office, picked up the telephone, and started dialing.

Chapter 14

Less than a mile from the ridge that the two monks and the driver had just climbed down, a boy of fourteen ambled after his small herd with tired feet.

Despite the early wake-ups, the boy did like the mornings best, as did all seven of his father's goats. The sun was still low, the valley cloaked by the long shadows of the hills surrounding them. The cool breeze was a welcome alternative to the sun that would soon be bearing down on them, and the purple hues of the barren landscape were also easier on the eyes and, if he allowed himself to think of them that way, more inspirational.

Humming a tune he'd recently heard on his father's radio, he rounded an outcropping of rocks and stopped in his tracks at the unexpected sight before him. Three men—soldiers, it seemed, from their outfits—were loading equipment into a dust-caked, canvas-topped pickup truck. Equipment like he'd never seen before. Like the sand beige, drumlike object, perhaps three feet wide but only five or six inches deep, that snared his attention.

Even though the boy had frozen in place and stopped breathing, the men spotted him instantly. His eyes drew a line of hard, unforgiving stares that seared through the black Ray-Bans the men were wearing. He barely had time to register the familiar gear he'd seen on countless news broadcasts of the war in Iraq—the sand-colored camouflage BDUs, the boots, the sunglasses—before one of the men spat out a brief word and the others dropped what they were doing and took quick strides toward him.

The boy started to run, but he didn't make it far. He felt one of the men rush up to him and tackle him from behind, bringing him down into the parched soil head-first.

With his heart in his throat, he wondered what the hell they wanted from him, why they'd wrestled him to the ground, why he was biting into the sand and grit that also pricked painfully at his eyes. In a mad frenzy of terror, he tried to squirm around and get onto his back, but the man who sat on him was too heavy and had him solidly pinned down.

He heard another man's footsteps crunching their way closer, then glimpsed a pair of military boots from the corner of his eye, looming over him like a demigod.

He didn't hear a word.

He didn't see the nod.

And he didn't feel a thing after the big, practiced hands of the man sitting on top of him quickly and efficiently took up their positions—one around the side of his neck, the other around the other side of his head—and tightened their grip before twisting suddenly and fiercely in opposite directions.

Swift, silent, deadly.

It was, without a doubt, a well-earned motto.

Chapter 15

"If you figure anything out, call me, okay? Just call me, anytime." Gracie gave out her satphone number, hung up, and heaved a sigh of frustration.

Another dead end.

She mopped her face with her hands before sweeping them tightly through her hair, massaging some life into her scalp. She'd managed to coax some good video bites from Simmons and some of the other scientists on board, and while Dalton was editing it all into a high-def report to broadband back to the news desk in D.C.—much better than the jumpy, grainy Began live feed they'd used for the first broadcast, more *Armageddon,* less *Cloverfield* this time around—she'd been working the satphone.

Her years on the job had allowed her to build up a beefy Rolodex, and right now, she was mining it for all its worth. She spoke to a contact of hers at NASA, a project director she'd met while covering the space shuttle *Columbia*'s disaster back in 2003. She also called contacts of hers at CalTech and at the Pentagon, as well as the editor of *Science* magazine and the network's science and technology guru.

They were all as baffled as she was.

She'd hardly hung up when the satphone rang.

Another reporter, angling for a comment.

"How are they managing to get hold of this number?" she groaned to Finch.

He pulled a who-knows face and grabbed the phone for yet another polite, but firm, rebuff. For the moment, it was their exclusive—for better or for worse.

It was not that she was camera shy, or that she didn't like being in the public eye. Far from it. Her career as a TV correspondent wasn't an accident: She'd wanted it ever since high school. She'd pursued every opportunity to get those breaks, and once she did, she'd worked damn hard at grabbing her share of airtime and overcoming the endemic misogyny and the subtle bullying in the industry. She thrived on the stories she covered and the experiences she shared with her viewers, she loved stepping in front of that camera and telling the world what she'd found out, and undeniably, the camera loved her back. She had that unquantifiable magnetism that went beyond the purely physical. People just tuned in and enjoyed her company. Focus groups confirmed her broad appeal: Women weren't threatened by her, they took a possessive pride in her expertise, and in an age where public image was everything and every word was carefully weighed for effect, her candor and honesty were a big draw; men, while readily admitting that they fancied the pants off her, more often than not pointed out how they found her brain to be just as much of a turn-on.

And so she'd gone from local reporter at a network affiliate in Wisconsin to weekend anchor at a bigger affiliate in Illinois and eventually to anchor and special correspondent for the network's flagship Special Investigations Unit. In the process, she'd become a face America trusted, whether she was reporting from Kuwait in the run-up to the invasion of Iraq, on board a Greenpeace vessel stalking Japanese whaling ships, or following the unfolding tragedies of the tsunami in Thailand and Hurricane Katrina in New Orleans.

More recently, she'd been unwittingly drawn into the emotionally charged debate on global warming. She'd approached the issue as a skeptic, her instincts compelling her to question—on air—the often lazy assumptions of the ever-more-fashionable, almost religious, environmental movement. She knew how unreliable long-term forecasts were, how history was littered with the failed predictions of the most brilliant minds on everything from population levels to oil prices, and she hadn't minced her words when voicing her skepticism. Up until then, her honesty and integrity had served her well. On this issue, her candor proved to be a problem. The reaction had been nothing less than incendiary. She was lambasted for her doubts from all corners, and her career had hung in the balance.

She decided the subject matter merited her attention, whichever side of the fence she ended up on. She pitched a comprehensive, no-holds-barred, in-depth documentary tackling the issue, and the network's brass signed off on it. And so, with the vast majority of her colleagues mired in the quicksands of the marathon election campaign back home, she focused her energies on examining all the available data on the climate issue and meeting everyone who mattered. She was soon convinced that greenhouse gases had undoubtedly risen in the last few decades, and the earth did appear to be warming, but she still needed to find out if the connection between the two was as direct as it was now being portrayed. And so she'd crisscrossed the globe, from the remote science station of Cherskii in Siberia, where 40,000-year-old permafrost was now thawing and, in the process, releasing huge amounts of greenhouse gases, to Greenland, where massive glaciers were sliding toward the sea at a rate of two yards every hour, taking a forensic look at every new report on the matter during her travels.

Her investigative claws sharpened when she looked into the Global Climate Coalition, the Information Council of the Environment, and the Greening Earth Society—all of them cleverly misnamed, created and funded by the automotive, petroleum, and coal industries with the sole purpose of deceiving the public by spreading disinformation and callously repositioning global warming as *theory* rather than *fact*. It didn't take long for her to become more and more convinced that the planet was indeed in trouble because of us. What was far less clear, however, was what we could realistically—and pragmatically—do about it. That was a far more contentious, and troubling, debate, and one she felt very passionate about.

But she hadn't expected it to lead to this.

She breathed out with exasperation. "I'm getting nothing here. You having better luck?" she asked Finch as she got out of her chair and walked over to the window to scan the skies.

Finch had been talking to the news desk back in D.C. and trawling through his own contacts list. "Nope. If it's natural, no one's seen anything like it. And if it's not, they're all telling me the technology to pull off something like this just doesn't exist."

"We don't know that," Dalton objected, looking up from his monitor. "I'm sure there's a lot of stuff out there that we don't know about."

"Yes, but what we don't know about doesn't really matter in this case, because there's nothing we know about that even comes close."

"You lost me."

"Technology breakthroughs—they have to start somewhere," Finch explained. "They don't just come out of nowhere. No one suddenly came up with cell phones. It started with Alexander Graham Bell two hundred years ago. There's a progression. Regular phone, cordless home phones, digital phones, and eventually, cell phones . . . Stealth fighters—we didn't know about them, but they're just evolutions of other fighter planes. You see what I mean? Technology evolves. And that thing we saw . . . There doesn't seem to be anything out there that we can point to and say, 'Well, if we took that and made it bigger, or more powerful, or used it in such a way, it could explain it.' It's in a whole different ballpark. And everyone's trying to figure it out. I mean, look at this." He pulled up the latest e-mail from D.C. "It's going ballistic," he enthused. "Reuters, AP, CNN. They're all carrying it. Every station from London to Beijing is running it. Same for the big news blogs. Drudge, Huffington. It's been voted up to number one on Digg, and we've crossed two hundred thousand hits on YouTube. And the chat rooms are just going nuts over it."

"What are they saying?"

"From what I can see, people are in one of three camps. Some of them think it's some kind of harmless stunt, a CGI, *War of the Worlds* kind of thing. Others also think it's a con but they see something more sinister in it, and they're throwing out all kinds of crazy ideas about how it could have been pulled off, none of which seem to hold water if you read the mocking replies they're getting from people who seem to know what they're talking about."

"Is there anyone who doesn't think we're behind it?"

"Yep. The third group: the pro camp. The ones who believe it's the real thing—real as in God, not ET. One of them called us 'the heralds of the Second Coming.'"

"Well, that makes me feel so much better," she groaned, her chest tightening with unease. Greed and fear were tugging at her. Part of her was thrilled by the idea of being the face of the hottest story around—she couldn't deny that—but the more reasoned side of her was clamoring for restraint. She knew what she'd seen; she just didn't know what it was. And until she did, she was uncomfortable with how it was all spiraling out of control. If it turned out to be something less momentous than everyone was suggesting, she could already picture Jon Stewart ridiculing her into an early retirement.

Finch spun the laptop back and tapped some more keys. "And speaking of ET," he said as he glanced pointedly across at Dalton, "a guy I know at the Discovery Channel sent me these." He turned the screen back so it was facing them. "Some of them are the ones you'd expect, like clouds and Concorde contrails that make people think they're seeing UFOs. I don't know if I should be surprised, but he tells me there are over two hundred reported UFO sightings a month in America. *A month*. But then, there's a whole slew of historic references to unexplained sightings going back thousands of years. We're talking hundreds of references throughout history about bright balls of fire, flying 'earthenware vessels,' luminous discs. It's not just a modern phenomenon. I mean, check out these historical records: 'Japan, 1458: An object as bright as the full moon and followed by curious signs was observed in the sky.' Or this one: 'London, 1593: A flying dragon surrounded by flames was seen hovering over the city.'"

"Opium'll do that to you every time," Dalton half joked. "Seriously. Drugs were legal back then, weren't they?"

"Besides, none of these references are even remotely verifiable," Gracie added.

"Sure, but the thing is, there are so many of them. Written continents apart, at a time when traveling from one to another was virtually impossible, when most of the world was illiterate. Even the Bible's got them."

"Big surprise there," Gracie scoffed. A charged silence hung between them. "So what are we saying? What do you think we saw?"

Finch pulled off his glasses and used his sleeve to give them a wipe as he thought about it. "I'd have said mass hallucination if it wasn't for the footage." He shook his head slowly in disbelief, slipped his glasses back on, and looked up at Gracie. "I can't explain it."

"Dalton?" she asked.

His face clouded with uncertainty. He leaned back in his chair and ran his hands tightly through his hair. "I don't know. There was something . . . ethereal about it, you know? It didn't look flat, like something projected, but then it didn't look like something hard and physical either. It's hard to explain. There was something much more organic, much more visceral about it. Like it was part of the sky, like the sky itself had lit up—you know what I'm saying?"

"I do," Gracie agreed uncomfortably. The sight of the bright, glowing sign, as vivid as when she first saw it, materialized in her mind's eye. An upwelling of elation, the same one she felt when she first saw it, overcame her again as she remembered how it had formed itself out of nothing. *It was as if the air itself had been summoned by God, lit up from within into that shape,* she found herself thinking. Which didn't sit well with her. She'd stopped believing in God when her mother died, ripped away from her young daughter by an unrelenting tumor in her breast. And now, here it was, this unexplained thing in the sky. As if it were taunting her.

She pushed the thought away. *Get a grip. We're running ahead of ourselves here. There's got to be a logical explanation for it.*

But a nagging question kept coming back.

What if there isn't?

Gracie stared out the window, scanning the sky for another sighting, her jumbled mind desperate for an answer. The satphone rang, and as Finch stretched across the table to answer it, her mind migrated to a UFO hoax from a year earlier. The clip, showing a UFO buzzing a beach in Haiti, had clocked up over five million viewings on YouTube within days of its posting, hogging chat rooms and news aggregator sites across the Web and popping up on every FunWall on Facebook. Millions were taken in by it—until it turned out to be something a French computer animator had put together in a few hours on his MacBook, using commercially available software, reluctantly explaining it away as a "sociological experiment" for a movie—about a UFO hoax, natch—that he was working on. With the advances in special effects and the proliferation of faked videos of such high quality that they managed to convince even the most staunch of skeptics, a subtle question arose in Gracie's mind: Would people recognize a "true" event of this kind when—as it seemed—it really happened? She knew what she saw. It was right there in front of her, but everyone else was only seeing it on a screen. And without seeing it with their own eyes, could they ever accept it for what it was, something wondrous and inexplicable and possibly even supernatural or divine—or would it be drowned in a sea of cynicism?

"Gracie," Finch called out, covering the phone's mouthpiece with his hand.

She turned.

His face had a confused scrunch to it. "It's for you."

"Now what?" she grumbled.

"I'm not sure, but . . . it's coming from Egypt. And I think you need to take it."

Chapter 16

Boston, Massachusetts

There were no cabs around, but it didn't take too long for Matt to get back to his car. The van hadn't traveled that far from the bar before he'd dived out of it. He would've made it back sooner, but he wasn't at his best. He felt groggy and nauseous, his skin had been scraped raw in several places, and every bone in his body felt like it had been hammered by a blacksmith on steroids. And, as if to add insult to injury, it was snowing again.

He was relieved to find his car, a highland green 1968 Mustang GT 390 "Bullitt" Fastback that was his next restoration project, still where he'd left it, close to the bar on Emerson. It hadn't even occurred to him to check for his keys before he got to it, but, mercifully, they were also still there, safely ensconced in the pocket of his peacoat.

Just a couple of small miracles to cap off a magical night.

Less miraculous, though, was the fact that he'd lost his cell phone. He guessed it had probably flown out of the pocket of his coat during his hard landing on the asphalt, though he didn't dwell on it. He had more pressing concerns.

He leaned against the car and caught his breath, and the brutal images of a helpless Bellinger getting fried and injected roared back into his mind's eye. He had to do something to try to help him, but he couldn't see a move that made sense. He couldn't report it to the cops. The van was long gone, and the inevitable questions he'd be asked, given his record, would only cloud the issue. More to the point, he didn't think the risk of flagging his whereabouts to the goon squad who'd come after Bellinger was outweighed by any positive effect it would have on helping the cops find Bellinger and bringing him back safely.

Which, somehow, he didn't think was going to happen anyway.

The traffic was light and scattered as he drove home, the city now tucked in under a thin blanket of snow. He was on the expressway within minutes, and from there, it was only a short hop down to Quincy and the studio apartment he lived in over his workshop. As he cruised south, his mind ground over what had happened to him, trying to make sense of the rush of events that had come at him from nowhere and figure out what the right move would be.

Bellinger had called. He'd asked for a meeting, one that couldn't wait. He'd then hit him with the news that his brother might have been murdered, or that his death might have been faked and that he might be locked up somewhere. How had he put it, exactly? *Working on it, against their will?*

Danny, alive—but locked up somewhere?

The thought flooded Matt's gut with equal doses of elation—and rage. Matt and Danny had always been close, which never failed to amaze their friends, given how different they were. For a start, they didn't look anything like each other. Matt, three years older, had inherited his dad's olive skin, dark hair, and solid build, whereas Danny—two shades fairer and fifty pounds lighter—took after his mom. The stark difference between them extended to, well, pretty much everything else. Matt had no patience for classes or for schoolwork, whereas Danny had an insatiable appetite for learning. Matt lettered in as many sports as he could cram into his schedule. Danny couldn't sink a basket if he was sitting on the backboard. Off campus, the contrast between the two brothers wasn't any less pronounced. Matt was irreverent, wild, and reckless—in other words, a babe magnet. Danny was far more introverted and preferred the company of the computer he'd found in a junk shop and rebuilt in his bedroom. Still, despite it all, they had a bond that was unshakable, a deep understanding of each other that survived the nastiest taunts and the most callous temptations that high school could throw at them.

Their friendship had also survived Matt's repeated collisions with the law.

As with a lot of cases like his, things had started small. Matt had built his first car at the age of thirteen, hooking up an old washing-machine engine to a soapbox derby car that became something of a fixture around his neighborhood. The local cops were amazed and even the hardheaded sticklers among them couldn't quite bring themselves to take away his pride and joy—a relationship that would change dramatically over the years. For as he grew older, the disparity between his love of cars, on the one hand, and the bleak part-time work prospects available to him in the Worcester area and his parents' wafer-thin bank account, on the other, became more frustrating. Headstrong and impatient, Matt sought to redress that imbalance his own way.

Those early escapades were classic Matt. He didn't go after any old ride. He would trawl the more affluent neighborhoods of Boston for specific cars on his hit list. He also never crashed or trashed the cars he stole, nor did he ever try to sell them. He would merely abandon them in some parking lot once he'd had the chance to sample them. He managed to test-drive quite a few before he got caught. The judge he came up against on that first conviction wasn't amused or impressed by his antics.

That inaugural stint behind bars proved to have far-reaching consequences. Upon his release from jail, it didn't take long for Matt to realize how his life had changed. Work prospects dried up. Friends shied away from him. People looked at him in a different way. He had changed too. Trouble seemed to come looking for him, as if sensing it had a willing customer. His hard-working, God-fearing parents were overwhelmed and paralyzed by his wild streak. They didn't have the good sense or the strength of character to offer him the guidance he needed. His underpaid and corrupt parole officer was even less of a candle in the dark. And despite Danny's repeated, frustrated arguments about where this was headed, Matt ended up dropping out of high school before graduation, and from there, his life just spiraled out of control. He spent the next few years rotating in and out of jail for theft, criminal damage to property, and battery, among other things, his future withering away while Danny's blossomed, first at MIT, then at a highly paid job in a tech company based nearby.

As he motored across the Neponset River, Matt ruefully remembered how he hadn't seen much of Danny before his death. Matt had only been released from jail a few months before Danny had been offered the job with Reece, and he hadn't seen much of him after that. Matt had been busy setting up his business—with the help of a life-altering loan from his kid brother, he thought with a twinge of shame. In a sense, he owed him his life.

It was Danny who'd sat him down and talked some sense into him—finally. Made him realize he couldn't keep doing this. And got him to straighten up.

The way out Danny had suggested was simple. Turn what did the damage in the first place into something positive. Use it to carve out a new life. And Matt listened. He found a small car shop in Quincy that was closing down, and took over the lease. The plan he and Danny came up with was for him to find and fix up classic cars. Matt had a soft spot for American muscle cars from the sixties and seventies, like the Mustang he was now driving, a highly collectible model, a car he and Danny had fantasized about owning ever since they'd watched Steve McQueen catapult one across the streets of San Francisco—a movie they'd only seen about three dozen times. He knew it would be hard to part with it once he was done restoring it, but with a bit of luck, he'd be able to sell it for seventy grand, maybe more, probably to some deskbound executive in need of a weekend toy. In the heady days before the credit crunch, Matt had built up a solid reputation in car enthusiast circles. He'd even sold a couple to guys whose cars he'd stolen years earlier, not that they knew it. Things had been looking up for him, all while Danny had been sucked into the black hole of his new job. A black hole that had ultimately swallowed up his life.

Or had it?

Was it possible that Danny was still alive?

Bellinger had made a convincing argument for it. And he'd been grabbed seconds after making it. That had to mean something.

Whether Danny was still alive or not, the idea that they'd all been lied to, that someone knew the truth and had kept it from them—*the idea that someone, not fate, had taken Danny away from them*—felt like acid in his throat.

He wasn't about to let it slide.

He took the Willard Street exit and turned into Copeland after the roundabout, and his fury swelled even more as he thought back to how the news of Danny's death had devastated their parents. It was bad enough their eldest son was a convicted felon. To lose Danny too—their pride and joy, the redeemer of the family name—was too much to bear. Their mom had died a couple of months later. Despite the complicated medical terminology the doctors insisted on using, Matt knew it was simply a case of a broken heart. He also knew he was partly to blame. He knew the havoc raging in her veins started the day he'd been arrested that first time, if not earlier. His dad hadn't fared much better. Danny's job came with life coverage, and though the insurance payout paid for the nursing home had allowed their dad some minor touches of additional comfort, he'd been left a demolished man. He and Matt had hardly spoken at his mom's funeral, and Matt hadn't been out to see him since that bleak day in January. Then almost a year to the day later, the local sheriff, a craggy old nemesis, had managed to track Matt down to his garage in Quincy and given him the news of his dad's death. A stroke, he'd said, although Matt had his doubts about that too.

Bellinger's words echoed in his mind. Someone had taken Danny, and it was linked to something that just happened in the skies of Antarctica. It sounded outlandish and surreal. Only it clearly wasn't. The guys he'd just gone up against were very real. Highly professional. Well equipped. Ruthless. And not overly concerned with discretion.

The implications of that last point were particularly worrying.

He coasted east on Copeland, the Mustang's forty-year-old headlights struggling to break through the swarm of cottonlike snowflakes. With no other cars around, the snow had had time to settle, covering the road ahead with a thin, undisturbed white duvet. He passed Buckley and motored on until he reached the 7-Eleven and the turnoff into the alleyway that led to his shop, and just before turning in it, a remote corner of his mind registered a set of tire tracks in the fresh snow.

They belonged to a single car that had veered off Copeland. He couldn't see down the alley. His shop was tucked away about a hundred yards back from the main road, and there were no streetlights that way, but the tire tracks were more than enough to trip his internal alarm, as they could only have been heading to his place. There was nothing else down there.

Problem was, he wasn't expecting anyone.

Which didn't bode well for the rest of his magical night.

Chapter 17

Amundsen Sea, Antarctica

"You need to come here. There's something you need to see."

The caller wasn't a native English speaker, and Gracie couldn't place his accent. And although he spoke slowly and deliberately, his words were laced with an urgency that came through loud and clear, despite the less-than-crystal clarity of the satellite link.

"Slow down a second," Gracie said. "Who are you exactly, and how'd you get this number?"

"My name is Ameen. Brother Ameen, if you like."

"And you're calling from Egypt?"

"Yes. From Deir Al-Suryan—the Monastery of the Syrians, in Wadi Natrun."

Her internal kook-alert monitor, which had already moved up to yellow before the man had even started talking, got a slight nudge up to blue.

"And how'd you get this number?" she asked again, a slight edge to her voice now.

"I called your Cairo bureau."

"And they gave it to you?"

Much as her vexation was clear, the man wasn't going out of his way to placate her. Instead, he simply said, "I told them I was calling on behalf of Father Jerome."

The name bounced around Gracie's tired mind for a moment, before landing on the obvious association. "What, *the* Father Jerome?"

"Yes," he assured her. "The very same."

Her monitor took a step back to yellow. "And you're calling on his behalf from Egypt? Is that where he is?"

It suddenly occurred to her that she hadn't read anything about the world-famous humanitarian for quite a while. Which was unusual, given his highly public, if reluctantly so, profile, and given the huge organization that he'd founded and still ran, as far as she knew.

"Yes, he's here. He's been here for almost a year."

"Okay, well, now that you've got me on the line," she said, "what's this about?"

"You need to come here. To see Father Jerome."

This surprised her. "Why?"

"We saw your broadcast. You were the one to see the sign. You brought it to the world."

" 'The sign'?"

Dalton and Finch were eyeing her curiously. She gave them an I'm-not-sure-where-this-is-going shrug.

"For whatever reason," Brother Ameen said, "divine or otherwise, you were there. It's your story. And, of course, I'm familiar with your work. People listen to you. Your reputation is solid. Which is why I am telling this to you and you only."

"You haven't told me anything yet."

Brother Ameen paused, then said, "The symbol you witnessed, there, over the ice. It's here too."

An altogether different alarm blared inside her, one that sent her pulse rocketing. "What, you've got it there too? In the sky?" Her words also visibly snagged Dalton and Finch's attention.

"No, not in the sky."

"Where then?"

"You need to come here. To see it for yourself."

Gracie's kook monitor fluttered upward again. "I'm going to need a little more than that."

"It's hard to explain."

"Why don't you try?"

Brother Ameen seemed to weigh his words for a moment, then said, "Father Jerome's not exactly here, at the monastery. He was here. He came to us several months ago. He was . . . troubled. And after a few weeks, he . . . he went up into the mountain. There's a cave, you see. A cave that provides the basics—you know, a shelter with a bed to sleep in, a stove to cook on. Men of God go there when they're looking for solitude, when they don't want to be disturbed. Sometimes, they stay there for days. Sometimes, weeks. Months even."

"And Father Jerome is there?"

"Yes."

Gracie didn't quite know what to make of that. "What does that have to do with me?"

The man hesitated. He seemed uncomfortable with what he was about to tell her. "He's a changed man, Miss Logan. Something . . . something we don't quite understand has happened to him. And since he's been up in the cave, he's been writing. A lot. He's been filling one journal after another with his thoughts. And on some of their pages, there's a drawing. A recurring drawing, one he's painted all over the walls of the cave."

Gracie's skin prickled.

"It's the sign, Miss Logan. The sign you saw over the ice."

Gracie's mind scrambled to process what he'd just told her. An obvious question fought its way out of the confused mire. "No offense, Brother, but—"

"I know what you're going to say, Miss Logan." He cut her off. "And of course, you've every right to be skeptical. I wouldn't expect any less of you, of someone with your intellect. But you need to hear me out. There isn't a television up in the cave. We don't even have one here at the monastery, nor a radio for that matter. Father Jerome hasn't seen your broadcast."

Gracie's kook-o-meter was having trouble sticking to one direction. "Well, I'm not sure your word on that's gonna get me hopping on a plane just yet."

"No, you don't understand," Brother Ameen added, the restraint in his voice struggling to contain the urgency he clearly felt. "It's not something he only just started to do."

An unsettling realization chilled her gut. "What are you saying? When did he start drawing this sign?"

His answer struck her like a spear.

"Seven months ago. He's been drawing the sign over and over again for seven months."

Chapter 18

Quincy, Massachusetts

Pure instinct took over and Matt turned in early, pulling into the lot of the 7-Eleven just before the alleyway.

Being a twenty-four-hour store, it was open, but there were no other cars outside. He flicked the Mustang's lights off but left the engine gurgling, and just sat there for a moment, bathed by the alternating red-and-green flicker of the store's Christmas lights, taking stock of the situation.

They were here already. Waiting for him. Had to be.

How?

He quickly segued back to Bellinger's abduction. They must have been watching Bellinger. Maybe even listening to his calls. And if they were, they knew about his call to Matt. And if this was about Danny, then they knew all about Matt already.

And Matt had obviously become a problem for them.

Wonderful.

He gave his immediate surroundings a quick scan but didn't notice anything that jarred. They had to be waiting for him near his garage. He put himself in their place and could almost picture the perfect spot where they'd have parked, out of sight, ready to ambush him on his return. *Bastards. How could they react so quickly?* It had only been, what, not even an hour since he'd leapt out of their van?

They weren't short of resources.

Which wasn't helping on the worrisome front.

He switched the engine off, pulled up his coat collar, and climbed out of the car, his eyes stealthily alert for any movement. He took a few quick steps over to the store and huddled under its awning, using the pause to give the area another quick once-over.

Nothing.

Just the single set of tracks headed down the alleyway to the side of the 7-Eleven, disappearing into the darkness, taunting him.

He stepped inside, triggering a two-toned electronic chime that brought him to the attention of Sanjay, the store's congenial owner, who was busy restocking the hot-dog grill.

Sanjay smiled. "Hey, Matt." Then he noted the dusting of snow on Matt's head with a bemused expression and said, "It's really coming down, isn't it?" In midsentence, his forehead crinkled with confusion as he registered Matt's battered condition.

Matt just nodded absently, his mind still processing the situation while he made sure there was no one else around. "Sure is," he finally replied after the distracted beat; then his face darkened and he said, "Sanjay, I need to go out the back way."

Sanjay stared at him for a moment. "Okay," he said. "Whatever you need, Matt." They'd known each other ever since Matt had taken over the lease on the garage down the road. Matt had been a good customer and a reliable neighbor, and by now, Sanjay knew him well enough to know that Matt wouldn't be asking if it wasn't important.

He led him to the back of the store and unlocked the door.

Matt paused at the doorway. "Don't lock it just yet, will you? I won't be long."

Sanjay nodded hesitatingly. "Okay." He glanced away, then turned back and added, "You sure you're okay?"

"Not really." Matt shrugged, then slipped out the door.

There were no cars around. He stayed low and close to the wall of the back lot and headed away from the main road, making his way past Sanjay's car and the Dumpsters. Any light from the store quickly petered out, and he was soon in total darkness with only a diffused moonglow to guide him. He ducked into a patch of trees and over to a low, single-story brick structure that housed a small law firm. As expected, all of its lights were out, and no cars were around. With his left leg and hip blazing with pain with every step, he scuttled along the back wall of the building quietly until it ran out.

He bent down and chanced a peek around the corner. He'd read it right. A dark Chrysler 300C was parked in one of the law firm's spots, huddled behind the far side of the building, about twenty yards from the entrance to his shop. He could just about make out the silhouettes of two figures inside.

They were waiting for him. Either that, or they were about eight hours early for their appointment with their lawyer, and no one was that enthusiastic about meeting a lawyer.

Matt inched back into cover, his mind racing through his options. His first instinct was to charge in, beat them to a pulp, and pound the truth out of them. A few years back, he might have done just that, despite the odds. But right now, the odds weren't good, and much as he was desperate to take them on, he grudgingly forced himself to accept that it would be the wrong move. He was hurting all over, and his left leg was barely holding him up. He wouldn't stand a chance, and he knew it.

He had a momentary lapse and thought of calling the cops, but again kiboshed that idea. He didn't trust them. Never did and never would. Besides, as far as the cops were concerned, he could always count on losing any his-word-against-theirs contest. And, as he'd realized, the guys in the Chrysler seemed to have a solid setup, which meant they had connections. All he had was a rap sheet that would dry up an ink-jet cartridge.

Another idea, a more promising one, elbowed its way into that one's place. He quickly put it through its paces, looking for flaws, and decided it was his best option. His best option out of a total of one, actually. He sneaked a last glance at the Chrysler, convinced himself that they weren't going anywhere just yet, then made his way back to the 7-Eleven.

He cut through the store, past Sanjay, who gave him a worried, quizzical glance. Without breaking step, Matt flicked him a stay-put, though not hugely reassuring, gesture.

"I need some tape," he told him. "Something solid and sticky, packing tape, that kind of thing."

Sanjay thought for a beat, then nodded. "I'll get you what I have," he said as Matt disappeared out the front door.

A quick glance around yielded no visible threats. Matt walked to the back of the Mustang and popped the trunk. With practiced fingers, he pulled back the lining along its side wall. He reached in behind it and found the small niche he was looking for. In it was a small black box, not much bigger than a packet of cigarettes. Matt pulled it out and stuffed it in his inside breast pocket. He then pulled out the lug wrench from the spare wheel's tool kit, closed the trunk, and ducked back into the store.

Sanjay was waiting for him. In his hands was a roll of two-inch-thick duct tape. Matt just grabbed it, blurted out a guttural "Perfect," and kept going.

He crept back to the corner of the brick building and peered around its corner. The Chrysler was still there, as he'd left it. He checked the perimeter, backed up, and crept into the shrubs and trees behind the parking bay, keeping low. He maneuvered to a spot around fifteen yards behind the Chrysler, making sure he wasn't in the line of sight of their mirrors. From there, he dropped to the ground and crawled the rest of the way.

Matt advanced on elbows that were still suffering from his leap out of the van. He ignored the pain and kept going until he was right behind the Chrysler. He paused to catch his breath and check for a reaction. None came. Satisfied that he hadn't been spotted, he rolled onto his back and pulled himself under the car. He quickly found a strut that would suit his purpose. He reached into his pocket, pulled out the tracker, and taped it to the strut.

He was almost done when he felt a small weight shift in the car, which was followed by the click of an opening door. He turned his head sideways, to the passenger side of the car, and froze as he saw first one foot, then the other, drop to the ground, faintly illuminated by the cabin's inside light. They crunched into the snow, and the light dimmed as the man swung the door back quietly without clicking it shut.

He felt a surge of panic as a sudden realization hit him. Very slowly, he angled his head sideways to look behind the car and saw the trail he'd left behind in the snow. It led right up to the car, a black streak through the pearlescent shimmer of the light snow cover.

His body tensed up as he watched the man take a few steps. He was heading to the back of the car. Matt's eyes stayed on him, fast-forwarding to the moment the man would spot the trail and what the best move would be. With his heart in his throat, he followed the man's feet around past the rear wheel, farther back to the edge of the car—then they stopped. Every nerve ending in Matt's body throbbed with alarm, and his fingers reached under his coat and tightened against the handle of the lug wrench. He was about to swing his legs out in an attempt to kick the man off-balance when he turned so he was now facing the wall. Matt then heard a zipper open, and his body pulled back from Defcon one as he realized the man was just out there to take a leak.

He waited for him to finish, then watched without moving an inch as the man got back into the car. Matt made sure the tracker was solidly attached, then slid back out from under the car and retreated along the same path he'd taken, only pausing briefly to commit the car's license plate to memory.

He found Sanjay standing by the cash register, clearly unable to do much, out of worry.

Matt gave him a firm nod of gratitude as he reached over for a pencil and scribbled down the Chrysler's license plate on a flyer. He tucked it into his pocket, then turned to Sanjay. "Do me a favor. Anyone asks, you haven't seen me, not since lunchtime. Okay?"

Sanjay nodded. "You gonna tell me what's going on?"

Matt's expression clouded under competing instincts. "Better you don't get involved. Safer for you that way."

Sanjay acknowledged his words somberly, then hesitated and said, "You'll be careful, won't you?" in an uncertain tone, as if unsure about how much he should say or get involved.

Matt half-smiled. "That's the plan." Then he thought of something, took a few steps to the fridge, and pulled out a can of Coke. He held it up to Sanjay and said, "My tab still good?"

Sanjay visibly relaxed a touch. "Of course."

And with that, Matt was gone.

Chapter 19

Amundsen Sea, Antarctica

"So what's the verdict? Do we believe this guy?"
Gracie leaned her head against the cold glass of
the conference room's window. Outside, the light was
virtually unchanged, the sky infused with the same gray-
ish pallor, which didn't help her flagging spirit. She
needed to rest, to take a step back and give her mind a
chance to reboot, if only for an hour or two. It had to be
the equivalent of way past midnight, and the continuous
daylight of the Antarctic's austral summer had already
wreaked havoc on her body clock, but there were still
too many questions that needed to be answered.

"Gracie, come on," Dalton replied. "He's talking
about Father Jerome."

"So?"

"Are you kidding me? The guy's a living saint. He's
not gonna fake something like this. That'd be like—I
don't know—like saying the Dalai Lama's a liar."

Father Jerome wasn't technically a living saint. There
was no such thing, since dying was a prerequisite to receiving the honor of sainthood, at least as far as the Vatican was concerned. But he was pretty much a shoo-in for
beatification, if not canonization, at some point in the
future.

In his case, though, the term *saint* was more than appropriate.

He'd begun his life in 1949 as Alvaro Suarez, the son of a humble farming couple in the foothills of the Cantabrian Mountains in northern Spain. His youth was far from cosseted. His father died when he was five, leaving his mother with the unenviable task of providing for six children in a Spain that was still under Franco's iron fist and recovering from years of war. Raised a Catholic, the young Alvaro—the youngest of his siblings—showed a great resilience and generosity of character, especially during a harsh winter when a viral epidemic almost took away his mother and two of his sisters. He credited his faith with giving him the strength to forge ahead despite overwhelming odds, and with helping his mother and sisters pull through, and their salvation further solidified his bond with the Church. Throughout his youth, he was also particularly drawn to the stories of missionaries, of selfless souls doing the work of God in the less fortunate corners of the planet, and by the time he was in his teens, he knew he would devote his life to the Church. Having narrowly escaped becoming one himself, he chose to concentrate on helping orphans and abandoned children. He left home at seventeen and began his journey, joining a seminary in Andalusia before crossing into Africa, where he soon founded the first of many missions. En route, he took his first vows a few months short of his twenty-second birthday, choosing the name of Jerome after Jerome Emiliani, a sixteenth-century Italian priest and the patron saint of orphans. The modern Jerome's hospices and orphanages were now scattered across the globe. His army of volunteers had turned around the lives of thousands of the world's poorest children. His charitable work, as it turned out, had even outshone that of the historic figure who inspired him.

Forget the technicalities. The man was indeed a living saint, and Dalton's point was hard to ignore. Provided what the monk had told Gracie really did involve Father Jerome.

"Yeah, but that wasn't Father Jerome on the phone, was it? We don't even know if the caller was really calling from Egypt, much less from the monastery," she argued.

"Well, we do know Father Jerome is really there," Finch pointed out.

The reports they'd pulled up after the call confirmed that Father Jerome was indeed in Egypt. He'd fallen ill while working at one of his missions there, close to the border with Sudan, a little over a year ago. After his recovery, he'd pulled back from active duty—he was just shy of sixty now—only going so far as to say he needed to take some time for himself, "to get closer to God," in his own words. He'd subsequently retreated entirely from public view. Crucially, a couple of brief wire reports did have him traveling north and seeking out the seclusion of the monasteries of Wadi Natrun.

"And how could he actually have drawn what we saw? I mean, how would you draw it?" Gracie argued.

"We need to get a copy of that tape," Dalton suggested.

Before ending his call, Brother Ameen had offered them a tantalizing piece of corroboration. A British film crew, working for the BBC, had visited the monastery several months earlier. They'd spent a few days there, filming part of a multi-episode documentary that compared the dogmatic approach to faith in Western churches with the more mystical approaches found farther east. They'd managed to get a quick peek inside the cave and shot some footage there, before being turned away by Father Jerome. Brother Ameen assured Gracie it included footage of the priest's handiwork across its ceiling and walls.

It was proof that Gracie desperately needed to see. The problem was, getting hold of it would most likely alert the filmmakers to its significance—something they didn't seem to have clicked to, so far—and Gracie could lose the lead on the story. A story that was still virtually exclusively hers.

She let herself sink into the sofa and heaved a sigh of frustration as she pondered Dalton's suggestion. "No," she decided, "not yet. We can't risk it."

She looked over at Finch, who nodded. After a moment, he said, "So what do you want to do?"

Gracie felt the air around her resonating with expectation. Warring sensations were tugging her in opposite directions, but, deep down, she knew that she'd already made the decision before she'd put down the phone.

With a conviction that surprised her, she said, "I have to go there." Her eyes danced from Finch to Dalton and back, hoping to find some support.

"I want to believe him," she explained. "I mean, look, none of this makes sense, right? But what if it's all real? Can you imagine? If what he's saying is true . . . Jesus." She sprang to her feet, pacing around now, gesturing with her arms, her decision somehow liberating her, unleashing a surge of energy that was intoxicating. "I don't know how this happened, I don't know what's really going on here, but, like it or not, we're part of it. We're caught up in something . . . exceptional. And the story's not here anymore. It's in Egypt. It's in that monastery. And that's where I need to be." She fixed on them fervently. "I mean, what are we gonna do? We can't stay on this ship forever. We sure as hell can't go home, not while this thing isn't resolved." She paused, studying them, willing a reaction out of them; then she reiterated, "The story's in Egypt."

Finch looked thoughtfully at Dalton, turned back to her,

and, after an uncertain, so-pregnant-it-must-be-triplets pause, he smiled.

"Let's do it. Even if it means disappointing the kids. Again." Finch had two under-tens, a son and a daughter. And although he was divorced, he was still friends with his ex-wife and had been planning to spend Christmas Day with them.

Gracie acknowledged Finch's comment with a sheepish, clenched expression. She knew it would be tough on him. She didn't have that problem. She was single and wasn't seeing anyone special. She wasn't a huge fan of the end-of-year holidays anyway. As a kid, she'd hated them, especially after her mom died. The cold weather, the short days, the passing of another year, one less year of life—it all felt morbid and sad to her. She turned to Dalton. He nodded, his expression pensive but supportive. He was in too.

Gracie beamed back. "Great."

"I'll go talk to the captain," Finch said. "See how quickly he can get us choppered off this ship. You guys start packing."

A lesser producer would have debated the point to death before covering his ass by getting his news director's approval. Finch was rock solid, and right now, Gracie was hugely grateful to have him in her corner. He looked at her, as if reading the thoughts written across her face, gave her a nod of unflinching support, then left the room.

She crossed over to the window again and looked out. The shelf was still disintegrating, but the sign was long gone. In her mind's eye, she saw it again, and as she relived the shock and awe it had generated in her, in everyone on that ship, a shiver of doubt crept into her.

Her back still to Dalton, she asked, "What do you think? Are we making the right call here?"

He joined her at the window. She glanced over at him, and thought she'd rarely seen him wearing such a solemn expression.

"We're talking about Father Jerome," he said, his voice lacking any traces of uncertainty. "If you're not going to believe him . . . who are you going to believe?"

Chapter 20

Boston, Massachusetts

Matt guided the Mustang back onto the expressway and headed north, toward the city. He was cruising on autopilot, without any specific destination in mind, just putting some distance between himself and the guys in the Chrysler.

He felt shattered. His brain was all tangled up, and he was having trouble making sense of what had happened since Bellinger called him. After the adrenaline rush from tagging the Chrysler, his body was now crumbling from under him. He needed to rest and think things through, but there were no obvious spots where he could crash out and no one to take him in. No spunky-and-resourceful girlfriend, no reluctantly supportive buddy, no irritable-but-still-smitten ex-wife.

He was on his own.

He rode up the expressway for a while, then drifted onto the South Station off-ramp and ended up at a fifties-style diner on the corner of Kneeland, the only place in town that he knew would be open this late.

He looked like a real mess and drew a couple of contemptuous glances as he stepped inside, which wasn't ideal. The last thing he needed right now was to get noticed. He disappeared into the men's room and cleaned himself up as best he could, then grabbed a stool at the far end of the bar. He ordered himself a coffee and decided to add on a cheeseburger, not knowing when he'd have a chance to eat in peace again, and hoping the caffeine-and-protein boost would help carry him through until daybreak.

Although his body still ached from his fall, the food and the coffee helped clear his mind. He asked the waitress for a refill and sifted through his options. He didn't hold out much hope of being able to do anything to help Bellinger. It seemed pretty clear to him that the hit team that came after them was connected to whatever had happened to Danny, and they weren't messing around. He was facing pros with serious resources and no inhibitions, and his options were limited, especially given that he didn't really know much beyond the cryptic words Bellinger had left him with—and the idea that Danny could still be alive. If he was going to get anyone to help him—the press, maybe even the cops; he wasn't sure who at this point—he needed to know more about what was going on. He could think of two threads to tug. One was the tracker. The other was Bellinger. Or, more accurately, whatever it was that Bellinger knew that put him in their crosshairs. His heart sank at the thought of the harmless scientist, his brother's buddy, and the dire situation he must now be in, and he seethed with frustration at not being able to do something about it.

Not yet, anyway.

He needed to check the tracker's position, and he also wanted to see what he could find at Bellinger's place. And for both lines of attack, he needed to go online.

By now, it was well past midnight, and hotel business centers were the only option at this hour. He asked his waitress and got directions to a nearby Best Western, raided an ATM three doors down from the diner, and pulled into the hotel's parking lot fifteen minutes later.

The business center by the soulless lobby was open all night, but it was restricted to hotel guests. Given that his home was off-limits for the time being, the idea of a safe bed and a hot shower had its merits, so he gave the receptionist a fake name, took a single, and paid in cash. He was soon ensconced at a workstation with a high-speed connection pumping information to his screen.

He logged onto the tracker's Web site and checked its position. Having been a car thief, he appreciated the value of trackers more than anyone, especially when it came to covetable, high-value classics like his Bullitt Mustang. Right now, he was more grateful than ever for having it. The contract he'd taken out had the tracker set up to transmit its location every thirty seconds when the car it was attached to was on the move. It would hibernate and ping its location once every twelve hours if the car was stationary. Assuming the car wasn't spending a lot of time on the road, the tracker's battery would normally last around three weeks between recharges, only Matt was pretty sure it was near the end of that cycle and running low on juice. It probably wouldn't last more than a few days before conking out.

It hadn't moved. Which was both good and bad. If the goons were still there, it meant they weren't on his tail, but then again, it also meant they weren't giving up easily. He moved on and trawled the online white pages for Bellinger's home address, which he found with ease. Clearly, Bellinger wasn't too fussy about his privacy, though it was frightening how much information one could find about anyone online. It was over in Inman Square, a trendy, upmarket enclave in neighboring Cambridge that Matt had visited a few times. Danny had lived there too, right up to his disappearance, Matt thought, preferring the sound of that to the words he would have used before tonight: his death. At this hour, it was only a quick hop there. One that couldn't wait.

Matt jotted down the address and was about to log off when he thought of something else. He Googled "Antarctica" and "sky" and "news" and let the billion-dollar algorithms do their thing. He hadn't taxed them too hard. Almost instantly, they presented him with over a million hits. The first page was dominated by news reports about a huge ice shelf breaking off, and Matt clicked on the first link, the one of the Sky News channel, and read through the report.

It was less than enlightening. He sat back and digested it, perplexed as to how it could possibly be linked to Danny or lead to the vicious reaction that targeted Bellinger. He reread it and was none the wiser, and was about to get up when a link below the article caught his eye. It mentioned an "unexplained sighting" on the frozen continent. He clicked on it, and it took him to a related article that had an accompanying, YouTube-like video clip.

This one had more bite.

He felt a tightening at the back of his neck as he read the report and watched the short video of the reporter and the apparition over the ice shelf. He reread the report and viewed the clip a second time, his face flickering with confusion. He dug deeper and initiated a new search, and got a geyser of hits related to the unexplained sighting, and as he skimmed through them and let the implications they debated sink in, a grim realization dropped further into the roiling pit of his stomach.

This was no small event.

If Danny was somehow involved in it—*against his will*, Bellinger had insinuated, though Matt couldn't even begin to imagine what his involvement could have been—then the stakes were much higher than Matt had imagined.

Minutes later, the Mustang was crossing the Longfel-
low Bridge and veering onto Broadway, a lone car gliding
across the desolate cityscape. There was a stark beauty to
the stillness around him, but Matt didn't feel any of it. His
mind was swirling with wild theories, and with them came
an increasingly uncomfortable feeling, a sense of a sinister
malignancy closing in on him.

He tried to stay focused as he made his way to the
intersection with Fayette and a three-story Victorian
house that matched Bellinger's address. He did a precau-
tionary drive-by, looped back on himself a couple of
blocks up the street, and cruised past the house again for
another look. It had stopped snowing, and the neighborhood was now huddled under a couple of inches of white
frosting. The lights of a lone Christmas tree blinked out
of a bay window on the ground floor, but otherwise, the
rest of the building was dark, and the street seemed
equally comatose. He also noticed that the snow outside
the house was undisturbed.

He pulled into a small alley that separated the house
from the similar, slightly larger one next door, and
switched off the throaty V-8—not the most discreet of
engines. He waited a moment to make doubly sure he
was alone, then climbed out of the car. Everything
around him was eerily quiet, the air cold and torpid under a moon that shone more brightly now that it wasn't
filtered by a veil of snow. He rummaged through his
glove compartment and found what he needed, his
trusted Leatherman multitool and a small, stiff piece of
wire, and pocketed them, then climbed out of the car,
pulled up his collar, and walked briskly over to the
house's front porch.

The labels on its buzzer showed three occupants,
which matched the number of floors—one apartment
per floor. Bellinger's name was on top, which Matt took

to mean that he had the penthouse. The lock on the communal entrance didn't pose too much of a challenge. It was a five-pin tumbler, a standard household lock that was surprisingly easy to pick, even without his preferred tools for such a job—a pair of paper clips. Getting past the lock on the door to Bellinger's place, up the stairs and on the third floor, was equally effortless. Matt had had way too much practice over the years.

Easing the door closed behind him, he slipped in quietly without turning the lights on, his eyes quickly adjusting to the darkness. He stepped deeper into the apartment, wishing he had a flashlight. The small entrance hall opened up to twin, open-plan living and dining rooms with a two-sided gas fireplace between them, its mantelpiece lined with a dozen or so Christmas cards. Moonlight bathed the wide, bay-windowed space with a delicate, silvery sheen that ushered him farther in. He advanced carefully, all senses on high alert. He spotted an upright halogen lamp with a dimmer switch in a near corner, by a large leather couch and away from the windows, and decided it wouldn't be too visible from the outside on a low setting. He chanced it, barely turning it up. The dimmer buzzed slightly as the lamp suffused the room in a faint, yellowish gleam.

The room was impeccably arranged and ordered. A sleek, glass-and-chrome desk faced a wall on the opposite side of the room, away from the window. Matt angled across to it. It was covered with neat piles of newspapers, books, magazines, printouts, and unopened mail. The clutter of a busy professional with an inquisitive mind. Matt spotted a small box of Bellinger's business cards, picked one up, and pocketed it. He could see that something was prominently missing from the man's desk. A computer. A large flat screen was still there, as was an orphaned docking station for a laptop, and a wireless mouse. The laptop itself was, it seemed, gone.

Had they been here already?

Matt tensed up and gave the room another scan, his ears now listening intently for the slightest disturbance. They wouldn't have had any trouble getting in. They had Bellinger, which meant they had his keys. He thought about it for a beat. If they had been here, they were probably already long gone. It had been maybe three hours since he and their van had parted company.

Still, he had to be sure.

With an even lighter step, he crept across the hallway and checked the rooms at the back of the apartment. He found two bedrooms, one a large master suite overlooking the side street and the back, the other smaller and sparsely furnished, both empty. He checked the bathrooms, also clear. He relaxed a touch and made his way back to the living room, where a blinking light on a coffee table caught his eye. It came from the base unit of a cordless phone that had waiting messages—just one of them, according to its LED display.

He clicked the PLAYBACK button. An androgynous, digital voice informed Matt that the message came in at 12:47 a.m., which piqued Matt's interest. People didn't normally get calls at that hour.

"Dude, where the hell did you disappear to?" a hyper voice on the machine quizzed. "What's going on? You're not home. You're not picking up your cell. Come on, pick up the damn phone, will ya? This thing's gathering some serious mass. The blogs are going loco over it. You gotta see this. Anyway, call me back. I'm staying locked on the news in case it decides to make another appearance. Call me, or . . . whatever. I'll see you at the ranch tomorrow." He sounded deflated before he hung up.

Matt grabbed a pen, picked up the handset, and hit

star-69. Another digital voice recited the caller's number to him. It was local. As he wrote it down on the back of Bellinger's business card, a faint noise intruded at the edge of his hearing, a car pulling up outside the building, shortly followed by the dull thuds of car doors closing.

He crossed to the window, but the crackle of brief radio transmissions told him what it was before he peered out and saw the two men walking away from an unmarked sedan and disappearing into the building.

Coming to check out Bellinger's place.

Which meant one of two things.

Either they were more goons, on the same payroll as the guys who'd stuffed him into their van, or they were plainclothes cops and Bellinger's body had already turned up.

Matt could just imagine how that one would play out.

He flinched as the entry phone in Bellinger's apartment buzzed, then sprinted to the front door and cracked it open. He waited, listening intently, his heartbeat thudding in his ears; then it buzzed again, this one longer, more impatient.

The buzzing seemed to confirm the latter scenario. The hit team had Bellinger, meaning they had Bellinger's keys. They wouldn't need to ring up. Matt felt the blood seep from his face, and a crippling sense of further unreality swept through him as he pictured what might have happened to Bellinger. He waited by the door, his mind racing through possible outcomes, none of which seemed promising.

The entry phone stayed ominously silent.

He decided to take another look, and leaving the door slightly ajar, he scuttled back to the bay window and peeked out.

He could see the two men standing by their car, which

he could now tell was a standard-issue Crown Vic. One of them was on his cell phone, but Matt couldn't hear what he was saying. Matt relaxed somewhat. They came, they buzzed, no answer, they'd leave. Or so he hoped. Then he saw the other man cock his head toward the entrance, as if reacting to something, before disappearing under the porch again.

Matt's instincts sharpened. He slipped back to the door and, very quietly, picked up the entry phone's handset. He came in midconversation.

"—on the second floor," a woman's voice was explaining. "Bellinger's got the penthouse directly over me." She hesitated, then asked, "Is everything okay?"

The man ignored her question and asked her, "Does Mr. Bellinger live alone, ma'am?"

Does, Matt thought, for a second. Not *did.* Present tense. Maybe Bellinger was all right.

The cheery thought was quickly overruled. The guys in the van hadn't looked like they were kidding. Bellinger was dead, he knew it. Why else would these guys be here? Why would they be asking if he lived alone?

The woman's voice had a nervous quaver to it. "Yes, I think so. I mean, he's single. I don't think he lives with anyone. But I'm surprised he's not picking up. I'm pretty sure he's home."

Her comment struck Matt like a bucket of ice water.

"What makes you say that?" the man asked, his voice snapping to attention.

"Well, I heard him come back. These are old houses, and even with the refurb, the floorboards have this creak in them that's always there, and I can hear him coming in and out, especially when it's late and it's quiet outside—"

"Ma'am," the man interrupted abruptly, clearly impatient.

"I think he came in earlier," she said with more urgency, "and then he went out again. But then he came back."

"When did you hear him come in?"

"Not long ago. Ten minutes, maybe? He should be upstairs."

Matt's nerves went haywire.

He heard the man's tone take on a much harder edge as he ordered the woman, "I need you to let us in, ma'am, right now," followed by a shout to his partner and the distinct sound of the entrance door snapping open.

Seconds later, heavy footfalls were charging up the stairs.

Chapter 21

Amundsen Sea, Antarctica

Gracie's stomach fluttered as she watched Dalton rise off the deck of the royal research ship. Unlike the *Shackleton*, its stablemate, the *James Clark Ross* wasn't endowed with a helipad. Transfers at sea could only be made by winching passengers to and from a hovering chopper. Which, in subzero weather and with a gargantuan wall of ice collapsing a few hundred yards away, wasn't for the fainthearted.

It was now six hours since the sign had first appeared. After their extended, high-definition clip was broadcast and carried by the other channels, the news had simply exploded. It was all over the news updates, splashed across the world's TV screens, and on every Internet news site. Armies of reporters and pundits were talking about it, wondering about it, offering wild theories. People across America and in the rest of the world were being interviewed and asked what they thought the sightings meant. As expected, some of the responses were glib and dismissive, but most people were seriously intrigued. And it was still the middle of the night across North America. Most people there were asleep. The next day, Gracie knew, was when the real frenzy would begin. Her satphone hadn't stopped ringing with requests for interviews and comments, and her in-box was also flooded.

Across every channel, every news network, one expert after another was being wheeled in to try to explain it. Physicists, climatologists, all kinds of scientists, dragged in from every corner of the planet. None of them had a clue. They couldn't offer any remotely convincing insight into how or why it was happening, and while that excited some people, it also scared a lot of them. The religious pundits were faring better. Faith was one explanation that didn't carry the burden of proof. Priests, rabbis, and muftis were voicing their thoughts on the sign with increasing candor. On one clip that Gracie had watched, a Baptist pastor was asked what he thought about it. He replied that people of faith everywhere were watching it very closely, and wondered if there was anything other than the divine to explain it. It was a view that several other interviewees also expressed—and that perspective was gaining ground. Faith, not science, was where the true explanation lay. The thought consumed Gracie as she strained against the downdraft from the Lynx's powerful rotor and shielded her eyes to watch Dalton's slow ascent. A small smile cracked across her face as he waved to her from above, coaxing a wave back. Consummate filmmaker that he was, he held a small camcorder in one hand, capturing every hair-raising moment.

She noticed Finch turn, and followed his gaze to see the ship's captain join them. He looked up, taking stock of the transfer's progress, which had to be swiftly executed, as they were already at the edge of the helicopter's operating range, even with its additional fuel tanks, then turned to Finch and Gracie.

"I got a call from someone at the Pentagon," he informed them, shouting to be heard against the deafening rotor wash.

Gracie glanced over at Finch, both of them visibly and suddenly on edge.

"They wanted me to make sure no one left the ship before their people got here," the captain added. "You in particular," he specified, pointing his finger at Gracie.

She felt a paralysis of worry. "What did you tell them?"

The captain grinned. "I said we were in the middle of nowhere and I didn't think anyone was going anywhere for the time being."

Gracie breathed out in relief. "Thanks," she said and beamed at him.

The captain shrugged it off. "It wasn't even a request. It was more like an order. And I don't remember signing up for anyone's army." His words were laced with bemused indignation. "I'll expect you to kick up a big stink if they ship me off to Guantánamo."

Gracie smiled. "You've got it."

He glanced overhead at the chopper, then leaned in closer. "We're also getting flooded with requests from journalists and reporters from all over the place. I'm thinking we should seriously bump up our room rate and rake in some cash."

"What are you telling them?" Finch asked.

He shrugged. "We've hung up a no-vacancy sign for the moment."

"They'll keep asking," Gracie told him, "if they're any good at what they do."

"I know," the captain said, "and it's hard to say no, but this is a research ship. I don't want to turn it into a Carnival cruise. Trouble is, we're the only ones out here. The only other ships within a couple hundred miles are a Japanese whaler and the Greenpeace vessel that's hounding it, and I don't think either of them's in a particularly hospitable mood." His deep-set, clear eyes twinkled mischievously at Gracie. "Looks like it's still your exclusive."

She smiled back, the gratitude evident in her expression. "What can I say? I must be blessed."

"I'm kind of surprised you're in such a rush to get off my ship while everyone else seems so desperate to get on," the captain queried with playful, barely disguised suspicion.

Gracie glanced at Finch; then, without trying too hard to throw their host off the trail, she grinned and told him, "That's what makes us the best damn investigative reporting team in the business. Always one step ahead of the story."

As if to rescue her from the uncomfortable moment, the harness appeared again, and a crew member helped Gracie strap herself into it. Once she was safely locked in, he waved to the winch operator in the chopper, and the slack in the cable began to tighten up.

"Thanks again, for everything," she yelled to the captain, emphasizing the last word in reference to Finch's request that he keep their departure under wraps. He'd graciously agreed, without asking questions, and she felt a slight pang of guilt at not being able to share the whole story behind their hasty exit with him.

He flicked her a small parting wave. "It's been our pleasure. Just let us know what you find out there," he added with a telling wink. "We'll be watching."

Before she could react, the cable went taut, yanking her into the ice-speckled air. She breathlessly watched the ship recede beneath her, dreading the marathon journey ahead and the uncertain reward awaiting her at its end.

Chapter 22

West Antarctic Ice Sheet

The four ghosts on the ice shelf stayed low and watched as the Royal Navy chopper glided over the ship, just under half a mile west of their position.

They weren't worried about being spotted. Their gear would more than take care of that. They just lay there, hugging the packed snow, invisible in their full "snow-white" camouflage parkas and pants, faces hidden behind white balaclavas, eyes and mouths peeking out from unsettling round openings. Even the soles of their boots, which they scrubbed down every morning before heading into action, were white. Four snowmobiles, also white and without markings, squatted nearby. Hidden under white camouflage netting, they were also virtually undetectable from the sky.

The team leader monitored the chopper through his high-powered binoculars as it lifted the last of the news crew off the ship. A hint of a smile of satisfaction flitted across his chapped lips. Things were going as planned. Which wasn't a given, considering how tight the timing had been and how frantic the deployment of his unit had been.

The operation had gone live four days earlier. They'd left their training camp in North Carolina and flown to

Christchurch in New Zealand, where an Air National Guard C-17 Globemaster had been waiting on the tarmac to whisk them down to the National Science Foundation's McMurdo Station, on the ice continent's Ross Island. From there, an LC-130 Hercules aircraft fitted with skis had ferried them to an isolated staging area on the ice shelf itself, fifteen miles south of their current position. Snowmobiles that they'd flown in with them had carried them on the last leg of their thirteen-thousand-mile journey.

The extreme change of climate and the travel through multiple time zones were brutal and would have debilitated most people, but it didn't affect them. They'd trained extensively for this operation and knew what to expect.

To say the job was a high-value, priority-one assignment was underselling it, big-time. He'd never experienced anything quite as intense, nor as uncompromising, as the rigorous interview process and psychological profiling he'd undergone before getting the job. Once that was settled, no expense had been spared in either the training facilities or the gear that was made available to him and his team. The client clearly didn't have budget issues. Then again, a lot of the firm's clients were governments—the U.S. government being its biggest—and they could usually afford what the job requirements would dictate.

In this case, however, it was clear to the team leader that the stakes were higher than on any of his previous assignments. Beirut, Bosnia, Afghanistan, then Iraq—he now saw those frenzied, violent years as mere stepping-stones. They'd led him here, to being selected to lead this unit.

It was, without a doubt, the gig of a lifetime.

And now, after all the preparation and after an interminable wait, it was finally under way. He'd started to think it would never happen. After completing their training, he and the rest of the small team of "contractors"—the spin-speak name always made him smirk, but he was more than happy to avoid the disdain associated with the more accurate "mercenary" label— had been put on standby. They'd waited for the go signal for months. The team leader didn't like getting paid to sit still. It wasn't his style. Like the others in his squad, he was ex–Force Recon, the U.S. Marines' equivalent to the Navy's SEALs or the Army's Delta Force. *Swift, Silent, Deadly,* the Force Recon motto, didn't exactly apply to sitting around watching endless hours of TV in isolated, if comfortable, barracks. The world out there— misguided, tyrannized, *evil*—was waiting.

Something in his pack warbled. He glanced at his watch. The call was expected.

He checked on the chopper's position again. It was banking away in a wide arc. He pulled out his satellite phone, a tiny Iridium handset. It was no bigger than a regular cell phone, if not for the ten-inch antenna that pivoted out from it and the STU-III voice encryption module clipped onto its base. He pressed the ANSWER key. A sequence of beeps mixed with static told him the call was bouncing its way halfway across the planet. He waited for the red LED to tell him the call was secure, then spoke.

"This is Fox One."

After the briefest of lags, a computerized male voice responded. "What's your status?"

It sounded like Stephen Hawking was calling, and he knew his own voice sounded just as robotic at the other end. Although he and the project's overseer had dodged bullets together on more than one continent, the military-level, 256-bit voice encryption made their voices unrecognizable, in case someone was eavesdropping. Which was unlikely enough, but one could never be too careful, which was also why a second safeguard was built into his phone's microchip, enabling a hybrid of hopping and sweeping scrambling. Only another phone fitted with the same chip could decode their transmissions. Any other phone would only pick up a burst of ear-piercing static.

"We're ready to roll," Fox One replied.

"Any problems I should know about?"

"Negative."

The synthesized voice came back. "Good. Pull your men out and initiate the next phase."

The team leader terminated the call and glanced up at the sky. It was back to its monotone, off-white, bleak self again.

Not a trace, he mused. *Perfect.*

Chapter 23

Cambridge, Massachusetts

Matt slipped the phone back into its cradle and eased the door shut before darting through the hallway and into the main bedroom.

He had to get the hell out of there. They were only seconds away.

He ignored the near window in the bedroom and went straight to the back wall where, in the pale moonlight coming in through the window, he'd earlier spotted a half-glazed door that gave on to a ten-foot-square balcony. With his heartbeat throbbing in his ears, he peered out and saw that, as he'd suspected, it led to a fire escape.

He joggled the door handle, but it was locked. He looked left and right for a key, but there was nothing in plain sight. He pulled and yanked at it again, a hopeless, desperate gesture, the door stubbornly refusing to budge, then was glancing back toward the hallway, his brain tripping wildly, like the ever-accelerating countdown of a time bomb, wondering how much time he still had, visualizing the two men bursting into the apartment, when a heavy knock pounded the front door.

"Open up. Police."

He didn't want to get caught in there. He was sure

Bellinger was dead, and here he was, in his apartment, an apartment he'd broken into, the apartment of a dead man who was last seen running away from him after they'd had a bust-up in a crowded bar.

A slam-dunk with any jury—if it ever got to that.

Somehow, he didn't think he'd make it that far.

His reflexes took over.

He grabbed a side table by the bed, swung it back, and hurled it through the window of the balcony door. Glass exploded as the heavy wooden console flew out and thudded heavily onto the decked floor. The posse outside the door must have heard it, as a more pointed shout of "Open up. Police" echoed from the stairwell, a shout with a distinct finality to it. Matt dashed across the room, only he didn't go for the balcony. Instead, he scurried in the opposite direction, away from it, and dived behind the door to the bedroom just as the front door erupted inward.

Two men thundered in, quickly got their bearings, and charged into the master bedroom, rocketing up to the shattered balcony door. Matt squeezed himself tightly against the wall and heard one of them yell, "He's gone down the fire escape," adding, "Check out the rest of the place" while using the muzzle of his handgun to sweep away the shards of glass that stuck up from the window frame, before clambering over and disappearing into the darkness outside. His partner darted past Matt, and just as he felt him go by, Matt slipped out from his hiding place and launched himself after him.

The man was halfway through the dark hallway when Matt tackled him from behind. They tumbled onto the hardwood floor, spilling over each other, something metallic clattering across the floor away from the downed cop. A handgun, by the sound of it. The man wasn't too tall or bulky, but his thin arms had a fierce, coiled energy within them and he fought back like a caged mongoose, twisting around and lashing out with rapid-fire blows to try to get out from under Matt. Matt knew he didn't have time on his side and had to end this fast. He weathered a couple of sacrificial blows to his ribs to set up an opening for a solid hit, then saw one and let loose with an anvil of a punch that caught the downed man just below the left ear and pounded the air out of him. The man curled over, groaning heavily. Matt used the brief respite to roll him back onto his front and felt something under his jacket. He reached under it and found a pair of handcuffs in a belt pouch. He pulled the groggy man a couple of feet to the wall and quickly locked his arms around a radiator pipe. A quick glance around yielded a coatrack overhead that held some jackets, caps, an umbrella, and a scarf that Matt yanked down and stuffed into the man's mouth before roping it around his head a couple of times and tucking it in to secure it in place.

Without even glancing back, he sprang to his feet and flew out of the apartment, hurtling down the stairs three at a time. He plowed to a sudden stop at the main entrance to check out front. There was no sign of the man who'd gone down the fire escape. He took a deep breath to clear his senses, steeled himself for the move, and slipped out into the cold night.

The street was disconcertingly quiet, oblivious to his plight. He scuttled down the steps and crept over to the parked sedan, pulling out his Leatherman and slashing one of the car's front wheels with its blade. He watched for a split second as its air rushed out, then leapt over the small picket fence by the pathway that led up to the house and skirted the front façade, avoiding the sidewalk and scanning ahead and back until he reached the alley.

The Mustang was still there, squatting in the shadows, waiting for him. He slid into it as quietly as he

could, and pulled the door half-shut. With his breathing
still coming short and fast, he spurred the engine to life
without switching on the headlights, and just as it ticked
over, the other cop appeared at the mouth of the alley,
behind him, backlit by the streetlights. He hollered,
"Stop. Police," reaching for his handgun and holding his
other arm up, palm out and flat. He was blocking the
way, leaving Matt no way out but to back out and charge
him, risking a game of chicken that could end really badly
for the one of them who wasn't cocooned inside two
tons of steel. It was either that, or—

Matt cursed under his breath, slammed the car into
gear, and floored it. The Mustang's wheels spun slightly
in the thin snow cover before biting into the asphalt, and
the car leapt forward, howling angrily through the alley,
rushing deeper into its dark recess. Matt strained to see
where he was headed, what waited for him at the end of
the alley, and when it finally came into view, it wasn't
good. The alley ended in a mound of bushy terrain that
rose into a thicket of trees. A Hummer might have had a
chance. The Mustang wasn't built for this. It didn't have
a hope in hell of making it through.

He slammed hard on the brake pedal, the Mustang
sliding to a halt at the edge of the asphalt, the engine
purring in anticipation, waiting to be unleashed again.
He glanced in his rearview mirror. He could see the
shadowy silhouette of the cop coming at him, weapon
raised.

Matt was out of options. He ground down on his
teeth and slammed the car into reverse. The car lurched,
thundering through the alley—*backward*—its V-8 roaring angrily. Matt hugged the passenger headrest as he
steered the car, riding virtually blind. In the best of light
conditions, the fastback didn't have the greatest visibility
through its rear windshield, and here, in the dark and

narrow alleyway, with only the Mustang's feeble reversing light to guide him, all he could do was keep the car in a straight line and hope for the best—hope he could avoid the walls, and hope the cop didn't have a death wish. He stayed as low as he could, tensing up while awaiting the inevitable gunshots, and sure enough, a shot reverberated in the narrow space, followed by several more, one of them drilling through the rear windshield and slamming into the passenger headrest, another pinging off the A-pillar somewhere to his right.

Within a heartbeat, he was almost at the cop's level. Matt twitched the steering wheel to angle the car right up against the wall closest to him, across from where the cop was firing. The Mustang shuddered and squealed furiously as it scraped the side of the house, and with the cop flattening himself against the opposite wall, Matt managed to thread it through without hitting him. More shots followed him as he bounced out of the alley and onto the main road, where he hit the hand brake, spun the car so it was aimed right, and powered away.

He glanced in his mirror and saw the cop emerge into the street and rush to his car, but Matt knew he wouldn't be following him. Still, he wasn't in the clear. An APB concerning his less-than-low-key car would be heating up the airwaves any second now. He had to ditch the car—quickly—and lie low until dawn.

What he'd do the next day, though, was far less certain. He still had the rest of the night to get through first.

Chapter 24

Washington, D.C.

Keenan Drucker felt electric. He was well rested, having managed to tear himself away from surfing the news channels and the Internet soon after midnight and get a decent night's sleep. In the morning, over a hearty breakfast of waffles and fruit, he'd gone through the newspapers with quiet satisfaction, something he hadn't felt for years. A feeling he hoped he'd be able to build on as the day wore on.

Presently, sitting in his tenth-floor office on Connecticut Avenue, he pivoted in his plush leather chair, away from his wide desk—nihilistic in its lack of clutter, with nothing on it except for a laptop, a phone, and a framed photograph of his deceased son—and looked out across the city. He loved being in the nation's capital, working there, playing a role in shaping the lives of the citizens of the most powerful country on the planet—and, by extension, the lives of the rest of the world's inhabitants. It was all he'd ever done. He'd begun working his way up the system soon after leaving Johns Hopkins with a master's in political science. He'd spent the next twenty-odd years as a congressional staff member, serving as senior policy advisor and legislative director to a couple of senators. He'd helped them grow in prominence and power while ensuring his own rise in stature, working quietly, behind the scenes, shunning the more visible positions that were constantly on offer—although he'd flirted with taking on that of undersecretary of defense for policy when it had been offered. He preferred the continuity afforded by pulling the strings from behind the curtain, and only left the Hill after an offer that was too good to turn down came in, giving him the opportunity to create and run a well-funded, far-reaching think tank of his own, the Center for American Freedom.

He was made for this life. He was a ruthless and imaginative political strategist, he had a mind like a steel trap, and his appetite for detail, combined with a prodigious memory, made him a master of procedure. And as if that weren't enough, his effectiveness was further enhanced by an easygoing, gregarious charm—one that masked the iron resolve underneath and helped when one was a dedicated polemicist ready to take on the red-button issues that were splitting the country.

The last few years, though, had instilled a new sense of urgency within him. Groups of civilian advisors had firmly gripped the reins of policy—both domestic and foreign—and steered the country to their vision. Their unapologetic, unbridled sense of mission was, to a political animal like Drucker, a thing of beauty; their methods and tactics, breathtaking.

Most impressive, he thought, was their use of "framing"—the cunning technique of dumbing down complex, controversial issues and policies by using powerful, evocative, emotive catchphrases and images in order to prejudice and undermine any potential challenge to those policies. Framing had been elevated to a fine art in the new century, with deceptive expressions like "tax relief," "war on terror," and "appeaser" now firmly embedded in the public psyche, pushing the right emotional buttons and creating a misguided belief that anyone who argued against such measures had to be, by definition, a villain trying to stop the innocent sufferers' champion from giving them their medication, a coward shying away from a full-blown war against an aggressor nation, or— even worse—one too spineless to stand up to Hitler.

Framing worked. No one knew that as well as Keenan Drucker. And he was now ready to do some framing of his own.

He checked his watch. A late-morning meeting had been hastily scheduled with the available senior fellows of the Center to discuss the unexplained apparition over the ice shelf. He'd already spoken to several of them by phone, and they were—understandably—as excited as they were unsettled.

After that, he'd monitor the news channels to check on the project's status. Which seemed well on track, apart from that small complication in Boston. Drucker wasn't worried. He could trust the Bullet to take care of it.

His BlackBerry pinged. The ring tone told him it was the Bullet.

As he reached for his phone, Drucker smiled. *Speak—* in this case, *think—of the devil* rarely had a more appropriate or literal embodiment.

◄◦►

WITH HIS HABITUAL CURT EFFICIENCY, Maddox updated Drucker on Vince Bellinger's fate, Matt Sherwood's subsequent escape, and his foray into the now-dead scientist's apartment.

Drucker had absorbed the information with admirable detachment. Maddox didn't like much about Drucker. The man was a politician, after all. A Washington insider. But he liked that about him. Drucker didn't question or second-guess when it came to matters in which he was no expert. He didn't have any ego issues, nor did he assume the annoying air of superiority Maddox had often seen—and enjoyed deflating—in deskbound executives and, even more so, in politicians. Drucker knew to leave the dirty work to those who were comfortable trudging through the muck, something Maddox had never shied away from, and still didn't, even though his "security and risk management" firm had grown healthily since he first founded it three years ago, not long after he'd been wounded in Iraq.

Maddox was a hands-on kind of guy. He had a tough, single-minded work ethic, an unwavering discipline forged out of a twenty-year career with the Marines and their Force Recon outfit, where he'd initially earned the sobriquet "The Bullet" because of his shaved, slightly pointed head. It was a name that took on an even more disturbing connotation after his squad was cut to bits in a savage firefight in the apocalyptic town of Fallujah.

The tragedy that had first brought him and Drucker together and united them.

His unit had been doing good work in the mountains of Afghanistan. Hitting the Taliban and their Al Qaeda buddies hard. Weeding them out of the mountains and caves across the border from Pakistan. Closing in on Bin Laden. Then, frustratingly and inexplicably, they'd been pulled out and reassigned. To Iraq. And nine months into that war, Maddox lost fourteen men and an ear that horrific afternoon. Those who'd survived that attack had left arms, legs, or fingers behind. The word *wounded* rarely conveyed the horror of their injuries—or the permanent, crippling effect on their lives. It was a day Maddox remembered every time he caught a glimpse of his hideous self reflected in a windowpane or a colleague's sunglasses. It was branded on his face, a star-shaped burn that spread out from the small, mangled flap of ear skin that the surgeons had been able to salvage.

He hated looking in the mirror. He relived that day every time he caught a glimpse of himself. Not just that day, but the aftermath. The inquests. The way his superiors had let him down. The way he'd been mistreated and spat out by the system. And if that wasn't bad enough, he then found out he'd been lied to. The whole country had. The war was a sham. A catastrophic sham. And then, to add insult to injury—literally—he watched as the same lying bastards who'd sent him to war, from the lowliest congressman to a war hero who'd come close to becoming president, were voting against funding increases for those who, like him, had come home with debilitating physical and mental injuries. He watched as soldiers were hauled in, tried for every minor trespass of the rules of engagement, and sacrificed for political expediency by men who'd never been within a hundred miles of a firefight. And with each new revelation about the lies and manipulations behind the war—the ones that had cost his buddies their lives, and him his face—he got angrier. More bitter. More vindictive. And out of the anger and the bitterness came a realization that he had to take matters into his own hands if he was going to change anything.

His wounded status made it easier for him to set up shop. Before long, he had dozens of highly trained, properly equipped men on his payroll, working for him in the hellholes of Afghanistan, Iraq, or anywhere else people were paying him to send them. Doing jobs that no one else wanted to touch. Jobs no one wanted to be seen doing. Jobs where they weren't subject to arbitrary rules drawn up by politicians sipping twenty-year-old Cognac. And somehow, with each new job, he found more solace, more satisfaction. It became a revenge fix he couldn't live without. And despite the hundreds of thousands of dollars in government contracts and fees his little operation was pulling in, despite having a small army of trusted, battle-hardened men ready and able to do whatever he asked them to do, he was still out there, on the front line, with them. And when this job came up, he immediately realized it was one he couldn't delegate. To be doing it was satisfying on a whole different level.

If this thing could really achieve what they thought it could, then he sure as hell was going to make sure nothing went wrong.

Still, Drucker didn't sound thrilled by his news.

"I'm not comfortable with Sherwood out there, running around," Drucker told him. "You need to put him away before it gets out of hand."

"Shouldn't take long," Maddox assured him. "He's a murder suspect. He doesn't have too many options."

"Let me know when it's taken care of," Drucker concluded, before ending the call.

Maddox set his phone down on his desk and stewed on the night's events. Matt Sherwood had proven far more resilient than his brother. They were clearly cut from a different cloth, something Maddox had already known, given Matt's record. All of which necessitated a more concerted approach.

His men were monitoring police communications, but that wasn't enough. Matt Sherwood was taking impulsive, unexpected initiatives like breaking into Bellinger's apartment. Unexpected initiatives that could prove to be a major nuisance.

Maddox cleared his mind and put himself in Matt's shoes, replaying every step the ex-con had taken, trying to get a better feel for the way Matt thought. He extrapolated ahead, looking for the straws Matt would be grasping at, straws he needed to cut down before Matt got to them. He thought back to the reports his men had called in and decided to plow that field.

He turned to his screen and brought up the phone logs of all the peripherals linked to Bellinger and to Matt. His eye settled on the last entry—the phone call from a co-worker of Bellinger's by the name of Csaba Komlosy. He clicked on the small icon by the entry and listened to the phone call, a message left on Bellinger's home phone. He listened to it a second time, then went back and listened to the first call between the two scientists. The one that had precipitated the previous evening's confrontations.

The Bullet checked his watch and picked up his phone.

Chapter 25

Boston, Massachusetts

Larry Rydell stared blankly at his BlackBerry's screen for a moment before setting it down on his desk. He'd just gotten off the phone with Rebecca. Again. Two calls from his daughter in less than twenty-four hours. Far more than he was used to. They were close, for sure, despite his divorce from her mother almost a decade earlier. But Rebecca was nineteen. She was wild and fabulous and free, in her second year at Brown, and although surprisingly grounded for someone with the world at her feet, regular phone calls to Daddy had—as expected—been increasingly crowded out of the whirlwind of activity that her life had become.

He loved chatting with her. Loved seeing her so excited, so enthralled, so curious about something, even with the undercurrent of fear in her bubbly voice. Loved hearing from her twice a day.

But he hated lying to her.

And he had. Twice now, in less than a day. And, no doubt, he'd have to go on lying to her—if all went well, for the rest of his life.

He felt a small tearing inside at the realization; then the tear widened as the bigger picture of what was going on hit him again.

It's really happening.

It was out there now. There was no turning back.

The thought terrified and elated him in equal measure.

It had all seemed so surreal when he'd first considered the possibility, just four years earlier. And yet it had all come about so fast. The breakup of the ice shelf had been expected. They'd been monitoring it through satellite imagery, but it had come sooner than they projected. And they'd been ready. Ready to capitalize on it.

Ready to change the world.

He thought back to that fateful evening with Reece, three years earlier. A great dinner. A bottle of Brunello di Montalcino. A couple of Cohiba Esplendidos. A long, inspired late-night chat about the possibilities of the manufacturing breakthrough that Reece had achieved. The many and diverse applications it could be used for. The leaps of imagination that great minds sometimes conjured up and actually turned into reality. And then, the mere mention of a word.

Miraculous.

One word. A catalyst that sent Rydell's mind tripping into uncharted territory. Dark, mysterious, wonderful, impossible territory. And here he was, less than four years later, and the impossible had become a reality.

Reece. The brilliant scientist's face drifted into his consciousness. Other faces materialized alongside it— young, talented, dedicated, all of them—and with them, a familiar cold, hard feeling deep inside him. He felt his very soul shrivel at the memory of that last day in Namibia. After the last test. After they'd all shared the elation of watching their hard work bear fruit in such spectacular, bone-chilling fashion. And then it all went wrong. He could still see Maddox, standing there beside him, pulling the trigger. He could hear himself shout, hear the bullet thumping into Reece's back, see his friend's body jerk before toppling into Danny Sherwood's arms.

The sounds and images of that day had been gnawing away at him ever since.

He hated himself for not having been able to stop it. And despite what the others told him, none of the platitudes, none of the clichés about the greater good or about sacrificing the lives of the few for the lives of the many—none of it worked.

He hadn't read them properly. He hadn't realized to what lengths they were prepared to go. And it was too late to do anything about it. They needed each other. If everything he'd worked for was to succeed, he just had to swallow it all and keep going.

Which he did, even though it wasn't easy. He could still feel it, deep inside, eating away at him, piece by piece. He knew it would eventually get him. One way or another, he'd die because of it. He had to. But maybe, before that happened, maybe, if all went well—maybe their deaths would amount to something in the end. Although he knew their ghosts wouldn't let go of him, not even then.

Chapter 26

Boston, Massachusetts

Sheltering behind a tall hedge in the brisk, early-morning chill, Matt waited and watched, trying to make sure no unpleasant surprises were in store for him at the hotel before breaking cover and making his way in. Tense and alert while avoiding eye contact, he slipped past a few bleary-eyed businessmen who brought a semblance of life to the drab, cookie-cutter lobby, took the elevator to the fifth floor, and reached the refuge of his room.

He was as tired as he was pissed off.

He'd had to dump the Mustang a few blocks from Bellinger's place, and that only fueled his anger. The car represented a personal milestone for him, a notable and particularly satisfying step on his road back from the edge. Danny had not just guided him onto that road, but paid the toll and given him fuel money to boot. And now Matt had been forced to abandon the car on some dark side street, all because of the same bastards who had taken Danny away.

He was seriously pissed off.

After parking the Mustang, he'd scuttled in the shadows for a couple of blocks, then crossed to the north side of Broadway, where he'd hot-wired a defenseless, decade-old Ford Taurus. He'd then cut west, heading out of town before looping back on the turnpike, on the look-out for any blue-and-whites. He'd parked in an incon-spicuous corner on the back lot of a small shopping center around the corner from the hotel and walked the rest of the way.

He stood by the window of his room, watching the city as it sprang to life. It was another overcast, wintry day, the sun struggling to break through the pasty gray cloud cover. He lay down on his bed, his muscles and nerves ravaged by tension and fatigue. He hadn't slept, and his body was crying out for a break. He hadn't put it through such a ringer for years. But he knew that would have to wait. He opted instead for a long, hot shower to reinvigorate him and help settle his mind. It bought him a renewed, if rapidly dwindling, lease on life. Twenty minutes later, he was back at a workstation in the austere and windowless business center.

He used the white pages' Web site to do a reverse list-ings search on the phone number he got off Bellinger's answering machine. The number yielded the curious name of Csaba Komlosy, with a home address—no sur-prises there—in the same geek-central catchment area straddling Harvard and MIT that Bellinger—and Danny—lived in. He thought about calling him. Accord-ing to his message, he and Bellinger had been discussing what was happening in Antarctica just before Bellinger had met Matt, and Matt sensed that this Csaba—he wasn't sure how to pronounce it—could fill in some of the blanks. He decided against making that call. The goon squad seemed to be avid wiretappers. A face-to-face would be better anyway. He jotted down the ad-dress, an apartment by the sound of it, clicked on the map link for a more accurate read of its location, then, deciding he couldn't duck it anymore, pulled up the Web site of the *Boston Globe* and hit the link for the local, breaking news section.

It was the first item.

His face contorted with sadness—and rage.

The report wasn't long. A stabbing. Close to a bar in South Boston, shortly after midnight. They'd identified the body as Bellinger's. There was a brief mention of a brawl in the nearby bar, but nothing more. A murder investigation was under way.

The report didn't mention Matt—yet. But he knew there'd be more to come on that front.

They'd make sure of it.

He exhaled heavily, rubbed some alertness into his face, and re-read the article. Its dry, clinical words pushed a caustic bile of anger up to his throat, burning him with their finality. His fists hovered over the keyboard, clenched bloodless white tight, as he summoned up every drop of restraint inside him to keep from bashing it against the desk and ripping the whole workstation to shreds.

It was that simple for these bastards. They could just pluck someone off the street, cut him open, dump him in the snow, and move on to their next assignment without batting an eyelid. A man's life—an innocent, decent man's life, snuffed out in its prime, and all because of what . . . a phone call? An idea?

Matt was boiling.

He took in a deep breath and let it out slowly, willing his fury to subside. A moment later, he raised his concentration back to the screen, keyed in the home page of his tracker, and logged in.

The Chrysler was no longer outside his place.

A detailed map displayed the car's itinerary in thirty-second increments. Backtracking to the first movement that his GPS tracker had registered, Matt saw that the goons had finally given up their stakeout—or, he thought, merely passed the baton to the next team—almost an hour ago. Which, he noted, was after he'd made it out of Bellinger's place. He wondered if that meant that they were already aware of his little excursion to Cambridge. If they were, it meant they had insights into police activity, either through radio scanners or courtesy of someone inside the department. He made a mental note of it and zoomed in on the Chrysler's current location.

It was parked on a street in Brighton, not far from St. Elizabeth's Medical Center, and hadn't moved for twenty-three minutes. The tracker's Web site featured a built-in link-up with Google Maps. Matt clicked on the "street view" option, moved the little orange avatar to the Chrysler's current location, and clicked again. A wide-angle shot popped up, as clear and detailed as if he were standing right in the middle of the street—not in real time, of course, but whenever the Google van with the panoramic camera had done its survey, which couldn't have been that long ago, given that this wasn't exactly Cold War–era technology. It afforded him a detailed view of what the place looked like. He full-screened it, scrolled up the street and back for a virtual drive-by, then rotated the camera to get a good look at the opposite sidewalk.

The narrow, residential street had a string of small, two-story clapboard houses. The fix, accurate to within three yards of the tracker's location if you believed the pitch of the well-oiled salesman he'd bought it from, fell on a tired-looking, seal gray house with a small balcony over the front porch and a gabled window in its roof.

He needed to take a closer look. A live one.

It didn't take long to get there at this early hour, given that he was heading against the rush hour traffic. The light snow from the previous night was mostly gone, and the old Taurus was, well, functioning. He turned into

Beacon and headed west, his mind busy imagining the different ways things could play out once he found them. He tried to rein in his primal instincts. Yes, they were vile, bloodsucking scum, and he knew he'd find it hard to resist beating the crap out of them if he ever got the chance. But there was no need to turn this into a suicide mission. If they were there, he needed to find out more about them—who they were, what they were doing, who had hired them.

What they knew about Danny.

What happened to him.

Once he got all that—well, there was no reason to let them live, really.

The notion just came to him, and it didn't make him flinch. Which surprised him. He'd never killed anyone before. Sure, he'd had his share of fights. Before prison. In prison. He'd taken some serious beatings over the years, but he'd cracked a few skulls too. He hadn't started out that way. He was wild and reckless and played by his own rules, but he wasn't a thug and he never set out to hurt anyone. And although prison had a way of hardening a man, physically as well as mentally, it didn't change what he was about. He was more prone to letting his temper erupt, less shy about using his fists, but he never took pleasure from it. It was always in self-defense, and never went beyond doing no more than was necessary to neutralize any threat facing him.

This felt different. And right now, he wasn't too worried about that. *Que será, será*. He had to find them first.

He turned right on Washington and headed north, his pulse nudging upward with each passing block as he closed in on his target. He hit a red light at the big intersection with Commonwealth, and as he sat there waiting, sitting behind an equally tattered pickup truck in dire need of new piston rings, his gaze was drawn beyond it to the aggressive, toothy grin of a familiar grille—that of a Chrysler 300C. It was waiting at the opposite light, facing him, left indicator on.

He squinted, focusing on it, trying to ascertain whether or not it was "his" 300C, craning his neck to get a better look past the smoking pickup blocking his view. The opposite light must have changed to green, as the Chrysler cut across the intersection just beyond the truck and motored up Commonwealth, trailing a couple of small imports behind it like a shark with its remoras. As it streaked past, Matt leaned across and got a look at the guy in the front passenger seat, and although his hard features fit the bill, Matt wasn't sure. He'd only seen the goons fleetingly, outside the bar and in the van, and in the shadows outside his place. Sealing it for him, though, was the 300C's license plate. He managed to catch a glimpse of the last two numbers on it, and they matched the number he'd seen on the car that had been parked outside his garage.

It was them.

His pulse rocketed as his eyes followed the rapidly receding car and he wondered what to do, needing to make a split-second decision. He spun the wheel and hit the gas, jinking the car around the pickup truck and ramping its right wheels over the curb, and turned into the avenue, following in the Chrysler's wake.

It was more of an instinctive reaction than a rational move, but as he trailed a few car lengths behind the silky sedan, his decision grew on him. He didn't know what the location was that the tracker had kicked up, whether it was their base or just a random stop they wouldn't be returning to. Besides, there were only two of them in the car, and he didn't mind those odds. Not with the way he was feeling right now.

They drove east on Commonwealth, then turned left on Harvard and took the bridge into Cambridge. As they headed up River, a cold, uncomfortable feeling twitched inside him. They were heading back to the Inman Square area, the one he'd only just escaped from a mere hour or two earlier. His unease flared into full-blown dread when he saw the name of the street the Chrysler turned into and spotted the number of the building where it pulled up.

There was no mistaking it, as it was an address he'd only just looked up.

They were parked right outside Csaba's place.

Chapter 27

Cambridge, Massachusetts

Matt coaxed the Taurus past the parked Chrysler, casually turning away as he drove by the brooding sedan, to deny its occupants a glimpse of his face. He kept going and took the first side street he found, and pulled over.

This wasn't good.

He sat in the car, stewing in his thoughts, unsure about what this meant. Was this Csaba character working with them? Had he helped them set up Bellinger, alerted them to what he was up to? Matt didn't know what to think anymore, although somehow, it didn't ring true. The message Csaba had left for Bellinger sounded genuine enough. They were discussing the apparition, and Bellinger—it seemed—had abruptly cut the conversation short.

If Csaba wasn't working with them, then they had to be here for the same reasons they'd gone after Bellinger. Which didn't give Csaba much of a rosy future. Not to mention that the very fact that the goons were after him meant that he knew something, something that could help explain what they were so hell-bent on protecting—and that could shed light on what had happened to Danny.

What *they'd* done to Danny, Matt reminded himself.

He had to do something.

He slipped out of the Taurus and crept over to the corner. He edged out carefully and looked down the street. The Chrysler hadn't moved; the two silhouettes were still inside.

They were watching. Waiting.

Stalking Csaba. Matt was now sure of it.

He had to get to him first.

He sized up the block, looking for a way past the goon squad. He couldn't see one. Csaba lived in a modern, six- or seven-story apartment block. The guys in the Chrysler had a controlling view of the street and a clear line of sight to the building's landscaped approach and its entrance lobby, which deep-sixed any notion of going in that way. There was, however, a ramp going down along its side, the kind of ramp that normally led to an underground garage. Problem was, it was also within their sight line.

He pulled back from the corner and sprinted farther up the side street, and found a narrow alley that ran between two houses. He cut into it and advanced cautiously, moving in parallel to the main street, closing in on Csaba's apartment block—only to hit a dead end and a five-foot-tall wooden fence after the second house in. He could see Csaba's building looming ahead, past another couple of houses and fences. He clambered over the fence and kept going. A few minutes later, he reached a side passage that ran alongside the ramp and led back to the street.

Matt peered out. The Chrysler was still there, and he still couldn't make it onto the ramp without them seeing him. From his vantage point, he noticed another problem. The ramp had a keypad-controlled entry. Not only that, it was the kind where the buttons didn't have any numbers printed on them. Instead, the buttons would light up with randomly assigned, nonsequential numbers appearing on them when someone attempted to key a code in, in order to prevent anyone watching from mimicking the sequence and gaining entry.

Just then, Matt heard a mechanical snap, followed by a low, creaking rumble. Although he couldn't see it from where he was, he knew it was the garage door opening. He tensed up and edged back. The nose and roof of a large, black Escalade emerged from the garage. The SUV obliterated a gallon of gas as it charged up the ramp and stopped where it met the street.

Momentarily blocking the Chrysler's view.

Matt seized the opportunity. He charged out and leapt over the low wall that gave onto the ramp. He landed heavily, his bones juddering in protest. It had to be at least a ten-foot drop, more if you counted the height of the wall. He rolled on himself before righting into a low squat. Just then, he heard the Escalade thundering off, turning onto the street, and exposing him to the Chrysler. Matt dived through the garage door as it closed, and took cover to one side, hoping he hadn't been spotted.

He peered out, but didn't sense any movement from the car.

He seemed to be clear.

The apartment numbers were listed next to the floor buttons in the elevator. He rode it to the third floor and made his way to Csaba's door and was about to hit the doorbell when he noticed that the door had a peephole in it. He pulled back, looked up, then took off one of his boots, slipped it on his right hand, and quietly smashed a couple of lightbulbs in the hallway, plunging it into darkness. He slipped his boot back on and rang the bell, which chimed inside. Some footfalls echoed and drew near; then a shadow fell across the bottom of the door.

"Who is it?" It was the same, slightly wired voice from the answering machine.

Keeping a wary eye on the elevator, Matt winged it. "I'm a friend of Vince. Vince Bellinger."

Matt heard some shuffling behind the door, as if Csaba were right up against it, trying to get a better look through the eyepiece—not easy given the now-dark hallway.

"A friend of Vince?" Csaba's voice had a stammer in it. "What's—what do you want?"

Matt tried to sound earnest and unthreatening, but firm. "We need to talk. Something happened to him."

A beat, and more shuffling; then, as if with great reticence, Csaba said, "Vince is dead, man."

"I know. Would you open the door so we can talk?"

A paralyzing dread seemed to tighten around Csaba's voice box. "Look, I don't . . . He's dead—he's been murdered—and I don't know what you want, but—"

"Listen to me," Matt interjected bluntly, "the same guys who killed him are parked outside your building right now. They heard your phone calls last night, they know what you were talking about, and that's what got him killed. So if you want me to help you not end up like he did, open the goddamn door."

A charged silence followed for a brief moment; then a decision was evidently reached, as the lock snapped and the door cracked open. A wide, boyish face surrounded by a shock of shaggy hair peered through the slit—then Csaba's eyes suddenly widened in panic at the sight of Matt's face.

"Shit," Csaba blurted as he tried to push the door shut.

Matt stuck his boot through and shoved the door

back and charged in. He shut it behind him as Csaba stumbled back into the room. The big man raised his arms defensively, tripping over himself as he backed away from Matt.

"Don't hurt me, please. Don't kill me. I don't know anything, I swear," he muttered, gesturing frantically.

"What?"

"Don't kill me, man. I don't know anything."

"Calm down," Matt shot back. "I'm not here to kill you."

Csaba stared at him in muted terror, droplets of sweat popping up all over his face. Matt studied him for a brief moment—then his attention was torn away by an image on the TV behind Csaba.

The big man noticed Matt's sudden distraction and sidestepped hesitantly, giving him a full view of the screen. It was on one of the twenty-four-hour news networks and showed the same glowing sign he'd seen earlier, only this wasn't the same footage. A loud banner on the bottom of the screen proclaimed, "Second unexplained sighting, now over Greenland."

Matt inched closer to the screen, his forehead furrowed in confusion. "This isn't the same one as before, is it?"

It took Csaba a second to realize he was being engaged in conversation. "No," he stammered. "This one's in the Arctic."

Matt turned to Csaba, feeling lost. It must have come across clearly in his expression, as Csaba was now shaking even more visibly.

"What?" Matt snapped angrily.

"Don't kill me, dude. Seriously."

Matt was missing something. "Stop saying that, all right? What is wrong with you?"

Csaba hesitated; then, as if against his will and with a hollow voice, he said, "I know you killed Vince."

"What?"

Csaba's hands rocketed up again. "Your face, dude. It's on the news."

Alarm flooded through Matt. "My face?"

Csaba nodded, still riven with fear.

"Show me," Matt ordered.

Chapter 28

Cairo, Egypt

Gracie spotted the man in the black cassock, with the anxious expression, angling for her attention among the throngs of people lining the plate-glass windows of the arrivals hall at Cairo International Airport. She caught Brother Ameen's eye and gave him a hesitant wave, which the monk acknowledged with a discreet, aloof wave of his own before moving sideways through the crowd to meet her.

The journey there had been fretfully long. After the chopper had deposited them at Rothera Station, a DASH-7 had flown them to Mount Pleasant Airport, a military airfield in the Falklands. There, they'd boarded an ageing RAF Tristar that provided commercial service for the long flight to the aptly named Wideawake Airfield on the Ascension Islands and onward to RAF Brize Norton in Oxfordshire. A cab to Heathrow led to the final leg on EgyptAir.

They'd had a brief, tense moment at Ascension, where they'd ducked out of sight and narrowly avoided being spotted by a British film crew headed in the opposite direction. They'd used the journey time to read up about the Coptic religion and, more specifically, the monastery's history. They'd checked their phones for messages at each stop, now that they were back in GSM-land, but hadn't replied to any of the messages that had been left for them. No one back in D.C., apart from Ogilvy, the network's global news director—not even Roxberry, much to Gracie, Dalton, and Finch's bemusement—had been told they'd left the ice continent, or where they were headed. Gracie and Ogilvy knew full well how ravenous their colleagues and competitors could be. The exclusivity of their story had to be ferociously guarded from the rest of the pack.

The new terminal, a gleaming, modern steel-and-glass structure, had surprised Gracie with its efficiency, even more so given that Egypt usually out-*mañana*ed the other countries of the region, no slouches themselves when it came to, well, slouching. The line through pass-port control had moved swiftly and courteously. The baggage had showed up on the carousel almost at the same time as they did. Even more surprisingly, people seemed to be observing the airport's recently introduced no-smoking policy, no small feat in a country where laws were routinely ignored and where more than half the male population were smokers practically from birth.

More pressingly, Gracie, Dalton, and Finch were al-ready aware of the new apparition over Greenland. Just after the 777 had landed, their BlackBerries had sprung to life almost in unison with urgent messages from the news desk and beyond. The bracing, electrifying news had shaken the tiredness out of their bones and injected them with renewed vigor. And as they sat in the back of Yusuf's Previa, inching their way through the bustling early evening traffic and into the city, they couldn't get their questions in to the overwhelmed Brother Ameen fast enough.

He told them he'd seen it too, on the news, and con-firmed that, as far as he could tell, it was identical to the one they'd seen over the ice shelf—and identical to the symbol lining the walls of Father Jerome's cave. The ones he'd started drawing seven months earlier.

Gracie was now certain she'd made the right choice in heeding the monk's call and coming to Egypt. Despite the continent hopping and its associated aches, she couldn't remember the last time she'd felt this energized. The rare, but coveted, sensation—the thrill of the exclusive scoop—was off the charts in this case, given the sheer scale and impact of what was unfolding. Still, there were many questions she needed answered. Starting with the reason for their trip, Father Jerome.

"How and why did he come here in the first place?" she asked the monk.

Brother Ameen hesitated. "The truth is," he winced, "we're not sure."

Gracie and Finch exchanged a questioning glance. "He was working in Sudan, wasn't he?" Finch queried.

"Yes. Over the last few years, as I'm sure you know, Father Jerome was very concerned with what was happening in Darfur. Earlier this year, he opened another orphanage there, his fourth, just inside Sudan, near the border with Egypt. And then, well . . . he doesn't quite understand it himself. He left the orphanage one night, by himself, on foot, with no belongings, no food or drink. He just walked out, into the desert."

"Just like that? He'd just been sick, hadn't he? Weren't they worried he'd be kidnapped or killed? He was very critical of what the warlords were doing out there," Gracie pointed out. "He would have been a big prize for them."

"The fighting, the massacres in Darfur . . . they affected him deeply. It weakened him, and he got very sick. It was a miracle he pulled through." The monk nodded to himself, his tone heavy with sadness at the thought. "The night he left, he told a few of his aides there that he needed to go away for a while . . . to 'find God.' Those were his words. He said he might not return for a while and asked them to make sure their good work continued during his absence. And he just walked away. Five months later, some bedouins found him collapsed, in the desert, a few kilometers south of here. He was in a simple *thawb*—a robe, torn and filthy. The soles of his bare feet were all cut up and calloused; he was delirious, lost, barely alive. He didn't have any water or food with him, and yet . . . it seemed that he'd crossed the desert. On his own. On foot."

Gracie's eyes flared up with puzzlement. "But it's, what, five, six hundred miles from here to the border, isn't it?"

"It is," Brother Ameen confirmed, his voice unnervingly calm.

"But he couldn't have . . . not in these conditions." Gracie was struggling for words. "There's nothing but desert out there. The sun alone, his skin . . . Wasn't he badly sunburned? How did he survive?"

The monk turned out his palms quizzically and looked at her with an expression that mirrored her confusion, but said nothing.

Gracie's mind raced ahead, processing his story. It was possible, maybe—but there were too many unknowns to his story. "What does Father Jerome say happened? He didn't say he walked here all the way from Sudan, did he?"

"He doesn't remember what happened," the monk explained. He raised a finger, his eyebrows rising as his words took on a more pointed tone. "But he believes he was meant to come here, to our monastery, to our cave. He believes it was his calling. Part of God's plan." The monk paused; then a hint of remorse crinkled his face. "I really shouldn't be speaking on his behalf," he added. "You can ask him yourself, when you meet him."

Gracie snatched a glance at Finch. He tilted his head in a discreet gesture that mirrored her bewilderment.

"What about the documentary?" she asked. "Tell us about that."

"What do you want to know?"

"How it came about. Were you there? Did you meet these guys?"

Brother Ameen shrugged. "There's not much to tell. They contacted us. They said they were making a documentary, that they'd heard about Father Jerome's being up in the cave, and could they come over and film him. The abbot wasn't keen. None of us was. It's not in our nature—it's not what we're used to. But they were coming from a very respectable network, and they were very courteous, and they kept on asking and insisting. Eventually, we accepted."

"Lucky you did," Finch told him. "We wouldn't be here otherwise."

"Oh, I don't know," Brother Ameen replied, a hint of a smile in his eyes. "God works in mysterious ways. I imagine he would have found another way to bring you here, don't you?"

Chapter 29

Cambridge, Massachusetts

Csaba hesitated. Then, without turning his back to Matt, he took a few steps back to his desk. It was a mess of piles of magazines and printouts. Coffee cups teetered over them like cardboard watchtowers. Clearly, he and Bellinger were far from twins on more than just the physical front. A large Apple flat screen rose out of the morass and dominated it. It too showed the light over the ice shelf. Flicking his eyes from Matt to a wireless keyboard, Csaba tapped in a few keys and brought up another Web site. He turned to Matt with an expression that straddled sheepish and terrified.

Matt joined him at the desk. The news report he'd pulled up was a brief crime report. Bellinger's body had been found in an alleyway not far from the bar. The report featured two black-and-white shots from a security camera inside the bar. One was a wide shot, showing Matt and Vince in midtussle. The other was a close-up of Matt's face, taken from another frame.

He was pretty recognizable.

Matt's eyes ate up the text voraciously. He didn't see his name anywhere in it, although he knew that wouldn't last. The article mentioned several witnesses, including an "unnamed woman" who claimed she was outside the bar when she saw Matt chase Bellinger furiously down the street. Which he hadn't done. They'd grabbed them right outside the bar. Matt frowned, his mind flashing back to the woman in the van. He could picture her profile, back-lit against the streetlights, the shoulder-length bob framing her face. One and the same, he was certain. He pictured the police showing up at his place, search warrant in hand. He also pictured them finding the murder weapon bob-girl and her buddies must have planted there.

He noticed Csaba scrutinizing him nervously.

"I know how this looks," Matt told him, "but that's not what happened. These guys came after Vince because of this thing in Antarctica." He pointed angrily at the TV screen. "He thought my brother might have been mur-dered because of it. They killed Vince. I didn't. You have to believe me."

Which, reading Csaba's jittery eyes, seemed like a tall order.

"You and Vince," Matt asked. "You were talking about it, weren't you? Before he bailed on you?"

Csaba nodded reluctantly.

It was all Matt had time for right now. "I need you to tell me what you guys said, but that can wait. They're outside. We need to get out of here."

" 'We'?" Csaba flinched, reaching for his phone. "Hey, I'm not going anywhere. You can do what you want. I'm calling the cops and—"

"We don't have time for that," Matt flared up fiercely as he grabbed the phone from him and slammed it back down close to its cradle. "They're here. Now. Because of your little chat with Vince. Same deal. So if you want to live, you're gonna have to trust me and come with me." His gaze drilled into him, dead-committed.

Csaba hesitated, his eyes locked onto Matt's, his breathing hard and fast—then he nodded.

"Do you have a car?"

"No."

"Doesn't matter. Come on." Matt sprinted toward the door.

"Wait," Csaba blurted, holding up one hand in a stalling gesture. He grabbed a backpack off the floor and started throwing things in it.

"We need to go," Matt insisted.

"Just gimme a sec," Csaba countered as he stuffed his MacBook laptop, charger, and iPhone into the backpack before flicking one last look around the room and joining Matt at the door.

Seeing the phone tripped something in Matt's mind. "Your cell," he told Csaba. "Switch it off."

"Why?"

"They can track us with it. You must know that."

Csaba's mouth dropped an inch. Then the words clicked into place. "Yeah, right," he said in a daze, and repeated "You're right" as he fished out the phone and turned it off.

Matt glanced over at the screen for one last look—the blazing sign was still there, taunting him enigmatically—then he dashed out, with Csaba on his heels.

They took the elevator down to the garage. It was home to a dozen or so cars. Matt glanced around, not exactly spoiled for choice. Csaba's neighbors seemed partial to Priuses and Japanese compacts, the Escalade owner notwithstanding. He settled on a marginally beefier Toyota RAV4, a car he was also pretty sure wouldn't resist his charms.

He moved fast. He grabbed a fire extinguisher off the wall and smashed the driver's window with it, then reached in and flung the door open. "Get in," he ordered Csaba as he swept the tiny glass flakes off the seat with his hand.

The big man just stood there, slack-jawed. "That's Mrs. Jooris's car," he said ruefully. "She's gonna be seriously pissed, dude. She worships that car."

"It's just a window. Get in."

In the time it took Csaba to relent and cram himself into the passenger seat, Matt had popped the hood, yanked out the transponder fuse from the power relay center, and gotten the engine running. He climbed back in, threw the car in gear, and screeched up to the garage door. An unseen sensor had already instructed it to open. As it rose, the ramp appeared ahead, unobstructed, curving to the left and hugging the building.

"Buckle up," Matt said.

Csaba gave him a look and glanced down wryly at his bulging midsection. The buckle and its stalk were out of sight, smothered by his doughy thigh. "You wanna help me with that?"

"Maybe not," Matt answered with a dry half grin. "Hang on."

His fingers tightened against the steering wheel as the garage door rose enough to let them out. Matt nudged the RAV4 up the ramp, slowly at first—there was no point alerting the goons to their presence earlier than necessary. They'd see him soon enough—which happened the instant the small SUV cleared the side of the building.

Matt locked eyes with the two startled men facing him in the Chrysler, committing as much of their features to memory as he could in that nanosecond, his foot poised on the accelerator. He'd already played out his move in his mind's eye. A quick charge across the street diagonally, right at the parked goons, aiming the Toyota's left front bumper at the Chrysler's right front wheel well, hitting it at a slight angle and with enough force to bend its wishbone and disable the car while allowing his own vehicle to keep going, bent but otherwise operational. It was a gamble, and a sacrifice he had to make. He'd lose the benefit of being able to track them, as they'd need to use another car from here on, but he had no choice. The Toyota was no match for the Chrysler. He wouldn't be able to lose them.

He was about to floor the pedal when he sensed something coming from his right. He ripped his gaze off the Chrysler and spotted a car coming down the street toward him. Something clicked into place in his mind. He waited a second or so for the car to get nearer, Csaba watching, not understanding the wait and giving him a low, anxious "Dude, come on," the killers in the Chrysler looking at them slightly perplexed now, not sure why they were still there, itching to bolt out of their car after them, probably pulling their weapons out of their holsters and ramming cartridges into their chambers—

—and just as the approaching car was almost at his level, Matt jammed his foot against the accelerator and charged into the street right in front of it, cutting it off. The car, a lumbering old Caprice from the bygone days of cheap and plentiful fuel and a blissful insouciance about destroying the planet, scraped against the Toyota and bounced off it, its driver—a nervy, ponytailed man wearing thick bone spectacles—swerving into the opposite lane evasively and screeching to a stop almost right alongside the Chrysler. Matt hit the gas and tore down the street, headed in the opposite direction to the one the Chrysler was facing. He watched in the rearview mirror as the Caprice's hapless driver got out of his car and mouthed off at him angrily, and saw the goons climbing out of the Chrysler to get the man to move his car so they could get their car turned around to take up pursuit.

Matt dived into the first turn he saw, pulling a scream-

ing left before charging down one empty street after another, changing directions often as he wove his way out
of Cambridge and onto the expressway, all while keeping
a wary eye on his mirrors for any sign of the Chrysler.

It was gone.

He relaxed a little and eased off the gas as he pointed
the borrowed SUV north, heading out of the city, putting some much-needed miles between him and the
streets that seemed determined to ensnare him in their
deathly clutches.

He glanced sideways at Csaba. The man's round face
was still flushed and glistening with sweat, but his posture relaxed a touch as he gave Matt a pinched acknowledgment. And with a small shake of his head, he said,
"Mrs. Jooris is gonna go mental when she sees this."

"How you pronounce your name anyway?" Matt
asked him.

"'Tchaba.' But you can call me 'Jabba,'" he replied
without a hint of annoyance. "Everyone does."

Which surprised Matt. "Really?"

Jabba nodded. "Sure."

"And that doesn't bother you?"

Jabba's expression was one of laid-back, casual bewilderment. "Should it?"

Matt thought about it, then shrugged. "Okay then.
Let's ditch this car and find us a safe place, somewhere
they won't find us. Then I'm gonna need you to tell me
exactly what you and Vince were talking about and help
me figure out what the hell is going on."

Chapter 30

Deir Al-Suryan Monastery, Wadi Natrun, Egypt

Before long, the Previa had left the desert behind and was trudging through the snarled traffic leading into Cairo. There was no avoiding cutting across the sprawling city, as the new airport was east of it, with Wadi Natrun to its northwest. By now, it was early evening, and the low sun's fading light punctuated the mist of exhaust fumes and dust that choked the overcrowded, run-down metropolis.

"Does he know what's going on yet?" Gracie asked Brother Ameen. "Have you told him about the signs?"

"No," the monk regretted. "Not yet." He glanced back at her uneasily, his look signaling that it was something she'd soon be a part of. "Actually, he doesn't know you're coming. The abbot doesn't know either."

Gracie was about to ask him to clarify, but he beat her to it. "The abbot—he doesn't know what to do. He didn't want the outside world to know about it."

"But you did," Finch prompted.

The monk nodded. "Something miraculous is happening. We can't keep it to ourselves. It's not ours to keep."

Gracie looked over at Finch. They'd been around such situations before: uninvited guests traveling into trouble spots to talk to reluctant interviewees, people whose first instinct was to shut themselves off from outside scrutiny. Sometimes, Gracie and Finch managed to get through; other times, they were locked out. In this case, they had to make it happen. They hadn't flown halfway around the globe to leave empty-handed. Not when the whole world was waiting for an explanation.

The appearance of the tips of the pyramids at Giza told Gracie they were finally leaving the city behind. She'd seen them before, but the sight never failed to inspire awe, even in the most jaded observer. On this occasion, something else stirred inside her, the majestic, stone peaks that jutted out of the sand oddly reminiscent of the nunataks—the rocky crags that rose out of the fields of snow—that she'd looked down on only hours ago from the window of the chopper. The noisy, chaotic mess of Cairo quickly gave way to sleepier, scattered clusters of houses, and as they passed the small town of Bir Hooker, the last town before the desert and the monasteries, they lost the signals on their cell phones. The monk informed them that they'd be limited to the sat-phone from there on.

Ever since his first call, Gracie hadn't been able to place his accent. "By the way, where are you from?" she asked him.

"I'm from Croatia," he explained. "I come from a small town in the north, not far from the Italian border."

"Then you must be Roman Catholic."

"Of course," the monk confirmed.

"So Ameen isn't your real name?"

"It's not my birth name," he corrected with a warm smile. "I was Father Dario before I came here. We all take on Coptic names once we join the monastery. It's the tradition."

"But the Coptic Church is Orthodox," she queried.

Long before the Protestant Reformation in the 1500s, the Christian world had already been rocked by the great schism in the eleventh century. The long-standing rivalries and theological disputes between Rome and its Eastern counterparts in Alexandria and in Antioch had been festering since the earliest days of Christendom. These petty squabbles finally came to a head in 1054 and split Christendom into two: the Eastern Orthodox Church and the Roman Catholic Church. The Greek word *Orthodox* meant, literally, "correct belief," which pretty much summed up the Eastern Church's belief that it was the true keeper of the flame, that its adherents followed the authentic and uncorrupted traditions and teachings that had been passed down by Jesus and his apostles.

"Orthodox, yes, but not Eastern Orthodox," the monk specified. Gracie's confused expression was obviously no surprise, nor was it limited to her. The monk glanced at his three visitors and waved the issue away. "It's a long story," he told them. "The Coptic Church is the oldest of them all, it out-orthodoxes the Eastern Orthodox Church. It was actually founded by the apostle Mark in the middle of the first century, less than ten years after the death of Jesus. But it's all nonsense, really. Ultimately, all Christians are followers of Christ. That's all that matters. And the monasteries here don't make those distinctions either. All Christians are welcome. Father Jerome is Catholic," he reminded her.

Before long, they rounded the nearby monastery of Saint Bishoi, and Deir Al-Suryan appeared at the end of a dusty, unlit lane. It looked like an ark adrift in a sea of sand—an image its monks had long embraced, believing the monastery to have been modeled on Noah's ark. Details soon fell into focus as the people carrier drew nearer to it: the two tall bell towers; the cubical, squat, four-story keep—the *qasr*—guarding the entrance gate;

the small domes with big crosses on them strewn irregu-
larly around the various chapels and structures inside the
walled complex; all of it surrounded by a thirty-foot fortified wall.

They filed out of the minivan, and Brother Ameen led
them past the keep and across the inner courtyard, which
was presently deserted. The enclosure was deceptively
large. It was roughly the width and length of a football
field, Gracie noticed, and just as flat. Every exterior surface, wall and dome alike, was covered with a clay-and-
limestone adobe of uniform color, a pleasing, sandlike
beige, the corners and edges rounded, soft and organic.
The walls of the keep were dotted with tiny, irregular
openings in place of windows—to keep the heat out—
and narrow staircases led in all kinds of directions. With
the setting sun's warm, orange gleam adding to the
walled sanctuary's otherworldly feel, and its stark contrast to the cold, bleak landscape of the ice continent
whose chill still lingered in her bones, Gracie felt as if she
hadn't just leapfrogged across whole continents. It felt as
if she'd stumbled onto Tatooine.

As they approached the entrance to the library, a
monk stepped out and paused at the sight of them, looking at them first curiously, then with a dour expression
on his face. Gracie guessed it was the abbot.

"Please wait here," Brother Ameen told Gracie and
Finch. They stayed behind while he stepped ahead and
intercepted the clearly irate abbot. Gracie gave Finch a
here-we-go look as they both did their best to observe
the heated chat without appearing too interested.

A moment later, Brother Ameen came back with the
abbot. He didn't seem thrilled to see them, and wasn't
doing much to hide it.

"I'm Bishop Kyrillos, the abbot of this monastery,"
he told them dryly. "I'm afraid Brother Ameen over-

stepped his bounds by inviting you here." He didn't offer his hand.

"Father," Finch said, "please accept our apologies for arriving here like this. We weren't aware of the, um," he paused, trying to find the most diplomatic way of saying it, "internal debate going on here regarding how to deal with it all. We certainly don't mean to inconvenience you or to impose in any way. If you'd like us out of here, just say the word and we'll head back home and no one needs to know about any of this. But I ask you to keep two things in mind. One, no one knows we're here. We only told one person back at our headquarters—our boss—he's the only one who knows where we are. So you mustn't worry about this suddenly becoming a media circus because of us. We won't let it happen."

He paused again, waiting to see if his words were having any effect. He wasn't sure they were, but thought he detected a softening in the man's frown.

"Two," he pressed on, "we're only here to help you and Father Jerome as you—as we all—try to understand the extraordinary events that we're witnessing. I assume you know that we were there. In Antarctica. We saw it all happening right in front of us. And if we're here, it's first and foremost as expert witnesses. We won't broadcast anything without your permission. What we see and discuss here remains between us until you allow otherwise."

The abbot studied him, glanced over at Gracie and at Dalton, shot an unhappy frown at Brother Ameen, then turned his attention back to Finch again. After a brief moment, he nodded slowly as he seemed to reach a verdict, then said, "You want to talk to Father Jerome."

"Yes," Finch replied. "We can tell him what we saw. Show it to him, show him what we filmed. And maybe he can make sense of it."

The abbot nodded again. Then he said, "Very well."

He then raised a stern finger. "But I have your word you won't let any of this out before talking to me about it."

"You have my word, Father." Finch smiled.

The abbot kept his gaze locked on Finch, then said, "Come."

He invited them into the most recent addition to the complex, a stuccoed, simple three-story building that dated from the seventies. Finch and Gracie followed while Dalton scooted off down the courtyard. Brother Ameen had told them the monastery didn't have a television, and they were aching to see the footage from the Arctic and the reaction to it.

Gracie and Finch gratefully accepted a drink of water and a small platter of cheese and fresh dates, and they'd barely had time to exchange casual pleasantries when Dalton popped his head through the door.

"We're up."

They rushed out. Dalton had linked his laptop to the foldable Began satellite dish and was on the network's Web site. Gracie, Finch, the abbot, and the monk huddled around him while he played the news clip of the sighting over Greenland.

A graphic showed the location of the sighting, by the Carlsbad Fjord on the eastern coast of Greenland, four hundred miles north of the Arctic Circle. The video clip that followed was eerily familiar. The footage was jerkier and grainier than their own. It wasn't filmed by a professional crew. Instead, the sighting had been captured on tape by a team of scientists who were studying the effects of meltwater on the Arctic island nation's glaciers. The apparition had taken them by surprise, with the breathless excitement and hectic activity coming through vividly on the screen. One of them, a white-bearded glaciologist with the National Snow and Ice Data Center in Boulder, Colorado, was then interviewed live, his face heavily pixelated and breaking up from the webcam-linked satellite phone they were evidently using.

"First, Antarctica, and now here," the offscreen anchorman's voice asked him. "Why do you think this is happening?"

There was a two-second lag; then the scientist's professorial face reacted to hearing the question. "Look, I'm . . . I don't know what it is or where it's coming from," he answered with a gruff voice. "What I do know is that it can't be a coincidence that this—this *sign* is showing up over what can only be described as disaster areas. I mean, that ice shelf in Antarctica that's crumbling, and this glacier here—they're ground zero. I've been studying these glaciers here for over twenty years." He turned and waved a gloved hand at the gray-white expanse behind him. "You'd look out across the land there and it used to be pure white. Nothing but snow and ice, year-round. Now you look at it and it's more blue than white. It's melting so fast that we've now got lakes and rivers all over the place, and that water's working its way down to the bedrock and loosening the bases of the glaciers, which is why they've started to slide out to sea. And if this one goes," he pointed out gravely, "we're talking a three-foot rise in global sea levels. Which could then trigger all kinds of nightmare upheavals. So, you ask me what I think is happening? I think it's pretty obvious. Nature's flashing us a red alert here, and I think we need to take that warning seriously, before it's too late."

Gracie stood there, rooted in silence, as the report cut away to a montage of reactions to the sign's second appearance. The images were breathtaking. A large crowd congregated in Times Square, watching the scenes unfold on the huge screen, the crawler underneath announcing the sighting in bold letters. Similar scenes were captured in London, Moscow, and other major cities. What the first appearance seeded, this second one reaped in spades, in terms of impact. The world was sitting up and taking notice.

Gracie glanced over at Dalton and Finch, and felt a surge of trepidation. Something unprecedented was happening, something big and wonderful and baffling and terrifying all at the same time—and she was right at the heart of it.

The satphone startled her and dragged her attention away from the screen. It was Ogilvy, calling from his cell, as per their agreed communication protocol.

"I just got a call from the Pentagon," he informed her. "Two DIA guys just landed in McMurdo and found out you'd skipped town. They're pretty pissed off," he said with a light chuckle.

Gracie frowned. "What did you have to tell them?"

"Nothing. It's still a free country. Sort of. But they'll track you to Cairo Airport pretty quickly, if they haven't done it already. From there . . . who knows? You might want to switch off your phones."

"There's no signal out here anyway," she told him, "but we need to keep in touch. We're pretty cut off out here."

"Check your satphone every hour; I'll text you if anything comes up." Ogilvy impressed her with his sangfroid.

"We'll do that," she confirmed. "And I'll get you the landline of the monastery too, just in case."

"Good." Ogilvy's voice took on a more serious tone. "Did you meet him yet?"

"No, we just got here."

"Talk to Father Jerome, Gracie. Do it quickly. The whole world's watching. And we've got to keep our lead on this thing. It's ours for the taking."

Gracie felt a hard lump in her throat. She glanced uneasily at the monks as she stepped away and turned her back to them, lowering her voice. "We've got to be careful here, Hal. We can't just announce this without taking the necessary precautions."

"What do you mean?"

"I mean, this is a Muslim country. I'm not sure they'd react kindly to something that smells like a Second Coming, especially not in their own backyard."

"It's where it happened the first time," Ogilvy remarked dryly.

"Hal, seriously," Gracie shot back, "we need to tread carefully. In case you hadn't noticed, this isn't the most tolerant corner of the planet. I don't want to put Father Jerome in any danger."

"I don't want to put anyone in danger either," Ogilvy countered, slightly testily. "We'll be careful. Just talk to him. We'll take it from there."

Gracie didn't feel overly relieved. She relented—"I'll call you after I meet him"—then snapped the phone shut and turned to the abbot. She needed to get something out of the way. "The documentary footage they filmed in the cave. Can we see it?"

"Of course. It's on the DVD they sent us—I haven't watched it as we don't have a player here."

"This laptop'll play it," Dalton told him, tapping his computer.

The abbot nodded and left them.

Dalton glanced worriedly at Gracie and Finch. "What if the shot we need didn't make the final cut?"

It was a disheartening possibility neither of them wanted to consider right now, as it meant they would then have to contact the filmmakers for the outtakes. The abbot interrupted their concern by reappearing quickly, DVD in hand. Dalton loaded it up and fast-forwarded through it until the screen showed the small film crew climbing up the mountain and approaching what looked like an old door cut into the rock face.

"There," the abbot exclaimed. "That's Father Jerome's cave."

Dalton reverted to play mode, and the screen showed the cameraman's point of view as he entered the cave. Gracie watched, heart in mouth, as it tracked through the dark chamber, an ominous, first-person voice-over describing the cave and its sparse, simple furnishings, giving her a preview of what she would imminently be visiting—then the camera banked around and, in a sweeping pan, covered the curving ceiling of the chamber.

"Right there," Gracie burst out, jabbing the screen with her finger. "That's it, isn't it?"

Dalton hit the PAUSE button, backtracked a few frames, and played the clip again in slow motion. They all leaned in for a closer look. It was just a brief shot, no more than a passing glimpse at a curiosity within the cave—but it was all they needed. Dalton froze the image on one of the painted symbols. It was an elegant construction of concentric circles and intersecting lines that radiated outward. Despite its simplicity, it somehow managed to convey what they'd seen over the ice shelf and now, on the video, with surprising ease and clarity.

It was unmistakable.

Gracie turned to the abbot. Her nerves were buzzing with anticipation. "When can we go there and meet Father Jerome?"

He checked his watch. "It's getting late. The sun will be gone soon. Tomorrow morning, first thing?"

Gracie winced, her heartbeat having a hard time pulling back from the frenzied quickening brought on by the footage on Dalton's screen. "Father, please. I don't mean to be a burden in any way, but . . . given what's happening, I don't think we should wait. I really think we ought to talk to him tonight."

The abbot held her gaze for an uncomfortable beat, then relented. "Very well. But in that case, we should go now."

◄o►

LYING UNDER A SAND-COLORED CAMOUFLAGE net four hundred yards west of the monastery's gate, Fox Two watched through high-powered binoculars as Gracie, Finch, and Dalton, accompanied by the abbot and another monk, climbed into the waiting people carrier.

His Iridium satphone vibrated. He fished it out and checked it. The text message told him Fox One and his team had just landed. On time. As expected.

He locked the phone and tucked it back into his pocket and watched as the Previa drove away in a swirl of dust.

He waited until they were half a mile away before pushing himself to his knees. Crouching low, he carefully folded the netting, stowed it in its pack, then slipped away to rejoin his two men, who waited nearby.

The mountain beckoned.

Again.

Chapter 31

Woburn, Massachusetts

The motel was grubby and run-down, but it provided Matt and Jabba with the basics: four walls, a roof, and the anonymity of a check-in alcove manned by a weedy daytime television addict who could barely string together a sentence. And right now, that was what they needed most. Shelter and anonymity.

That, and some answers.

Matt was sitting on the floor, leaning against the bed, his head tilted all the way back, resting against the lumpy mattress. Jabba, on the other hand, couldn't sit still. He was pacing around and making repeated checks out the window.

"Would you stop doing that?" Matt grumbled. "No one's coming for us here. Not yet, anyway."

Jabba grudgingly let go of the thin, stained curtain and embarked on another lap up and down the room.

"Just sit the hell down," Matt snapped.

"I'm sorry, all right?" Jabba fired back. "I'm just not used to all this. I mean, it's just insane, dude. Why are we even here? Why can't we just go to the cops and tell them what you know?"

"'Cause what I know is nothing compared to what

the cops think they know, and I don't fancy sweating this one out behind bars. Now do me and this carpet a favor and sit down."

Jabba stared at him for a beat, then relented. He looked around, frowned at a rickety chair that looked like it would disintegrate if he even thought of sitting in it, and set himself down on the marginally sturdier bed instead. He palmed the remote and changed channels on the small TV that was bolted onto the wall. It matched the room: basic, run-down, but functional. Matt glanced at its screen. The picture was grainy and the set had a meek, tinny sound, but that didn't matter. He could see what he needed to see.

News of the Greenland apparition had whipped up the media into an even bigger frenzy. Coming on the heels of the Antarctic event, it was an irrefutable confirmation that no one could ignore. It was on every channel—endless blathering that ultimately couldn't offer any explanation beyond replaying the same clips over and over and exploring past mystical sightings for any relevance. Clips about previous claims, from Fatima to Medjugorje, were getting airtime, only they paled in comparison. This wasn't a handful of kids claiming to see the Virgin Mary in a field.

The world was, simply, entranced.

Matt tilted his head back again and exhaled wearily. "Tell me what you and Vince talked about."

"Tell you what we talked about?" Jabba rambled. "We talked about everything, dude. Where do you want me to start?"

"Last night," Matt specified testily. "What did you guys talk about last night?"

"Last night. Last night, right," he muttered, pinching the bridge of his nose between two fingers. "We were watching this thing," he said, pointing at the screen. "The first one, anyway. Trying to work out how it could be done."

Matt sat up. " 'Done'? You think it's a fake?"

Jabba gave him a look. "Dude. Come on. Something like this happens, your first instinct has to be it's a fake. Unless you buy into that whole 'the truth is out there' mind-set."

"Which, I'm guessing, you don't?"

"No, hey, I'm open to it. I'm sure there's some weird stuff they're not telling us about. But there's so much bullshit out there, whether it's from the government or from people who are out to make a fast buck, you've got to look at things with a cynic's eye. And we're scientists, man. Our instinct is to ask questions first."

Matt nodded, trying to stay focused. "So you and Vince bounced around some ideas. You come up with anything?"

"No. See, that's the thing." Jabba leaned forward, and his voice livened up. "Nothing stuck. Nothing at all. We couldn't even begin to figure it out. If this thing's a fake, then whoever's doing it is using some technology that's straight out of Area 51."

Matt frowned. He was missing something. "What is it you guys do, anyway? I mean, if it *was* a fake, what made you think you and Vince could figure it out?"

"We're electrical engineers. We work on . . . I mean, me and Vince, we . . ." He stumbled with visible discomfort. "We design computer circuits, microchips, that kind of thing."

Matt glanced at the screen dubiously. "That doesn't sound particularly relevant to this thing."

"I'm not talking about Radio Shack walkie-talkies, dude. Or even iPhones. I'm talking sci-fi-level stuff. Like right now, we're building these micro-RFID chips—you remember that scene in *Minority Report*? When Tom Cruise is walking through a mall and all these holographic panels know it's him and start talking to him and showing him these tailor-made ads?"

"Not really." Matt shrugged. "I've missed out on a few movies over the years."

"Too bad, man. Awesome movie. Right up there with *Blade Runner*, the only other Philip K. Dick story Hollywood didn't manage to screw up." A look from Matt put him back on track. "Anyway, we can do that now. Not the screen. I'm talking about the recognition part. Tiny chips embedded in the actual fabric of your shirt, that kind of thing."

"It still doesn't tell me why you think you'd be able to figure this out."

"What we do . . . it's not just a job," Jabba explained. "It's a calling. You live it, breathe it, dream it. It takes over your life. It *is* your life. And part of it is keeping track of everything that's going on, not just the stuff that's directly related to your work. You've got to want to know about what everyone else is doing, whether it's at NASA, in Silicon Valley, or in some lab in Singapore. Because everything's interconnected. One of their breakthroughs could be combined with what you're doing in ways neither one of you intended and could open up a whole new door in your brain. It can give you the one thing you need to make that quantum leap and send your work in a completely new direction."

"Okay." Matt didn't sound too convinced. "So you and Vince kept an eye on what other brainiacs were dreaming up."

"Pretty much."

Matt still felt confused. "Well, if the two of you couldn't figure it out, then why was your conversation a threat to anyone? Do you think you might have hit on something without knowing it?"

Jabba did a quick mental rummage of his chat with Bellinger. "I doubt it. Everything we talked about is public knowledge—at least, among the other 'brainiacs' out there. If any of it was relevant in any way—and I don't think it was—someone else would have made the connection too by now."

"So why come after Vince? And why did it make him think that my brother was somehow involved?"

Jabba's face signaled he was now missing something. "Who was your brother?"

"Danny. Danny Sherwood."

A name that clearly struck a chord. A resonant one. "Danny Sherwood was your brother?"

Matt nodded. "You knew him?"

"I knew *of* him, sure. Distributed processing, right? Progamming's holy grail. Your brother's cred was rock solid on that front." He nodded wistfully. "Vince loved your brother, man. Said he was the most brilliant programmer he'd ever seen." He let the words settle as his mind tried to fill in the blanks and see the connections. "What did Vince tell you, exactly?"

"Not much. He said someone called Reece hired Danny to work with him on something. You heard of him?"

"Dominic Reece. They all went down in that chopper, didn't they? I'm sorry, man." Jabba's expression tightened. "Vince told you he thought they'd been murdered? All of them?"

"Maybe. Maybe not." He didn't want to lose his thread. "He said they were working on some kind of biosensor project. Does that mean anything to you?"

"No. But Vince and Danny were close. Closer than close. He might have told him something in strict confidence. Something he wasn't supposed to spread around. Like maybe the patents hadn't been applied for yet. In our business, one slip of the tongue could lose you a billion-dollar advantage."

Matt rubbed the exhaustion from his eyes. The sign over Greenland was on the screen again, taunting him. It was hypnotic, and Matt was finding it hard to take his eyes off it. "You and Vince. Last night. He cut the conversation short, didn't he?"

Jabba nodded.

"What was the last thing he said? Do you remember?"

Jabba concentrated. "He didn't say it. I did. I was just saying that it looked like the air itself was being lit up. Like the air molecules themselves were on fire. Only that's not possible."

Matt studied the grainy image on the screen. "What if it is?"

"Setting the air on fire? I don't think so."

"What about a laser, a projector . . . something that needs the skill set of one hell of a programmer?"

Jabba just shook his head. "Nothing I know of can do that. And if anyone else knew how it could be done, they'd be on every channel."

Matt shut his eyes and leaned back, frustrated. He was having a hard time concentrating and getting his head around it all. It didn't help that he was running on empty. He was exhausted, physically as well as mentally. He hadn't slept for well over twenty-four hours, hours that he hadn't exactly coasted through. And it didn't look like whatever it was that had him in its grip was about to let go anytime soon.

"There's a reason they killed Vince. And it has to do with what happened to Danny and the others. Whether this damn sign is real or not, someone's doing something."

Jabba's face sank. "And you want to find out who's doing it."

"Yep."

Jabba looked at him like a kid studying a three-eyed panda at the zoo. "Are you nuts? 'Cause that's the wrong play, dude. The right play is we lose ourselves until they're done with whatever it is they're doing. We disappear, maybe drive up to Canada or something. We sit tight and we wait until it's all blown over."

Matt eyed him like he was now the alien species. "You think?"

Jabba frowned, a bit discomfited by Matt's sardonic expression. "You asked me what made me and Vince think we could figure this out. What makes you think you can? I mean, what are you, an ex-cop or something? Ex-FBI? Some kind of ex-SEAL special ops hard-ass maybe?"

Matt shook his head. "You've got me pegged on the wrong side of that fence."

"Oh, well, that's just wonderful," Jabba groaned. He shook his head again; then his tone turned serious. "Dude, seriously. These are bad people. We're talking about guys who kill people by the chopper-load."

Matt's mind was elsewhere.

Jabba could see it. "You're not listening to me, are you?"

Matt shook his head.

Jabba's face sank again in exasperation. "We're screwed, aren't we?"

Matt ignored the question. "Can you find out who else was on that chopper? What their specialties were? And also . . . who was funding them?"

Jabba sighed. "Like I have a choice?" He reached into his backpack and pulled out his laptop.

Matt pointed at it. "Think you can get an Internet connection in this dump?"

"I seriously doubt they have wi-fi here, but . . ." Jabba held up his iPhone and flashed Matt a cheesy, knowing look. Then he remembered and his face clouded. "Forgot. Can't use this. Dammit." He rubbed his face with his meaty fingers, thought about it, then looked up. "Depends on what you need. I can fire it up for forty seconds max. Any longer than that and they'll get a fix on where we are."

Matt grimaced. "You get that from watching *24,* or is this for real?"

Jabba held up the phone. "Dude. First thing I did when I bought this thing? I took it apart to jailbreak it. Just to piss off AT&T."

"Meaning?"

"Meaning I've set it free. I can hook up its Edge data connection to my laptop."

"Okay. But just to play it safe, maybe the guy at reception'll let you use his computer."

Jabba frowned. "Why? What else do you need?"

"A little update," Matt said. "On where our friends with the Chrysler are hanging out."

Chapter 32

Mountains of Wadi Natrun, Egypt

Father Jerome looked very different from what Gracie had imagined. That didn't surprise her. In her experience, people often looked different in the flesh than they did in pictures or on film. Occasionally, the change was for the better, though mostly—and more commonly these days, given the amount of Photoshopping that went on—it led to disappointment. In this case, Gracie had expected him to look different, given what he'd been through since the last coverage she'd seen of him. And he was: thinner, more gaunt-faced, seemingly more fragile than she remembered. But even here, in the light of three gas lanterns and a few scattered candles in the oppressively dark cave, his eyes, a piercing green-gray that blazed out of the tanned corona of his face, were more captivating than on film and made up for any frailty his recent ordeal had exacerbated.

"So you don't remember anything at all of your journey?" Gracie asked him. "You were out there for weeks, weren't you?"

"Three months," the old man answered, his eyes never leaving hers. Gracie, Finch, and Dalton had been pleasantly surprised by the fact that he hadn't refused to see them. Far from it, he'd been warm and welcoming.

He was unperturbed, his voice unwavering and soothing, his words clear and slow. He hadn't lost the trace of
Spanish that colored his words. Gracie had immediately
warmed to him, no doubt predisposed by her great ad-
miration for the man and the selflessness and humility he
inspired.

"And it's just . . . blank," she added.

"It's not something I've ever experienced. I have
vague recollections, fleeting images in my mind . . .
Walking, alone. I can see the sandals on my feet, walking
in the sand, the endless landscape surrounding me. The
blue sky, the burning sun, the hot air . . . I can smell it. I
can feel the heat on my face, the hot air in my lungs. But
that's all they are. Snippets. Momentary flashes of consciousness in an otherwise blank slate." He shook his
head in despair, slightly, to himself, as if chiding himself
for that failing.

Although Dalton and Finch were sitting there with
her in the cave, along with the abbot and Brother Ameen,
Gracie had decided not to ask for this first interview to
be filmed. It hadn't been an easy decision. Although she
felt it was best to spend a bit of time with Father Jerome
first, to get to know him, to get him comfortable with
them, she also wasn't sure how he'd react to seeing the
footage of the signs in the sky. And she felt uneasy and
disingenuous at the thought of springing the news on
him with a camera rolling.

She glanced up at the roof of the cavern. The white
swirls, unsettling representations of the sign she'd witnessed over the ice shelf, were all over it.

"Tell me about these," she asked him, waving her
hand across the ceiling.

The priest looked upward thoughtfully, studying the
painted symbols above their heads, and thought about
her question for a brief moment, before letting his eyes

settle on her again. "Shortly after I arrived here," he told her, "a clarity that I'd never experienced came over me. I began to understand things more clearly. It was as if my mind were suddenly liberated of its clutter and freed to see life for what it really was. And these thoughts, these ideas . . . they started coming to me with such clarity, and such power. I just need to close my eyes and they start flowing through me. It's beyond my control. I've been writing them down, there." He pointed at his desk. A few notebooks sat on its worn surface, some others on the ledge by the window. "Like a faithful scribe," he added with a faint smile.

Gracie couldn't take her eyes off him as he spoke. Most unsettling was how steady his voice was, how utterly normal he sounded, how casual his tone was. It was as if he were describing nothing more than the most mundane of experiences. "And this symbol?" she reminded him, pointing upward again. "You painted these, didn't you?"

He nodded slowly, his face slightly pinched in confusion. "It's something I can't quite explain. When the thoughts come to me, when I hear the words in my head just as I hear you, I also see that," he explained, pointing at the sign. "It's just there, burning brightly in my consciousness. And after a while, I found myself drawing it, over and over. I'm not sure what it means, but . . . it's there, in my head. I can see it, clearly. And it's . . . it's more than this," he added almost ruefully as he gestured at the roof of the cavern. "It's . . . clearer. Richer. More resplendent. More . . . alive." He glanced away, hesitating to go further. "It's hard to explain. Forgive me if this sounds too vague, but . . . it's really beyond my understanding. Or control."

"Could it be something you saw in your dreams?"

Father Jerome shook his head and smiled. "No. It's

there. I just need to close my eyes and I can see it. Anytime."

Gracie felt a shiver at the base of her neck. "So you've never actually seen it? I mean, physically?" she specified, weighing her words—then an idea swooped into her mind. "Could it be something you saw while you were out in the desert? Something you saw but don't remember?"

"Saw? Where?" he asked.

She hesitated, then said, "In the sky?"

The priest tilted his head slightly, his eyebrows raised, as he mulled her suggestion for a moment. "I suppose it's possible," he finally conceded. "Anything's possible, given how those weeks are nothing but a blur."

Gracie glanced over at Finch, then at the abbot. With the slightest nods, they seemed to agree with what she was thinking. She turned to Dalton, who had cottoned on and was already keying in the commands on his laptop.

She felt a tightening in her throat as she coaxed the words out. "I'd like to show you something, Father. It's something we just filmed, something we saw in Antarctica, just before coming here to see you. I'm a bit wary of showing it to you like this, without preparation, but I really think you need to see this. It has to do with this symbol you've been drawing." She paused, scrutinizing his face for signs of discomfort. She didn't find any. She swallowed hard and asked, "Would you like to see it?"

The priest looked at her quizzically, but, calm as ever, nodded. "Please," he said, spreading his hands invitingly.

Dalton got up and placed the laptop on a low table in front of the priest, and turned it so that they could all watch it. He hit the PLAY button. The video from Antarctica, the edited piece they had sent the network, played. Gracie kept her gaze locked on Father Jerome, studying his face as he absorbed the images unfurling before him.

She watched, on edge, expecting to see any one of a number of emotional responses to the clip—surprise, consternation, worry, fear even—and hoping it didn't make the priest distraught. It didn't. But it seemed to confuse him. His posture visibly stiffened as he leaned in for a closer look; his mouth dropped slightly; his forehead furrowed under the strain.

When it was finished, he turned to them, looking bewildered. "You filmed this?"

Gracie nodded.

The priest was at a loss for words. His eyes took on a haunted, pained expression. "What does this mean?"

Gracie didn't have an answer for him. From the silence around her, it didn't seem like anyone else did either. She winced a little as she said, "There's been another sighting like that. In Greenland this time. Just a few hours ago."

"Another one?"

"Yes," Gracie confirmed.

Father Jerome pushed himself to his feet and shuffled over to the window. He stared at his desk, shaking his head in disbelief, then reached down and picked up one of his notebooks. He riffled through its pages until he found what he was looking for, and just stood there, staring at it. "I don't understand it," he mumbled. "It's what I've been seeing. And yet . . ." He turned to face Gracie and the others, the open notebook in his hand. Gracie hesitantly reached out. He placed it in her hand, a faraway, haunted look in his eyes. She looked at the pages before her, then leafed through a few more pages. They were all similar: packed densely with an elegant, handwritten script, and dotted, here and there, with more elaborate renderings of the sign. She looked over at Finch and passed him the notebook, her fingers quivering slightly under the weight of what she'd seen on its pages.

"When I see it," the old priest continued, "it . . . it speaks to me. Somehow, it's as if it's putting the words and ideas in my head." He studied their faces intently, his gaze magnetic, his eyes jumping from one to another, searching for comfort. "Don't you hear them too?"

Gracie didn't know what to answer. She felt the others shifting uncomfortably, not knowing what to say either. The abbot got up and crossed over to Father Jerome. He placed a comforting arm around his shoulder. "Perhaps we should take a small break," he suggested, nodding at Gracie. "Let the good father's mind settle down. It's a lot to take in."

"Of course," Gracie agreed with a warm, supportive smile. "We'll wait outside."

The three of them left Father Jerome with the abbot and the younger monk and stepped out into the small clearing outside the cave's entrance. The last vestiges of day that they'd witnessed on the climb up were now gone. With a total absence of ambient light as far as the eye could see, the ink-black dome above them looked unreal, blazing with a dazzling array of stars, an astounding and humbling display the likes of which Gracie had rarely seen.

No one said anything. They each seemed to be processing what the priest had said, looking for a rational explanation to it all. Gracie glanced absentmindedly at her watch, and saw that it was coming up to the hour. She suddenly remembered what they'd agreed with Ogilvy. "Where's the satphone?" she asked.

Finch retrieved it from his bag, which he'd left at the door of the cave, inserted the battery back into it, and switched it on. Within seconds, it pinged with several text messages. The one that caught his eye was from Ogilvy. It simply said, in loud, capitalized letters, "CALL ME AS SOON AS YOU GET THIS." He handed it to Gracie. "Something's up."

The curtness of the message unsettled her as she thumbed the redial key. Ogilvy picked it up inside of one ring, the words somersaulting out of his mouth.

"They just aired the documentary footage from the cave."

Gracie froze. "What?"

"They showed it," Ogilvy reiterated, breathless with urgency. "It's out. The whole thing's out. Father Jerome, the monastery, the symbol he's painted all over his cave. It's on every TV screen from here to Shanghai as we speak," he told her, uncharacteristically nerve-racked, clearly struggling to process the implications himself. "This thing's just blown wide-open, Gracie—and you're standing right at ground zero."

Chapter 33

Boston, Massachusetts

Larry Rydell was having a hard time focusing on what his chief advertising strategist and his director of interactive marketing were saying as they stepped out of the elevator. He'd had trouble concentrating on the conversation throughout their lunch at the firm's laid-back canteen—a moniker that seriously understated the fine sushi and Mediterranean cuisine that were on offer. He knew both executives well. They were part of the brain trust that ran the firm—his firm, the one he'd founded twenty-three years earlier, before he'd dropped out of Berkeley. He used to thrive on their informal meetings. They were part of what fueled the company to its global success, and he normally enjoyed them with the enthusiasm of a young entrepreneur hell-bent on conquering the world. Lately, though, he'd been more distant, less focused, and today, he was only there in strictly physical terms. His mind was entirely elsewhere, locked on the events that were taking place continents away.

He gave them a casual half smile and a small wave as they parted, then strode down the wide, glass-covered hallway to his office. As he reached the secretarial pool stationed outside his door, he saw Mona, his trusted senior PA, and his three other assistants clustered around the bank of wall-mounted LCD screens that were constantly tuned to the major international news channels.

The sight surprised him somewhat. They'd already watched the Greenland sighting that morning. Mona turned and spotted him. She waved him over while gesturing at the screen. "Did you see this?" she asked. "It's from a documentary they filmed six months ago in an old monastery in Egypt. You've got to see this."

He felt a pinch of concern as he stepped closer to the screen; then the blood drained from his face as the significance of what it was showing sank in.

He managed to mask his unease and feigned sharing in their excitement for a minute or two before retreating into the sanctuary of his office, where he studied the news reports in private. He was familiar with Father Jerome, of course—who wasn't?—but he'd never heard of the monastery. Close-ups of the markings on the cave wall were everywhere he looked, and were definitely renderings of the sign. Which sent Rydell's mind cartwheeling in all kinds of deeply troubling directions.

He flicked around TV channels and Web sites feverishly, looking for something, anything, to put his mind to rest. Nothing came to his rescue. On the screens, legions of commentators on the news networks were competing to make sense of it.

"Well, if what we're seeing here is true, if this footage was really filmed when they're saying it was," one notable pundit was saying, "then clearly, it's an association between this unexplained phenomenon and a highly regarded man of faith, and not just any faith—a Christian man of faith," he emphasized, "who somehow foresaw these events we've been witnessing, while staying in one of Christianity's oldest places of worship . . ."

The implications of the footage were obvious and inescapable, and it was already creating a huge stir. Evangelists and born-again Christians, parishioners and preachers alike, had begun staking their claim on the sign and making all kinds of prophetic proclamations. The followers of other faiths—predictably—didn't share in their euphoria and felt excluded and threatened. A few angry denunciations had already been voiced by Muslim scholars. More would inevitably come, and from other religions too, Rydell was certain.

Which wasn't part of the plan.

He pulled back and engaged his mind in a broader, less prejudiced analysis of what this might be. He knew there were a lot of other possible explanations for it. They'd expected people to claim the sign all along. They knew that crazies in every dark corner of the planet would be coming out of their rabbit holes and making all kinds of nonsensical declarations. But this was no nutcase. This was Father Jerome. *The* Father Jerome.

No, he was sure of it. Something was very, very wrong.

He'd misjudged them again.

And that possibility—that certainty—sent a bracing shot of ice rushing through his veins.

He did all he could to keep his anger in check as he picked up the phone and punched the speed-dial key for Drucker.

◄◦►

SEATED COMFORTABLY IN HIS OFFICE on Connecticut Avenue, Keenan Drucker watched his TV monitor with avid interest. He marveled at how quickly the media pounced on any development and whipped it around the planet. The content beast needed to be fed, and ever since the first appearance of the sign, it was positively feasting.

He felt a deeply rooted satisfaction at how things were unfolding, and his gaze ratcheted back from the plasma screen on his wall and dropped down to a framed picture on his desk. Jackson, his son—his dead son—beamed back at him from behind its thin glass plate. Drucker felt the same stab of grief he suffered every time he glanced at the picture. He tried to keep that image of Jackson in his mind—alive, vibrant, handsome, proudly turned out in his crisp officer's dress uniform, the young man's eyes blazing with a sense of pride and purpose—and not let the horrific images from the mortuary seep in and overpower it. But he never could. The images from that visit to the base, when he and his wife were presented with what was left of their son, were permanently chiseled into his hardened soul.

I'll make things right, he thought to Jackson. *I'll make sure it never happens again.*

He tore his eyes off his son's face and looked up at the screen. He surfed away from the mainstream news networks and trawled the Christian channels instead. The sound bites coming through were promising. The footage from the caves was whipping up a storm of excitement; that much was clear. The people in the street were lapping it up. The preachers, however, were being more cautious. He watched as one televangelist after another gave cagey responses about what was going on, clearly unsure about how to handle this unexpected intrusion into their cosseted worlds.

Typical, he thought, knowing they had to be seriously threatened—but also aware that they'd be watching one another, waiting to see who'd be the first to jump into the pool.

"If he's the real deal," he heard one pundit remark on air, "these preachers will soon be falling over themselves to embrace him and claim him as their own."

They'll get there, he mused. *They just need some encouragement.*

Covert encouragement, to be precise.

Which, as it happened, was something Keenan Drucker excelled at.

His BlackBerry pinged. He dragged his concentration away from the monitor and glanced at the phone. It was Rydell.

As expected.

He inhaled a long, calming breath, then picked it up. Rydell's voice was—also as expected—agitated.

"Keenan, what the hell's going on?"

Time for damage control. Something else he excelled at.

"Not on the phone," he replied curtly.

"I need to know this isn't what I think it is."

"We need to talk," Drucker just repeated, his words slow, emphatic. "In person."

A beat later, Rydell came back. "I'll fly down first thing in the morning. Meet me at Reagan. Eight o'clock." And he was gone.

Drucker nodded slowly to himself. Anticipating Rydell's reaction, and his call, hadn't exactly taken an act of supernatural-level divination. It was simple cause and effect. But it meant he needed to initiate an effect of his own.

Maddox picked up his call within two rings.

"Where are you?" Drucker asked him. "Where are we with Sherwood's brother?"

"It's under control," Maddox said. "I'm dealing with it myself."

Drucker frowned. He didn't expect the Bullet to dive in himself unless things were getting out of hand. He decided now was not the time to delve further on that front. He had a more pressing message to convey, in the form of three short words.

"Get the girl" was all he said. Then he hung up.

◄o►

ALMOST TWO THOUSAND MILES EAST, Rebecca Rydell was still in bed and enjoying a late lie-in. By conventional standards, it was past lunchtime, but Costa Careyes was far from conventional. And at the Rydells' sprawling Casa Diva, moreover, as in the other villas and casitas on the sun-kissed Mexican coast for that matter, life was unfettered by such mundane limitations.

She'd been up most of the night, with her friends. They'd watched the latest sighting on the big screen in the open-air living room before adjourning to the beach and wondering about it over ceviche, grilled shrimp, margaritas, and a big bonfire under a pearlescent moon.

Vague recollections of the evening drifted into her mind as she stirred, half-awake, her senses tickled to life by the delicate scents of bougainvillea and *copa de oro* that wafted through the house. She usually liked to sleep with the French doors open, preferring the sound of the ocean's waves and the salty taste of the air to the clinical hum of the air conditioner, but it had been a particularly hot week, hotter than she could ever remember. Still drowsy, she realized something else had nudged her awake. A faint noise outside her bedroom. Footsteps, getting closer.

The door to her room swung open, and Rebecca almost jumped out of her skin at the sight of the two men who hurried in. She knew them, of course. Ben and Jon. The bodyguards her father had insisted should accompany her whenever she left the country. Especially when she was in Mexico. They were normally very discreet and stayed well out of sight, particularly here, in the sleepy, remote playground of Careyes, far removed from kidnap-central Mexico City and the drug war zones farther north. She'd known the two men for over a year now, and she liked and trusted them—which was why she sat up briskly, a sudden ripple of fear rushing through her. For them to be barging into her bedroom like this, without so much as a knock, meant that something very, very bad had happened.

"Get dressed," Ben told her bluntly. "We have to get you out of here."

She pulled the sheet right up against her chest and shrank back against the headboard, her breath coming short and fast. "What's going on?"

Ben's eyes fell on a light, floral-patterned dress that was strewn across a bench at the foot of her bed. He picked it up and flung it at her.

"We have to get you out here now. Let's go," he ordered.

Something about the way he said it, something about the way Jon's eyes were dancing back and forth warily, made her uneasy. Her hand fumbled to the night table, and she grabbed her cell phone. "Where's my dad? Is he okay?" she asked as she hit the keypad.

Ben took a couple of quick strides to her bedside and snatched the phone out of her hand. "He's fine. You can talk to him later. We have to go now." He slipped her phone into his pocket and looked at her pointedly.

The finality of his words pummeled her into submission.

She nodded hesitantly and reached for her dress. The two men half-turned to give her some privacy as she pulled it on. She tried to calm herself, to placate the terror that was coursing through her. The two men were professionals. They knew what they were doing. This was what they were trained to do. She shouldn't be asking questions. She knew her dad only hired the best of the best. She was in safe hands. She'd even met her bodyguards' boss, the slightly creepy guy with the granite eyes whose firm handled all aspects of security for her dad's businesses, a man who didn't look like he did anything halfheartedly.

Everything would be fine, she tried to convince herself.

She slipped her sandals on. Seconds later, they were rushing her out of the house and into a waiting car that charged out of the estate and barreled down the bumpy road, heading for Manzanillo.

Everything's going to be fine, she told herself again, although somehow, deep inside, a little voice was telling her she was wrong.

Chapter 34

Brighton, Massachusetts

Matt was parked across the street and six car lengths back from the target house. He'd been there for over an hour, sitting low, watching, waiting. Thinking about his options. Not really liking any of them.

He'd ditched the RAV4 and picked up a bathtub-white Camry, pre-'89 and hence pre–car key transponders. Probably the blandest car he'd ever stolen—it even out-blanded the Taurus, which was no mean feat. Regardless, he'd felt a pang of guilt as he'd hot-wired it. Several people were now facing the unpleasant task of dealing with their insurance companies regarding their stolen cars, all because of him. Still, he didn't really have a choice. He figured they'd probably understand if they knew what he'd been going through.

The gray house he was watching was equally unremarkable. Small, run-down, two floors, clapboard siding, gabled roof. Probably leased in the name of a shell company. Rent paid in advance. Practically untraceable, Matt imagined. It squatted there anonymously, its gray boards mirroring the dreary wintry sky overhead, looking as bleak and lifeless as the bare-limbed red oaks that dotted the quiet neighborhood. A small driveway ran alongside it and led to a covered single-car garage out back. The

Chrysler was parked outside, as was the van—the one he'd last seen barreling down the snow-lined avenue after he'd jumped out of it.

His nerve endings bristled with impatience and anticipation. The answers he so wanted were probably inside that house, but he couldn't exactly waltz in there and get them. He needed to bide his time. Watch. Study. And come up with a plan. One that had half a chance of working. One that wouldn't end up with him dead.

He'd come up with one earlier, back at the motel, before driving over. A grand plan, one that had him excited—for a short spell, anyway.

He'd call the cops. Do the "anonymous-tip" thing and tell them Bellinger's real killers were in the house. They'd send a car to check it out. The cops—maybe the ones who showed up at Bellinger's apartment that night—would come up to the door and knock. One of the goons—not bob-girl, presumably, since she was one of the "witnesses" who'd "seen" Matt chase down Bellinger—would answer. They'd have a little Q&A. Dance around some questions.

And then Matt would ramp things up a notch.

He'd pick up a couple of empty bottles from a Dumpster on the drive over, along with any old rag he could find. He'd buy a jerrican of fuel and a lighter at a gas station. He'd fill the bottles with fuel. He'd shred the rag into strips and stuff them into the necks of the bottles and use them as wicks. And then he'd firebomb the house.

Maybe from the back. Or from the side. Just sneak up to a spot where he wouldn't be seen and chuck a flaming bottle or two through a window. And watch. It would take them all by surprise. The cops would want to go in to help put out the fire. The goons would probably resist, not wanting them in the house where their gear might be on show. Their behavior would certainly be less than ingenuous, and they would probably behave suspiciously. The cops would get curious, especially given the reason they were there in the first place. They'd probably call for backup. A standoff would ensue. The goons would have a lot of explaining to do. In looking into the unexplained arson attack, the cops would find some forensic evidence in the van, linking it to Bellinger's murder. The goons would get mired in a procedural swamp. They'd be off Matt's back, and, with a bit of luck, Matt would be off the hook for the stabbing.

Maybe.

On the other hand, it could all go wrong and he could get shot by the cops and the case would be closed. And either way, he wouldn't get the thing he most wanted: to find out what they had done to his brother.

So he dropped that plan. Decided to play it more cautiously. Take things one step at a time. Maybe try to get some one-on-one time with one of the goons. In which case a weapon would be good. The van—and the car—could yield one. Something he could use to even out the odds a little. And maybe, with a bit of luck, he could then grab one of the killers and get the answers he wanted.

Maybe.

No one had gone in or out of the house since he'd been there, but the cars and the lights in the front ground-floor room suggested the goons were in. He tried to think back to how many were in the van—four, he thought. Which was bad enough. He didn't know if the two in the Chrysler were part of that crew, or if they were additional, in which case there'd be six of them in there. Which would be even worse.

The house next door looked dark and empty by comparison, with no sign of life apart from a Christmas tree that blinked on and off mind-numbingly in its front window. A five-foot-tall hedge ran between the houses, alongside the target's driveway. Matt thought of waiting till it got dark, to give him more cover, but he didn't feel like loitering around that long and wasn't sure how long they'd be staying in there.

He decided to chance it.

He scuttled alongside the hedge and made his way to the back of the house. He skulked behind the Chrysler and peeked out. He couldn't make out any movement at the back of the house. It was just dark and still. He looked through the 300C's window. Couldn't see anything inside, but the glove compartment and the trunk were the areas of real interest. The car's doors were locked, which was expected—and unhelpful. It was a new car, high-specced, with robust locks and both perimetric and volumetric alarms as standard. Which meant that before he could get inside the cabin he'd need to get under the hood without disturbing the car too much. Not the easiest car to break into, certainly not with the basic tools he had at hand.

He crept over to the van. It was slightly older and had a more basic locking mechanism that would surrender more easily. He glanced inside. Again, nothing on view, but once inside, things could prove different.

He knelt by the passenger door and was about to start jimmying the lock when he heard a car slow down by the house and turn in to the driveway. He ducked down and slipped quickly around to the front of the van as the other car, a black S-Class Mercedes, pulled up and stopped alongside the house.

Matt crouched low and peered out from under the van. He heard the Merc's door open and watched as a man climbed out of it and walked up to the back door. Matt leaned over and risked a side glance off the van's left fender. The man was close to six feet tall and had a sharp, accurate step. He walked with purpose. He had a shaved head and wore a dark suit that he was subtly packed into, but not with fat. Matt recognized the build from his time in prison. The slightly bowlegged step, the arms cocked out just a touch, limbs whose natural rest positions were impeded by the bulk of muscle. Not huge. Not in-your-face. But there, lurking under the otherwise-slender build, waiting to inflict damage.

As he turned, Matt saw the missing ear and the spiderwebbed burn scar spreading out from it. The unsettling sight took him by surprise. Matt wondered if the man was ex-military. Maybe they all were. And judging by the step, the suit, and the car, this guy didn't seem to be just another one of the drones. He was their boss. As if to confirm it, the rear door of the house creaked open as the man in the suit approached it. One of the goons stepped out and took an instinctive glance around as the hard case in the suit walked right past him without acknowledging him and disappeared into the house. A moment later, the goon followed him in and shut the door behind him.

Matt crouched low, his mind working double-time at interpreting this new variable and adjusting his options accordingly. One move sprang to the forefront of his mind immediately. He embraced it, sneaked over to the 300C, and slid under it.

Chapter 35

Mountains of Wadi Natrun, Egypt

"It's not safe," Gracie told Father Jerome. "We have to get you out of here."

She quickly related to the three holy men what Ogilvy had told her. "Trust me on this," she concluded. "I know how it works. The news vans are already on their way and the satellite hookups are already booked. It'll be a zoo out there before sunrise. At least at the monastery, you'll have four walls around you to keep the world at bay until we figure things out."

What she didn't want to mention was another problem—not the bullying of the press, but an altogether more dangerous one. They were in an overwhelmingly Muslim country, in an overwhelmingly Muslim region. Sure, 10 percent or so of the country was Christian—Coptic, specifically—but that still left more than seventy million other Egyptians out there, and countless others in neighboring Muslim countries, who might take issue with what was unfolding. This was, after all, a region where the moon landings were still believed to be a hoax to promote American superiority, where everything had a "Christian plot" angle to it, where the Crusades still cast a long and angry shadow.

Father Jerome's face sagged with dismay at the news,

but he didn't object. He'd witnessed the savagery that men in the region had a long habit of inflicting on one another for no reason other than what tribe they belonged to or what religion they were born into. The abbot and the young monk didn't argue with Gracie's read of the situation either. What she was suggesting seemed to be the sensible move.

"We should take what we can with us," she told them, casting her eyes around the cave's spartan interior before pointing at the journals. "Everything you wrote, Father. And anything else that's of value to you. I don't know what condition the cave will be in next time you see it." She looked up at the markings on the ceiling with a sense of foreboding, wondering how long it would be before they'd be defaced, and asked for permission to film their exit, which was given. She got Dalton to shoot a quick take of the cave and of its ceiling while the others helped Father Jerome gather his belongings.

Before long, they were back under the stars and heading down the mountain.

Chapter 36

Brighton, Massachusetts

Matt was just sliding out from under the big Mercedes when he heard the back door of the house creak open.

He huddled against the car's front passenger door and froze. He couldn't risk a look, but he didn't need to. The odds were, it was the hard case in the suit, but he knew he was in trouble regardless of who was coming out of the house. The Merc was blocking the Chrysler and the van. Before either of them could be driven out, the Merc would have to be moved first. And the Merc itself was exposed. It had yards of open air in front and behind it, the side and rear of the house to its left and the five-foot hedge that separated the two houses to its right, behind Matt. All of which meant that if anyone was driving anywhere, the Merc was about to move, and Matt was about to find himself out of cover.

He was stuck. He'd known it was a possibility going in, but he'd still gone ahead with it, thinking it worth the risk. Right now, as he listened to the approaching footsteps, he sorely regretted not going with his original firebombing plan. Then again, everything looked better with hindsight, especially when your back was up against a wall—or, in this case, a dense, impenetrable five-foot hedge.

There was more than one set of footsteps, and he figured there were at least two of them approaching. If they were going into the Merc, he'd have someone in his face in a matter of seconds. He crouched down, cheek to the ground, trying to get a handle on how many of them there were and which way they were heading. The backyard sloped upward. He couldn't see anything for a tense moment; then one pair of shoes appeared—black brogues, the hard case's shoes, he thought—closely followed by another. Two of them. Headed for the Merc. The hard case must have hit his alarm key fob, as the car beeped and the locks popped open with a loud snap.

Matt didn't have a choice.

He coiled up, waiting, his ears straining to pick up the approaching footsteps. He heard a door click open, the driver's door—and then a figure appeared on his side of the car, rounding the front right fender, a guy with high cheekbones and a brush cut that Matt thought he recognized from the car staking out Jabba's place. Matt just sprung up before the guy could react, catching him by surprise and landing a crushing fist on his chin. Brush Cut's face juddered sideways, twisting unnaturally around his neck, a loud, wet wheeze rushing out of his chest and mouth. He was tough and didn't go down. Instead, he tried to turn in and fight back, but Matt was now close enough to inflict more serious damage and hooked him with a ferocious uppercut that lifted Brush Cut momentarily off his feet before sending him staggering backward.

Matt heard movement on the other side of the car and, from the corner of his eye, saw the hard case in the suit stepping back and reaching under his coat. Brush Cut was groggy and having a hard time staying on his feet. Matt grabbed him from behind, curling his left hand around the guy's neck while diving his right hand under the guy's jacket, praying his fingers would find a gun somewhere. On the other side of the Merc, the hard case had his own gun out. He chambered a round and raised the gun at Matt, with Brush Cut between them.

Matt hit pay dirt. Brush Cut had a handgun tucked under his jacket, in a belt holster on his right hip. Matt's fingers found the gun's ribbed grip and yanked it out. He raised it, his right arm extended, level with his hostage's ear, and aimed it straight at the hard case.

"Get back," Matt shouted, swinging the gun to his hostage's head and back at the hard case.

He sidestepped to his left, putting the car between him and the hard case, who raised his left hand in a calming gesture while keeping his gun aimed at Matt's face.

"Easy, Matt," he said. "Just take it easy."

"Who the fuck are you people?" Matt yelled, still edging sideways, his eyes darting left and right nervously, keeping tabs on the front and rear of the house.

"I'm impressed that you made it here, Matt," the hard case said, clearly trying to work out how Matt had found them. "In fact, I'm pretty impressed by everything you've done since this thing started."

Matt was now at the back corner of the Merc. The hard case wasn't backing away. He was actually tracking Matt, sidestepping smoothly and moving closer to the Merc that was now between them, eyeing the surroundings with radarlike focus. There was something deeply unnerving about him. The missing ear and the scar, the bald head that tapered up in the shape of a bullet—and they only served as a backdrop to the real darkness that emanated from the ceramic-black eyes that looked like they'd been to hell and back without blinking, the dark, eyeliner-like eyelids that rimmed them, and the sharp eyebrows framing the stygian mask that brooded out of the center of his face.

"And what is this thing?" Matt rasped. "What the fuck's going on? What happened to my brother?"

The hard case shook his face slightly, in a condescending, tut-tutting way. "You know what, Matt? You're too concerned with the past. You need to think more about your future."

Matt backed up another step. "What did you do to my brother?" he yelled again. "Is he still alive?"

The hard case didn't flinch. He stayed unsettlingly calm, his cold eyes seemingly assessing Matt's position and evaluating possible outcomes. "You're messing around with something you really don't want to be messing with," he finally told him. "My advice to you is to let it go. Find yourself a nice, deep hole, bury your head down, and forget any of this ever happened. Or better still—"

—and he just squeezed the trigger, once, with no discernible emotion, just made a decision and acted on it without a trace of emotion. The round hit the guy Matt was holding up squarely in the chest—

"—let me put you in it."

Matt felt Brush Cut jerk and felt a sudden burn at his own side, by his left ribs, but he didn't have time to pause and check it out. He had to stay on his feet as everything rushed into a frenzied blur.

Brush Cut's legs gave and he started to fall just as the hard case fired again, then again. One of the shots hit Brush Cut in the shoulder, the bullet exiting close to Matt's crouched head, whizzing past his ear and splattering his face with blood and bone shards. Matt struggled to keep Brush Cut up, using him as a shield while firing back at the hard case, who ducked behind the Merc. He faltered backward, his eyes scanning around, the burning sensation in his left flank getting stronger with each step. The hard case came up for another shot, got Matt's hostage in the thigh. Two more bodies rushed out of the back of the house, guns out. They saw Matt, crouched into firing positions, but they were wide-open and Matt got one of them in the shoulder a split second after he realized it was the auburn-haired girl from the van, the night they took him and Vince Bellinger. She tumbled sideways as if her feet had been knocked out from under her. The other shooter dived behind the Merc and joined the hard case. Matt kept moving, still using the bloodied-if-not-dead Brush Cut as a shield, lugging his heavy body back toward the street, step by step, inch by inch, firing away every time he spotted a flash of skin. A couple of shots whizzed by and he retaliated with three more of his own; then his gun's magazine spat out its last round and the slide locked in its open position.

He saw that the hard case and the other shooter cottoned onto it as soon as he did, and they emerged from cover with little concern. He looked around frantically and realized he was now only a couple of yards from the sidewalk. Summoning whatever energy he could muster, he dragged Brush Cut's deadweight back a few steps before letting go of him and bolting into the street.

He didn't look back. He just kept running, the spent gun in hand, hugging the parked cars before sprinting across the street and leaping onto the opposite sidewalk, putting a barrier of cars between him and the shooters' line of fire, hoping one last round wouldn't find him before he got to his Camry, wondering how badly he'd been hit already and whether or not he'd get the chance to find out.

Chapter 37

Deir Al-Suryan Monastery, Wadi Natrun, Egypt

As Gracie had predicted, they'd barely managed to beat the news crews to the monastery, and were now safely ensconced behind its walls. A growing number of cars and vans were gathering outside the gates. With the rest of the monks alarmed by the sudden activity—the monastery was home to almost two hundred of them—the abbot set out to calm them while dispatching Brother Ameen to talk to the journalists. The younger monk told those crowding the gates that Father Jerome had no comment as yet, and asked them to respect his privacy. The reporters protested loudly, but to no avail.

The siege had begun.

Gracie's satphone was back up and running. There was no point in staying under the radar any longer. On the contrary. She, Dalton, and Finch were supremely well placed to trump their peers on this story, which was now monopolizing the screens at all the major news channels, commanding continuous coverage and constant live updates. Their exclusive was alive and well, and less than half an hour after getting back, they were sending their first "live" footage from the roof of the keep that abutted the monastery's entrance gate.

Standing on top of the large, sand-colored cube, Gracie weighed her words carefully as she faced the lens of Dalton's camera.

"He hasn't yet made a statement, Jack. As you can imagine, he's overwhelmed by what's happened in the last couple of days. All I can confirm to you at the moment is that Father Jerome is indeed here with us at the monastery."

"But you've talked to him, haven't you?" Roxberry asked, through her earpiece.

"Yes, I have," she affirmed.

"And what did he tell you?"

Roxberry's frustration was coming through loud and clear, and Gracie's cagey replies weren't helping. She'd avoided mentioning to him that they'd shown Father Jerome the footage of the sightings, and hadn't shared what he'd told them in the cave. She and Finch had sifted with great care through what she would or wouldn't say, deciding that it wasn't their place—not yet, anyway—to announce things that the priest had said in confidence and that could be taken wildly out of context and distorted at will, which was inevitable. Hard as it was to keep a huge scoop like that to themselves, they'd agreed that it was more appropriate to give Father Jerome the chance to tell his story himself, if and when he chose to do it. They'd approach him for a live interview as soon as he'd had a chance to rest and let it all sink in.

"He asked us to respect his need for a bit of peace right now, which we fully understand."

She could almost feel Roxberry's rising blood pressure throbbing through her earpiece.

She and Finch had also debated whether or not to use the material they'd shot inside the cave. Gracie felt they'd been granted a privileged viewing, and she had misgiv-

ings about airing the footage, feeling as if she'd be betraying the priest's trust. But, as Finch had pointed out,
they couldn't not use it either. It was too good for that;
it was part of the story, and besides, the British documentary crew had been allowed to film it for broadcast
purposes. It was already airing around the world. He
couldn't see the harm in simply confirming it, and Gracie
had agreed.

She signed off, expecting an instantaneous and irate
callback from the news desk, and stepped over to the
edge of the flat roof. The roof had nothing but a low,
three-inch lip around it, and Gracie felt a bit uneasy looking at the sharp drop-off. As she gazed beyond it at the
flat, barren landscape outside the monastery's walls, she
also had a different kind of bad feeling. The trickle of
headlights bouncing across the desert was growing ominously as more and more cars converged on the monastery. She knew the region well enough to know how
quickly things got out of hand, how suddenly religious
passions got inflamed and escalated into bloodshed. She
tore her gaze away from the eerie light show and joined
Finch and Dalton, who were huddled around the open
laptop, watching the Al Jazeera reporter's live broadcast
from outside the gates.

"Weird, isn't it?" she observed, overcome by a sudden
tiredness and setting herself down cross-legged beside
them. "Sitting here, inside the gates, watching ourselves
from the outside in."

"It's like a bizarro-world version of a hostage situation," Dalton intoned.

Gracie noticed a shift in the shadows coming out of
the roof hatch to her left, and saw Brother Ameen's head
pop out. He gave them a subdued nod and climbed up
the rickety ladder to join them.

"How's Father Jerome?" Gracie asked.

He shrugged wearily. "Confused. Scared. Praying for guidance."

Gracie nodded in empathy, frustrated that she couldn't give him any answers herself. She knew that the pressure he was under was only starting. Watching the streaming news reports on the laptop only confirmed it. The reports coming in from Cairo and Alexandria were troubling. The revelation that Father Jerome had effectively foreseen what was still unexplained was causing a huge stir across the country. The polarization of opinions was already clear, even though the story had barely broken. The clips chosen for broadcast showed the local Christians to be confused, but generally excited, by the news. For them, Father Jerome had long been a beacon of positive transformation, and on the whole, they seemed to be embracing his involvement as something inspirational and wanted to know more. The Muslims who were interviewed, on the other hand, were either dismissive or angry. And, Gracie thought cynically, probably chosen for how inflammatory—hence attention-grabbing—their reactions were. Clerics were denouncing Father Jerome and calling on their followers not to be swayed by what they were already describing as trickery.

She glanced over at the young monk. His face was tight with tension.

"What is it?" she asked him.

He kept his eyes on the screen for a moment, then turned to her.

"I don't understand what this thing is that you all saw. I don't understand Father Jerome's visions either, or how they're both related. But there are some things I do know. Egypt's not a rich country. Half the people around here have little or no education and live on less than two dollars a day. Even doctors in public hospitals don't get paid more than that. But we're also a very religious country," he continued, his eyes drifting off to the chaotic light show below. "People take comfort in their religion because they don't see hope in anything else around them. They don't have faith in their politicians. They're tired of traffic and pollution and rising prices and falling wages and corruption. They have no one else to trust but God. It's the same everywhere else in this part of the world. Religious identity matters more to people out here than their common citizenship. And here, in this country—we're on a knife edge as far as sectarian differences are concerned. It's taboo to talk about it, but it's a real problem. There have been a lot of incidents. Our brothers at the Abu Fana Monastery were attacked twice in the last year. The second time, they were beaten and whipped and made to spit on the cross." He paused, then turned, his eyes bouncing between the three of them before settling on Gracie. "There's a lot of tension and a lot of misunderstanding between the people of this country. And there are millions of them within an hour's drive of here."

Gracie understood. It wasn't a good mix.

"Bringing Father Jerome down from the cave was a good move," he added. "But it might not be enough."

She'd been thinking the same thing. An alarming vision coalesced inside her: that of two seriously antagonistic groups outside the gates, Coptic Christians on a pilgrimage of sorts to hear what Father Jerome had to say, and Muslims out to repel whatever outrage the *kuffar*—the blasphemers—were perpetrating.

Again, not a good mix. Unless you were cooking up some nitro.

"Where's the army?" she asked. "Don't they know what's going on here? Shouldn't they be sending people here to protect the monastery? And the cave—it's gonna get trashed if things get out of control."

"Not the army," the monk said somberly. "The internal security forces. They're twice as big as the army, which tells you where the government perceives the real threat. But they don't usually send them out until after a problem catches fire. And when they do show up, things generally get worse. They don't have a problem with using force to bring things back to normal. A lot of force."

A swell of unease rolled through her. She turned to Finch. "Can you get hold of someone at the embassy? Maybe they can rustle something up."

"I can try, but—I think Brother Ameen is right. Might be better to get out of here before it gets out of hand. And that goes for Father Jerome too."

Dalton indicated the crowd below with a nudge of his head. "It's not going to be easy."

Gracie's expression darkened further. "We have a car and a driver. And it's still calm out there. We should leave at first light. While it's doable." She faced Finch again. "We can take Father Jerome to the embassy. We need to let them know we're coming. We'll figure the rest out from there."

"What if he doesn't want to leave?" Finch asked.

Gracie turned to Brother Ameen. He gave her an uncertain shrug. "I'll talk to him, but I don't know what he'll say."

"I'll go with you. We've got to convince him," she insisted as she got off the floor. Brother Ameen nodded and crossed over to the open hatch. Gracie turned to Finch. "First light, okay?" She gave him a determined look before gripping the sides of the hatch and disappearing into the heart of the keep.

Chapter 38

Houston, Texas

The Reverend Nelson Darby's cell phone rang just as the tall, elegant man was stepping out of his chauffeur-driven Lincoln Town Car. He was in great spirits, having just witnessed a dress rehearsal of the hundred-person choir's Christmas show. The caller ID on his screen prompted him to wave his assistant on, and he stayed back to take the call on the wide stairs that led to the handsome manor that housed the administrative core of his sprawling "Christian values" empire, an empire whose flagship was the resplendent 17,000-seat glass-and-steel megachurch Darby had built, one of a growing number of full-service Christian cocoons the likes of which hadn't been seen since the thirteenth-century cathedral towns of Europe.

"Reverend," the caller said. "How are things?"

"Roy," Darby answered heartily, as always pleased to hear Roy Buscema's measured voice. A fit man in his early forties, Darby had an angular face, deep-set eyes, and thin lips. With his backswept, perfectly coiffed jet-black mane and Brioni suits, he looked more like a pre–credit crunch investment banker on the make than a preacher. Which wasn't inappropriate, given that both involved managing multimillion-dollar enterprises in a highly competitive marketplace. "Good to hear from you. How are things with you?"

Buscema, a gregarious journalist for the *Washington Post*, had met the pastor a little over a year earlier, when he'd been commissioned to write a feature profiling him for the newspaper's Sunday magazine. The finely observed and highly complimentary article that he'd written had laid the groundwork for the friendship that followed, a friendship that grew into an unofficial consigliere-godfather relationship with all the hours they spent discussing and strategizing the pastor's endorsements in the marathon presidential primary of the last year. Buscema's take on the events had been impressively astute and always correct, and he'd let the pastor in on more than one scoop that had borne itself out. The pastor was converted. He saw in Buscema a savvy analyst who had the pulse of the people and knew where to go to get his prognoses corroborated, and as such—and given that Darby was one of the Christian Right's political bigwigs—he was an invaluable man to have at hand.

Especially now, with all this going on.

"Crazier than ever," Buscema replied. "But hey, I can't complain really. It's what we're here for. Say, you been watching that thing over the ice caps?"

"Who isn't?"

"What do you think?"

"To be honest with you, I'm a bit befuddled by the whole thing, Roy," the pastor confided with his usual disarming candor. "What in God's name is going on out there?"

Buscema's tone took on a slightly more serious edge. "I think we ought to talk about it. I'm gonna be in town tomorrow," he told the pastor. "If you have some time, why don't we get together?"

"Sounds good," Darby replied. "Come out to the house. I'm curious to hear your take on it."

I bet you are, Buscema thought as they agreed on a time. He said good-bye and hung up. He then scrolled down his contacts list and made a second, almost identical, call.

A third, similar call followed soon after that.

As did six other carefully coordinated calls, made by two other men of a similar profile to his, to other influential evangelical leaders across the country.

Chapter 39

Woburn, Massachusetts

The bullet hadn't done as much damage as Matt had first feared. It had clipped him just below his bottom left rib, punching a small hole through him less than an inch in from his side. Not exactly a graze, but not a major-organ buster either. Still, he had a couple of half-inch holes gouged out of him. Holes that needed to be sealed. Which meant stitches. And given that going to a hospital or to a doctor was out of the question, whatever sewing talents Jabba had would need to be summoned.

Jabba was holding up surprisingly well. He'd managed not to throw up when Matt first staggered back into their room, his clothes soaked with blood. He'd made it to the closest drugstore and picked up the items on a shopping list Matt had hastily dictated to him: iodine to clean the wound; any anesthetic cream he could find, to numb the skin; sewing needles, along with a lighter to sterilize them; some nylon thread; painkillers; bandages.

Most impressively, he'd so far managed to complete three sutures on the entry wound without puking, which he'd come close to doing while attempting the first stitch. Three more would do the trick on that front. Then he had the exit hole to take care of.

They were huddled in the far-from-antiseptic bathroom of the motel room. Matt was in his shorts, on the floor with his back against the tiled wall by the bathtub, grinding down his teeth as Jabba pushed the needle through the caldera of skin that rimmed his raw, open wound. The sensation was far worse than the immediate aftereffect of getting shot, when the wound was still warm and the pain receptors hadn't started their furious onslaught up his spine. He felt weak and nauseous and was fighting hard not to pass out. He swam through it by telling himself, over and over, that it would pass. Which it would. He just had to get through this part. He'd had a couple of bad wounds before, and although he'd never been shot, he tried to convince himself that this wasn't any worse than a nasty cut from a blade. Which was something he'd had. Only then, he'd been sewn shut by a real doctor who'd used a proper anesthetic, not an over-the-counter cream more suited to hemorrhoids and leg waxing.

He blinked away tears of pain as the needle came out the other side.

"This look right to you?" Jabba's fingers trembled as he pulled the thread through.

Matt didn't look down. His sweaty face winced under the strain. "You're the movie buff. You must have seen them do it a few times, right?"

"Yeah, but I usually turn away when they're doing it." Jabba grimaced as he pulled the two sides of the wound closer to each other and tied a knot in the thread, adding, pointedly, "Which, by the way, they usually do to themselves."

"Yeah, but then they end up with these Frankenstein-like scars, whereas with Dr. Jabba on the case . . ."

". . . the Frankenstein look's guaranteed," Jabba quipped as he cut the end of the thread off. It wasn't a particularly elegant piece of stitching, but at least the wound wasn't bleeding anymore. "See?"

Matt shrugged. "Don't sweat it. I hear the ladies just love the hard-ass scars," he cajoled him. "When you're done with me, maybe you could take a look at mending that hole in my jacket? It's kind of an old favorite, you know?"

Seven stitches and half an hour later, they were done.

As he cleaned up the bloody mess around them, Jabba filled Matt in on what he'd discovered while he was out, which wasn't much. He'd given the deadbeat receptionist ten bucks to let him use his computer. He'd logged into his Skype account and made a few calls while burrowing through the Internet, trying to find out more about the team that had died in the helicopter crash.

He'd managed to come up with two other names to add to Danny's and to Reece's—a chemical engineer by the name of Oliver Serres, and a biomolecular engineer named Sunil Kumar.

"Both were at the top of their game and highly regarded," he told Matt. "But it's weird, dude. I mean, Kumar's a biologist. So far, we've got him, a chemist, Reece—an electrical engineer and computer scientist—and Danny, a programmer. The last three, I get. But Kumar . . . what's a biomolecular engineer have to do with this?"

The nuance was beyond Matt at the best of times. In his current state, it just streaked past him. "What do you think?"

"I don't know, man," Jabba said with visible discomfort. "These biomolecular guys, they're into rearranging DNA, playing around with the building blocks of life. Pulling apart and rearranging atoms and molecules like they were Lego bricks. And this sign in the sky, the way it looks organic, alive even . . . the gray area between biology and chemistry, between life and nonlife, you know? It's giving me a creepy feeling. Like maybe what they're doing has more to do with some kind of designed life-form than a projected image."

Matt frowned, trying to wrap his head around what Jabba was saying. "You've spent too much time watching *The X-Files*."

Jabba shrugged, like it wasn't a bad thing. "These biotech guys, they're always getting flak for messing around in God's closet. God's closet, man. Who knows what they found in there."

He let it drift and ran the cold tap. He drank from it, then splattered water across his face before filling up a glass and handing it to Matt. He didn't have much more to tell him. He hadn't been able to find any mention of who was backing Reece's project, let alone what it involved.

Darkness was closing in fast outside their room, which suited Matt just fine. He wasn't going anywhere tonight. He needed to rest. Jabba went back out and picked up some blood-free clothes for Matt and brought back some food and some Coke cans. They wolfed it all down greedily while watching the news. The footage from the cave in Egypt was hogging the airwaves, and the warm pizzas, though welcome, weren't doing much to quell the cold, dismal feeling inside them.

"This is getting bigger," Jabba noted glumly. "More elaborate."

Matt nodded. "They know what they're doing."

"That's not what I mean."

"What then?"

"These people. They've got serious resources at their disposal. Think about what they're doing. First, they rustle up some major brain power, put them to work somewhere for, what, a couple of years? Then they kill them all off." He noticed a hint of resistance on Matt's face and quickly amended his words. "Or, whatever, maybe lock them up somewhere and fake their deaths—even more complicated to pull off. But no one seems to know anything about what this scientific dream team was working on, and there's no record of who they were all working for. The one thing that's sure is that there's some serious moolah involved. Danny, Reece, and the others, they wouldn't have gotten involved if they didn't know they had all the backup they needed. And the kind of research they do, it ain't cheap. Plus the rest of it, all this," he said as he waved at the screen. "Seriously deep pockets, dude."

"Okay, so where'd the money come from?"

Jabba thought about it for a second. "Two possibilities. Reece could've raised the money privately," he speculated, "though not from a VC or a public company. There'd be a trace of it, especially after the deaths. No, it would have to be private money. Not easy, given the scale of it. And practically untraceable, given that the entire creative team was supposedly wiped out."

"What's the other possibility?"

"Reece was doing this for a government agency. A highly classified project. Which sounds about right to me."

Matt's face darkened with uncertainty. He'd been wondering about the same thing. "Any particular candidates?"

Jabba shrugged. "DARPA. In-Q-Tel."

Matt looked a question at him.

"DARPA. The Defense Advanced Research Projects Agency. It's part of the DoD. They fund a ton of research. Everything from microbots to virtual battlefields. Any technology that can help us win these wars and defeat those who hate our freedom," he added mockingly.

"And the other one?"

"In-Q-Tel. It's the CIA's venture capital arm. They're early-stage investors, which is actually very savvy of them when you think about it. Get in on the ground floor. Find out about any useful technology while it's still being dreamed up. They've got their fingers in a lot of tech companies—and that includes a few of the big household-name Internet sites you and I use on a daily basis." He gave him a pointed, big-brother-is-watching-you look.

Matt absorbed what Jabba was trying to say. "A government op."

"It's pretty obvious, isn't it? I mean, if what we're saying is true, if they've really faked this thing, they're on their way to convincing everyone out there that God's talking to us. Maybe even through the good Father Jerome. Who else would try to pull off something like this?"

Matt could see the sense in what Jabba was saying, only deep down, something was nagging at him. He winced with doubt. "You're probably right, but . . . I don't know. Something about the guys in the van. Their place down in Brighton."

"What?"

"They're a small unit. Working with good resources, but not overwhelming ones. Bunkered down in a small house in a quiet neighborhood. I don't know. If it is a black op, it's not just off the books. It's way off the books."

"Even worse, then," Jabba added emphatically. "Officially, they don't exist. Whoever sent them's got full deniability. They can do anything they want to us and no one will ever know they were there." He fixed Matt with a sobering stare. "We need to quit asking questions and disappear, dude. Seriously. I mean, I know he's your brother and all, but . . . we're outgunned."

Matt processed his warning. He was too tired to think straight, his nerves numb with fatigue and apprehension.

But one thought kept coming back to him, a steadying keel that was keeping his head above water in the storm of confusion that swirled around him. He looked at Jabba, and just said, "What if Danny's still alive?"

Jabba took in a long, sobering breath. "You really think he might be?"

Matt thought back to the hard case's reaction when he'd asked him that question. The man had an impenetrable poker face, and he hadn't been able to read him. "I don't know, but . . . what if he is? You want me to just forget about him and run?"

Jabba held his gaze for a moment, a conflicted glimmer in his eyes. It was as if his mind was desperately looking for a way to flush Matt's words back out of his system and was failing miserably to do so. Then he nodded. "Okay."

Matt acknowledged his acceptance with a small nod of his own. After a quiet moment, he asked Jabba if he could hustle a few more minutes of online time from the receptionist and check the tracker's Web site.

Jabba left him alone, then came back a few minutes later armed with some printed screenshots. He handed them to Matt. The tracker had moved within what Matt estimated had been mere minutes of his escape from the house in Brighton. Which was expected. Neighbors would have reported the shooting. The place would have been swarming with cops pretty quickly.

They'd obviously vacated their safe house in a rush. Hastily. Panicked. Matt's incursion had screwed them up. Which lit a tiny fire of satisfaction deep in his gut.

He checked the tracker's current position. It was stable, at a location in the Seaport district of the city. Which meant the big Mercedes—the hard case's car, the one he'd moved the tracker onto—was there.

Matt glanced over at the handgun on the night table,

then let his head loll back against the pillows. His eyelids rolled down and blocked out the world, and the last image that floated into his mind before everything went quiet was the hard case's face.

The man had the answers Matt needed. And hard case or not, one way or another, Matt knew he'd have to wrest them out of him.

Chapter 40

Deir Al-Suryan Monastery, Wadi Natrun, Egypt

By dawn, the desert plain outside the monastery was teeming with life. Dozens of cars were scattered far and wide, strewn across the parched wasteland beyond the monastery's walls and all along the narrow road that led up to its entrance gate. People—men, mostly—milled around by their cars or stood in small groups, tense, uncertain, waiting.

It was time to go.

Gracie and Finch sat on either side of Father Jerome in the middle row of the people carrier, with Dalton riding shotgun—his camera locked and loaded—next to Yusuf and Brother Ameen in the back.

The noise coming from outside the walls was disconcertingly subdued for such a large crowd. The general silence only accentuated the tension and the anticipation, like the wait between lightning and thunder. There were some pockets of activity, here and there. Hints of music wafted in from small groupings of worshippers, their heads down in prayer as they chanted traditional Coptic hymns. But there were also many pockets of disturbance, farther back, away from the monastery's walls. Several firebrand clerics were angrily spouting invective, denouncing the priest and the sign to clusters of willing followers. The internal security forces were nowhere to be seen, and while the two opposing groups hadn't collided, it was clear that the plain could erupt into violence at any moment.

Gracie fretted. *It can't last. They're going to be at each other's throats any minute now.* Which was why Father Jerome had agreed—reluctantly—to leave. He was the lightning rod. And if he left, perhaps the storm could be avoided.

She watched as the abbot pushed the people carrier's door shut. He peered in through the dark, tinted glass and gave them a small farewell wave, his face etched with concern. Father Jerome returned the wave with a forlorn look. He seemed even more lost now than he had in the cave.

The abbot waved to two monks manning the gate. They nodded and pulled its huge doors open. As the ancient cedar leaves pivoted inward slowly, creaking on their rusty hinges, a rising cacophony gushed in with them as the crowd outside took note and sprang to life.

Gracie's pulse quickened as she heard the ambient noise rise around her. She shifted uncomfortably in her seat, staring out of her window, the combination of the car's powerful air-conditioning and the musty smell of incense from Father Jerome's cassock making her feel even more heady.

"Time to rhumba," Dalton said, shifting his camera from the side window and aiming it forward.

Gracie swallowed hard.

The old people carrier lurched forward and charged out of the gate. It advanced quickly along the monastery's wall, and almost immediately, people started swarming across the scrub and converging on it. As the van cleared the perimeter wall and turned down the road that led away from the monastery, the crowd around it swelled. Countless hands reached out, trying to stop their escape. Yusuf had to slow down as the wedge of clear space ahead of him disappeared. With his hand pressed against the horn, he managed to keep going another thirty yards or so at a sputtering crawl before coming to a complete stop, blocked by a wall of people.

Gracie leaned over and looked out past Yusuf and Dalton, who was panning his camera around to capture the pandemonium all around the van. Desperate faces were pressed against the Previa's tinted windows, calling out Father Jerome's name, trying to see if he was inside, pleading for him to talk to them. They rattled the door handles, fighting the locks, their pained, intense features distorted from being squeezed against the van, their sweaty, dusty hands streaking the windows. Father Jerome shrank into his seat as he darted nervous glances left and right at the faces that looked all the more threatening behind the dark glass.

"We've got to go back," Finch urged Yusuf. "We've got to get back to the monastery."

"We can't," Gracie said as she craned her neck back and saw the mass of bodies pressing against the car from all sides, the loud thumps against the roof and windows echoing like war drums. "We're boxed in."

◄◦►

AT THE EDGE OF THE CROWD, on a small rise by the crumbling remnants of an old wall, three men in a canvas-topped pickup truck surveyed the unfolding chaos with great interest through military-issue, sand-colored, high-powered binoculars.

As the people carrier disappeared behind the swarm of bodies, Fox Two watched and decided it was time to act.

He signaled his men with a curt hand.

One of his men peeled up a corner of the canvas top, enough to expose the tripod-mounted, drumlike device that lurked underneath. Another man, positioned behind it, looked through its targeting scope and aimed it at the scrum of men crowding the back of the Previa.

He double-checked the settings on the device.

Then he hit the trigger.

◄o►

THE CRUSH OF PEOPLE pressed against the people carrier recoiled for the briefest of moments, as if struck by an unseen force, their faces contorted in discomfort and pain, their hands rising to block their ears.

The effect only lasted a second, but it was long enough for Finch to catch it—as did Brother Ameen. As the mob jerked back, a crater of clear space opened up behind the Previa.

Brother Ameen caught Finch's eye—both their faces were locked in confusion—then he pointed back frantically and yelled, "Go back," to Yusuf.

The driver and Gracie swung their heads back and spotted the opening.

"Back. Go back now," Brother Ameen shouted again.

Yusuf hesitated.

"Let's go. Come on, back up," Gracie yelled at him, also pointing back fiercely.

The driver nodded reluctantly, slammed the car into reverse, and—with his hand still on the horn—eased the car backward. The men flinched back in surprise, widening the opening behind the Previa.

"Keep going," Gracie insisted, scanning in all directions. "Get us back to the gates."

The Previa gathered momentum, Yusuf taking advantage of the faltering crowd and keeping his foot down. They swerved around the bend at the far corner of the monastery, and the going got easier as they rushed up its long perimeter wall, still in reverse gear and chased by the frenzied horde. Fighting broke out as people lashed out and grabbed at one another, with Father Jerome's followers trying to block the followers of the Islamic firebrands from getting to the van. The Previa kept moving, slipping past the tangle of fists and blood, finally making it to the monastery's gates, which swung open just as it reached them. Yusuf skillfully managed to thread the Previa through the opening before the gates slammed shut and blocked off the crazed posse's advance.

They all tumbled out of the car in a daze, hearts thumping, veins drowning with adrenaline. Dalton was still filming, capturing every moment of their escape.

"Let's go up there," Gracie yelled to Dalton and Finch, pointing up at the keep that stood next to the gate, jutting in from the perimeter wall.

Finch nodded and said, "Let's get the Began up," lifting the compact satellite dish out of the Previa. "The guys on the outside are getting this live."

Gracie turned to Father Jerome. "Please go inside, Father. You need to be somewhere safe, away from the gate," she cautioned. She glanced at the abbot, whose grave face nodded with agreement.

Father Jerome didn't seem convinced.

He didn't acknowledge her words. He seemed distant, his mind preoccupied elsewhere. He was staring beyond her, beyond the gate even, at the people crowding it and shouting out his name, and seemed curiously calm.

"I need to talk to them," he finally said, his voice settled and certain.

His eyes traveled back to Gracie and to the abbot. Then, without awaiting further words, he stepped away from the car and headed toward the keep.

"Wait, Father," Gracie called out as she rushed in after him, closely followed by the abbot and Brother Ameen.

"I must talk to them," Father Jerome insisted, without turning or stopping as he reached the narrow staircase and began marching up its stone steps.

They followed him across the second-floor drawbridge, into the keep and all the way up until they reached the top floor. The rickety wooden ladder still stood there, in a corner of the chapel, poking out through the small hatch. Moments later, they were all standing on the roof.

Gracie, Finch, and Dalton inched forward for a peek at the crowd below.

The scene below was unnerving. Hundreds of people were massed against the gates of the monastery, chanting, shouting, waving their hands and pumping their fists into the air, starved for a response, looking nervously over their shoulders as, behind them, the violence was growing, the pockets of fighting spreading like wildfire, threatening to engulf the entire plain.

Dalton got the live feed hooked up while Finch got through to Atlanta on the satphone. Gracie grabbed her earpiece and mike, mentally running through what she would soon be telling a world audience while watching the old priest as he stood by the hatch, staring ahead at the edge of the roof twenty feet in front of him, the only barrier between him and the clamoring mob below. From where he was standing, he could hear them, but he couldn't see them yet. The abbot and the young monk were talking to him, pleading with him not to expose himself in that way, telling him someone below could easily have a weapon and might take a shot at him. Father Jerome was having none of it. He was calmly shaking his head, a strange mix of resolve and fear radiating from him. His arms were hanging down listlessly, his fingers

straight, his sandaled feet idle. He turned his head sideways and met Gracie's gaze, and, with the smallest, most
stoic of nods, he started moving forward.

Gracie turned in alarm to Finch and Dalton. They
were huddled by the small, cross-topped dome that occupied a corner of the otherwise flat roof. Dalton had his
camera up and was tracking the priest in a low crouch.
Finch gave Gracie the sign that they were live. Gracie
held up the mike but felt momentarily dumbstruck as she
edged forward, tracking the old man, who soon reached
the edge of the roof.

He stood there and looked down, and the crowd
erupted in a mix of whoops and cheers and angry shouts.
The throng pressed forward, calling his name out and
waving, the euphoria of the faithful at the front of the
mob only riling even more those opposed to Father Jerome's appearance, and the fighting farther back gained
in intensity. Shouts of *"Kafir,"* Blasphemer, and *"La ilah
illa Allah,"* There is no God but Allah, resounded angrily
across the plain as incensed protestors started throwing
rocks up at the keep.

Father Jerome stared down at the raging maelstrom
below, beads of sweat trickling down his face. Slowly, he
raised his arms, stretching them high and wide in a welcoming gesture. Again, as his mere appearance had done
a short moment earlier, the gesture only seemed to polarize the crowd below even more and fuel the fighting.

"Please," he yelled out in an Arabic that was heavily
accented. "Please, stop. Please stop and listen to me."
His pleas could hardly be heard over the chaos raging
below, and had no effect on the commotion. With rocks
still pelting the wall of the keep and flying wildly past
him, he remained steadfast and shut his eyes, his face
locked in deep concentration, his arms held high—

—and suddenly, the crowd gasped in shock. Gracie

saw people pointing upward—not at the priest, but higher up, at the sky above him, and she spun her head up and saw a ball of light, perhaps twenty feet or so in diameter, swirling over the priest. It hovered there for a moment, then started to rise directly above him, and as it did, it suddenly flared up both in size and in brightness and morphed into the sign, the same one she'd seen over the ice shelf. It now blazed overhead, a massive, spherical kaleidoscope of shifting light patterns, its lower edge hovering no more than twenty feet or so directly above Father Jerome.

The throng below just froze, rooted in place, entranced, staring up in openmouthed awe. The stones stopped flying. The brawls ended. The shouting died out. The sign was just there, shimmering brilliantly, rotating very slowly, almost within reach, closer now than it had been over the research ship, its radiant lines and circles mesmerizing.

Dalton was lying on his back at the very edge of the roof, filming the sign and panning back down to get the crowd's reaction. Gracie was still crouching near him, fifteen feet or so away from Father Jerome, who had his head tilted back and was staring up at the blazing apparition above him, dumbfounded. The camera swung back, stopping momentarily to settle on Gracie. She stared into the dark abyss of the lens, tongue-tied. She wanted to say something; she could feel the whole world watching, hanging on the edge of their seats, willing her to tell them what it felt like to be there, but she couldn't do it. The moment was simply beyond words. She looked up at the blazing sphere of light; then Father Jerome brought his head back down, and as he did, she caught his eye. She could tell that he was shivering, and saw a tear trickle down his cheek. He looked scared and confused, his stricken expression telegraphing an am-I-really-doing-this anguish to her and quietly pleading for some kind of confirmation, as if he didn't believe what was happening. She mustered up a confirming nod and a supportive smile—then his expression shifted, as if something had suddenly startled him from within. He closed his eyes, as if locked in concentration; then, a few seconds later, he turned to face the crowd. He looked down on them for a moment; then he spread his arms expansively and tilted his head upward to face the sign. He shut his eyes again and breathed in deeply, basking in the sign's radiance, drinking in its energy. The masses below were still paralyzed, staring up in shocked silence, their arms stretched upward toward him, reaching out, as if trying to touch the hollow globe of light.

Father Jerome maintained his outstretched stance for the better part of a minute; then he opened his eyes to face the crowd.

"Pray with me," he bellowed out to them, his voice thick with emotion, his arms raised to the heavens. "Let us all pray together."

And they did.

In a stadium wave–like reaction that spread slowly and silently from the front to the back of the crowd, every single person outside the monastery—Christian and Muslim, believer and protestor alike—fell to their knees and bent forward, all of them dropping their foreheads to the ground and prostrating themselves in fearful adulation.

Chapter 41

Washington, D.C.

"What the hell are you doing? I thought we had an agreement."

Rydell was seething. He'd been up through the night, monitoring the news. The images from Egypt had exploded across his TV screen a little after midnight, and right now, pacing around the cabin of his private jet by a quiet hangar at Reagan National Airport, his senses still throbbed with the burns of their visual shrapnel.

"We never agreed on it, Larry," Drucker replied smoothly from his lush, padded seat. "You just wouldn't have it any other way."

"So you just went out and did it anyway?"

"We both have a lot invested in this. I wasn't about to jeopardize it all because of your stubbornness."

"Stubbornness?" Rydell flared up. "You don't know what you're doing, Keenan. Have you even thought about where this goes from here?"

"It's working, isn't it?"

"It's too early to tell."

Drucker tilted his head slightly. "Don't be disingenuous. It demeans you."

"I don't know if it's working, but—"

"It's working, Larry," Drucker interrupted emphatically. "It's working because that's what people are used to. It's what they've been used to for thousands of years."

"We didn't need it."

"Of course we did. What did you expect? Did you think people would see the sign and just 'get' it?"

"Yes. If we gave them a chance."

"That's just naive. What people don't understand they just push away to the far corners of their minds and eventually it fades away and gets forgotten. 'Cause it's safer that way. No, people need someone to tell them what to believe in. It's worked before, many times. And it'll work again."

"And then what?" Rydell fumed. "Where do you go from here?"

Drucker smiled. "We just let him grow his following. Get the message across."

"That's untenable and you know it," Rydell flared up. "You're building up something that's going to be impossible to maintain."

"Not if you graft it onto an existing structure. One that has staying power. One that can last."

Rydell shook his head. "I can't believe you're saying this. You, of all people."

Drucker chuckled. "You should be enjoying the irony of it. You should be sitting back and laughing instead of getting all worked up about it."

"I can't even begin to . . ." Rydell's mind was overwhelmed with indignation. "You don't get it, do you? You don't see how wrong you are."

"Come on, Larry. You know how the world works. There are only two surefire ways to get people to do what you want them to do. You either put on an iron glove and make them do it. Or you tell them God wants them to do it. If God wills it," he scoffed, "it shall be done. That's when they listen. And given that we don't live under an Uncle Joe or a Chairman Mao—"

"That was the whole point," Rydell protested. "God was supposed to be willing it. God. Not His self-appointed, holier-than-thou representatives."

"That wouldn't work, Larry. It's too vague. Too open to interpretation. You're asking people to decipher the message on their own, and that would be giving them far too much credit. That's never worked. They're not used to figuring things out for themselves. They like to follow, to be led. They need a guide. A messenger. A prophet. Always have. Always will."

"So you create, what, a Second Coming?"

"Not exactly, but close. And why not? A major chunk of the planet's expecting something like this. All this talk of End of Times and Armageddon. It's a golden opportunity."

"What about the other religions? 'Cause you do know there are others on the planet, right? How do you think they're going to react to your manufactured Messiah?"

"He won't be exclusive. It's been factored in. His message will embrace all."

"Embrace all and encourage them to follow Jesus?" Rydell said acidly.

"Well," Drucker mused with a mischievous twist to his mouth, "that's not the main message he'll be bringing, but I suspect it may well be a secondary effect of his preaching."

"Great," Rydell retorted fiercely. "And in doing that, you'll be propping up this mass delusion we haven't been able to shake for thousands of years. Can you imagine the field day these preachers are gonna have with this? Can you imagine how much power you'd be handing to all those blow-dried, self-serving egomaniacs out there? You'll turn every born-again politician and every televangelist into a saint who can do no wrong. And before you know it, they'll reclassify the pill as a form of abortion and ban it, the *Left Behind* books will become required reading in schools in between mass burnings of Harry Potter, kids will be saying Hail Marys for detention, and we'll have a creationist museum in every town. If that's the trade-off, I think I'd rather stick with global warming."

"It doesn't have to be that way. See, you're forgetting one thing," Drucker pointed out as he leaned forward, his face animated with expectation. "We control the messenger. Think about it, Larry. We've got a chance to create our own prophet. A Messiah that we own. Just imagine the possibilities. Think of what we can make people do."

Drucker studied Rydell through cold, calculating eyes.

"You know we're right," he continued. "You know this was the only way to go. These people don't read newspapers. They don't research things on the Internet. They listen to what their preachers tell them—and they believe them. Fanatically. They don't question what the preachers say. They don't bother to fact-check the bullshit they hear in their megachurches. They're happy to swallow it whole, no matter how ridiculous it is, and not even an army of Pulitzer Prize–winning thinkers or Nobel Prize–winning scientists with all the common sense or scientific evidence in the world could convince them otherwise. They'd just dismiss them as agents of the devil. Satan, trying to cloud their minds. We need these windbags. We need them to sell our message. And what better way to get them on board than to give them a new prophet of their own to sell on to their flocks?"

Something in his words jarred within Rydell. "What about the rest of the world? You're talking as if we're the only problem here."

"We're the biggest polluters, aren't we? So let's start here. The rest of the world will follow." He paused, gauging Rydell for a moment, his gaze unwavering. "Our focus hasn't changed. We're still in this for the same reasons. This is still about survival. It's still about the singular threat facing the planet. It's still about leading people away from the dangerous path they're on."

"By sending them back to the Dark Ages? By giving those poor deluded sods out there a real reason to believe in their Bronze Age superstitions?"

"See?" Drucker answered him with a smile. "Now you're getting the irony." He scrutinized Rydell, then added, "For better or for worse, the whole movement has become a religious one, Larry. You know that. It's the same old story, the same classic myth that's hardwired into our brains, and in this case it fits like it was tailor-made. It's a story of salvation, after all, isn't it? We're sinners. We're all sinners. We took this perfect Garden of Eden that God bequeathed to us and desecrated it with our orgies of consumption. And now we have to pay. Now we have to make huge sacrifices and flagellate ourselves by driving smaller cars and using less electricity and cutting down on flying and other luxuries we take for granted and choking our economies to death to make things right. We have to defeat the Antichrist that is pollution and seek out the salvation of sustainability and save ourselves before Judgment Day rolls over us and wipes us out in an Armageddon of abrupt climate change. That's how it's playing out, Larry. And the reason it's become that is that people like these religious myths. They thrive on them. Sooner or later, they turn everything into a crusade. And this crusade needed a prophet, not just a sign, to get the word across and make it happen."

Rydell shook his head and looked away for a moment.

He was still struggling to fully register that they were actually having this conversation. That, after they'd debated it many months earlier and put the issue to rest—or so he thought—he was actually sitting there facing it in its full, catastrophic glory today. "The others . . . they're all with you on this?"

"Without hesitation."

"And where does it end?" Rydell countered. "Do you really think you can keep Father Jerome in line forever? You really think you can keep this lie alive indefinitely? Sooner or later, someone's gonna figure it out. Something'll screw up, someone'll slip up, and it'll all come out. What happens then?"

Drucker shrugged. "We're running a very tight ship."

"Even the best-laid plans eventually come unstuck. You know that. I thought that was one of the main reasons you agreed not to go down this route."

Drucker wasn't budging. "We'll keep it going as long as we can."

"And then?"

Drucker thought about it, then waved it off like a minor nuisance. "Then we'll figure out a graceful exit."

Rydell nodded stoically, processing it all. He just sat there, hobbled by the shock of it all, his eyes staring into the distance as if he'd just been told he had a week to live. "No," he finally told Drucker, his voice thick with dismay. "This is wrong. This is a huge mistake."

Drucker's eyes narrowed a touch. "Take some time to think this through properly, Larry. You'll see that I'm right."

The words didn't really sink in with Rydell. The image of the priest standing on the roof of the monastery in Egypt, with the sign hovering over him and hundreds of prostrate worshippers before him, shot to the forefront of his mind again. "Even with the best intentions, even given what we're trying to do . . . I won't be a part of this. I can't help you make this . . . this virus any stronger than it already is."

"You're gonna have to. We both have too much at stake here," Drucker reminded him dryly.

"It's wrong," Rydell flared. "The plan was to scare them, Keenan. To make them sit up and think about what they're doing. That was it. A few carefully chosen appearances; then it's gone. Keep it unexplained. Keep it mysterious and unsettling and scary. We were in agreement on this, goddammit. We agreed that it would be a good thing if people didn't know where this was coming from, if they ended up thinking it was coming from some alien presence, from some higher intelligence out there. The beauty of this whole plan was that beyond making them sit up and listen, it might also help them pull away from this childish notion they have of this God of theirs, this personal God, this old man in a white beard who listens to every pathetic request they make and who sets down ridiculous rules about what they should eat or drink or wear or who they should bow to, and help them grow into the notion of God being, if anything, something that's unfathomable and unexplainable—"

"—and nudge them to the half-assed mind-set of agnostics," Drucker commented mockingly.

"Well, yes. It's a step in the right direction, isn't it?"

Drucker was unmoved. He shook his head. "It's a noble thought, Larry, but . . . this was the only way it was ever going to work. The world's not ready to give up its obsession with religion. Far from it. It's becoming more fundamentalist by the day. And it's not just our enemies. We're doing it too. Look at what's happening in this country. We don't have a single congressman or senator who can admit to being an atheist. Not one. Hell, we had ten presidential candidates on a podium last year, and not one of them dared raise his hand and say he believes in evolution."

"And you're helping make it even worse."

"It's a trade-off. It's a message they'll understand."

Rydell shook his head again. "No. It's wrong. There was no need to do it this way. You might help get rid of one evil, but you'll be feeding one that's just as vile. One that'll turn our world into a living hell for any rational person." His face darkened with resolve, and he fixed Drucker with a hard stare. "We need to figure a way out of this. We need to stop it before it gets too big."

"You saw what just happened in Egypt. It's too late."

"We have to stop it, Keenan," Rydell insisted.

Drucker shrugged. "We might just have to agree to disagree on that one."

"I still have a say in this."

"Within reason. And right now, you're being unreasonable."

Rydell thought for a moment, then said, provokingly, "You need me for the smart dust."

"I do," Drucker nodded calmly.

"You can't do this without it."

"I know that."

Rydell was momentarily thrown by Drucker's lack of even the slightest hint of agitation. "So?"

"So . . ." Drucker winced, as if pained by something. "So I had to take out some insurance."

Rydell studied him, unsure of what he meant—then it fell into place. "What?" he hissed. "What have you done? What have you done, you son of a bitch?"

Drucker let him stew on it for a moment or two, then just said, "Rebecca."

The word stabbed Rydell like an ice pick. His eyes turned to saucers as he yanked out his phone and stabbed a speed-dial button. After two rings, a voice answered.

Not Rebecca's. A man's voice. Rydell instantly recognized it as the voice of Rebecca's bodyguard.

"Ben, where's Becca?"

"She's safe, Mr. Rydell."

Rydell's heart somersaulted with relief. He shot a victorious glance at Drucker.

The man's face was unnervingly serene.

A bolt of worry ripped through Rydell. "Put Becca on," he ordered the bodyguard, hoping for an answer he knew he wasn't going to get.

"I can't do that, Mr. Rydell."

The words coiled around his gut and twisted it, hard. "Put her on," he growled.

The bodyguard's voice didn't waver. "Only if Mr. Drucker gives the word, sir."

Rydell threw his phone to the ground and charged at Drucker. "Where is she?" he yelled.

Drucker sprang out of his seat and deflected Rydell's attack, grabbing his hand and elbow and twisting his arm sideways and back. As he did so, he kicked out Rydell's leg from under him. The billionaire tumbled to the floor heavily, slamming against one of the seats. Drucker eyed him for a beat, then took a couple of steps back.

"She's fine," he said as he straightened his jacket. His face was slightly flushed, his breathing slightly ragged. He took in a calming breath before adding, "And she'll stay fine. As long as you don't do anything foolish. Do we understand each other?"

Chapter 42

Deir Al-Suryan Monastery, Wadi Natrun, Egypt

Tucked away behind the crumbled wall four hundred yards west of the monastery and veiled by their desert camouflage netting, Fox Two and his two men watched silently through their high-powered binoculars, and waited.

Beside them, nestling under the truck's canvas top, the long-range acoustical device unit sat patiently, ready to wield its unseen power again. It had been painted a matte sand-beige in preparation for their mission, a color that had been matched perfectly to blend in with the terrain outside the monastery and farther up, on top of the mountain, above the cave. They'd left the directional microphone in its casing on this occasion. Today's event had been planned strictly as a one-way conversation, unlike the long hours they'd spent during all those weeks and months, up on the mountain, when Father Jerome had occasionally seen fit to ask a question or two.

Fox Two studied the restless crowd below. So far, he'd been able to push the right buttons and generate the responses he needed without a problem. Father Jerome had reacted as expected to the gentle prodding he'd given him on the rooftop, after the sign had appeared above him—but then, he'd been well primed to react that way. A few whispered words, aimed at the more visibly heated pockets in the mob, were also enough to trigger a cascading reaction, to nudge them into a frenzy at the sight of an escaping car. A high-frequency, ultraloud pulse using the crowd-control setting was more than enough to hobble their fervor when it was no longer needed and get them to pull away in order to facilitate an escape.

Remarkable, he still thought, even after using the LRAD device so often that it had become second nature to him. A simple concept, really—projecting noise in a tightly focused audio beam, the same way a film projector's lens magnifies and focuses a shaft of light, so that only the persons—or person, for it was as accurate as a sniper's rifle—in the device's crosshairs could hear it. Even at that distance. And either make it appear as if someone's voice, live or taped, was actually inside the target's head, or—using the less subtle crowd-control mode—send an unbearably loud, caustic sound pulse into the target's ears that, at its highest setting, caused nausea and fainting and crippled the toughest enemy.

Simple, but hugely effective.

His master's voice, Fox Two mused.

The power of suggestion was particularly effective in this case, when the subjects were already burning with the desire to do what was required of them, as in the case of the selected targets in the mob outside the monastery, or, as in the case of Father Jerome, when they'd undergone weeks of forced indoctrination. Electroshocks and sleep deprivation sessions, followed by cocktails of methohexital to take the edge off. Transcranial mental stimulation. A complete psychochemical breakdown. Tripping the switches inside the brain, disarming it entirely before bombarding it psychologically. Implanting visions, thoughts, feelings. Conditioning the brain to accept an alternate reality, like hearing the voice of God or over-coming one's humility in order to embrace the notion of being the Chosen One.

He panned his binoculars across the desert, west of his position. Even though he knew what he was looking for, it still took him the better part of a minute to locate Fox One and his unit. The four men and their gear were also virtually invisible, huddled under camouflage netting in the sand dunes a couple of hundred yards away. Their contribution had been flawless, as expected. Its effect, staggering. He'd seen it before, in a video of a test in the desert. But not like this. Not live. Not in front of an unsuspecting audience.

It had taken his breath away. Even for a battle-hardened cynic like him, it was a heart-stopping moment. A one-two punch that, he knew, would resonate around the world.

Fox Two turned his attention back to the hordes at the monastery's gates. He'd soon be able to leave this dump for good, he thought with a degree of relish. It had been a hellish assignment. Living in hiding, on call at dawn and at dusk, climbing up and down the mountain, lugging the gear, day in and day out. He'd been out here in the desert way too long. He missed the feel of a woman's skin and the smell of a good barbecue, but most of all, he missed living among people.

Soon, he thought.

But before he could do that, he needed to make sure that the mission ended as smoothly as it had begun.

Chapter 43

Woburn, Massachusetts

The smell of fresh coffee tripped Matt's mind and coaxed him out of a dreamless sleep. Everything around him looked hazy. He tried to sit up, but did so too quickly and almost blacked out and had to try again, a bit slower this time. His head felt like it was filled with tar as he took in his surroundings and awareness trickled in.

The TV was on, though Matt couldn't really make out what it was showing. He tried blinking the fogginess out of his eyes. Jabba was sitting by the small table next to the window, watching the TV. He turned and grinned at Matt, a smoking cup of coffee in one hand— a venti or a grande or whatever quirkily-original-yet-misguidedly-obnoxious name coffee shops had replaced *large* with these days—and a half-eaten glazed dough-nut—or was that "glazé"?—in the other, with which he pointed at the two other oversized cups and the box of doughnuts on the table.

"Breakfast is served," he said, in between mouthfuls.

Matt acknowledged the venti-sized scientist with a weary smile before noticing the daylight streaming in.

"How long was I out? What time is it?"

"Almost eleven. Which means you've been out for"—

Jabba did a quick mental calculation—"sixteen hours or so."

Which Matt had needed.

Badly.

He also noticed a couple of newspapers on the table. The headlines were in an unusually large font—the type only used when a major event had occurred. An almost quarter-page photograph of the apparition, in color, was also emblazoned across the front pages, next to older, file portraits of Father Jerome.

Matt looked up at Jabba. Jabba nodded, and his expression took a detour into more ominous territory. "The Eagle has landed," he said somberly, aiming his half-eaten doughnut at the TV.

Matt watched the footage from Egypt in silent disbelief. Breathless reports coming in from around the world also showed the explosive reaction to what had happened at the monastery.

In St. Peter's Square in Vatican City, tens of thousands of people had assembled, hungrily awaiting the pope's guidance on how to treat the apparition. In the Praça da Sé in São Paulo, hordes of euphoric Brazilians spilled into the square from in and out of the city, invading every available inch of the Sé Cathedral, also looking for answers. The reactions reflected the local variations in faith and the different levels of appetite for the supernatural across the planet. The scenes were repeated in frenzied massings outside churches and in city squares in other centers of Christianity, from Mexico to the Philippines, but were different elsewhere. In the Far East, the reaction was generally more muted. Crowds had taken to the streets in China, Thailand, and Japan, but they were mostly orderly and there were only pockets of disturbance. The hot spot of Jerusalem, on the other hand, was very tense, with worrying signs of polarization already apparent among its religious groups. Christians, Muslims, and Jews were taking to the streets, looking for answers, conflicted and unsure about how to treat what many of them saw as a miraculous, supernatural manifestation—but one that didn't match anything prophesized in any of their sacred writings. The same thing was going on in the Islamic world. Confused worshippers had taken over city centers, town squares, and mosques across the Arab world and farther east in Pakistan, Bangladesh, and Indonesia. As always, moderate voices seemed to be either holding back or crowded out by those of the more radical clerics. Reports were coming in of scattered skirmishes and brawls in several cities, both between followers of different religions as well as infighting among members of the same faith.

Around the world, official reaction was only starting to trickle in, but so far, government and religious leaders had refrained from making public statements about the phenomenon—apart from some fiery rhetoric that a few fundamentalist firebrands weren't shy to express.

Throughout the coverage, Father Jerome's face was everywhere. It was plastered across the front page of every newspaper in the country, if not the world. It beamed down from every channel, the frail priest suddenly thrust into megastardom. Every news outlet was locked in on the story. Anchors and talking heads across the language spectrum were struggling to hold back on the superlatives—and failing. The whole world was firmly gripped by the unexplained event.

As Matt drank and ate and watched the screen, Jabba told him what had happened during the night. The caffeine and sugar worked its magic on him again, slowly injecting a semblance of life back into his veins; the wall-to-wall footage from Egypt and from the rest of the world reached the parts the caffeine had missed. And with each new report, with each new video clip, Matt felt a crippling chill seep through him. The stakes were growing exponentially, along with the realization of the enormity of what he was facing.

When the doughnuts ran out, Jabba turned the volume down and filled Matt in on what he'd been up to. He'd been busy. After Matt had conked out and before the breakfast run, he'd gone back out to the reception alcove, handed the weedy receptionist another ten-dollar bill, and worked late into the night, and again this morning.

He'd gotten an update on the tracker's position, and handed Matt the printouts. They showed that the Merc had left the Seaport district, the last position they had for it, sometime before ten the previous night. It had traveled to the downtown area where the signal had been lost—presumably boxed in by concrete walls deep in the underground parking lot of some building. It had appeared again soon after seven that morning and returned to the same location in the Seaport district, and hadn't moved since.

Jabba had then spent most of his time trying to beef up the thin sketch they had managed to compile on the doomed research team and its covert project. He'd made more calls to contacts in the industry and had given Google and Cuil's search algorithms a real workout, and although he hadn't come up with much, what he didn't find also told him something.

Even though his experience was in non-defense-related research projects, the secrecy surrounding his and his peers' work was often military-like in its intensity. And although defense-related projects were even more cloaked, there was often a whisper, a hint, something that had seeped through the cracks and gave an idea, however vague, of what ballpark the project was in. The critical piece of information to protect was more often than not how a goal was to be achieved; the goal itself was, in most cases, at least obliquely known, especially within the most well-connected techie circles. In this case, however, no one knew anything. The project had been born, and had died, in total and utter secrecy. Which told Jabba that it was unlike anything he'd ever encountered. It also spoke to the resources and determination of those behind it, which made the prospect of going up against them even less appealing—if that was even possible.

He had, however, managed to unearth a real nugget, one he kept for last.

"I tracked down Dominic Reece's wife," he informed Matt with no small satisfaction beaming across his weary face. "Maybe she has some idea of what her husband and Danny were doing out there in Namibia."

"Where is she?" Matt asked.

"Nahant, just up the coast," Jabba replied, handing him a slip of paper with a phone number on it. "We can be there in half an hour."

Matt thought about it for a moment, then nodded. "Sounds good. But let's see what the tracker's got for us at the Seaport first."

Chapter 44

Deir Al-Suryan Monastery, Wadi Natrun, Egypt

Gracie had been doing almost continuous lives ever since the frenzied moment on the roof of the keep. She'd faced Dalton's lens every half hour or so, feeding the connected world's insatiable hunger for new information, regardless of how much—or how little—new information she actually had. Her throat felt numb, her nerve endings raw, her legs rubbery, but she wouldn't have had it any other way. The whole world was sitting up and listening, hanging on every tidbit of information they could find. Every news broadcast was carrying the story. And she was right there, at the heart of it all, the singular face and voice that everyone on the planet was now hooked on.

And yet she still couldn't believe it was happening, still couldn't fathom the fact that she was there, doing this, living through the epochal events right alongside the man who was quite possibly an envoy from God.

They'd brought Father Jerome down off the roof for safety, given the mob that was massed outside the gates. After the dawn appearance of the sign, the crowd had grown tenfold, and more people were still streaming in from all corners. Father Jerome had been escorted into the bowels of the monastery by the abbot and Brother Ameen.

He'd been baffled by the whole experience, and looked visibly drained. He needed time to recover and take stock of what had happened. Dalton, Finch, and Gracie had climbed back up onto the roof on a couple of occasions, and Dalton had crept right up to the edge and filmed the scene outside the monastery's walls. He'd been desperate to use the skycam, but he'd reluctantly agreed with Gracie and Finch that it would be unwise, given the highly volatile nature of the crowd.

So far, ever since the sign had faded fifteen minutes or so after it had first appeared over Father Jerome, things out there were calm, if tense. The violence hadn't flared up again, but the crowd had entrenched itself into separate areas, rival camps that were eyeing one another nervously: Christians who were gathering there to worship and pray, Muslims who were enthralled by the miracle they had witnessed and had joined the others in prayer even though they were unsure about how to interpret the appearance of the sign over a priest's head, and fired-up groups of more fundamentalist Muslims who rejected any suggestion of a new prophet and whose mere appearance was pushing the more open-minded moderates among them to the sidelines.

In between broadcasts, Gracie, Finch, and Dalton were monitoring news reports streaming in from across the globe and getting updates from the network's contacts in Cairo. The first major religious figure to make an official comment on what was happening was the patriarch of Constantinople. Unlike the pope, who was the undisputed leader of Roman Catholics and whose word they considered infallible, the patriarch had little direct executive power in the fragmented world of the Eastern Orthodox Church. It hadn't stopped him from using his resonant historical title to promote his concern for the environment, presenting it as a spiritual responsibility.

And in that context, he'd just released a statement that asked the people of the world to pay heed to what they were witnessing and to express his interest in meeting with Father Jerome to better understand what was happening.

Presently, as Gracie looked out over the teeming plain below, she felt increasingly uneasy about their situation. The air was heavy with a charged silence. The threat of a bigger eruption of violence was palpable. She gratefully accepted some fresh lemonade from one of the monks and sat down, cross-legged, on the far end of the roof, her back against a pack of gear. Dalton and Finch, glasses in hand, joined her.

They sat in silence for a moment, allowing their brains to throttle back and their pulses to settle.

"Amazing, isn't it?" Finch just said, looking out over the irregular, domed roofs inside the monastery's walls. "How everything can change like that, in a heartbeat?"

"Weren't we just freezing our nuts off in the South Pole, like, yesterday?" Dalton asked in a weary, incredulous tone. "What just happened?"

"The story of our lives, that's what happened," Gracie replied.

"That's for sure." Dalton shook his head, a wry smile curling up one corner of his mouth.

She caught it. "What?"

"Weird how these things happen, isn't it? I mean, I don't know what you want to call it. Luck. Fate."

"What do you mean?"

"We could have missed all this so easily. Imagine . . . If you hadn't taken that call from Brother Ameen, back on the ship. Or if he hadn't been able to convince us to come. If the documentary guys hadn't been here before us and shot Father Jerome's wall paintings. We might have passed, right?" His eyes swung from Gracie to Finch and back. "We wouldn't be here right now, and maybe none of this would have happened."

Gracie thought about it for a beat, then shrugged. "Someone else would be here. It'd just be someone else's story."

"But would it? What if the documentary guys hadn't shot that footage? What if no one had showed up here to talk to him? The mob wouldn't be out there. Father Jerome wouldn't have been up here on the roof. There'd be no sign up there." He raised his eyebrows in a think-about-it manner. "Makes you wonder if he's the first, or if there were others before him."

"Others?" Gracie asked.

"You know, kooks. Nuts with voices in their heads, painting weird signs all over their walls or filling journals with their ramblings. What if there were others, before him? Others who were also the real deal. But no one knew." He nodded, to himself, his mind mining that vein further. "And what about the timing of it?" he added. "Why now? There were other times when we could have used a sign, a message. Why not just before Hiroshima? Or during the Cuban missile crisis?"

"You always get this lucid with lemonade?" she asked.

"Depends on what the good monks put in it." He grinned with a raised eyebrow.

Just then, Brother Ameen popped his head through the roof hatch, his expression knotted with concern. "Come with me, please. You need to hear this."

"Where?" Gracie asked as she got up.

"Down. To the car. Come now."

They climbed down and followed him to the Previa, which was still parked by the gates. The abbot arrived as they did. The car's doors were open, and Yusuf and a couple of monks were huddled around it, heads hung in concentration as they listened to an Arabic broadcast coming through on its radio. They looked thoroughly spooked.

Another religious leader was making a pronounce-ment, only this one wasn't as inspirational as the earlier one. Gracie couldn't understand what was being said, but the tone of the speaker wasn't hard to read. It sounded just like the other furious, inflamed rants she'd heard countless times across the Arab world. And even before Brother Ameen explained it, she understood what was happening.

"It's an imam, in Cairo," he told them, his voice quaking slightly. "One of the more hotheaded clerics in the country."

"He doesn't sound happy," Dalton remarked.

"He's not," Brother Ameen replied. "He's telling his followers not to be deceived by what they see. He's say-ing Father Jerome is either a *heela*—a trick, a fabrication of the Great Satan America—or he's an envoy of the *shaytan* himself, an agent of the devil. And that either way, they should consider him a false prophet who's been sent to sow fear and confusion among the true believ-ers." He listened some more, then added, "He's telling them to do their duty as good Muslims and to remember the preachings of the one true faith."

"Which is?" Finch asked.

"He's asking for Father Jerome's head," Brother Ameen replied. "Literally."

Chapter 45

River Oaks, Houston, Texas

"I've got to tell ya, I'm really confused," the pastor grumbled as he set down his tumbler of bourbon. "I mean, what the hell's going on out there? This isn't how it's supposed to happen."

"How what's supposed to happen?"

"The Second Coming, Roy," he answered. "The End of Times. The Rapture."

They were seated across from each other in the large conservatory, a huge glass house that dwarfed most single-family homes but looked like an outhouse next to the rest of the pastor's massive mansion. An oval-shaped pool lay beyond the chamfered windows, huddled under a glistening tarp cover and waiting for warmer days. The fence around Darby's tennis court winked out from behind a row of poplars that skirted the left edge of the property.

Although they'd met countless times over the last year, Roy Buscema still studied the man before him with the fascination of an anthropologist discovering a new species. The Reverend Nelson Darby was an intriguing specimen. Modern in all things technological and where business practices were concerned, but immovably medieval when it came to anything relating to scripture. Genteel and measured, and yet a fierce right-wing culture warrior and unrepentant agent of intolerance. In all the times they'd met, Darby was never less than a charming, relaxed, and earnest host, nothing like the bombastic, fire-and-brimstone preacher he morphed into onstage. He was also always impeccably groomed, an elegant man who appreciated the finer things in life. Fortunately for Darby, God—according to the inerrant scripture he bequeathed us, in any case—took pleasure in the prosperity of his servants, and the pastor was nothing if not a loyal servant.

His refined style extended to his home. Nestling at the end of a leafy road in River Oaks, it occupied a privileged site, directly overlooking the fairways of the country club. It was a stately, white-columned mansion that dated back to the 1920s—stately, but tasteful and restrained, not a vulgar temple to Prosperity Theology. Darby was particularly proud of his conservatory. He'd had it custom-designed by one of London's leading purveyors of garden houses, who'd then flown over a team of four carpenters to install it. He liked to take meetings there. It was away from the eyes and ears of the small army of staffers who toiled in the sprawling offices on his megachurch's campus. It was a chance to show off and impress his visitors. And, of course, it inspired him. The glass house seemed, to Darby, a prism for the sun's rays, a white hole that sucked in the faintest glimmer of light on even the bleakest of days. It normally helped instill a further sense of wonder in him than he already possessed. It was here that he prepared his most fiery sermons, the ones in which he took on homosexuals, abortion—even in the case of victims of rape and incest—condoms, evolution, stem cell research, and elitist, quasi-Muslim presidential hopefuls, even directing his bombastic, venomous rants at the Girl Scouts, whom he'd branded as agents of feminism, the Dungeons & Dragons game, and, still more bizarrely, SpongeBob SquarePants. It was here that he drafted the sermons he reserved for special occasions, like Christmas, which was now only days away.

Today, though, any inspiration was hobbled by the confused thoughts swarming inside him.

"Maybe this isn't the End of Times," Buscema suggested.

"It sure as hell isn't," the pastor agreed huffily. "Can't be. Not yet. Not when none of the prophecies of the Good Book have happened." He leaned forward, a studious stare in his eyes, and did the parallel-vertical-karate-chops thing with his hands for emphasis, as he did at his pulpit. "The Bible tells us the Messiah will only return *after* we've had the final battle between God's children and the army of the Antichrist out there in Israel. It's only after that happens that we can be saved by the Rapture." He shook his head. "This isn't right. Hell, we're still waiting for the Israelis to bomb the crap out of Iran and kick-start the whole thing."

"God's giving us a message, Nelson," Buscema put in thoughtfully. "He's given us a sign—two signs—over the ice caps. And he's sent us a messenger."

Darby scoffed. "An Arab. And a Catholic at that, if you can get your head around that one."

"He's not Arab, Nelson. He's Spanish."

Darby swatted the correction away. "Same difference. He's still Catholic."

"It doesn't matter. What did you think the Messiah of the Second Coming was gonna be? Lutheran?"

"I don't know, but . . . Catholic?" Darby groaned.

"That's an irrelevant detail right now. He's Christian. More important, he happens to be one of the holiest men on the planet. He's spent the last few months holed up in some cave near a monastery in Egypt. Which is part of the Holy Land. Jesus Himself hid in that same valley when He was being hounded by the Romans."

"What about all that Coptic business?"

"The monastery where he's staying is Coptic, but he's not a Copt. You know much about Copts?"

"Not yet," Darby answered with a self-effacing smile.

"They're the Christians of Egypt. Maybe ten percent of the population. But they're the ones who've been there longest. They were there long before the Arabs invaded in the seventh century. In fact, they've been there since day one. Uninterrupted. The purest, oldest uncorrupted Christians you'll find, Nelson," Buscema insisted. He paused to let his words sink in, then continued. "You do know who started the Coptic Church, right?"

"No," Darby said.

"Mark. As in Matthew, Mark, Luke, and John. That Mark. He went out there to preach the gospel, about thirty years after Jesus's death. He didn't have too much of a hard time getting the people there to sign up. They already believed in everlasting life, had done so for thousands of years. Difference was, Mark told them it wasn't just for pharaohs. No need to be mummified and put inside a huge pyramid and have priests perform all kinds of weird rituals for it to happen. Everyone was entitled to go to heaven, provided they believed in the One God and asked him to forgive them for their sins. Which, as you can imagine, was music to their ears. And that's where it all started, where Christianity first took shape. The symbolism, the rituals. A lot of it came out of there. Look at the ankh—the ancient Egyptian symbol of eternal life—and the cross. Think about their God, Ra—the God of the sun—and our holy day, Sunday. And that valley where Father Jerome is holed up? It's holier than you think. Those monasteries out there? They're the oldest monasteries in the world. They hold some of the earliest holy books anywhere. Fourth- and fifth-century gospels. Priceless manuscripts. Piles of them. Just lying there. They're still translating them. Who knows what they'll find in them? It's a deeply religious place, Nelson. A deeply religious, *Christian* place. And Father Jerome . . . well, you know all about him. Everything he's done. God's work. How he's helped spread the word. If God was going to choose someone, it seems to me like Father Jerome fits the bill nicely."

Darby nodded, grudgingly allowing his advisor's sermon to sink in. "But why now? And why the signs over the poles?"

Buscema's brows rose with uncertainty. "Maybe he's telling us to watch out. Maybe he'd like us to stick around a bit longer. And who knows?" He smiled. "You might find people end up preferring that message to the End of Times prophecies you've been telling them about. Regardless of how much they've been looking forward to that." He smiled inwardly at that last little dig.

Darby's eyes narrowed as it registered. He let it pass. "It's our destiny, Roy. That's what the Bible says. That's how those of us who've accepted Jesus Christ as our savior are going to be saved. Before Armageddon. Before the earth is reaped. Besides, you don't really believe these greenhouse gases are gonna end up wiping us all out with their tidal waves or with that new ice age they've been harping on about?"

Buscema gave him a noncommittal shrug. "I'm not sure it couldn't happen."

"Hogwash," Darby shot back. "War's gonna bring about the End of Times, Roy. Nuclear war between the forces of good and evil. Not global warming." He sighed and sat back. "The good Lord created this earth. And if you remember your Genesis, He said, 'It is good.' Which means, He's happy with how it turned out. It's His divine creation. And He's the Almighty, for crying out loud. You think He'd design it in a way that puny little man could destroy it just by driving some SUVs around and setting the A/C on high? His divine creation? It can't happen. He wouldn't let it happen. Not like that."

"All I'm saying is," Buscema countered in his calming manner, "there's a sign popping up over the planet's climate change tipping points. It's a sign, Nelson. And I just saw the first national polling numbers."

That fired up a totally different subsection of the pastor's brain, and his face sharpened with keen interest. "What do they say?"

"People are taking notice. They're listening."

Darby exhaled with annoyance. "I bet those 'creation care' jugheads are smiling now."

" 'The Earth is the Lord's, and the fullness thereof,' " Buscema quoted playfully.

Darby frowned. "Thanks for reminding me."

"It's in the Bible, Nelson. 'The Lord God took the man and put him in the Garden of Eden to work it . . . *and to take care of it*,' " he pointed out. "People are worried about the kind of world their kids are going to grow up in. It's a powerful hook."

"They're misguided. And dangerous. We've got to be careful, Roy. What are we talking about here? Are we saying the planet's holy? Are we supposed to worship nature? That's a slippery slope. We can't go out there and tell people to love Mother Earth and look after her. Hell, that's what the Indians believed in."

Buscema smiled. The man understood the subtleties of faith. And he was smart; there was no denying it. A branding whiz, as well as a mesmerizing orator who knew how to entrance his audience. There was a reason thousands of people endured punishing traffic jams every Sunday morning to hear his rousing sermons. Why millions of others tuned in to catch their slick broadcast on national cable and network TV. Why the man's opinions, despite being primitive and bigoted and containing such brain-dead inanities as blaming 9/11 on gays, had helped him build an empire that extended to over fifty different ministries and a global network of over ten thousand churches, a school and a university, a conference center, twenty-three radio stations, and a couple dozen magazines.

"It doesn't have to get to that," Buscema said. "Think of it more in terms of man's sinful desires that have led him astray. He needs to see the road to salvation. And it's your job to hold his hand and show him the way." Buscema studied him, then leaned in for emphasis. "Unless I've got the wrong end of the stick here, you're pro-life, right?" He teased him by letting the question hang for a beat, always perplexed—and pained—by how pro-lifers applied their zeal to the smallest cluster of cells, no matter how tragically disabled or conceived, but not to any other living species or to the habitat we all shared. "That's what saving the planet's all about, isn't it? Life?"

Darby breathed out heavily, clearly not liking this, and steepled his hands, buttressing his chin with his thumbs.

"Why aren't any of those bozos in Washington saying anything?"

"They will," Buscema said, his expression leading Darby to assume he knew more than he was saying.

Darby bought it. "What have you heard?"

"He's the real deal, Nelson. They know it. They're just mapping out how best to handle it."

Darby frowned. Small crinkles overpowered the Botox and broke through around his eyes. "They're worried about the same thing I am." He waved his arms expansively. "You build all this, you get to the top of the heap, king of your castle . . . then someone shows up and wants you to call him massa."

"It's happened, Nelson. We can't change that. And he's out there. I just don't want you to miss the boat, that's all."

Darby asked, "What do you think I should do?"

Buscema thought about it for a beat, then said, "Grab him. While you can."

"You want me to endorse him?"

Buscema nodded. "Others are thinking about doing it."

"Who?"

Buscema held his gaze for a beat, then confided, "Schaeffer. Scofield. And many others." He knew mentioning the names of two of Darby's biggest competitors in the soul-saving sweepstakes would generate a reaction. One of them even had the affront to have his megachurch in the same city as Darby.

Judging by Darby's expression, the names hit the sweet spot he was aiming for.

"You sure of that?" the pastor asked.

Buscema nodded enigmatically.

I should know, he thought. *I spoke to them before coming here to see you.*

"The man's a friggin' Catholic, Roy," Darby grumbled, a flutter of panic in his eyes.

"It doesn't matter," Buscema answered flatly. "You've got to endorse him and endorse him big. Big and loud. Look, you're already lagging on this front. The others, your fellow church leaders who signed up for the global-warming initiative two years ago . . . they're on board." Buscema was referring to the eighty-six Christian leaders who, despite strong opposition from many of their evangelical brethren, had signed up for what became known as the "Evangelical Climate Initiative." Some of the most prominent church leaders, however, such as the president of the National Association of Evangelicals, had resisted publicly supporting the movement, even if they privately backed it. "This is your chance to leapfrog over them and take control."

Darby frowned. "But what about that sign that keeps popping up? What is it? If it was a cross or something clearly Christian, then fine . . . but it's not."

"It doesn't matter what it is. What matters is that it's there. It's up there and everyone's looking at it and wanting to be part of it." Buscema leaned in and fixed Darby with unflinching resolve. "You're missing the point here, Nelson. Catholic, Protestant, Baptist, Presbyterian, Quaker, or Amish—or even Mormon, Jew, Muslim, Buddhist, or Scientologist for that matter. None of it matters now. You're right that it's not a cross up there. But it's not a Star of David or a crescent or anything linked to any of the other major religions either. It's a game-changer. An entirely new paradigm. It could be the start of something bigger than anything we've seen before, something new, something global. And as we've seen throughout history, when these things happen, they spawn big organizations. Right now, there isn't one. There's nothing. There's just a man and a sign in the sky. But people are coming to him in droves. And you need to decide whether or not you want to be part of it. Right now, you can get a jump on the others by hitching your wagon to him before the rest of them. Things can change . . . in the twinkling of an eye." He just couldn't resist throwing that one in. "Because even if it isn't specifically, obviously Christian," he pressed on, "if you haven't embraced it while everyone else has, you just might find yourself with a whole bunch of empty pews. And that wouldn't be a good thing, would it?" He winced, trying to stop himself from taking another dig using an End of Times catchphrase, but he couldn't resist, and he kept his voice as even as he could and added, "You don't want to be left behind, now, do you?"

◄o►

"Did he buy it?" Drucker asked Buscema.

"Please," the journalist said mockingly, the sound of rushing air coming through his car phone. "He's so into it it's almost painful to watch."

"You gonna see Schaeffer again?"

"He's left me two messages since I last spoke to him," he confirmed. "Same with Scofield. I'll let them sweat it out a little bit before calling them back."

Good man, Drucker thought. It sounded like they'd already reeled in one major marlin. With a bit of luck, they'd be bringing in a record haul.

Chapter 46

Boston, Massachusetts

Matt and Jabba were in the bloodstained Camry, parked outside a modern, six-floor office block in the Seaport district.

Matt's face was screened by the shadow of his baseball cap and the upturned collar of his coat. He sat in the passenger seat and eyed the building with quiet fury. It was a bland, architecturally bankrupt tile-and-glass box with a large parking area out front. There was no corporate signage by its front entrance; instead, various tenants probably leased suites there, moving in and out in accordance with the ebb and flow of their earnings. A thin blanket of snow from an early-morning flurry covered the asphalt and trimmed the bare branches of the trees that dotted the lot.

They'd been parked there for half an hour, and had seen only one person walk into the building. There had been no sign of the hard case.

The painkillers had taken the sting out of Matt's wound, but it still hurt every time he moved. He still felt a bit light-headed, which he attributed to the loss of blood. His body was pleading with him to give it time to heal, but the pleas were falling on deaf ears. He could walk, and right now, that would have to do.

"I'm going to have a look," he told Jabba. He reached for the door handle, grimacing with discomfort as he pulled on it.

Jabba reached out to stop him. "Not a good idea, dude. You shouldn't even be here. Look at you."

"Just a look," Matt repeated; only as he pushed the door open, Jabba put a hand on his shoulder and stayed him.

"I'll go," Jabba said.

Matt looked at him.

"I'll go," he protested-insisted, his voice rising a notch, before concern flitted across his eyes. "If I'm not out in five minutes, call the cops," he added, slapping his iPhone into Matt's hand. Then he caught himself, and grinned. "God, I never imagined I'd ever hear myself say that."

Matt brushed it away, dead serious. "Just don't get too nosy."

Jabba looked at him askance. "Seriously, sometimes, it's like you don't even know me," he mock-griped, then climbed out of the car.

He scanned left and right as he ambled across the lot, slightly overdoing the casual don't-mind-me attitude, but there was no one around to notice. Matt watched him disappear inside the building's entrance lobby.

Less than a minute later, he emerged.

"Well?" Matt asked.

Jabba gave him a piece-of-cake smile, but his body told a different story. He was breathing fast, and his face was sprinkled with sweat droplets that weren't there before.

"No receptionist. Five names on the roster, one per floor. Third seems unoccupied, or they've been too lazy to put their name up," he informed Matt in between sharp breaths. "But I think I know which one we want. Just need to go online somewhere to confirm it."

Matt thought about it, then said, "Okay. Do it here."

Which totally threw Jabba. "What, you want me to use my phone?"

"Yep," Matt confirmed, sure of it.

"Dude, they could track our position. My iPhone's got A-GPS, as in 'assisted.' Makes their job even easier."

"Fine. Do it. And stay on long enough for them to be able to do it."

Jabba looked at him like he was nuts. "You *want* them to know we were here?"

Matt nodded. "Yep."

Jabba was now looking at him like he'd sprouted little green antennae from his ears. "Why?"

"I want to fuck with them a little. Shake them up. Keep them unbalanced."

"It's my phone, dude," Jabba specified. "All they'll know for sure is that I was here."

"Same difference. They know we're together."

Jabba looked like he wanted to object more, but he gave up, raised his hands in surrender, and turned on his phone. He checked his watch, then fired up his Macbook and connected it to the phone, using the phone's Internet connection. Matt watched as Jabba's fingers danced across the keyboard and tapped the touchpad a few times. He then swung the laptop so Matt could see the screen.

It was on the home page of a company called Centurion. A slick slideshow showed an oil refinery in a desert location at sundown, then what looked like a gated compound somewhere in the Middle East, then a convoy of cars, again in the same sunny, dusty environment. The last picture showed a steely guy in pristine quasi-military gear, black gloves, and surfer-cool wraparound shades, poised behind a large-caliber machine gun. A slogan flashed up with each image, the last of them announcing the company's motto, "Securing a Better Future."

Matt and Jabba read through the "About Us" paragraph, which described Centurion as a "security and risk management company with offices in the U.S., Europe, and the Middle East" and a "security provider to the U.S. government and a registered and active UN contractor." Jabba clicked on the "Management" link, and a black-and-white portrait of Maddox leapt out at them. The hard case was the firm's founder and CEO, and the accompanying blurb described his long, stellar career in the Marines and his achievements in the field of "security consulting."

"Ouch," Jabba said, flinching at the unsettling and unapologetic mug shot of Maddox. He glanced around nervously, clearly uneasy at the thought of taunting this man. He checked his watch again and held up his phone. "Eighty-five seconds. Can we please switch this off now and get the hell out of here?"

Matt was still absorbing every word of Maddox's bio in silence. After a moment, he said, "Sure."

Jabba turned it off as Matt fired up the car and pulled away.

He looked over at Matt. "So?"

Matt nodded to himself, his eyes a bit distant, his expression dour. "So now we know who we're dealing with."

"Dude, the man's got a private army," Jabba pleaded, his pitch doing its worry rise. "We've got a white Camry and a handgun with no bullets in it."

"Then we've got some catching up to do," Matt replied. "But let's see what Reece's wife has to say first."

◄◦►

"You're sure?"

Maddox wasn't shouting. In fact, his voice was unnaturally calm, given the news he'd just been given. But his displeasure was coming through loud and clear to his contact at Fort Meade.

"Absolutely," came the answer. "Komlosy's phone signal popped up on the grid for just over a minute before powering down."

Maddox walked over to his office's window and looked down. Nothing unusual caught his eye. The parking lot and the street beyond were glacially quiet.

Two unexpected appearances from Sherwood in as many days, he fumed. The second one in the immediate vicinity of his office.

The man was good.

A bit too good for Maddox's liking.

"How long ago?" he asked.

"It just went dead."

Maddox seethed quietly. "Can't you track him with his phone switched off?"

"Looking at his contract, it seems he's got an iPhone, a 3G one," the NSA monitoring agent told him. "If he keeps it on long enough, I can remotely download some burst software onto it that'll let me track it even if it's powered down."

"I need you to do better than that," Maddox insisted.

"We're working on some stuff. But for now, it'll get better every time he switches it on. The tracking software will have a head start on him; it'll keep adding data every time he powers up. We won't need as long to get a lock."

"Okay. Let me know the second it powers up again," the Bullet ordered. "And get that download done as soon as you get a chance." With that, he hung up, stuffed the phone into his pocket, checked his watch, and glared out his window again.

Chapter 47

Deir Al-Suryan Monastery, Wadi Natrun, Egypt

"Don't we have anyone who can get here sooner?" Dalton asked. "Where's the damn sixth fleet when you need it?"

They were standing around uneasily by the base of the keep—Gracie, Finch, Dalton, Brother Ameen, and the abbot. An expectant hum of voices reverberated across the plain, beyond the monastery's thick walls. Closer by, the imam's hateful voice droned on from the people carrier's radio, an angry, never-ending call to arms that was echoed on countless other radios outside the walls. "Yeah, that'll look real good," Finch commented wryly. "American troops flying in to safeguard a Christian holy man in a sea of angry Muslims. That'll clinch the hearts-and-minds battle right there."

"We need to get Father Jerome out of here," Gracie said.

"I agree," Finch said, "but how?"

"What about bringing a chopper in to whisk him out?" she asked.

"Where's it gonna land?" Finch queried. "There's nowhere wide enough for it to put down, not inside the monastery's walls."

Gracie pointed up at the keep. "What about up there?"

Finch shook his head. "The roof's not strong enough. It's hundreds of years old. There's no way it can hold the weight. And I don't think winching him out is gonna work either. He's too old to take that, and even if he could, someone could take a potshot at him."

Dalton slid a forlorn nod over at the keep behind them. "So what do we do? Bunker down?" He pointed up at the keep's second-floor drawbridge, sitting above them. "This thing still work?" he asked the abbot, only half-joking. The fortified keep, with its food stores, water well, library, and top-floor chapel, had been used as a refuge in times of attack, but that hadn't happened in over a thousand years.

"No, but . . . we should just stay here and wait for the security forces to arrive. They're bound to send them in now. Besides, there aren't just Muslims out there," the abbot reassured them. "A lot of them out there, they're our people. Christians. They'll defend Father Jerome if they have to."

"I'm sure they would, but that's not the point," Gracie pressed. "It'd be better to get him out of here before anything like that happens. To make sure it doesn't."

"There might be another way out," Brother Ameen offered.

All eyes turned swiftly to him. "How?" Gracie asked.

"The tunnel," he said, turning to the abbot with a questioning look.

"There's a tunnel? Where to?" Gracie asked.

"It goes from here to the monastery closest to us— the one we drove past on the way in."

"The Monastery of Saint Bishoi," the abbot confirmed.

"What, the one across the field?" Gracie was pointing northeast, trying to visualize the second monastery's relative position from when she'd last seen it, from the roof of the *qasr*.

The abbot nodded. "Yes. The tunnel is older than this monastery. You see, our monastery was built over what was once the monk Bishoi's hermitage, the cave he used to retreat to. Because of the constant threat from invaders, the monks decided to build an escape route from Saint Bishoi's monastery, and they chose his old cave as the exit point. Years later, as the danger receded, a small chapel was built over his cave, and that small chapel eventually grew into this monastery."

"You think it'll still get us there?" Finch asked.

"The last time anyone went down there was years ago, but it was clear then. I don't see why it should be any different now," the abbot replied. "We haven't had any earthquakes or anything like that."

Gracie glanced doubtfully at Finch. Still, it was all they had.

"If we can make it across, can we get a car to drive us from there? Discreetly?" she asked.

The abbot thought about that for a moment, then looked around at the driver of the Previa and the others, smoking nervously as they listened to the radio. He stepped over to Yusuf and spoke to him in Arabic. Yusuf replied; then the abbot turned back to Gracie. "Yusuf's brother-in-law also drives a car like his. If he can use your phone to call him, we can get him to meet you at Bishoi."

"Okay, but then what? Where do we go?" Dalton asked. "The embassy?"

"It'll be the same thing there," Ameen put in. "Maybe even worse. It's safer to fly him out of the country."

Finch frowned, thinking ahead, stumbling over the logistics. "Easier said than done. Does Father Jerome even have a passport?"

"We have to sneak him out," Gracie opined. "If anyone sees him, it'll get complicated."

"He can use my passport," the abbot offered. "With his robe on and with his hood down, they won't look too closely. And Ameen will be with you to deflect any questions."

Gracie looked to Finch for approval. He thought about it quickly, then nodded. "Okay, it's worth a shot. I'll call D.C.," he told her, "see how quickly they can get a plane over to us." He turned to the monks. "How long do you think this tunnel is? Half a kilometer maybe?"

"I'm not sure," the abbot said. "Maybe a bit more."

Finch frowned. "We're not going to be able to lug all our gear through." He turned to Dalton. "Let's bring it all down. We'll grab as much as we can."

The speech on the car radio flared up, the speaker's voice rising fiercely. Gracie flashed on iconic, violent images from the region's turbulent recent history, all of them fueled by religious fervor—the storming of the U.S. embassy in Tehran, the stoning and burning of the Danish embassy in Beirut, the beheadings in Iraq and Afghanistan. She didn't want to become one of them, not in that sense, anyway.

"We'd better get moving." She turned to the monk and the abbot. "You need to talk to Father Jerome."

Ameen nodded. "I'll go now," he said, before leaving them and disappearing into the doorway, closely tailed by the abbot.

◄◦►

"THEY'RE TRYING TO GET HIM OUT," Buscema informed Darby.

"Already? Who?"

"I just got a call from my guy at the network," the journalist told the reverend. "They've still got that news crew there with him, and they're not waiting for an official reaction. They're handling him themselves."

"Of course they are," Darby chortled. "That inside track's not exactly bad for their ratings, is it? How are they going to do it?"

"I'm not sure. They're scrambling to get a plane out to them as soon as possible."

"Where are they planning on taking him?" Darby asked.

"I don't know. I don't think they know. They just want him out of there before the whackos rip him to pieces."

The reverend went silent. After a moment, he exhaled slowly, as if he'd reached a decision, and said, "Let's bring him here."

"Here?"

"Hell, yes. This is God's country, isn't it?" he boomed.

"It's not gonna be easy. Everyone else will want him," Buscema goaded him. "Did you see the rallies in Rome?"

"The pope hasn't announced his position on this whole thing yet, has he?" An unusual, slight panic creeped into his words.

"No. The Vatican's not exactly famous for its quick reactions."

"So where else is he gonna go? France?" Darby scoffed.

"Spain, maybe. He's from there originally. And the Brits are usually quick to put out the welcome mat for anyone in trouble."

"No way. We've got to get him over here. Besides, like you said," he added, "he's polling through the roof. People here want to hear what he has to say."

"The government hasn't even made an official statement about him yet."

"Just as well," Darby said, gloating. "Gives me a chance to do it myself and save him from ending up with those heathens back east."

There it is, Buscema thought. "You want to handle this yourself?" His voice rose with mock surprise.

"God's sending us a message," Darby asserted. "I'm going to make sure everyone hears it, loud and clear."

Buscema went silent for a moment, then said, "If the State Department gives the embassy the green light—and they will—it'll be over. If you want to make it happen, you're gonna have to move fast."

The reverend's tone was as smooth and sharp as a blade. "Watch me."

◄o►

GRACIE, DALTON, AND FINCH had brought the rest of their gear down from the roof of the keep and were now sorting through it in the shade by the entrance to the library. The tunnel would be a long, dark trek through a narrow, dusty passage, and they hadn't thought they'd be able to take everything with them. The camera and live broadcasting gear and as many of Father Jerome's journals that they could carry made the cut. Dalton's skycam rig was almost a casualty of the forced triage before the abbot drafted in a few monks who would accompany them through the passage and help them lug the rest of their gear.

Finch had spoken to Ogilvy, who went to work on rustling up a jet that could fly them out without asking too many questions. They'd still have to get past whatever security checks were in place at the airport, but Finch knew that those controls would be far less stringent for a private plane than they were for commercial flights. Still, they'd have to, pun notwithstanding, wing it at the airport. It didn't give him too much cause for concern, though. They'd gotten out of trickier places before.

As Finch clicked his backpack shut, Dalton's observations from earlier were still bouncing around his mind. Something was nagging at him. As Dalton had noted, everything had hinged on the preexistence of the documentary footage. Without it, he thought, none of this would have happened. They certainly wouldn't have made the trip. Something else was bothering him too. The way the throng surrounding their car had recoiled and given them an opening to back up and return to the safety of the monastery. He couldn't quite put his finger on what it was that bothered him—the moment had been a blur of frenzy. Still, something wasn't right.

He thought again about putting in a call to the documentary's producer to find out more about how it had all happened. He checked his watch and was about to say something when Dalton, looking around impatiently, said, "Where are these guys? We need to go."

"I thought Ameen and the abbot went to get him," Finch answered.

"I'll see if I can find them," Gracie offered.

She headed down the courtyard, toward the small building that housed the monks' cells. Finch watched her go. He wiped the sweat off his brow and paced around for a beat, and decided to use the dead time to reach out to the documentary's producer. He checked his watch again, made a quick mental calculation of the time difference between Egypt and England, where the producer was based, and found he wouldn't be waking him up at some ungodly hour. He picked up the sat-phone, then patted his pockets, looking for his cell phone, only it wasn't there.

"You seen my BlackBerry?"

Dalton glanced around. "No. Why?"

He checked his backpack. "I've been thinking about what you were saying. Thought I'd put a call in to the documentary guys."

"So use the satphone. Your phone doesn't work here anyway, remember?"

Finch gave him a wiseass grin. "It's got my contacts list on it, numbnuts."

Dalton thought about it for a second, then said, "Last I remember, you had it out when we were up there," pointing at the *qasr*. "Before you took that call on the satphone."

Finch glanced up at the keep that towered over the monastery's walled-in courtyard, and frowned. "Must have left it up there while we were packing up," he said. "Be right back."

He left Dalton, cut across the courtyard and up to the drawbridge, before disappearing into the keep.

As with each time he entered it, it took a moment for his eyes to adjust from the glare of the Egyptian sun to the dusty darkness of the windowless, low-ceilinged interior of the keep. He made his way down a passage to the narrow stairs and climbed up.

The keep was deserted, as before. Some of its rooms were used for storage, as the darkness and the thick walls kept the temperature relatively cool; others hadn't been used for years, if not centuries. The ceilings were low; the windows were nothing more than thin slits cut into the thick walls—not the most inviting place to work, or sleep, neither of which was what it was designed for. He climbed the staircase up three floors and reached the top, then found the small landing with the wooden ladder that led up to the roof.

The BlackBerry was there, skulking in the dust behind a small stucco smokestack. Finch picked it up. He thought of edging forward for one last look at the teeming plain below, but decided against it. Instead, he found the phone number of the documentary's producer, pulled out the satphone, and called him.

The man, Gareth Willoughby, was a respected, globe-trotting filmmaker with an impressive CV of well-crafted documentaries covering all kinds of topics. Finch only managed to get through to his voicemail, and left him a brief message explaining what was going on and asking him to return the call.

He took one last look across the desert, then headed back down. As his foot settled on the bottom rung of the ladder that came down from the roof, he heard a voice, a low murmur coming from one of the small rooms behind the chapel. A man's voice, no more than a few words, but their rumble carried across the quiet, warren-like space. Something about it made him listen more closely. He stepped away from the ladder, quietly, and followed the voice around the narrow corridor to a room that faced out, away from the monastery. Finch couldn't make out what he was saying, but it struck him that the man was speaking English.

He reached the doorway and stopped just short of it, hovering, leaning in for a look. The man was inside, alone. It was a monk. Like the others, he wore the traditional black cassock with the distinctively embroidered hood, which was raised over his head. He had his back turned to Finch. Finch stood there, somewhat taken aback, as he realized the man was talking on a cell phone. In English.

"We should be leaving in ten, fifteen minutes," the man said. "Shouldn't take more than twenty minutes to get through." He paused, then said, "Okay," and hung up.

Finch stiffened as he recognized the voice, and it must have caused him to pull his foot back an inch, maybe less, nothing significant—except that it was significant enough for the monk to sense his presence and turn.

It was Brother Ameen.

The awkwardness of the moment was stifling. Finch's eyes were drawn to the phone and back—there was something unusual about it, but his frazzled mind didn't latch onto it immediately—and he looked the monk squarely in the eyes before he caught himself and relaxed his face into a casual, sheepish half smile.

"I, um," he said, wavering, then pointing up at the roof. "I forgot my phone up there."

Brother Ameen didn't answer him. He didn't return the casual half smile either. He just stood there, rooted in silence.

Finch sensed the monk's muscles going tight. His eyes drifted down to the phone; then he realized what he'd unconsciously noted. It wasn't just a regular cell phone. They didn't work out there. It was a satphone, with its distinctive, oversized flip-up antenna. Not only that, but it had a small box plugged into its base, which Finch knew to be an encryption module.

Chapter 48

"**M**ore than anything, Dom lived for his work," Jenna Reece was telling Matt and Jabba. "Even when the kids were around, he hardly ever managed to make it up here, and when he did, it didn't make much difference anyway. His mind was always back in his lab."

They were in the living room–slash-studio of her house in Nahant, a small town that squatted on a tiny crescent-shaped peninsula fifteen miles north of Boston. A couple of miles offshore, it was linked to the mainland by a narrow umbilical cord of sandbank. Reece's house, a fully modernized Dutch Colonial, faced the ocean on the town's western coast. It had once been Dominic and Jenna's summer home, she'd told them, but following her husband's death, she'd sold their place in the city and moved full-time out here, where she'd turned the double-height living room into a workshop and lost herself in her sculpture.

"I imagine your brother was probably the same, wasn't he?" she asked. "They all seemed consumed by their work." She shrugged wistfully and leaned down to stroke her dog, a ginger-haired retriever that dozed lazily by her feet. A small Christmas tree twinkled in a corner, by the floor-to-ceiling sliding doors that led onto the deck. "And look what it got them in the end."

Matt held her gaze and nodded solemnly. "What do you know about the project they were working on when they died?"

Jenna Reece let out a light chortle. "Not very much. Dom didn't really go into much detail about his work with me. Not with his ditzy wife," she laughed easily. "I haven't really got much of a scientific mind anyway, so it wasn't something I was normally curious about. It was his world. And, well, you must know how obsessive he and the rest of them were when it came to making sure no one knew what they were working on—not until they were good and ready to make their announcements and reap the glory. Which I always thought was a bit too paranoid . . . I mean, it's not exactly the kind of thing I would slip into casual conversations at the coffee shop, is it?" She smiled.

Matt shifted in his seat and leaned forward, steepling his hands under his chin, clearly discomfited by what he needed to ask her. "Mrs. Reece . . ."

"It's Jenna, Matt," she softly corrected him.

"Jenna," he tried again, "I need to ask you something, but you might find it a bit weird, and . . ." His voice trailed off and he looked at her, hoping for encouragement.

"Matt, you said you needed to talk and you drove all this way to see me, so I figure it has to be important." She fixed him squarely. "Ask me what you need to ask."

"Okay." He nodded gratefully. "I just wanted to know . . . Did you actually get to see your husband's body?"

Jenna Reece blinked a couple of times, and her eyes looked away before dropping down to her feet. She reached down and stroked her dog again, somewhat rattled by the memory. Outside, frothy December waves pounded the rocky outcroppings below the timber deck, their metronomic crashes punctuating the uneasy silence. "No," she said after a moment. "I mean, not his whole body. But you know how they died, and . . . the conditions out there . . ."

"I know," he offered, trying to avoid conjuring up any additional painful imagery. "But you're sure it was him?"

Her eyes were aimed at Matt, but they were looking through him, far beyond, beyond the room's walls and the town itself. "All they had for me was his hand," she said. The words caught in her throat and she shut her eyes for a moment. When she opened them again, they glistened with moisture. "It was his hand, though. His left hand. His wedding band was still on it. I didn't have any doubts."

"You're sure of it," Matt probed again, despite his misgivings.

Jenna Reece nodded. "He had these really lovely, fine hands. Like a pianist's. I noticed them the first time we met. Of course, it had been . . ." She brushed a painful thought away and straightened up. "I still knew it was his." She smiled through it at Matt. "Why do you ask?"

"Well, there wasn't anything left of my brother, so I was just wondering if . . . I was just hoping maybe someone had made a mistake," he obfuscated.

"You think your brother might still be alive?"

The way she cut to the heart of his thinking surprised him, and he couldn't help but nod.

She gave him a warming, supportive smile. "I wish I could tell you something that would help clear it up for you one way or another, but all I can tell you is what I know about my Dom."

Matt nodded, quietly grateful that he didn't have to explain any further. He thought back to the main reason for their visit. "Do you know who Dom was working for?"

"He didn't share that with me," she told him thoughtfully. "Not that he wasn't very excited about it. He was. But like the rest of them, he was cagey about details. And I'd seen it all before—every discovery of his had the potential to change the way we live. That's how they all thought; it was what they were all chasing after. And I guess some of these things can end up changing our lives, whether it's cell phones or the Internet or electric cars." She leaned forward, frowning with concentration, trying to see through the cobwebs in her mind. "But with this project . . . it was different. Like I said, Dom didn't say much about his work at the best of times, but with this one, he was particularly aloof. And I could see that this was different. It was the big one. Much as he tried to hide it, he had this burning enthusiasm about it, this optimism . . . He felt it could really change things, on a more fundamental level. I pressed him on it a couple of times, and he'd just say, 'You'll see.' And the day he got the green light on the funding—it was usually a big night out for us, a big celebration in some fancy restaurant. This one wasn't like that. He was delighted—don't get me wrong. But it was more than that. It was like the next phase of his life had begun. Like he was on a mission. And he was being more secretive than ever after that. I hardly ever saw him. Until . . ." She looked away, shaking the memory away.

"You didn't know anything about who was backing him? He must have said something about that," Matt pressed.

Jenna eyed him hesitantly, then said, "I'm not sure I should be telling you this."

"Please, Jenna," Matt said, palms open. "I really need to know. My brother was part of it."

Jenna studied him, then heaved out a sigh and nod-ded. "Well . . . I always assumed the money was coming from one of the big tech VCs he knew or maybe the gov-ernment. He only let it slip once, and that was by acci-dent," she confided.

"What?" Matt asked, gently.

"The money. It was coming from Rydell."

Matt looked at her, confused. Jabba took up the slack. "Larry Rydell?"

"Yes," she confirmed. "No one was supposed to know. I don't know why, but that's how they wanted it. Rydell has such a big public profile, and I guess he has his share price to worry about. Still, I was surprised—and more than a bit pissed off, to tell you the truth—when he didn't even show up at Dom's funeral. I mean, I can't complain. They took good care of me. I didn't have any trouble with their insurance people or anything, but still . . ."

Jabba looked at Matt pointedly. Matt knew the name—most people did—but didn't quite grasp the sig-nificance it seemed to have for Jabba.

"You're sure of this?" Jabba pressed.

"Yes," Jenna Reece replied.

Jabba looked at Matt with an expression that said they had all they needed to know.

Chapter 49

Deir Al-Suryan Monastery, Wadi Natrun, Egypt

"So . . . you've got a satphone?" Finch found himself asking, rhetorically, as if he were in a trance.

Brother Ameen didn't respond in any way.

"I didn't think you had one out here," Finch added, while trying to drain his tone of any hint of suspicion.

The monk still didn't say anything. He just kept looking blankly at Finch.

"It's funny," Finch continued, "'cause I just thought the whole point of being here was to isolate yourself from the rest of the world, to allow you to, you know, concentrate on God and . . . and yet you've got a satphone," he stated again, his attention traveling down to the phone in the monk's hand and back to his eyes.

Finch's forced smile dropped. It rose, fractionally, across Brother Ameen's face.

"I do," the monk finally said, almost regretfully. "And it's got an encryption box."

He held Finch's probing gaze. Finch tried to dismiss the comment with a no-big-deal grimace, but the monk wasn't buying.

"I know you recognized it when you saw it," the monk added. "It was obvious from your expression. I expect you've seen them before, given your line of work, the kinds of places you've been."

"Yeah, but . . ." Finch waved it away, mock-casually. "I see more and more of them these days. It's safer, isn't it? What with all the scanners and . . ." His voice trailed off as his mind went off on its own, rocketing back over all the events that had led to his being here, in this small, stuffy room; enlightening him with a barrage of revelations that he'd never imagined—and it suddenly hit him that he was in serious danger, an odd, instinctive reaction he didn't quite understand but one that still made him take a hesitant step backward.

The monk mirrored him with a soft step forward.

Finch frowned. "What are you doing?"

"I'm sorry," Brother Ameen said as he took another step toward him.

Finch's instincts flared red-hot—and he bolted backward and turned to head back to the stairs, but he'd barely made it past the door's threshold before the monk was right with him, moving lightning fast, slamming him back against the wall while driving a hard knee straight into his groin. Finch pitched forward, exhaling heavily from the kick. His glasses flew off his face as he bent over, and he pivoted around and raised his hands defensively, hoping to stave off another blow. For a split second, he caught sight of the monk's fist. Without the spectacles, it was a bit out of focus, but it looked like the monk had it bunched tight, with its middle knuckle extended, and it recoiled before lunging at his head, fast as a rattlesnake's strike. Its steely tap struck him on the side of his neck, just below his ear, pounding his carotid sinus with the force of a hammer blow. He felt his entire body tense up from the hit, before losing all motor control of his muscles and plummeting to the ground.

It was the oddest feeling—motionless, no control

over his muscles, like a big lump of Jell-O dropped on the ground. Through groggy, hazy eyes, he saw the monk hover over him, look away and then back down, think for the briefest of moments, then bend down, grab him by the arm, lift him up, and sling him over his shoulder.

◄◦►

"WHERE IS HE?" Gracie asked, scanning the monastery's courtyard.

She was standing with Dalton, ready to go. They'd been joined by the abbot and Father Jerome, and the other monks who'd be helping them carry their gear across.

Dalton tilted his head up at the top of the keep, cupped his hands around his mouth like a bullhorn, and yelled, "Finch. We're all set here. Time to move out, pal."

No answer.

Gracie looked around, then asked Dalton, "You sure he went up there?"

Dalton nodded. "It shouldn't be that long. He's just looking for his BlackBerry."

Gracie glanced around again, impatiently, then frowned at the keep. "I'm gonna see what's keeping him," she said, and stepped away.

She'd almost reached the doorway when something inside her made her look up—the barely perceptible noise of a wind rush, a hardly noticeable darkening of the ground to her right—and she turned and looked up just in time to see Finch's body hurtling to the ground and slamming into the hard sand a few feet away from her.

Chapter 50

Outskirts of Boston, Massachusetts

"It makes sense," Jabba concluded, all pumped up, his mouth motoring ahead. "He's got the money. He's got the technical chops to pull off something like this. And he's a major, major environmentalist." Jabba shook his head, his face locked in concentration. "Question is, how's he doing it?"

"Doesn't matter," Matt replied.

They were back on the mainland, heading down the Salem Turnpike, toward the city. Jabba had told Matt what he knew about Rydell—the way he championed alternative energy projects across the globe, the passion with which he lobbied Washington to take the climate change issue seriously, the support he gave to politicians and to groups who'd been fighting the mostly losing battle against the previous administration's callous disregard for environmental concerns. Every word of it added an additional pixel of clarity to the picture that was forming in Matt's mind: him getting in Rydell's face and hearing what they'd done to Danny straight from the horse's mouth.

"How is it you know so much about Rydell?" Matt asked.

Jabba looked at him askance. "Dude. Seriously? Where've you been living?"

Matt shrugged. "So he really thought he could start a new 'green' religion? Is that it?"

Jabba cracked a grin. "We're hardwired to believe from minute one, dude. It's all around us from the day we're born. There's no escaping it. And people will believe all kinds of crap. Look at what a third-rate sci-fi writer was able to pull off, and everyone knew he was only out to get stinking rich. Rydell . . . the man's in a whole different league. He's got state-of-the-art technology and all the money he needs at his disposal. And he's no fool. It's an awesome combination."

Matt nodded, taking it in. "And he's set this whole thing up to save the planet?"

"Not the planet. Us. It's like George Carlin said. The planet's gonna be just fine. It's been through far worse than anything we can throw at it. It was here long before us and it'll still be around long after we're gone. It's *we* that need saving."

Matt shook his head in disbelief, then glanced out the window. The traffic up and down the turnpike was already noticeably heavier, with the Christmas rush home starting to clog the nation's arteries.

"Do you think they knew what they were really working on?" he asked Jabba. "Danny, the others . . . do you think Reece and Rydell told them?"

"I don't know . . . They had to be aware of the power of what they were putting together." He glanced sideways at Matt. "The question isn't just whether or not they were told. It's whether or not they knew about it from day one. Whether or not they were working on it knowing what it was going to be used for."

Matt shook his head again with denial.

"He was your brother, man," Jabba added, hesitantly. "What do you think? Could he have been part of something like this?"

Matt thought about it. "A hoax like this? Scamming millions of people." He shook his head again. "I don't think so."

"Even if he thought it was for a good cause?"

That one was harder to answer. Danny wasn't any more religious than Matt was, despite their parents' best efforts, so there wouldn't have been any faith issues for him there. And although he was a high-minded, upstanding kind of guy, Matt didn't remember him being particularly concerned with the planet's environmental problems, no more than most well-read, levelheaded people. He certainly wasn't messianic about it. Still, they'd spent a lot of time apart, courtesy of Matt's stints behind bars, and when all was said and done, how well did anyone know anyone else, really?

Jabba was scrutinizing him, unsure about whether or not to say anything more. Matt noticed it.

"What?" he asked.

"I don't know, dude. I mean, I hate to say it, but it doesn't look good. It's been two years. If Danny didn't pull a disappearing act to be part of this, I don't see how they could have kept him locked up and muzzled all this time. He would've found a way to reach out to someone, to sneak a word out, don't you think?"

"Not if they know what they're doing."

"Two years, man," Jabba added with a slight wince.

Matt stared ahead, frowning. Suddenly, he was feeling a tightening in his chest. He didn't know what was better—to find out Danny was actually long dead, or that he was part of all this willingly. Part of something that had gotten his own best friend killed and his brother accused of his murder.

"No way," Matt finally said. "He'd never want to be part of something like this. Not if he knew what they were really doing."

"Okay," Jabba accepted and turned away.

They motored on for a mile or so; then Matt said, "Get us another lock on Maddox's car, will you?"

"Okay, but we really shouldn't be using this," Jabba cautioned as he pulled out his iPhone.

"Just don't stay on any longer than you think is safe. You can be in and out in less than your forty seconds, right?"

"Let's make it thirty," Jabba said and nodded reluctantly. He pulled up the tracker's Web site. He didn't need to key in the tracker's number—it was now stored on a cookie. He waited a couple of seconds for the ping to echo back, then zoomed in on the map.

"He's stationary. Somewhere by the name of Hanscom Field," he told Matt. "Hang on." He pulled up another Web site. Punched in his query. Waited a couple of seconds for it to upload. "It's a small airport between Bedford and Concord. And I'm logging off before they track us." He killed the phone, checked his watch—twenty-six seconds total—and turned to Matt.

Matt chewed it over quickly. A small airfield. He wondered what Maddox was doing there. He also liked the idea of maybe being able to surprise Maddox and get up close and personal with him outside the man's comfort zone.

He glanced at the clock on the dashboard. It wasn't far, even with the holiday traffic building up. A half hour, forty minutes maybe. "That's just outside the ninety-five, isn't it?"

Jabba's face sank. "Yep." He shrugged.

"Check it again in fifteen minutes or so, will ya? Keep making sure he's still there."

Jabba nodded grimly and sagged into his seat, sucking in a deep breath and anticipating the worst.

◄◇►

MADDOX HUNG UP with his contact at the NSA and scowled. He scanned the skies instinctively for the incoming jet, but his mind was now preoccupied elsewhere.

He'd received three consecutive calls. The first one was innocuous enough: The learning software had delivered on its promise, and the targets were just north of the city, heading into town. The second call told him the targets had changed direction and were now heading west on the Concord Turnpike, which, with hindsight, should have raised an eyebrow, but hadn't. The third call, though, was seriously troubling. The targets had turned north once they'd hit I-95, and were now less than five miles away from the airfield.

Which was, again, seriously troubling. For the simple reason that Maddox didn't believe in blind luck any more than he believed in coincidences. And it was the second time Matt had managed to track him down that day. Which meant he was either psychic, or he had an advantage Maddox wasn't aware of.

Yet.

His mind did a one-eighty and ran a full-spectrum sweep of everything that had happened since he'd first come across Matt Sherwood. He shelved details he thought extraneous and focused on establishing causal links between that first encounter and the present moment and ran them against the background skills he knew Matt possessed.

All of which colluded to draw his attention across to his car.

He took a half step closer to it, his eyes scrutinizing it as his operational instincts assessed what the likely culprit could be.

And frowned at the realization.

He wouldn't have time to have the car checked out.

Which meant there was a chance he'd have to leave it there for now. Which pissed him off even more. He really liked that car. He checked his watch. The jet's arrival was imminent.

He looked around. The airfield was quiet, as it normally was. Which was good. He decided it was time to put an end to Matt Sherwood's unexpected intrusions—permanently—and waved over two of his men who were waiting nearby.

"I think we're about to have some company," he told them.

Then he told them what he wanted to do about it.

Chapter 51

Deir Al-Suryan Monastery, Wadi Natrun, Egypt

"Finch!"

Gracie's cry shook the walls of the monastery as she dropped to the ground at his side. She was shaking. The blood drained from her face, and her hands shot up to her open mouth. Finch's body just lay there, in front of her, flat against the desert sand. He was on his front, motionless, the puff of dust that he'd kicked up when he'd slammed into the ground drifting back down and settling around him.

Slowly, her hands came down and hovered over him, not daring to touch him. The others, led by Dalton, all rushed to her side.

"Is he . . . ?" Dalton couldn't say it.

There were no visible open wounds, no blood seeping out. It didn't make the sight any less horrific. His head, which must have hit the ground first, was twisted sideways at an impossible angle. He had one arm bent backward, and his eyes were staring lifelessly at the parched soil.

"Oh my God. Finch," Gracie sobbed as she stared at him, not sure what to do. Her hands finally dropped down onto his body, her fingers pressing softly against his neck, searching for a pulse or for any sign of life she knew she wasn't going to find.

She looked at Dalton through teary eyes and shook her head.

Dalton was shaking. He put his arms around Gracie, his eyes also locked on his fallen friend's body. The monks, waiting hesitantly behind Father Jerome and the abbot, started murmuring some prayers. After a moment, Gracie pulled her hand back, then gently brushed a few errant strands of hair off Finch's forehead and gave his cheek a gentle caress, staring at him, wanting to slide his eyelids shut but not daring to touch them. She sensed movement behind her, turned, and saw Father Jerome advance hesitantly, his gaze locked on Finch. The holy man took a few more steps until he was standing right next to her; then he knelt down beside her, softly, his concentration still focused on Finch's dead body.

A shiver of anticipation rolled through her. *What is he doing?* She watched with rapt attention as he leaned in closer, held out his hands over Finch, and shut his eyes in silent prayer. For a fleeting moment, a wild notion rose within her, an impossible, absurd notion—that she was about to witness something miraculous, that Father Jerome was actually going to intervene with the heavens and bring her friend back from the dead. Her heart leapt into her mouth as she sat there, crippled with fear and hope, and she tried to hold on to that crazy possibility as long as she could, flashing to all the other impossible things she'd witnessed over the last few days and trying to convince herself that anything was now possible, clutching at it with raging desperation even as it slipped away as quickly as it had arisen, driven out by the sight of Finch's mangled, still-dead body and the cold logic that had always guided her. A devastating sense of grief soon came rolling back in and numbed every nerve in her body.

She looked over at Father Jerome, who opened his

eyes and made a cross over Finch's head. He turned to face her with a look of profound sadness, and took her hands in his.

"I'm so sorry," he said simply.

His expression, Gracie saw, was also riven with guilt. She nodded, but said nothing. He rose and shuffled back to join his brethren. The abbot and Brother Ameen were standing a few steps back, and as Father Jerome reached them, the abbot put a consoling hand on his shoulder, and he and the younger monk murmured some words to him. Gracie turned to Dalton, then glanced up at the top of the keep. Its sand-colored edge contrasted sharply against the backdrop of clear blue sky. It looked like a close-up one would find on a hip postcard or coffee table book, disconcertingly perfect with its striking pastel colors—too perfect to have hosted such an ugly death.

"How . . . ," she muttered. "How could he fall like that?"

Dalton shook his head slowly, still in shock. "I don't know." His eyes went wide. "Do you think someone out there took a shot at him? Was he shot?"

Gracie looked at him with sudden horror, then bent back down to Finch's side. Dalton bent down with her. She hesitated; then, with trembling fingers, she straightened Finch's arms and legs and, slowly, turned him over. She scanned his front, but couldn't see any bullet wound.

"It doesn't look like it," she said. "I didn't hear a shot. Did you?"

"No." Dalton looked mystified. He turned his gaze back up at the top of the keep. "The lip of that wall up there, it's so low. Maybe he was leaning over to tell us he found it and just . . ." His voice trailed off.

Gracie scanned the ground around them. The sat-phone glinted at her from a few feet away, half-buried in the sand. She scanned wider. Spotted it. A small black box, lying by the base of the keep's wall. Finch's Black-Berry. She got up, retrieved the satphone, then padded over to the wall. She picked up the BlackBerry and just stared at it, brushing the sand off it with her fingers, imagining Finch's last moments in her mind's eye as he found it on the roof and crossed over to the edge for— what, one last look? A wave? She wished there was some way to go back and stop him from climbing up there and having his life grind to a halt in one cruel and sudden moment. But there was no going back. She knew that. She'd seen enough deaths in her years and had learned, long ago, to accept their finality.

"What are we going to do?" she asked. Her eyes, still teary, drifted past Dalton, to Father Jerome, the abbot, and Brother Ameen, who were behind him, and the ma-cabre contingent of monks slightly farther back.

"We've got to go," Dalton told her, his voice hollow.

"What about Finch? We can't leave him here like this."

"We can't take him with us," he replied softly. "We just can't."

After a brief moment, she nodded, still reluctantly but with a hint of clarity seeping back into her. "You're right," she said. She looked over at the abbot. "Can you . . . ?"

Sparing her the need to say it, the abbot nodded sol-emnly. "Of course," he told her. "We'll take care of him until we can send him home . . . properly." He paused, as if to make sure she was all right with that, then glanced over at the Previa and the men huddled around it. She followed his gaze. The faint drone of the radio was still there, threatening like a malevolent siren.

"You should go now," he added, "as planned."

◄◦►

As THEY GATHERED THEIR GEAR, Gracie and Dalton watched as a few monks, aided by the driver, lifted Finch's body onto a makeshift stretcher—an old door that they'd lifted off its hinges—and carried him inside the main chapel. Four other monks picked up the rest of the news crew's gear, and the small troupe followed the abbot out of the sun-soaked courtyard and into the cool darkness of the monastery.

They trudged past the entrance of the Church of the Holy Virgin and the refectory, until they reached an ancient, unlit stairwell.

"You'll need the lamps from here on," the abbot instructed. The monks lit up a succession of small camping gas lanterns, casting a cool white pallor across the stone passage. Slowly, they descended a narrow staircase, kicking up a fine mist of pungent dust, and landed in another passage that led them past a couple of olive-oil cellars, where some of the world's earliest dated books—brought to the monastery by monks fleeing religious persecution in Syria and Baghdad in the eighth century—had been discovered in the mid-1800s, and on to the entrance of Saint Bishoi's cave.

The abbot pushed the crumbling timber door open and led them in. The cave was dark and narrow, no bigger than a small bedroom. Gracie held her lantern up for a closer look. The cave's floor was begrimed with dirt, its ceiling vaulted with rough-hewn stone. She saw nothing to support the legend she'd read about during the downtime on their journey over—the legend that Bishoi's devotion to his faith was so powerful that he used to tie his hair to a chain that dangled from the roof of the cave, to make sure he didn't fall asleep for days on end while awaiting the vision of Christ that he was praying for.

"It's this way," the abbot said.

Gracie swung her lantern in his direction. In a corner

of the cave, to the left of the doorway, skulked another rotting timber door, this one even smaller than the one leading into the cave. Two monks helped the abbot pull it open, smothering the tight space with more dust. Gracie edged closer and spotted the entrance to the narrow, low tunnel. It was no more than five feet high and three across, a black hole that sucked in the dim gaslight just as it had barely made it inside.

"God be with you," the abbot told Father Jerome as, one by one, they dropped their heads and clambered into the tight passage. Gracie was the last one in. She hesitated for a moment, still choking inside at the thought of abandoning Finch, before nodding a parting half smile at the abbot, clenching her jaw with stoic acceptance, and disappearing into the tunnel's oppressive darkness.

Chapter 52

Bedford, Massachusetts

Matt slowed the Camry right down as the woods on either side of the two-lane road gave way to a handful of low office buildings that dozed behind snow-dusted lawns.

He slid a sideways glance at Jabba and said, "Heads up," before scanning the surroundings.

There were no other cars on the road, and the area seemed very sedate. They cruised past the entrance to a small air force base that was tucked away to their right. A lone, bored guard manned its flimsy red-and-white barrier. The base shared its runway with the adjacent civilian airfield, but little else. From what they could see, it seemed austere and outdated, a stark contrast to the two swanky flight services buildings farther down the road that catered to the well-heeled clientele who favored flying their private jets into Hanscom Field to avoid the air traffic delays and heavy-handed security at Boston's Logan Airport—the twin wonders of twenty-first-century air travel.

The approach road led to the civilian air terminal, which wasn't exactly a hotbed of activity either. There, it doglegged left, then looped back on itself, ringing a disproportionately large, trapezoidal, asphalted central space that served as the visitors' parking lot. Matt counted less than a dozen cars parked there, and none that he recognized.

The hangars and planes were to his right, on the outside of the ring road, across the street from the parking lot. The high-pitched whine of a taxiing jet could be heard behind one of the two main hangars. Given that we lived in a post-9/11 world, the low-level security was surprising. A pretty basic chain-link fence, seven feet high at best, with an extra foot on top canted outward, was all that separated the road from the apron. You could practically reach through the fence and touch the planes that were dotted around the hangar area. As he drove around the return leg of the road, Matt saw two entry points to the airfield. Again, surprisingly basic: chain-link rolling fences, two cars wide, that slid sideways on small metal wheels. No guardhouses. No guards. Just a swipe-card reader and an intercom on a stalk for those who weren't regular visitors.

"Check it again," Matt told Jabba. "We need a tighter fix on the bastard."

"I don't know, dude," Jabba replied warily. "We're too close."

"Just don't break your forty-second rule and we'll be fine, right?"

Jabba studied him with a wry look. "You think that cocky optimism of yours might have anything to do with your getting that priority pass to prison?"

"Nah. Back then, I was just reckless," Matt quipped.

"Didn't really need to know that right now," Jabba groaned as he fired up his laptop and phone. He zoomed right in on the linked Google map, then killed the connection. The tracker was about four hundred yards ahead, at the far edge of the apron, just before the tree line, beyond the second hangar and what looked like a smaller outbuilding.

"What's he doing in there?" Jabba asked.

"Either dropping someone off or, more likely, meeting someone who's flying in." Matt twisted around, scanning the perimeter. He glimpsed a small private jet crossing from behind one hangar to another. It was rolling toward the tracker's position.

Matt's pulse quickened with a jolt of urgency. His instincts told him he needed to be in there—fast. He frowned at the near gate, giving his options a quick run-through, then saw the other gate, the one farther down and closer to the tracker, open up. He tensed—but it wasn't the Merc, or the 300C, coming out. Just a silver Town and Country minivan, idling as the gate rolled back.

He nudged the throttle, propelling the Camry forward, its narrow tires giving out a tortured squeal. The car accelerated down the ring road, the airfield's perimeter fence to its right. He was eighty yards away when the gate had rolled back far enough for the minivan to nose forward. Sixty yards away when the minivan had cleared the gate, turned right, and was driving off. Forty yards away when the gate had clicked to a stop and started to roll back. Twenty yards away when the gate was halfway shut—and closing. Which, given that it was two cars wide, meant the math wasn't on his side.

Matt didn't lift his foot. Fifteen yards from the gate, he twisted the steering wheel left to send the car swerving wide before flicking it right again while giving the gas pedal a violent kick. The Camry's soft shock absorbers went into cardiac arrest as the rear end swung around and the small car leaned dangerously to the left, the momentum shifting its entire weight onto its two left tires—but Matt got what he wanted. The car had fishtailed into a position perpendicular to the gate and was now rushing toward it. Matt kept his foot down and threaded the

Camry in, flying past the gate's fixed post, while scraping the car's right side against the incoming edge.

They were in.

◄◦►

THE BULLET WATCHED attentively as the Citation X veered left on the wide apron and pulled up between the out-building and the edge of the tree line, by the parked Merc and the 300C.

The X was a fabulous piece of engineering. Its Rolls-Royce turbofan engines took it to within a whisker of Mach 1, which meant it could fly twelve passengers from New York to L.A. in under four hours and in the height of luxury. Little wonder, Maddox mused, that it was the private-jet-du-jour for the lucky Forbes-level big hitters who weren't even aware there was a credit crunch going on: the biggest Hollywood stars, free-spending Russian tycoons—and evangelist preachers. Humble servants of the Lord like Kenneth and Gloria Copeland, who got their megachurch's army of faithful followers to stump up twenty million dollars for their customized X to help them follow God's personal directive and spread His word more efficiently.

The Bullet had used the spot before: It was tucked away at the far end of the airfield, away from prying eyes. It was well suited for whisking certain camera-shy clients in and out of the city unnoticed—usually, postoperative or postscandal celebrities, or masters of the universe putting together sensitive transactions.

In this case, things were different.

As the plane's tail-mounted engines whined down, a voice crackled in his earpiece.

"A white Camry just snuck in through the south gate," the operative said. "I think it's our boys."

Maddox casually raised his wrist to his mouth and

spoke clearly into his cuff mike. "Got it. Stay with them. And take them down once the package is in the car."

He stepped closer to the plane as its door snapped open, his eyes casually sweeping the environment. He didn't see anything suspicious, and turned his attention back to the plane, where Rebecca Rydell and her two bodyguards were now coming down the stairs.

◄o►

MATT TURNED LEFT and hugged the back of the first hangar. He reached its corner and stopped, then edged forward slowly, looking out. He whirred his window open, and he could hear the plane in the distance, powering down, but he couldn't see it, so he feathered the throttle again and crossed over to the second hangar. From what he could see on the frozen map on the laptop's screen, there was nothing but open tarmac from there to the tracker's position.

He edged forward. In the distance, about a hundred yards ahead, was the outbuilding, a low, concrete structure with no windows. He could see the tail of the jet sticking out from behind it, as well as the tailgate of a black Dodge Durango. A couple of private jets and a handful of smaller propeller-driven planes sat idly between the hangar and the outbuilding. They provided some kind of cover—which he needed if they were going to get closer without being spotted.

He decided to cut across and get behind the outbuilding. From there, they would be able to see what was going on—and, if feasible, Matt could make his move. He pulled out his handgun. Sat it on his lap. Noticed Jabba looking at him warily.

"You do realize it's empty, right?" Jabba said.

"They don't know that," Matt replied. "Besides, I don't plan on needing it."

Which, judging from Jabba's expression, didn't seem to reassure him much.

"You can get out here and wait for me, if you want," Matt told him.

Jabba looked left and right at the deserted area behind the hangar, then turned back to Matt. "I think I'll stick around. It's not exactly Grand Central Terminal out here, you know what I mean?"

Matt nodded and eased the car forward.

They shadowed the parked aircraft and pulled in behind the outbuilding. It was a power substation and had a low metal fence around it. Matt nosed forward, just enough to give them a view of the plane without exposing any more than the side of the car's A-pillar.

Two men were escorting a young, tanned blonde off the plane.

Jabba leaned forward, his jaw dropping with surprise. "Whoa."

Matt slid a reproachful glance at him. "Not now, tiger—"

"No, dude," Jabba interrupted urgently. "She's Rydell's daughter."

Matt studied her with more interest. She stepped off the stairs and glanced around uncertainly as the two men led her over to Maddox, who spoke to her briefly before leading them to the waiting Durango. As he opened the SUV's rear door, he glanced across the tarmac and over in Matt's direction, and their eyes met. Matt flinched slightly, but Maddox didn't. In fact, he didn't seem rattled at all. Which, given that he'd spotted them, could only mean one thing.

The hard steel muzzle that suddenly nudged Matt just above his ear confirmed it.

Chapter 53

Deir Al-Anba Bishoi Monastery,
Wadi Natrun, Egypt

Half an hour after climbing into the tunnel, Gracie,
Dalton, Father Jerome, Brother Ameen, and their
four black-robed sherpas all emerged into a musty old
cellar at the neighboring monastery. A few anxious
monks, led by the local abbot, were there to greet them.

Gracie laid her backpack down, dusted herself off, and
stretched her back as the abbot fussed over Father Jerome. He looked haunted. A compact, elderly man by
the name of Antonius, the abbot seemed completely
awed by the miraculous monk's presence as well as rattled by the turn of events—which was expected. She
watched his wrinkled fingers as they trembled while
clasping Father Jerome's hand tightly. "Praise God that
you're all right," he was telling him as he fired off a nervous prattle of words and led them up a stone stairwell
and into the monastery's refectory.

They were offered cold water and took a moment to
catch their breath before heading out into balmy daylight. The monastery had the same beige, Tatooine-like
feel as the one they had just left, and although it was
smaller, it was no less venerable. Many Coptic popes had
started off as monks there, including the current pope,
Shenouda III. It also enjoyed its share of religious myth.

The body of Saint Bishoi himself—his name was the Coptic word for "sublime"—was kept there, sealed inside a wooden container that was wrapped in clear plastic. He was believed to be lying perfectly preserved and uncorrupted by time, even today, a claim that was hard to verify given that the container was locked away in a coffin and the faithful told stories of his reaching out from inside it and shaking their hands, seemingly undeterred by the limitations of physics. The magic wasn't limited to him either. Nearby and similarly sealed were the remains of another monk by the name of Paul, a fellow ascetic who was rumored to have committed suicide—successfully—seven times.

They reached Yusuf's brother-in-law's taxi, a tired white VW Sharan people carrier. It was waiting for them in the shade by a small multidomed structure, Pope Shenouda's occasional retreat.

"Are you sure it's safe out there?" Gracie asked the abbot.

"It's relatively quiet here," Antonius informed her. "They're not interested in us. So far." He smiled uncomfortably. "Come, I'll show you."

They left the driver and the monks to pile the gear into the car and followed the abbot across the courtyard and up a maze of narrow outdoor stairs that snaked up to the top of the wall.

"Have a look," the abbot told them, "but stay low—just in case."

Gracie and Dalton rose slowly from their crouched positions. The familiar carpet of cars and trucks covered the plain between the two monasteries, but with one crucial difference. All attention seemed focused away from them, toward the monastery they'd just left. Which meant they had a reasonable chance of sneaking out unnoticed.

They climbed back down, thanked the abbot, and got into the car. This time, Dalton and Gracie sat on either side of Father Jerome, while Brother Ameen rode shotgun. Gracie felt a bubble of apprehension as she watched the gate creak open. She steeled herself and straightened up in her seat as the driver gave the throttle a gentle nudge and the Sharan rumbled out into the desert.

There were a few scattered cars and trucks parked on either side of the dusty trail that led away from the monastery. A few men loitered by each cluster of vehicles, talking, smoking, waiting. As their car got closer to the first group, Gracie turned to Father Jerome and raised his cassock's hood over his head, shielding him from view. Yusuf's brother-in-law kept calm, trying not to draw any attention to them as the Sharan cruised past slowly without eliciting more than a casual glance.

Gracie let out a small breath of relief. There weren't many cars or trucks up ahead. A few more minutes, she guessed, and they'd be free and clear. They were less than a hundred yards out from the monastery's gate when the road doglegged to the left by an old crumbling wall and a clutch of palm trees. A few more cars were parked there, with another bunch of men clustered against the wall, seemingly oblivious to the sun. Gracie felt a flutter in her gut as the driver slowed down to thread through the haphazardly strewn cars, which he managed without fuss—only to find a narrow ditch cutting across them. A lone man was walking toward them, alongside the trail, heading for the trees. Gracie spotted him and tensed up. She tried not to look over at him as the driver slowed right down to a crawl. They were halfway across the ditch when—just as Gracie feared—the passing man drew alongside them, and just as he glanced in, Father Jerome turned and looked sideways, casually, in his direction. It was enough.

The man reacted as if he'd been slapped. His relaxed features took on a sudden alarmed scowl as he put both hands against the car's side window and leaned right in against the glass, trying to see in, sidestepping alongside them.

"He's made us," Gracie exclaimed. "Get us out of here—now."

The driver glanced back, saw the man moving with them, and nudged the gas pedal. The Sharan's engine whined as the rear tires bounced across the ditch and kept going. The man tried to keep up, but couldn't, and quickly fell back into the car's dusty trail. Gracie watched him drift away, but she knew they weren't out of danger yet. Sure enough, she saw the man turn away and start running toward the cluster of men by the trees, waving his hands feverishly, trying to attract their attention. And then, he disappeared. She wasn't sure what had happened, as her view was partially obstructed by the gear in the back of the car and the dust the car was kicking up behind it, but one moment he was there, running and waving and shouting, and then he was gone. She thought she saw him clasp his hands to his head and fall to the ground, almost as if a sudden spasm had crippled him, but she wasn't sure. They weren't about to stop and find out. The driver kept his foot pressed against the pedal, and fifteen minutes later, they were on the highway with a seemingly clear run to the airport.

And then Gracie's satphone rang.

She'd been steeling herself to make that call to Ogilvy, to tell him about Finch, and thought he'd beat her to it. But as she reached for the phone, she didn't recognize the number it was showing. She only recognized the prefix as that of an American cell phone.

"Hello?" she queried curiously.

"Miss Logan?" the voice boomed back. "We haven't

met yet, but my name is Darby. Reverend Nelson Darby. And I think I can help you."

◄o►

FOX TWO WATCHED the white people carrier streak away down the desert trail, then turned his binoculars back to the stricken man. He was still on the ground, writhing with pain, his hands pressed against his ears. Fox Two relaxed somewhat.

It had been a close call—but they'd been prepared.

He knew the agitator would be down for a while. They'd hit him with a potent blast, just to make sure. Fox Two was surprised the man hadn't lost consciousness, though he knew he still might. Main thing was, he wasn't going anywhere or saying anything. Not for a while, anyway. Which was all the time they needed.

He raised a finger and spun it around, giving his men the signal to move out. Swiftly and silently, they powered down the LRAD and covered it up before pulling away and heading out as innocuously as they'd arrived, shadowing the van from a safe distance and looking forward to finally going home.

Chapter 54

Bedford, Massachusetts

The man kept the gun pressed against Matt's temple. "Easy." His voice was flat, his arm stable. With his left hand, he reached down to Matt's lap and pulled out his gun, which he stuffed under his belt. Matt cursed inwardly. He'd been so focused on watching the plane and Maddox that he hadn't noticed the man sneaking up on them from the back. Another guy—same general appearance, dark suit, white shirt, no tie, granite dark shades—appeared a few yards ahead, rounding the other side of the outbuilding, moving toward Jabba's side of the car. He also had a gun out, and it was also leveled at Matt's head. A big gun. A Para-Ordnance P14. It looked heavy. It looked like it could stop a charging rhino in its tracks. Which it could.

Matt's mind rocketed into a manic good news/bad news sift-through. Maddox's drones couldn't really kill them there and then; the airport authorities had to have a record of their being there. There had to be some CCTV cameras scattered around that would have recorded their presence. It was altogether too messy for them, too risky, had to be. Which definitely went under the good news column. But they had plenty of other options. The key was getting him and Jabba off the airport grounds, quietly.

They'd either lead them to their cars, or—the cleaner, more obvious option—one of the drones, or both of them more likely, would get into the Camry and lead him and Jabba, at gunpoint, to somewhere nice and quiet where they could pump a few bullets into them and leave their decomposing bodies for some hapless camper to discover. Which definitely went under the bad news column. Matt knew that if he let one or both of the drones into the car, he probably wouldn't be running these good news/bad news exercises ever again. Which in itself wasn't a bad thing, but he did feel like sticking around for other, less life-threatening, pursuits.

It was simple. He couldn't let them into the car.

Which meant he probably had no more than a couple of seconds left to do something about it.

Matt's hands and feet moved like lightning. His left hand shot up and grabbed the man's right wrist—his gun hand—and slammed it forward, crushing it against the inside of the A-pillar. A shot erupted out of it—a deafeningly loud explosion inside the car, a mere eighteen inches from Matt's face. He felt like he'd slammed face-first into a swimming pool. The shot's sound wave hit him like a lead fist that pounded both ears and numbed them into a soundless, disconcerting stillness in the same split second that the .45 ACP round obliterated the rearview mirror and punched through the windshield, a clean, supersonic jab that didn't shatter it but only spiderwebbed it around the bullet's clean, oval-shaped hole of an exit point.

Matt thought he heard Jabba yell out, but he couldn't be sure. He felt like he was still underwater, and besides, he wasn't focusing on him. The other guy was more his concern. So in the same instant that he shoved the first shooter's hand forward and jammed it against the windshield pillar, his right foot stamped on the gas pedal and his right hand twisted the wheel to the right. The car lunged forward and slewed right—straight at the second shooter. The guy to his left jerked backward, but Matt had his elbow locked and managed to keep the guy's gun hand pinned against the pillar long enough for the car to cover the three yards to the second shooter and slam into him before he had the chance to loose a shot, crushing him against the low metal fence that jutted out from the side of the outbuilding. The shooter's midsection was pulverized—his eyes popped wide and he let out a piercing yelp of agony before a gush of blood overwhelmed his vocal cords and came spewing out of his mouth and onto the Camry's virgin white hood.

Matt still had the first guy to deal with. For a second, the guy's face went rigid with shock at seeing his co-worker truncated; then he was all crunched up with renewed determination as he fought Matt's grip and struggled to angle his gun inward. Another round exploded—again mere inches from Matt's face, again deafening, dizzying, like a baseball bat to the ears—and whizzed past Jabba's face before spinning out through his open window. Matt saw the guy reaching down with his free hand—his left hand—moving to pull the gun he'd taken off Matt from under his belt, and Matt spun the wheel to the right—once, twice, full lock, using one arm—then dropped his hand down to the gearshift, slammed it into reverse, and mashed the gas pedal again. The car leapt back, courtesy of the standard tight gearing in reverse, and with the steering locked all the way to the right, the Camry's front swung sideways and outward violently and slammed into the first shooter. He was thrown back and, with his hand still pinned to the pillar, tripped over himself and stumbled to the ground—with the car still arcing backward. The Camry's rear end crunched against the outbuilding's concrete wall just as its left front wheel rode over the fallen shooter's ankles, tearing up bone and cartilage in its wake. The man howled with pain and his fingers let go of the gun, which tumbled into Matt's foot well. Matt threw the car back into drive and howled away in a squeal of rubber.

He threw a glance at the plane—the two bodyguards who were with Rydell's daughter were rushing toward him, guns drawn. He floored the accelerator again and tore back up the apron, found the gate through which he'd sneaked in—it was closed—plowed right through it and tore down Hanscom Drive and into the shelter of its tree line.

"They knew we were coming," he yelled at Jabba.

"What? How do you know that?"

"They knew. Maddox knew we were coming. They were waiting for us."

"But . . ." Jabba's mouth was stumbling for words, still in shock from the bullets slicing through the air right in front of him.

"Your phone—they're reading it," Matt stated flatly.

"No way," Jabba objected. "I haven't been keeping it on long enough—"

"I'm telling you they're reading it," Matt shot back angrily.

"There's no way, man." He held his iPhone up, examining it curiously. "No way they can lock onto it that fast, and I haven't had it on long enough for them to download any spyware onto it and—"

Matt just snatched it out of his fingers, and was about to flick it out the window when Jabba grabbed it with both hands.

"No," he yelled, "don't."

Matt looked at him angrily.

Jabba wrenched it out of his fingers and took it back.

"My whole fucking life's in there, man. You can't just throw it away like that. Just give me a second."

He looked around, checked the car's side pockets, the ashtray, then opened the glove compartment and rifled through it. He found some paperwork in a plastic sleeve—service documents and a receipt—held together by the very thing he was looking for, a paper clip. He plucked it off, straightened it, and stuck one of its ends into the tiny hole on the top face of the phone. The SIM card tray popped out. He pulled the card out of its slot and showed it to Matt.

"No SIM card. No signal. For all intents and purposes, the phone's dead. Okay?"

Matt frowned at him for a moment, then shrugged and nodded. "Okay." He felt his pulse ratchet its way back down. He had probably just killed two men. Which should have felt bad, but—strangely—didn't. It was, he told himself, a simple matter of kill or be killed. But he knew he'd have to be more careful if he didn't want to fall on the wrong side of that equation the next time it presented itself.

Jabba sat quietly for a moment, just staring ahead, then asked, "What are we going to do now?"

"What do you think?" Matt grumbled.

Jabba studied him, then nodded stoically. "Rydell?"

"Rydell," Matt simply confirmed.

Chapter 55

Wadi Natrun, Egypt

"I understand you're looking to get out of there in a hurry," Darby said in a casual tone.

Gracie stared ahead quizzically. "I'm sorry?"

Dalton leaned out and mouthed her a question. She gave him an uncertain glance back.

"You need a ride, Miss Logan," Darby observed somewhat smugly. "And I'm calling to offer you one."

Her mind scrambled to make sense of the call. She recognized the name, of course. She couldn't exactly count herself among the pastor's fans. Far from it, truth be told. But that didn't really matter now, nor did it tell her what she needed to know. "How did . . . ?" she stammered. "Who gave you this number?"

"Oh, I have a lot of friends, Miss Logan. Well-connected friends. I'm sure you know that. But that's beside the point, which is that you need to get yourself and my most esteemed brother in Christ out of danger. And I can help you do that. Are you interested?"

She tried to park his offer to one side while she dealt with the competing bits of information that were clamoring for attention and tried to figure out where they stood. Finch had called Ogilvy. The news director was supposed to be arranging a plane, but she hadn't heard back. Hell, she hadn't yet had time to tell him about Finch's death. She didn't even know what Ogilvy had told Finch exactly—whether or not he'd be able to get them a plane and, if so, how soon. She didn't even know where they were headed. The embassy in Cairo? The airport? They didn't have a specific destination—not in Egypt, and not beyond either. The overriding concern had been to put as many miles as possible between them and the mobs outside the monastery. The rest hadn't been mapped out. It was all happening too fast, and besides, that was Finch's domain, and he wasn't there to sort it out.

She needed to know more. "What do you have in mind?"

The reverend breathed a smile down the phone. "First things first. Father Jerome is with you, right?"

"Of course," she answered, knowing that was all he was interested in.

"Can you make it out of the monastery safely?"

Gracie decided to play it out on a need-to-know basis. "Yes," she answered flatly. "We have a way out."

"Okay, good. What I need you to do is get to the airport in Alexandria."

"Why Alexandria?" Gracie queried.

Dalton gave her another mystified glance. She flicked him a hold-on gesture.

"It's as close to you as Cairo is, but it's quieter," Darby told her. "More manageable. I'll have a plane on the ground in under two hours. How soon can you get there?"

Gracie thought about it. Alexandria made sense. Smaller airport, off the beaten path, far fewer commercial flights, far less chance of being spotted. "Shouldn't take too long," she replied. "We can be there before that."

"Perfect," Darby shot back. "I'll give you my number. Call me when you're on your way."

"Where are you thinking of flying us to?" she asked, feeling a stab of discomfort at the idea of giving up control and putting herself and Father Jerome in the reverend's hands.

"Where else, Miss Logan?" he boomed. "The one place we know we can keep the good Father safe." He paused, then proudly announced, "Home. You're coming home, Miss Logan. To God's own country. And you can take it from me, the people out here are going to be overjoyed to see you."

Chapter 56

Brookline, Massachusetts

Darkness was moving in impatiently, crowding the low winter sun against the horizon as Matt slowed down and pulled over by the side of the road.

The area was heavily wooded, the traffic sparse. Just ahead, two waist-high stone posts marked the entrance to the municipal service center, which was nestled between the forest of Dane Park and the thickets of oak trees that shielded the Putterham Meadows Golf Course. From where he was parked, Matt could make out the low, warehouselike office-and-garage structure of the Brookline Municipal Service Center, set way back from the road, the drive leading up to it lined with parked cars and lingering thin patches of dirty snow. There wasn't much going on in terms of activity, which suited Matt just fine.

They hadn't driven there directly from Hanscom Field. First priority had been dumping the battered, bloodstained Camry. Which wasn't too much of a problem. They'd ducked into a mall, pulled up to a far corner of its parking lot, and exchanged the car for an equally uninspiring, decade-old, dark polo green Pontiac Bonneville that didn't look like it had that much longer to live anyway.

Matt had wanted to get a few things first—more bullets for the handgun he'd taken off the shooter at the airfield, most important. His options were limited. He couldn't exactly walk into a gun store, not in his current wanted and bruised state. Jabba didn't possess an FOID card, so he couldn't buy them for him either. So they'd rushed down to Quincy, where they'd hooked up with a deeply concerned Sanjay, who'd met them away from the 7-Eleven, at his place. He came through for Matt with two boxes of Pow'RBall rounds, some fresh gauze dressing for his wound, and some cash. Matt had wanted to ask him for another handgun, or maybe his rifle—Sanjay kept a loaded Remington 870 Breacher behind his counter that would have been good to have in hand, given what Matt was planning. But he knew he couldn't ask his friend for it, not in these circumstances.

They'd also used Sanjay's computer to look up Rydell's home address—he lived in a big house in Brookline, where his planning applications to add to the existing house had caused a bit of a stink. Matt also got a refresher course in what Rydell actually looked like. Once that was done, Matt and Jabba had driven across to Brookline and scouted the service center and the area around Rydell's house before staking out the house itself.

They didn't have to wait too long.

Rydell's chauffeur-driven Lexus had pulled into the narrow lane that led to his house and to a couple of other mansions shortly after five o'clock. Matt had thought about making his move there and then, but decided against it. The Bonneville wasn't as meek as the Camry, but it was still weak on muscle, and the bodyguard and the heavyweight riding shotgun looked to be slightly too much to take on, given Matt's condition and whom he had riding shotgun next to him.

They'd watched the house for a while, making sure

Rydell wasn't going anywhere; then Jabba had stepped out of the car to keep an eye on the house while Matt climbed behind the wheel.

"Remember," Matt told him, "if this goes wrong, don't go to the cops. Don't trust anyone. Just do what you thought was the right play right at the beginning, remember?"

"You mean, make like D. B. Cooper?"

"Yep."

Jabba looked at him and shrugged. "Just make sure it doesn't go wrong then, all right? I'm already missing my stuff as it is."

Matt smiled. "I guess I'll see you in a little while."

He'd then left him there and looped back to the service center, where he was presently parked.

He double-checked the handgun, then tucked it in under his coat. He emptied one of the boxes of rounds into his pocket, checked the road ahead and the mirror, then got out and walked up the drive to the service center.

He'd taken some more painkillers, which had numbed the wound in his side, and found that he was able to walk halfway decently, in a way that didn't scream out "walking wounded." He followed the curving drive, past the parked cars, past the entrance to the reception area and offices, and past the building's "employees only" door. A couple of guys stepped out, their shift finished, heading home. He met their casual gazes with a small bob of acknowledgment, muttered a laconic "How's it going?" which only elicited a similarly muttered reply, and didn't break step until he reached the garage area out back.

There were several trucks parked in there, side by side, the wide letters on their grilles announcing they were Macks. Matt looked around. A couple of mechanics were working on a truck that was parked thirty or so yards away. One of them glanced over. Matt gave him a relaxed half wave and a nod, as if his being there was the most natural thing in the world, then walked toward the back wall of the garage with as much of a purposeful step as he could muster, so as not to appear out of place in any way. From the corner of his eye, he saw that the mechanic went back to work. Matt checked the back wall. He noticed a whiteboard with some shift lists marked up on it, then spotted the metal, wall-mounted box where the keys were normally kept. It wasn't locked, which wasn't a surprise—garbage trucks usually ranked pretty low on the "most stolen vehicles" lists, which probably had a lot to do with the fact that they were garbage trucks.

He quickly matched the number on the tag of one of the keys with the last three digits of the license plate on one of the trucks, and gingerly picked the keys off their hook. He climbed into the big truck's cabin, gave the surroundings another quick once-over, then stroked the engine to life. The big cab rumbled under him. He pressed down on the heavy clutch, selected first using the thin, long gearshift, and teased the accelerator. The hydraulic brakes hissed loudly and the truck nudged forward. The same mechanic looked over again, an uncertain expression creasing his face. Matt stopped the truck long enough to give him another friendly nod, then thought better of it and leaned out the window.

"You almost done there? Steve said he was having trouble getting this one into third," he bluffed matter-of-factly, using a name he'd noticed on the shift list.

The guy looked at him a bit perplexed, but before he could say anything, Matt added, "Clutch might need some work. I'll be back in ten," and gave him a short wave before pulling away.

He checked in the side mirror as he turned out of the

garage. The man looked his way for a second before shrugging and getting back to what he was doing.

A moment later, Matt was turning onto the main road and guiding the lumbering orange behemoth toward the exclusive enclave that surrounded Sargent Pond.

◄◦►

FEELING NUMB as he sat in the book-lined study of his mansion, Larry Rydell stared into his tumbler of Scotch and fumed in silence.

Those bastards, he seethed, flinching at the thought of any harm coming to his daughter. *If she so much as gets a scratch,* he flared, a surge of blood flooding his temples . . . but it was pointless. He knew he couldn't do anything about it.

He sagged in his chair and glared at his glass. He'd never felt as helpless in his life.

With his fortune and his power, he could and did take on the most aggressive hedge fund or shareholder revolt without blinking. He'd had heated debates in Senate chambers that didn't ruffle him in the least. He'd reached a point of his life where he felt he was untouchable. But he was powerless to deal with these . . . thugs. That was what they were, pure and simple. Thugs. Out to pervert his vision, to take his idea and twist it around and use it for . . . what, exactly?

It didn't make sense.

Much as he ground and turned over what Drucker had said, it didn't make sense. They were alike—all of them—when it came to what they believed in. They viewed the world the same way. They saw the risks facing the world—and those facing America—in the same light. They shared the same frustrations with some deeply entrenched aspects of the world's, and the country's, mindset.

And yet they were doing this? They'd created a fake Messiah? An envoy from God? One whose presence would reinforce and vindicate the mass delusion most of the world was suffering from?

It doesn't make sense, he thought again. And yet they were doing it.

He'd seen it.

Drucker had confirmed it.

They were actually doing it.

The backstabbing bastards.

His mind latched onto Rebecca's face, on the last time he'd seen her, shortly before her ill-fated trip to Costa Careyes. He'd wanted to join her there for the holidays—they really hadn't spent much time together, ever, not with everything he wanted to achieve in life, and it was something he now deeply regretted. But he hadn't been able to join her. Not with all this going on. Not with the biggest undertaking of his life in full swing. And, bless her, she hadn't voiced her disappointment. She never did. She'd gotten used to having a mythical dad, in the good and bad sense. Which was something he'd fix, he now thought—if he ever got the chance.

He had to find her.

He had to get her out, put her out of their reach, tuck her away somewhere safe. Nothing else mattered. Even saving the planet now paled into insignificance. He had to get her out of their hands. Then—and only then—he had to try to stop this. He had to find a way to kill it off, to shut it down before it got too big.

But how? He didn't have anyone else to call. He didn't exactly have an "A-Team" tab in his Rolodex. For years, he'd entrusted all his security requirements—personal and professional—to that rattlesnake Maddox. The security guards "watching over him" right now, at his house. His driver-slash-bodyguard. The vetting of his pilot, of the

staff on his yacht. The corporate security at his companies. E-mail, phones. Everything was covered by one
firm. Maddox's. On Drucker's recommendation. "Keep
it all under one roof" had been his advice. "Use someone you can trust. One of us," he'd said.

Clearly, Maddox was one of "us." Rydell himself, he'd
now found out, wasn't.

He felt like a fool.

They had him covered.

He'd been played. From the beginning.

He stared angrily at the heavy tumbler, then flung it
at the wall, by the huge, stone fireplace. It exploded and
rained shards of glass on the carpet. Just then, he heard a
rising whine at the edge of his hearing, the sound of a
large engine straining. Curious, he edged over to the
window and looked out, down the drive that sloped and
curved gently to the mansion's entrance gate.

◄o►

MATT SPOTTED JABBA as he approached the turnoff into
Sargent Lane. Jabba gave him the all-clear, a small
thumbs-up, before darting back into the trees. Matt
nodded, turned into the lane, and floored the gas pedal.

The Mack's muscular, three-hundred-bull-horsepower
engine growled as it raced ahead, straining with each additional mile-per-hour of speed that it managed to add.
Before long, the mansion's entrance gate appeared up
ahead. Matt stayed in gear, red-lining the engine, not
wanting to shift into a higher gear. He wasn't exactly flying, but that didn't matter. Speed wasn't what Matt was
after here.

It was bulk.

He reached the gate and wrenched the oversized,
horizontal steering wheel left with both arms, fighting
the lateral pull from the truck's tires. He didn't lift his

foot off the pedal. The truck screeched and leaned a few degrees sideways before its fifteen tons of solid steel plowed into the gate and obliterated it into toothpicks.

The truck charged up the driveway, its heavy footprint scattering gravel and leaving twin ruts in its wake. Matt could see the house through a scattering of stately trees, looming at the top of a manicured, landscaped rise. It was a Georgian revival mansion with separate wings jutting out of the main house and a multicar garage tucked off to one side. It had a circular gravel drive outside the main entrance. There was no sign of the Lexus or the muscle. Yet.

He aimed the truck right at the entrance and kept his foot down. Just as he reached it, one of the heavies—he thought he recognized him as the guy who'd been riding shotgun in Rydell's Lexus—rushed out of the house. His eyes went wide as he spotted the charging garbage truck, and he was already pulling his gun out from an under-shoulder holster.

Matt didn't bother going around the drive. He just beelined for the house's entrance. The truck bounced over the central floral bed and slammed into the body-guard before he had a chance to fire off a single round. The man splattered against the panoramic windshield, staining it with blood before the truck squashed him against the front door as it bulldozed its way into the house.

Brick, timber, and glass exploded inward as the Mack thundered ahead and came to a rest inside the house's cavernous foyer. Matt kept the engine running as he pulled his gun out and climbed from the cabin just as another heavy appeared from a side room, dumbstruck and gun drawn. Matt had the advantage of surprise and blew him away with two rounds to his chest. Matt stepped away from the truck, sizing up what was left of the house's entrance hall, and yelled, "Rydell."

Like a killer-bot on a mission, he advanced through the house, using his handgun like a divining rod, looking for his quarry. He checked the main living room, then a media room next to that, and was on his way into what looked like the kitchen area when a large double door in a hallway to his right opened up and Rydell's head popped out.

The man looked stunned and confused. Matt recognized him immediately. He looked more gaunt than the photos Jabba had shown Matt on his phone's browser, but it was definitely him.

Matt raised his gun, rushed to him, and grabbed him by his shoulder.

"Let's go."

He manhandled him back toward the truck, jabbing the gun into his back. Rydell's mouth dropped when he saw the truck squatting in the entrance hall, surrounded by debris, a twelve-foot-square gash eaten out of the house's front façade. As Matt nudged Rydell forward, he heard some approaching footsteps, turned, and saw another guard rushing at them. By now, the adrenaline coursing through him was in control, and Matt was riding its autopilot of heightened awareness. He swung the gun away from Rydell, aimed, and squeezed, dropping the man to the floor.

"Is that all you've got, huh?" he barked furiously at Rydell. "Is that the best you can do?"

Before the shell-shocked Rydell could answer, Matt grabbed him by the neck, pushed him to the back of the truck, and shoved him against it. Matt glared at him and pointed at its rear-loading bay.

"Get in," he ordered.

Rydell stared at him, terror-stricken. "In there?"

"Get in," Matt roared, raising the gun so it hovered a few inches from the bridge of Rydell's nose.

Rydell studied him for a beat, then climbed in. Matt glared at him crouched there, cowering, and hit the compacting switch. The hydraulic paddle churned to life and inched its way down, swinging over Rydell and herding him into the belly of the truck.

Matt hit the switch again to block the paddle in position, sealing the hold, then made his way back through the debris to the truck's cabin and climbed in. Another man appeared, another drone in a dark suit with a big gun aimed at Matt's face. He fired, the bullets punching through the windshield and hammering the back of the cabin behind Matt's head. Matt ducked, crunched the gear lever into reverse and floored the accelerator. The truck extricated itself from the battered house and emerged onto the gravel drive again. The man followed, still shooting, his bullets digging themselves into the truck's thick carcass. He wasn't doing much damage—the way the truck was built, it was like trying to stop a rhino with a blowpipe. Matt swung the orange beast around and slammed it into first. The truck's smokestack let out an angry bellow of black smoke—its engine probably hadn't ever had such a workout—before hurtling down the drive and out onto the narrow lane again.

He was halfway to the main road when the first of the armed response cars appeared, a yellow SUV with a blaring siren and a rack of spinning lights on its roof. The lane wasn't wide enough for both, and its driver knew it. He didn't stand a chance. He swerved just as the big Mack reached him, but there was nowhere for him to go. The truck plowed into the side of the SUV and flicked it out of its way and into the trees like a hockey puck. The second armed response car didn't fare much better. Matt encountered it just before the intersection of the lane with the main road, clipping its back and sending it pirouetting on its smoking tires before coming to a violent stop in a sewer ditch.

He slowed down at the mouth of the lane, picked Jabba up, and motored on, his neurons teeming with life. He had Rydell, which was good, and Matt was still alive, which was even better.

Chapter 57

Washington, D.C.

Too bad, Keenan Drucker thought.

He liked Rydell. The man was a great asset, in any circumstance. And none of this would've happened without him. The term *visionary* was bandied about a lot, but in Rydell's case, he truly was such.

Drucker's mind traveled back to how it had all started.

Davos, Switzerland.

The two-hundred-thousand-dollar-a-table black-tie dinner. The Aberdeen Angus beef and pink champagne jelly. Yet another gathering of the planet's rich and famous, the powerful elite who aspired to solve the world's big crises. Insecure egotists and well-meaning philanthropists, getting together not just to assuage their guilt by handing over some money to help a thousand or two poorer souls, but hoping to trigger change that could save the lives of millions.

Rydell and Drucker had sat together, late into the night, going over the growing mountain of data on global warming. Fourteen thousand new cars a day hitting the road in China. The booming industries there and in India building new coal-fired electricity plants every week. The developed world embracing cheap, coal-burning energy more than ever. Congress giving the oil and gas companies back home one tax break after another. The energy companies' disinformation campaigns helping people duck the issue and avoid making hard choices. Every new study confirming that if things looked bad, they were actually far worse.

They were both in agreement: The planet was hurtling toward the point of no return. We were living a defining moment, the defining moment for our continued existence on this planet, and we were ignoring it.

The question was, what to do about it.

Throughout, Drucker couldn't escape the feeling that Rydell was testing him, sounding him out. Seeing how far he'd go.

Drucker smiled inwardly as he remembered how Rydell had finally let it out.

Drucker had said, "All this," gesturing at the lavish setting around them, "it's something, but it won't change much. Governments, big business . . . no one wants to upset the apple cart. Voters and share options, they're the only things that matter. Growth. People don't really want change, especially not if it costs something. The price of oil has quadrupled so far this century, and nothing's changed. No one cares. The 'don't worry, be happy, it's all a load of crap' message the fuel lobby keeps pumping out—deep down, that's what everyone wants to hear. It's heaven-sent."

"Maybe heaven should send them a different message," Rydell had replied, a knowing—and visionary—blaze in his eye.

The rest had followed on from that.

At first, it had seemed Rydell was talking theory. But the theoretical soon became the possible. The possible became the doable. And when that happened, everything changed.

As far as Drucker was concerned, a whole host of possible uses were on the table. What Rydell and his people had come up with could be used as a weapon that could tackle any number of threats in different, and potentially spectacularly effective, ways. Problem was, Rydell wouldn't be open to that. As far as he was concerned, there was only one major threat facing us.

Drucker disagreed.

There were others. Threats that were far more immediate, far more dangerous. Threats that required more immediate attention. For although Drucker was a concerned citizen of the world, he was, more than anything, a patriot.

The Muslim world was growing bolder and wilder. It needed reining in. Drucker didn't think they'd ever be able to convert that part of the world, to pull its people away from their religion. But there were other ways of using Rydell's technology there. One idea he'd toyed with was using it to foment an all-out war between Sunnis and Shias. China was also a growing concern. Not militarily, but economically. Which was even worse. A spiritual message could have shifted things there. And there were other concerns that troubled Drucker even more. Concerns that were closer to home. Concerns about threats that had cost his only son his life. In any case, using the global-warming message as the first hook was the way to go. It was nonthreatening. It was a cause that everyone could embrace, one that transcended race and religion. It would help bring people on board from day one. The secondary message—the one that counted—would sneak in through the back door.

The strategy had to be carefully conceived. He had a head start, given the makeup of the country. Seventy percent of Americans believed in angels, in heaven, in life after death—and in miracles. Even better, fully 92 percent of Americans believed in a personal God, someone who took interest in their individual dramas and whom they could ask for help. The foundation was solidly there. Drucker had also drawn from the work of highly respected psychologists and anthropologists who studied the mental architecture of religious belief. What he was planning had to sit within the parameters such research had laid out. For one, the deception had to be minimally counterintuitive. It needed to be strange enough to capture people's attention and root itself firmly in their memory, but not too strange, so they wouldn't dismiss it. Studies had shown that convincing religious agents had to have just the right level of outlandishness. Also, the manifestation needed to have an emotional resonance in order for belief to set in. Religions used elaborate rituals to stir up people's emotions: soaring, dark cathedrals filled with candlelight, hymns and chants, bowing in unison. In that context, the environmental movement taking on a quasi-religious aspect was the perfect platform. It wasn't just us coming face-to-face with our mortality—it was the entire planet.

The timing was also helpful. The planet was living through scary times on many fronts. The environment. Economic meltdown. Terrorism and rogue nukes. Avian flu. Nanotechnology. Hadron colliders. Everything seemed to be out of control or have the potential to wipe us out. Our very existence seemed threatened on a daily basis. Which could only feed into the prophecies of some kind of savior, a Messiah showing up to sort everything out and bring about a millennial kingdom. And it wasn't just a Christian phenomenon. Every major religion had its own version of how a great teacher would appear and rescue the world from catastrophe. For Drucker, however, only one of them mattered.

Ultimately, though, he kept coming back to one main

stumbling block: the notion that at some point, something would go wrong. They wouldn't be able to fool all
of the people all of the time. Someone would let something slip. The technology would leak out. Something
was bound to screw up. Which was why he'd decided to
embrace that fallibility and use it as the starting point of
his strategy.

It proved to be an inspirational masterstroke.

Everything was in place. He'd recruited the right
partners to help him pull it off. He just needed to wait
for the right event, something big, something with
enough emotional resonance. He knew that, sooner or
later, it would come. The planet was roiling, writhing in
anger. More and more natural catastrophes were taking
place all around the globe. And the one he got came as if
gifted by the gods themselves. The best part of it all was
the role the media would play. They'd buy into the deception without hesitation. It was visceral, it was huge,
and—in its crucial launch phase, anyway—it was about
saving the planet, an issue that was dear to their hearts.

Too bad, Drucker thought again, his hands steepled in
front of his pursed lips. He would have preferred for
Rydell to be on board. To be part of it all. He'd tried to
convince him about the need to introduce a messenger—
a prophet—to the mix. They'd talked about it at length.
But Rydell wouldn't listen. Drucker didn't like doing
what they had to do to Rebecca either. He'd known her
for years; he'd watched her grow into an attractive, free-
spirited young woman. But it had to be done. Rydell was
too passionate. His commitment and his intensity came
with an inflexibility that couldn't be overcome. He'd
never be able to accept the trade-off. And, besides, he
couldn't be fully included anyway. He was part of the
endgame. The sacrificial pawn that was crucial to its successful closure.

Drucker's phone trilled. He glanced at its screen. The Bullet's name flashed up. The enabler. The man whose foot soldiers were making it all happen. The charred, deformed marine who had been Jackson's commanding officer. The man who'd left half his face in the same Iraqi slaughterhouse that had ripped Drucker's son to shreds.

Drucker picked up the phone.

The news wasn't good.

Chapter 58

Brookline, Massachusetts

The hydraulic compactor whined as it swiveled upward. Almost instantly, a sour stench wafted out of the truck's belly, even though the truck wasn't actually carrying any garbage. Matt let the compactor rise two thirds of the way up, then killed its motor. The heavy lid just held there, cantilevered over the yawning, stinking cavity of the truck's hold.

Matt leaned in. "Get out here," he ordered.

A short moment later, Rydell stumbled out, shielding his eyes from the day's glare.

The truck was parked in a deserted, narrow alley that ran parallel to and behind a busier, low-rise commercial street, at the back of a closed-down Blockbuster video store. It was six blocks from the municipal service center where Matt had stolen the truck. The green Bonneville was parked nearby. They stood by the mouth of a narrow passageway, out of view, shielded from any potential passing cars by the bulk of the truck.

Rydell stank. His clothes had rips in them, and he was battered and bruised from bouncing around the empty metal box. He was wheezing, his breath coming in brief, ragged bursts. A nasty, bleeding gash had been cut into his left cheek. He was wobbly, totally unbalanced, and had to lean against the truck, breathing in heavily, shut-ting his eyes, gathering his senses, and probably doing his best not to throw up.

Matt allowed him a few seconds to recover, then raised the big silver handgun the shooter at the airport had lost and held it inches from Rydell's face.

"What did you do to my brother?"

Rydell raised his eyes at him. They were still half-dead, drowning in a morass of pain and confusion. He glanced at Matt, then across to Jabba, who was hovering ner-vously a few steps back, but Rydell's head was still spin-ning and he still wasn't totally there. His eyelids slid shut and his head lolled forward again as his hands came up to rub his temples.

"What did you do to my brother?" Matt growled.

Rydell raised a hand in a stiff back-off-and-give-me-a-second gesture. After a moment, he looked up again. This time, his expression was alive enough to telegraph his not having a clue about who Matt and Jabba were or what Matt was asking him.

"Your brother . . . ?" he muttered.

"Danny Sherwood. What happened to him?"

The name resuscitated Rydell. His eyes flickered back to life, like a succession of floodlights getting switched on in a stadium. He winced, visibly struggling with how to answer.

"As far as I know, he's okay," Rydell said with a hol-low voice. "But it's been a few weeks since I saw him."

Matt flinched at his words. "You're saying he's alive?"

Rydell looked up at him and nodded. "Yes."

Matt glanced over at Jabba. Jabba put his almost-debilitating unease on hold and gave him a supportive, relieved nod.

"I'm sorry," Rydell continued. "We didn't have a choice."

"Of course you did," Matt shot back. "It's called free will." He was still processing the news. "So this sign . . . this whole thing. You're doing it?"

Rydell nodded. "I was."

"You 'were'?"

"The others . . . my partners . . . they're doing it their way now." Rydell sighed, clearly weighing his words. "I've been . . . sidelined."

"What really happened? In Namibia? Was Danny ever really there?"

Rydell nodded again, slowly. "Yes. That's where we did the final test. But there was no helicopter crash. It was all staged."

"So Reece, the others . . . they're also still alive?"

"No." Rydell hesitated. "Look, I didn't want any of that. It's not how I do things. But there were others there . . . They overreacted."

"Who?" Matt asked.

"The security guys."

"Maddox?" Matt half-guessed.

Rydell looked at him quizzically, clearly surprised by Matt's familiarity with the name.

"He got rid of them," Matt speculated. "When you didn't need them anymore."

"It wasn't like that," Rydell objected. "None of them knew what we were really planning. Not Reece, not your brother. And then when I finally told Reece, he didn't want to hear of it. I thought I could have convinced him. I just needed a bit of time . . . He would've come on board. And the others would have joined in too. But I never got the chance. Maddox just snapped and . . . it was insane. He just started firing. I couldn't stop him."

"And Danny?"

"He ran," Rydell said.

"But he didn't get away."

Rydell shook his head witheringly.

"And you kept him locked up, all this time."

Rydell nodded. "He designed the processing interface. It works perfectly, but it's very sensitive to the smallest variations in air density or temperature or . . ." He caught himself, as if he realized he was rambling on unnecessarily. "It was safer having him around."

"So all this time . . . you kept him alive, to use him now."

Rydell nodded again.

"Why would he keep doing what you asked? He had to know you'd kill him once it was all over." He studied Rydell, inwardly hoping he wouldn't hear the answer he was dreading. "He's not doing this of his own free will, is he?"

"No," Rydell replied. "We—they—threatened him."

"With what?"

"Your parents," Rydell said, then added, "and you." He held Matt's gaze, then dropped his eyes to the ground. "They told him they'd hurt you. Badly. Then they'd get you thrown back into prison, where they'd make sure your life was a living hell." He went silent for a beat, then added, "Danny didn't want that."

Matt felt an upwelling of anger erupt inside him. "My parents are dead."

Rydell nodded with remorse. "Danny doesn't know that."

Matt turned and stepped away, his face clouding over. He looked away into the distance, hobbled by Rydell's words. His kid brother. Going through hell for two years, living in a cell, cut off from the world, made to wield the fruit of his brilliance for something he didn't believe in . . . going through it all to protect him. To keep Matt safe.

After everything Danny had already done for him.

Matt thought of his parents, how they'd been devastated by the news of Danny's helicopter crash, and a crushing sense of grief overcame him. He glared back at Rydell and felt like ramming his fist down his throat and ripping his heart out.

Jabba watched Matt struggle with the revelation with a pained heart, but didn't interfere. Instead, he took a hesitant step closer to Rydell.

He couldn't help himself. "How are you doing it?" he asked him, his tone reverent, as if he still couldn't believe he was here, face-to-face with one of his gods, albeit a fallen, battered, and bloodied one.

Rydell tilted his head up to take stock of him, then just shook his head and turned away.

"Answer him," Matt barked.

Rydell looked at Matt, then back at Jabba. After a brief moment, he just said, "Smart dust."

"Smart dust? But that's not . . . I mean, I thought . . ." Jabba stammered, shaking his head with disbelief, a deluge of questions battering his mind as it stumbled over Rydell's answer. "How small?"

Rydell paused, reluctant to engage Jabba, then shrugged. "A third of a cubic millimeter."

Jabba's mouth dropped an inch. According to everything he'd read or heard about, that just wasn't possible. Not even close. And yet Rydell was telling him it was.

"Smart dust"—minuscule electronic devices designed to record and transmit information about their surroundings while literally floating on air—was still a scientific dream. The concept was first imagined, and the term coined, by electrical engineers and computer scientists working at the University of California's Berkeley campus in the late nineties. The idea was simple: Tiny motes of silicon, packed with sophisticated onboard sensors, computer processors, and wireless communicators, small

enough to be virtually invisible and light enough to remain suspended in midair for hours at a time, gathering
and transmitting data back in real time—and undetected.
The military was immediately interested. The idea of
scattering speck-sized sensors over a battlefield to detect
and monitor troop movements was hugely appealing. So
was sprinkling them in subways to detect chemical or
biological threats, or on a crowd of protestors to be able
to track their movements remotely. DARPA had kicked in
the initial funding, as, although the concept also had a host
of potential civilian and medical uses, the more nefarious
surveillance possibilities were even more alluring. But
funding doesn't always lead to success.

The concept was sound. Breakthroughs in nanotechnology were inching the dream closer to reality. Theoreti-
cally, manufacturing the motes was possible. In practice,
we weren't there yet. Not overtly, anyway. Making the
sensors small enough wasn't the problem. The processors
that analyzed the data, the transmitters that communi-
cated it back to base, and the power supply that ran the
whole minuscule thing—typically, some kind of minute
lithium battery—were. By the time they were added on,
they turned the dust-sized particles into hardly stealthy
clusters the size of a golf ball.

Clearly, Rydell's team had managed to overcome
those hurdles and achieve new levels of miniaturization
and power management.

In secret.

Jabba was struggling to order the questions that were
coming at him from all corners. "You were working on it
for DARPA, weren't you?"

"Reece was. The applications were endless, but no
one could figure out how to actually manufacture them.
Until he did. He told me about it before letting them
know he could do it. We stayed up late one night, imag-

ining all kinds of things we could use it for." He paused, reliving that night. "One of them stood out."

"So that whole biosensor story?" Jabba asked.

Rydell shook his head. "Just a smoke screen."

"But . . . how? Where are they coming from? You dropping them from drones or . . . ?" His voice trailed off, his mind still tripping over the very notion.

"Canisters," Rydell told him. "We shoot them up, like fireworks."

"But there's no noise, no explosion," Jabba remarked. "Is there?"

"We're using compressed air launchers. Like they're now using at Disneyland. No noise. No explosion."

The questions were coming to Jabba fast and furious. "And the motes . . . How are they lighting up? And how'd you get the power source down to a manageable size? What are you using, solar cells? Or did you go nuclear?" Sensing, sorting, and transmitting data used up a lot of juice. One option scientists were exploring was to sprinkle the motes with a radioactive isotope to give each mote its own long-term energy supply.

Rydell shook his head. "No. They don't actually need an onboard power source."

"So what are they running on?"

"That was Reece's brilliant brainchild. They feed off each other. We light them up with an electromagnetic signal from the ground. They convert the transmission into power and spread it across the cloud where it's needed."

The answer triggered a new barrage of questions in Jabba's mind. "But how do you get them to light up?"

Rydell shrugged. "It's a chemical reaction. They're Janus particles. Hybrids. They light up and switch off as needed to take on the shape we want, like skydivers in an aerial display. They burn up after about fifteen minutes, but it's long enough."

Jabba was visibly struggling to absorb the information and complete the puzzle. His voice rose with incredulity. "But they're constantly moving around. They've got to be. I mean, even the slightest breeze pushes them around, right? And yet the sign wasn't moving." He extrapolated his own answer; then his eyes widened. "They're self-propelled?" He didn't seem to believe his own words.

"No." Rydell shook his head, then glanced over at Matt, his expression darkening with remorse, his shoulders sagging, before looking away again. "That's where Danny came in. His distributed processing program . . . more like massively distributed intelligence. He designed it. He came up with this brilliant optical system based on corner-cube reflectors. It lets them communicate with each other very elaborately while using up virtually no energy. It literally brought the motes to life." He exhaled uncomfortably, then continued. "We needed the shape— the sign—to stay in one place. But you're right, the motes, they're so small, so light, they're floating around, moving in the air like dandelion seeds. So we needed them to be able to talk to each other. Several hundred times a second. When one mote that's lit up moves away, it turns itself off and the one that drifts closest to where it was lights up instead and takes its place and assumes its position in the display. So the sign appears stationary even though the dust particles are always changing position. Factor in that we wanted the sign to constantly morph in shape to appear like it's alive, and . . . it's a hell of a lot of processing power in a machine the size of a speck of dust." He lifted his gaze back at Matt, guiltily. "We couldn't have done it without Danny."

"Oh, well, in that case, I guess you did the right thing by locking him up all this time," Matt retorted.

"You think this has been easy?" Rydell shot back. "You think this is something I just got into on a whim? I've put everything on the line for this. And the way things are going, I'll probably end up dead because of it."

"It's a distinct possibility," Matt confirmed dryly.

"I had no choice. Something had to be done. This thing's getting out of hand, and no one's paying attention."

"Global warming?" Jabba asked. "That's what this is all about, right?"

"What else?" Rydell flared up, pushing himself to his feet. "You don't get it, do you? People out there—they've got no idea. They don't realize that every time they get into their cars, they're slowly killing the planet. Killing their own grandchildren." He was gesticulating wildly, all fired up. "Make no mistake, we're getting close to the point of no return. And when that happens, it'll be too late to do anything about it. The weather will just shift dramatically and that'll be the end of us. And it's happening faster than you think. We owe it to our kids and to their kids to do something about it. Sometime in the next hundred years, people will be living on what will undoubtedly be a very unpleasant planet to live on, and they'll look back and wonder why the hell no one ever did anything about it. Despite all the warnings we had. Well, I'm doing something about it. Anyone who's in a position to do something about it has to. It would be criminal not to."

"So you decided to go out and kill off a bunch of decent guys to get everyone's attention," Matt said.

"I told you, that wasn't part of the plan," Rydell snapped.

"Still, you're going along with it."

Matt's point must have hit home, as Rydell didn't have a quick answer for him. "What did you want me to do? Give up on the whole thing and turn Maddox and his people in? Waste everything we worked on for all those years, throw away a plan that could change everything?"

Matt didn't waver. "But did you ever even consider it?"

Rydell thought about it, and shook his head.

Matt gave him a small, pointed nod with his head. Rydell's face sank, and he looked at Matt blankly before turning away.

"What about Father Jerome?" Jabba asked. "He's not part of this too, is he?"

"I don't know. He wasn't part of the original plan," Rydell said. "They came up with that one all on their own. You'll have to ask them about it."

"He can't be in on it," Jabba protested. "Not him."

"It doesn't matter," Matt interjected firmly. "I just want to get Danny back." He turned to Rydell. "Where is he?"

"I don't know," Rydell said. "I told you, I'm out of the loop."

Matt raised the big handgun and held it aimed squarely at Rydell's forehead. "Try again."

"I'm telling you I don't know, not anymore," Rydell exclaimed. "But the next time the sign shows up, you'll probably find him there."

"What?" Matt rasped, thrown by Rydell's answer.

"That's why we needed him alive," Rydell pointed out. "To make the microadjustments in real time. On-site."

"'On-site'?" Jabba asked. "He has to be there? He can't do it remotely?"

"He could, but data transmission isn't foolproof over

such long distances, and even the smallest time lag could mess things up. It's safer having him on location, especially if the sign's gonna do more than just pop up for a few seconds."

"So he was out there?" Matt asked. "In Antarctica? And in Egypt?"

"He was in Antarctica," Rydell confirmed. "Egypt I don't know about. Again, it wasn't part of the plan. But from what I saw on TV, I'd guess he was there. He has to be within half a mile or so of the sign. That's the transmitter's range."

An approaching siren wailed nearby. Matt tensed. Through a narrow passage that led to the main drag on the other side of the low, commercial buildings that backed up to the alley, he spotted the flash of a police car blowing past.

It was time to vamoose.

He turned to Jabba. "We need to move." He flicked the gun at Rydell, herding him on. "Let's go."

"Where?" Rydell asked.

"I don't know yet, but you're coming with us."

"I can't," Rydell protested. "They—"

"You're coming with us," Matt cut him off. "They've got Danny. I have you. Sounds like a good trade."

"They won't trade him for me. They need him. Much more than they need me. If anything, they'd probably be happy to see me dead."

"Maybe, but if they haven't killed you yet, it means they also need you for something," Matt observed.

Which, judging by Rydell's expression, struck a nerve. But he seemed to quickly shelve it as he told Matt, "I can't go with you. They have my daughter."

Matt scoffed. "Sure." Rydell was, clearly, a cunning liar. Which suddenly put everything else he'd told Matt in question.

"I'm telling you they've got my daughter—"

"Bullshit. Let's go," Matt prodded him, though something about the intensity in his voice, in his eyes—was Matt missing something? His fury at Rydell didn't let it in and he plowed ahead. "Move."

"Listen to me. They grabbed her. In Mexico. They're hanging on to her as security. To make sure I don't rock the boat. They can't even know I talked to you. They'll kill her."

Matt wavered, suddenly unsure—and Jabba stepped closer.

"Maybe it's true, dude." He turned to Rydell. "She's here."

Rydell's head jerked forward with attention. "Here?"

"We saw her," Jabba informed him. "A couple of hours ago. Maddox and his goon squad flew her into a small airport near Bedford. We thought they were her bodyguards."

Rydell's expression clouded.

"They have your daughter, and you only think you've been 'sidelined'?" Matt's expression was heavy with contempt. "I don't know, man. Me, I'd take it as a definite sign that you guys are now enemies."

Rydell looked at him blankly, Matt's words clearly weighing him down.

Matt shook his head indignantly and just said, "Let's go." He motioned to Rydell with his gun.

Rydell's features fogged up as he desperately searched for a glimmer of clarity. He then shook his head and raised his hands in surrender, palms out, and took a step backward. "I can't." He took another step back, then another. "They'll kill her."

Matt's anger flared. "You should have thought of that before you started looking the other way while your people got bumped off."

"How many times do I have to say it?" Rydell blurted. "I didn't want any of that." He shook his head stoically. "Even if I wanted to help you, I can't. Not as long as they have her. So do what you want, but I'm not going anywhere with you."

Matt raised his gun at him, but Rydell didn't stop. He kept inching backward, his palms spread, his eyes darting around, taking stock of his surroundings.

"Stop. I mean it," Matt ordered.

Rydell just shook his head and kept backing up. He was now at the mouth of the small passageway that led to the main drag.

Matt hesitated. Rydell saw it. He gave him a small, knowing, almost apologetic tilt of the head before bolting into the passageway.

"Shit," Matt muttered as he took off after him. "Rydell," he yelled, his voice echoing through the narrow brick canyon as he charged down the grubby passage, Jabba in tow. Within seconds, they burst onto the main road. Matt stumbled to a halt. A few pedestrians stood there, on the wide sidewalk, motionless, eyes locked on Matt, taken aback by his sudden appearance and his gun. Behind them, Rydell was backing away, arms spread out in a calming gesture.

Matt felt too many eyes on him. Rydell was slipping away, and he couldn't do anything about it.

"Let's get the hell out of here," he told Jabba, before turning and rushing back down the passage toward the Bonneville. He'd lost Rydell, but Danny was alive, and right now, that was all that mattered.

Chapter 59

Alexandria, Egypt

The decision to avoid Cairo Airport proved to be an inspired one, although it hadn't started off that way. Gracie had gotten herself into a knot by picturing herself doing what Finch normally took care of—in this case, trying to sneak Father Jerome past an Egyptian passport clerk who would be either maniacally fastidious, sexist, anti-American, or any combination thereof.

The plane was waiting for them when they got there. Darby had come through, as promised. They made their way to the civil aviation office in order to access the tarmac without going through the main terminal, and kept Father Jerome well out of view. They were well aware that the merest glimpse of him could trigger a stampede. He was too recognizable—perhaps the most recognizable face on the planet right now. The clerk manning the small office turned out to be a Copt—a one-in-ten chance in Egypt—and a devout one at that. One look at Brother Ameen's cassock did the trick. Within minutes, their passports had been stamped, the gates had been opened, and they were climbing up the stairs of the hastily chartered jet. The plan was for the driver to wait and make sure the plane took off unhindered before letting the abbot know it was safe to announce that the priest was no longer at the monastery, in the hope of defusing the tense crowd besieging its walls.

Gracie started to relax as the Gulfstream 450's wheels lifted off the runway and the sleek fourteen-seater aircraft streaked upward to its cruising altitude, but her relief was short-lived. It only allowed darker thoughts to resurface. Thoughts about Finch. Visions of him, lying there in the sand. Dead.

A veil of grief descended over her. "I wish we hadn't left him there," she told Dalton. He was in the seat opposite her, facing back. "It feels awful. Us being here, while he's . . ." She let the words fade.

"We didn't have a choice," Dalton comforted her. "Besides, it's what he would have wanted us to do."

"And to think, just when he was covering the story of a lifetime." She shrugged, thinking back. "After everything he's been through, all the wars and the disasters . . . to die like that."

Dalton nodded, and they just sat there quietly, crippled by the loss. After a moment, Dalton said, "We've got to tell the folks back home about Finch."

Gracie nodded quietly.

"We need to give Ogilvy an update on our ETA," he added. "I'll go talk to the pilot. See if he can patch us in to the desk."

He pushed himself to his feet, but Gracie's hand reached out and arrested his move. "Not just yet, okay? Let's . . . let's just take a few minutes for ourselves, all right?"

"Sure." He glanced back at the galley and said, "I'll see if they have some fresh coffee. You want one?"

"Thanks." She nodded, then added, "If they're out, a couple of fingers of Scotch will do just as nicely."

◄◦►

THE FALSE PRIEST who had chosen to be called Brother Ameen watched Dalton rise from his seat opposite Gracie and head his way. He acknowledged the cameraman with a friendly nod as he walked past him to the back of the plane, then turned away and stared out the window.

It was his first kill on this mission, though he'd killed many times before. The war in his homeland had been brutal. It had turned a lot of young Serbian men like him into heartless killers. Once the war was over, some had been able to smother that aspect of their past and morph back into average, amiable folk. Others liked what they'd discovered in themselves. And some of those, like Dario Arapovic, also discovered that the talents that they'd forged in places like Vukovar and during operations like the Otkos 10 offensive were in strong demand. That region of the world was still unstable. It was an ongoing struggle, and any lull was but a temporary pause in the Great Game. A game that people like Maddox were actively participating in, a game where talents like Dario's were coveted—and richly rewarded. And his decision had paid off handsomely, for although Dario had taken great pride in playing a covert role in helping shape his homeland's future, his being picked by Maddox to play this key position in a far more important match was a source of even greater satisfaction.

He would have much preferred not to kill the producer. The risk of detection was high. Equally dangerous was the risk of disrupting a plan that had been working smoothly up until then. The news team had done everything that had been expected of them. They couldn't have done a better job had they been a covert unit themselves. Finch's death had disrupted that. They worked well as a team. They saw things and reacted the way they had been expected to. They were professionals, and professionals who knew what they were doing could be counted on to follow a well-thought-out methodology—and to listen to reason and act accordingly. Finch had been an integral part of that. With him gone, a new door had been opened. One that led down an untried path. Someone else would have to replace him. A new producer. A hard-head who might not be as easy to steer as Finch had been.

Still, he'd had no choice. There was no way out of it. He knew Finch wouldn't have bought into anything he could have come up with to explain his having a satphone, much less one that was encryption-module equipped.

He turned and glanced at Gracie. She was now sitting alone, her shoulders slightly hunched, looking out her window. He knew she wouldn't bow out because of Finch's death. She was a pro too. And like all pros, she had drive. Ambition. And the cold, rational ability to compartmentalize tragedies like her producer's death and carry on.

Which was good.

She still had a role to play. An important one.

◄◦►

HALF AN HOUR after the Gulfstream had taken off from the airport at Alexandria, another aircraft had followed it into the sky and was now shadowing it, a couple of hundred miles back, headed in the same general westerly direction.

The plane, a chartered Boeing 737, was a much larger, and older, aircraft. It had enjoyed stints with various airlines over its twenty-six years of service, though none was as unusual as the one it was undertaking today.

The jet's hold carried a highly covetable selection of state-of-the-art technology. It included a long-range acoustic device, canisters of nano-engineered smart dust, and ultra-silent compressed air launchers. Also stowed there was some decidedly less sophisticated, but equally effective, gear: sniper rifles, silencer-equipped handguns, tactical knives, camouflage gear. The jet's cabin held a load that was no less exceptional: seven men whose actions had entranced the world. Six of them were highly trained professionals: a three-man team that had spent over a year in the desert, another that had endured extreme weather all over the globe. The seventh was an outlier. He wasn't highly trained, nor did he share their sense of purpose.

Danny Sherwood was only there out of fear.

He'd been their prisoner for close to two years. Two years of tinkering, of testing and double-testing, of waiting. Two years of worrying, of coming up with devious, complicated plans of escape, of fantasizing about them, of ditching them. And then, finally, it had begun. It was why they'd kept him alive. It was why they needed him. And now it was in play.

He didn't know what their plans were or how it would all end. He'd heard snippets of talk. He thought he knew what they were up to, but he wasn't sure. He'd thought of sabotaging it, of screwing up their plans, of rejigging the software so that a giant Coca-Cola or Red Sox sign appeared instead of the mystical sign they had designed. But he knew they were keeping a close eye on his work, knew they'd probably figure out what he was up to before he got a chance to use it. He also knew that if he tried it, it would mean a death sentence for him, and, probably, for Matt and for their parents. And so he thought about it, he mulled it over and dreamed of it and enjoyed the brief satisfaction it gave him to imagine it, but he knew he'd never go through with it. He wasn't a fighter. He wasn't a tough guy.

If they'd taken Matt, he knew things would have been different. But Matt wasn't there. He was.

He sometimes wished his survival instincts hadn't kicked in just as the Jeep was launching itself off the canyon's edge. Wished his hand hadn't lunged out and pushed that door open. Wished he hadn't leapt out of the Jeep just as its front wheels ran out of ground. Wished he hadn't ended up clinging to life at the very edge of the abyss, staring up at the circling bird of prey that was about to land and take him away.

But he had. And he was here now, shackled to his seat, headed for another corner of the planet, wondering when his nightmare would ever end.

Chapter 60

Framingham, Massachusetts

The hamburgers were big and juicy and grilled just right, the buns soft but not crumbly, the coleslaw freshly cut and crunchy, the fries thick, crisp on the outside and the right side of mushy on the inside, the Cokes—in glass bottles, not cans—nicely chilled and served in tall, curvy glasses filled with ice cubes that weren't in a rush to melt. It was the perfect meal for Matt and Jabba, given their day—a solid, comfortable meal, a reassuring meal, the kind of meal that dragged one's mind away from troubled times and pulled it back to better days, a meal that drew one into its own comfy world with its hearty offerings and put all thoughts of heavy conversation on indefinite hold.

They sat facing each other in a booth in a small diner in Framingham, about fifteen miles west of Brookline. It was far enough, and busy enough, for them to feel relatively safe. They'd polished off a burger each and hadn't spoken more than ten words throughout. A lot had happened. It had been a charged day, a bad day right on the heels of another bad day. They'd seen a guy get crushed in half, another get his legs mangled up by a Japanese import. Bullets had whizzed by inches from their faces. Matt had shot several guys, possibly—probably—killing one or more of them, which was not something he'd done before. Not even close.

Thinking about it, revisiting those images in his mind's eye, he found it hard to accept it had all really happened. That he'd done all that. He didn't recognize himself. It all felt surreal, like he'd been on the outside, watching it. But it all became real again once he focused on the overwhelmingly good thing that had trumped everything else that had happened: the discovery that his kid brother was still very much alive.

They sat in silence. A small, wall-mounted TV over the cash register was set low. It was on a local channel and had been screening a rerun of an old *Simpsons* episode, one Jabba knew by heart and one Matt couldn't have been less interested in. The end credits eventually gave way to some staggeringly unimaginative ads before segueing into the evening news, starting with the latest update from Egypt. It brought reality roaring back into Matt's face in a flash.

The volume was too low for him to hear what was being said, but even before the waitress turned it up, the visuals themselves were deafening enough. A loud banner on the bottom of the screen informed them that Father Jerome hadn't been seen since the sign had appeared over him earlier that day. Another added that unconfirmed reports had said that he had actually left the monastery for destinations unknown. Reporters and pundits around the world were scrambling to figure out where he was and where he could have gone to. They wondered about whether he might be headed to Jerusalem, or the Vatican, or back home to Spain.

Elsewhere, gargantuan crowds were still massed in St. Peter's Square, in São Paulo, and in many more cities now, holding vigils and praying. The world was holding its breath, waiting for Father Jerome's next appearance.

Pockets of violence had cropped up in Pakistan, in Israel, and in Egypt, where men and women of all religions who had taken to the streets to proclaim their faith in Father Jerome had clashed with mobs of unswayed and unwavering believers who were sticking to the rigid tenets of their holy books. Riot police had been deployed, cars and shops had been set alight, and in each case, there had been deaths.

Matt stared at the screen for a moment, then finally said, "Wherever that priest's going, that's where we'll find Danny."

"You want to go to Egypt?"

Matt shrugged. "If he's still there, hell yeah."

Jabba's shoulders sagged. He took one last bite and pushed his plate off to the side of the table, wiped his mouth and cast a glance across the diner, then turned his attention back to Matt. Their fates were now intertwined, there was no escaping that. And though he hardly knew the man, he'd seen enough of him to recognize that look—a distant, frowning look that indicated something was bothering him, some kind of itch he needed to scratch. Jabba studied him for a beat, then prompted him by asking, "What is it, dude?"

Matt nodded his head a fraction, to himself, wheels visibly spinning in his mind. After a moment, he said, "We need Rydell. They screwed him over. They've got his daughter. Right now, he's real angry. Which makes me think he could help us get Danny back."

"Not as long as they've got his daughter," Jabba reminded him.

"Maybe we can change that."

"Dude, come on," Jabba protested.

"She's got herself caught up in this thing just like we have," Matt argued. "Through no fault of her own. You think this is going to end well for her? You think her dad's gonna kiss and make up with these guys? They're hanging on to her to get him to play nice. Once they're done, they're not going to let them live."

Jabba gave him a look.

Matt just batted it back. "You like the idea of Maddox and his storm troopers keeping her locked up somewhere?"

Jabba smiled despite himself and said, "Look, just because you throw in a *Star Wars* reference doesn't mean—"

"Seriously," Matt interrupted. "We need to do this. Besides, maybe that's where they've been keeping Danny too."

Jabba tilted his head at him, dubiously. "You don't really believe that, do you?"

"Not really," Matt conceded. Then he gave Jabba a slight grin. "What, you got something better to do?"

Jabba shook his head in defeat. "Even if I did, this is bound to be *so* much more fun."

◄◦►

JUST OVER THREE HOURS LATER, Maddox took the second call that night from his contact at the NSA.

"I just got another hit," the man from Fort Meade told the Bullet. "Very brief. Under twenty seconds."

"They know we're trying to track them."

"For sure. They're being very careful. But not careful enough."

"Location?"

"Same place," the caller told him. The GPS lock had placed Jabba's iPhone on a busy little commercial strip leading out of Framingham.

"Okay. Keep me posted. In real time. We're in progress."

Maddox hung up and hit a speed-dial key. The man

on the other end picked up the line before it had completed its first ring.

"How far are you?" he asked.

"Should be there in less than ten," the operative replied.

"Okay," Maddox said. "We just got another lock. Same location. They're probably in a hotel or a motel on that block. Let me know what you find."

Chapter 61

Boston, Massachusetts

The presidential suite on the sixth floor of the Four Seasons was as comfortable as it got in the city, or pretty much anywhere else in the world, but as far as Rydell was concerned, he could just as easily have been sitting in a cramped motel room with a coin-operated vibrating bed that didn't work. His mind wasn't registering his surroundings right now. It was elsewhere, stranded on a totally different plane. Grappling with a new reality.

He'd returned to his house after getting away from Matt. It had been swarming with cops and armed response guys—and Maddox. He'd convinced Rydell to give the cops a bullshit story about an attempted kidnapping. Rydell had told them he didn't know who was behind it, saying the men had worn balaclavas. He told them he'd managed to escape from his captors when they'd tried to transfer him from the garbage truck to another car and hadn't operated the compactor properly. He'd left it at that and, wanting to avoid the inevitable paparazzi onslaught, had checked into the Four Seasons. His lawyers could deal with the rest.

Maddox had arranged to have two of his men stationed outside the suite. That angered Rydell, but there was nothing he could do about it. Not as long as they had his daughter. And ever since, he'd been busy reliving his meeting with Drucker, Matt's intrusion, and grinding over what the two men had said.

If they haven't killed you yet, it means they also need you for something, Matt had told him. Which rang true. Worryingly true. But what did they need him for? When Rydell had threatened Drucker and told him they couldn't do it without him, Drucker had agreed. But that wasn't true. Not really. Rydell had left there believing his own bluff. With a rising dread, he now realized that actually, they could. And were. They had the technology. They knew where the smart dust was being manufactured and stockpiled. They could easily secure the facility. They had Danny.

They didn't need him to make it happen. Not anymore.

And yet they hadn't gotten Maddox to pump a couple of bullets into him.

The realization pulled his doubts regarding what Drucker had in mind back into focus. They'd gone into this together, brothers-in-arms, united for a worthy cause. Was that still the case? It suddenly dawned on him that maybe they weren't after the same thing anymore. Maybe the others were after something else. And in the process, they'd created a messenger that transcended the message. That dwarfed it and buried it in its shadow. The media's shifting focus confirmed his fears.

The story wasn't about God's warning anymore. It was about His messenger.

Drucker wouldn't make such a mistake. Unless he had a different message in mind.

Think of what we can make people do, Drucker had said. The phrase reverberated inside Rydell's head again.

A final thought confirmed his worst fears. Again, it was born out of something Matt had said.

Me, I'd take it as a definite sign that you guys are now

enemies. That was what he'd said. And it suddenly dawned on Rydell that Matt was right. There was no way this was ending well. Not for him. Nor for his ill-fated alliance with those bastards. They had Rebecca. There was no point in glossing over it. In pretending that it was a temporary difference of opinion. There was no going back from that. No way to salvage it. It was over.

They were the enemy.

His cell phone rang. It was Drucker. It didn't take long for him to voice the main question.

"What did you tell him?"

"All he wanted to know was what happened to his brother," Rydell said vaguely.

"And?"

"I told him I thought he was still alive. I told him I didn't know where he is. Then I ran."

Drucker went silent. After a moment, he said, "Nothing else?"

"Don't worry. He doesn't care what you're up to," he lied. "He doesn't know about you, for that matter, although maybe I should have mentioned it."

"Wouldn't have been ideal for Rebecca," Drucker reminded him coldly. He paused, clearly putting the news through its paces, then said, "All right. Stay at the hotel and avoid the press as much as you can. We might have to find you somewhere more discreet to stay until you can move back into the house."

Rydell hung up and thought about Rebecca again. Matt's words rang through his mind.

He was right. They were enemies now.

And maybe Matt was the only one he could turn to in order to do something about it.

Chapter 62

Skies over the Eastern Mediterranean

The sea stretched out as far as Gracie could see, a cobalt blue quilt snugly tucked in around the very edge of the planet. Up ahead and to the left, the sun was teasing the horizon. She leaned forward, right against the glass, and drank in the tranquil view. Although she hopped on planes as often as people took the subway, looking out from an aircraft at high altitude never failed to instill a sense of wonder in her. It was an almost mystical experience—looking out at the planet, the clouds, the sun, the infinite expanse of space beyond what she could see. She never tired of it. She'd normally just sit there and stare out and let her mind wander in all kinds of directions, enjoying that fleeting moment of blissful isolation before getting pulled back into the land of the living by some intrusion.

This time, the intruder was a question, voiced in the dulcet tone of Father Jerome. "How are you feeling?"

She looked up at him. It felt surreal. To be there, talking to him. After what she'd witnessed. When she wasn't sure what he really was.

She managed a partial smile and a soft shrug. "Frankly . . . a bit lost. Which is not a feeling I'm used to."

"You've been lucky," he commented. He looked uncomfortable, slightly stooped in the cabin despite the fact that its ceiling was an inch or two over six feet high and he wasn't a tall man.

Gracie noticed. She gestured at Dalton's empty seat. "Please. Won't you join me?"

He nodded, and as he sat down, Dalton came back from the galley.

"I'm sorry. I'm in your seat," the priest apologized.

"No, that's fine," Dalton replied breezily as he handed Gracie another coffee. "I need to talk to the pilot anyway. Find out what the plan is." He glanced back at Gracie to make sure she was okay with that, then moved forward toward the cockpit.

Gracie watched him go, then turned her attention back to the priest, recovering her train of thought. "You were saying I'm lucky?"

"I know what it feels like. To feel lost. Ever since I left the Sudan, I've often felt adrift myself. Unsure of where I was, what I was doing. It's been . . . hard," he said vaguely. "And now this . . ." He managed a half smile. "Just to confuse me even more." He waved his ramblings away and focused on her.

She studied him, then leaned closer. "Up on that roof," she asked. "What did it feel like?" She remembered his mystified look, when the sign was just there, over him, suspended in midair. "Did you have any control over what was happening?"

He shook his head softly. "It feels as strange to me as it does to you and to everyone else," he said. "There's only one thing that's clear to me."

"What's that?"

"If I've been fortunate enough to be chosen, then I must overcome my doubts and accept God's grace and His trust. I mustn't shy away from it or deny it. It's happening for a reason. It has to be." He eyed her reaction, then asked, "What do *you* think is happening?"

"I don't know. But it's just weird," she explained, "to be living it. To be there, watching it happen, to see it going out live, on TV, around the world. To actually have documented proof of this unexplained phenomenon, this miracle I guess, not just some," she hesitated at which words to use, then went with "questionable writings from a couple of thousand years ago."

Father Jerome's brow furrowed with curiosity as he tilted his head slightly to one side. " 'Questionable'?"

Gracie glanced away before her eyes came back to Father Jerome. "I have to be honest with you, Father. I don't believe in God. And I'm not just talking about the Bible or about the Church," she added, somewhat defensively, as if that made it potentially less offensive to him, "although I never bought into that either."

He didn't seem offended or perturbed at all. "Why not?"

"I guess I got that from my parents. They didn't buy into it, so I never had it drummed into me when I was a kid. Which is where it usually comes from, isn't it?"

He nodded.

"The thing is—again, no offense, Father—on the few occasions I did go to church, I never met a preacher I felt I could trust. I never felt they were in it for the right reasons, and none of the ones I met could ever give me an honest, intelligent, or convincing answer to the simplest questions I put to them."

"Like what?"

"How much time have you got?" she joked. He smiled back, inviting her to continue. "Anyway, once I was old enough to think for myself, I agreed with my parents and their take on the whole thing. I mean, again, no offense, Father, but historically? It doesn't stand up, does it? Let's be honest here. All those stories, from the Garden of Eden to the Resurrection . . . they're myths. Archetypal, clever, resonant—but still myths. I mean, I tried. I wanted to believe. I wanted that comfort, that crutch. But the more I read, the more I researched it, the more I saw what a primitive masquerade it all was, the more I realized that the faith I saw all around me was really nothing more than a bunch of old tales cobbled together a couple of thousand years ago by some very savvy guys to try and turn a superstitious world into a better place—and one they could control better. We're talking about a seriously primitive bunch of people here. One and a half thousand years later, people were still burning witches. So, to believe in it back then . . . that's one thing. But today? With everything we know? When we've mapped the human genome and sent space probes out to the very edge of our solar system?" She sighed, then added, "And then this happens and suddenly I'm not so sure anymore." She looked at him with a sheepish, defeated expression.

Father Jerome nodded studiously, allowing her words to sink in more thoroughly. "Not to believe in one religion or another, that's entirely understandable," he told her. "Especially for a well-educated woman like you. Besides, they can't all be right, can they?" He spread his palms out questioningly and smiled; then his expression turned more serious. "But you're saying something very different. Something much more fundamental. You're saying you don't believe in God."

Gracie held his gaze, and nodded. "I don't. I didn't. At least, not until these last few days. Now I don't know what to believe. Or not to believe."

"But before all this. Why not believe in God, outside religion? The idea of something wondrous and unknowable—and putting aside all the associations the word *God* has in the minds of religious people."

"Logic. You can boil it all down to the basic 'chicken and egg' question. The only reason—the only need—to believe in God is to try and explain where this all came from, right? Where we came from. Where we're headed. But it doesn't work. If there was a creator, a designer who created all this, well, then, there had to be a creator to create that creator, right? And one to create him. And so on. It doesn't hold water." She paused, thinking further, about something closer to her heart. A deep-seated sadness seemed to emerge from within her. "And then my mom died. I was thirteen at the time. Breast cancer. She'd been clear for five years; then it just came back and took her away in ten days. It was . . . brutal. And I couldn't see why anyone would create something that nasty or take away someone so wonderful." Even all these years later, her eyes glistened at the memory.

"I'm sorry."

"It was a long time ago." She studied him and hesitated, as if unsure about whether to mention something, then decided she would. "You know, back at the monastery. When you leaned down beside Finch. For a moment there, I . . ."

"You thought I was going to bring him back?"

She was taken aback by his insight. "Yes."

He nodded to himself, as if he had wondered about the same thing. "I have to say . . . I wasn't sure myself. Of what would happen. Of what I could do." He looked up at her, his expression foggy.

"But that's what I'm talking about," she said. "That's what I can't understand. One minute, something we can't understand—something that could well be what we call God—is sending us some kind of message, showing itself, and it's hopeful and inspiring and wonderful . . . and then, the next minute, a perfectly good man's life is taken away, just like that." Her whole face was questioning him. "It's like when my mom died. There wasn't a better, kinder soul on this planet. And I couldn't understand why something like that could be allowed to happen if there was any kind of superbeing watching over us. There was no way that could be justified. I talked to a couple of pastors at the time. They just gave me the standard sound bites about her 'being with God' and his 'testing us' and all kinds of other platitudes that, frankly, sounded like complete nonsense. Their words meant nothing to me."

Father Jerome nodded thoughtfully. "The reason your preacher couldn't help you is he's lost. He's still using the same words preachers used to try and comfort people five hundred years ago. But we're a bit more sophisticated than that now." He paused, as if pained by his own words. "That's the problem with religion right now. It hasn't evolved. And instead of being open and looking for ways to be relevant in today's world, it's gone all defensive and protective and it's regressed into lowest-common-denominator sound bites—and fundamentalism."

"But you can't reconcile religion with modern life, with all the knowledge we have, with science," Gracie said. "I mean, let me ask you this. Do you believe in evolution? Or do you think men and dinosaurs wandered around the planet together six thousand years ago . . . after it was created in six days?"

Father Jerome smiled. "I've lived in Africa for many years, Miss Logan—"

"Please, call me Gracie," she interjected.

He nodded. "I've been to the digs. I've seen the fossils. I've studied the science. Of course I believe in evolution. You'd have to be a blinkered halfwit not to." He studied her reaction as she flinched. "Does that surprise you?"

"You could say that," she laughed, still stunned.

He shrugged. "It shouldn't. But then, religion in your country is so focused on fighting science and all these compelling atheist voices that your preachers have lost track of what religion is really about. In our church—the Eastern Church—and in Eastern religions like Buddhism and Hinduism, religion isn't there to offer theories or explanations. We accept that the divine is unknowable. But for you and for a lot of rational people like you, it's become a choice. Fact or faith. Science or religion." He paused, then added, "You shouldn't have to choose."

"But they're not compatible," Gracie insisted.

"Of course they are. They shouldn't be in competition. The problem is with your preachers—and your scientists. They're stepping on each other's toes. With big, heavy boots. They don't understand that religion and science are there to serve different purposes. We need science to understand how everything on this planet and beyond works—us, nature, everything we see around us. That's fact—no one with a working brain can question that. But we also need religion. Not for ridiculous counter-theories about things that science can prove. We need it for something else, to fill a different kind of need. The need for meaning. It's a basic need we have, as humans. And it's a need that's beyond the realm of science. Your scientists don't understand that it's a need they can't fulfill no matter how many Hadron colliders and Hubble telescopes they build—and your preachers don't understand that their job is to help you discover a personal, inner sense of meaning and not behave like a bunch of zealots intent on converting the rest of the planet to their rigid, literalist view of how everyone should live their lives. In your country and in the Muslim countries, religion has become a political movement, not a spiritual one. 'God is on our side'—that's all I hear coming out of your churches. But that's not what they should be preaching."

"It didn't exactly work for the Confederacy, did it?" Gracie joked.

"It's very effective at rallying the masses. And at winning elections, of course," Father Jerome sighed. "Everyone claims Him at one point or another."

"The way they're now claiming you," she pointed out.

"Are they?" he asked, curious.

"We're in this plane, aren't we?"

Her comment seemed to strike a nerve, and he pondered it for a beat.

"Although," she mused, "they might be in for a bit of a surprise. *I'm* surprised. You're much less dogmatic than I imagined. Much more open-minded. Shockingly open-minded, in fact."

The priest smiled. "I've seen a lot. I've seen good, kind, generous people do the most charitable things. And I've seen others do the most horrific things you could imagine. And that's what makes us human. We have minds. We make our own choices and live by them. We shape our own lives with how we behave toward others. And God—whatever the word means—is just that. We feel His presence every time we make a choice. It's something that's inside us. Everything else is just . . . artifice."

"But you're a priest of the Church. You wear that," she said, pointing at a cross that hung from a leather strap around his neck. "How can you say that?"

She thought she detected some nervousness inside him, some uncertainty, as if it was something that had been troubling him too. He looked at her thoughtfully, then asked, "When the sign appeared . . . did you see a cross up there?"

Gracie wasn't sure what he meant. "No."

He smiled, somewhat uncomfortably, and his eyebrows rose as he opened out his palms in a silent gesture that said, "Exactly."

Chapter 63

Framingham, Massachusetts

At around midnight, the Chrysler 300C swung into the front lot of the Comfort Inn. Two men got out. Dark suits, white shirts, no ties. Lean, hard men, with flat glares and purposeful steps. A third man stayed in the car, behind the wheel. He kept the engine running. They weren't planning on staying long.

The two men entered the austere lobby. It was deserted, which was expected. Framingham wasn't exactly a hotbed of late-night merriment. They strode up to the reception desk. Behind it, a lone man of Latin origin and advancing years was huddled in a corner chair, watching a soccer match on a fuzzy screen. The lead man beckoned him over. His dark suit, surly expression, and sharp tone of voice got the receptionist on his feet in no time. The man reached into the breast pocket of his jacket and pulled out three items, which he spread out on the desk under the receptionist's nose: two photographs—headshots of Matt and Jabba—and a fifty-dollar bill.

The receptionist scanned the items, looked up at the man, looked back down, and nodded. He then reached out and, with a trembling hand, swept back the fifty and pocketed it. Then the man got his answer, but it wasn't the answer he wanted. They had checked in earlier that evening. Taken a room. Occupied it for a couple of hours. Then they'd paid and left. The guy behind the counter had figured something of a carnal nature was going down, and the mental picture it had inspired clearly wasn't one he was comfortable with.

They'd just missed them.

The man from the 300C frowned. He studied the receptionist for a beat, decided there was nothing more to be gained, and walked out. They'd paid, which meant they weren't coming back. Something about it didn't sit well with him. Why take a room for just a couple of hours? He figured something unexpected must have come up. Something that didn't come through on the fat guy's cell phone. Which wasn't good news. It meant they had some other way of communicating with the outside world, one that his own side wasn't aware of.

He led the other man back out, paused by the car, and gave the parking lot an instinctive once-over. Nothing suspicious caught his eye. He pulled out his phone and made the call. Informed his boss what he'd been told. Heard the irritation and anger in his boss's voice. And was ordered to head back to the safe house and wait for further instructions.

The two men climbed back into the 300C. Their driver waited for a passing car, then slid the beefy Chrysler onto the road and drove off, oblivious to the dark polo green Pontiac Bonneville that pulled out a safe distance back and was now tailing them.

◄◦►

MATT AND JABBA kept their eyes peeled on the taillights of the 300C and didn't say much. It was late, the traffic was sparse, the cars few and far between. It all made the risk of them being spotted that much greater. They had to be extra vigilant. No mouthing off or second-guessing their plan. No superfluous chitchat. Just total focus.

They'd baited them by lighting up Jabba's iPhone. The Chrysler's appearance had confirmed Matt's suspicion that Maddox and his goons had been able to track them, despite Jabba's precautions, what with the phone being switched on for such short bursts. Somehow, they had been doing it. Which gave Matt an opening to draw them in. And wait.

The 300C hung a right on Cochituate and curled around to meet the turnpike, which they rode east. There were more cars there, which ramped down the tension of getting spotted, but ramped it up as far as losing the 300C was concerned. Still, Matt had significantly better-than-average driving skills and a keen eye when it came to spotting subtle changes in the attitude of cars, which helped keep them in the game.

They weren't in the least bit sure of what they'd find when the 300C got to wherever it was headed. As Matt had conceded to Jabba, he didn't really think he'd find Danny there, but there was a small chance they'd find Rebecca Rydell. Maddox didn't seem to have an entire brigade of thugs dedicated to this. They were running a lean, mean operation. It wasn't beyond reason to think they weren't running more than one safe house, and that they might be keeping her stashed away at one. It would be the safest place to keep her, and saved resources. Matt started to reel back to what would have happened had he not moved the tracker over to Maddox's car in the first place, but gave up after finding it was taking away from his concentration. He didn't want to risk losing them. Beyond the possibility of finding Rebecca Rydell, this was also a chance to throw a wrench into Maddox's plans, which, to Matt, sounded pretty satisfying right now.

They dumped the turnpike for I-95, which they rode

north for a couple of miles before getting off at Weston. Matt pulled back as the traffic got lighter. He stalked the big car and its distinctive, boxy taillights east, all the way to Bacon, where it turned left and headed into Waltham. The going got dicier. There were far fewer cars here, and Matt had to drop way back to avoid being noticed. He also switched from main beams to daytime running lights at each change of direction to vary the front appearance of the Bonneville in the 300C's mirrors.

The 300C threaded through some residential streets before finally turning into an unlit driveway. Matt already had his lights off and pulled over a couple of houses back. He killed the motor and watched. The three men emerged from the car and headed into the house. The last of them, the driver, beeped the car shut. He hung back and gave the street a cursory sweep before following the two other goons in.

Moments later, the 300C's interior lights automatically faded to black and the car and the house were shrouded in darkness.

The house was a small, two-story structure. Matt knew those houses well—it wasn't far from where he'd grown up, in Worcester, and the internal layouts in that stratum of the housing market were pretty standard. Front or side entrance to a front living room, kitchen at the back, stairs in the middle going up to two or three bedrooms and a bathroom or two upstairs. There was also a basement, and Matt was pretty sure that was where they'd be keeping any prisoners.

There were no lights on in the upper floor, and the front living room was also dark. Traces of light from the back of the ground floor filtered through the bay window of the living room and cast a faint glow on its ceiling.

Matt glanced at Jabba and nodded. There was another

car in the driveway. The black Durango they'd seen at the airfield. The one Maddox's goons had stuffed Rebecca Rydell into.

The easy part was over. It was time to crash that party.

Luckily, they hadn't come empty-handed.

◄◦►

THE GUYS FROM THE CHRYSLER were in the kitchen at the back of the house, talking, having a smoke, sipping cold cans of Coke. Going over the events of the day. Winding down. Not really expecting to be called out again that night.

The loud crash changed things.

It blasted through the house and whipped them to attention. It came from the front, at ground level. From the living room. The distinctive sound of glass, exploding inward: something dense thumping heavily against the wall and landing in a dull thud while a shower of glass cascaded down onto the floor, where it exploded into tiny shards.

The guys moved as one, the lead guy from the hotel barking orders as he rushed to the front of the house, his gun already drawn and out in front. He got one guy to stay behind in the kitchen. Another followed him halfway through the house and stopped at the central staircase, positioning himself at a door that led to the basement. The third was hot on his heels as he burst into the front living room.

It had a wide bay window, and louvered half shutters ran a little over halfway up the glass, to a height of about five feet off the ground. In a defensive reflex, he didn't turn on the lights, relying instead on the dim light that spilled in from the hallway. The room should have been empty, as the rental was unfurnished, and it still was, except for the glass shards that littered the wood floor. They crunched noisily under the man's heels as he advanced into the room, sweeping his gun around. He stopped and looked up at the bay window and saw that its central portion had a huge hole punched out of it, the size of a large pumpkin. He glanced around, trying to make sense of what had happened, and spotted a rock, about the size of a football, at the foot of the back wall. His mind was still processing the idea of someone throwing a big rock through the window when something else came crashing in, something bigger and bulkier that clipped the edge of the broken glass, busted an ever wider gap through what was left of it, and narrowly missed him. It showered him with glass and splashed him with a sour-smelling liquid before it tumbled to the ground and clattered to a rest. He stared at it, dumbfounded for a nanosecond. It was a gas can. Lightweight polyethylene, red, threaded vent. Only its lid wasn't screwed on. In fact, it didn't have a lid. And it had spewed fuel like a Catherine wheel as it spun through the air on its inward flight, hosing him along the way and now spilling its load all over the floor.

"Fuck," he rasped as he lunged down and grabbed its handle, turning it upright to stem the flow of gas—only that didn't help, as small geysers of fuel were pouring out of it from all sides, drenching his arms and legs as well as the floor around him. He saw that crude perforations had been cut into it. There was no way to stop the fuel from pouring out. Which wouldn't have been that bad, except that a third projectile came flying into the room. This one was coming right at him, and it was lit.

◄◦►

MATT WATCHED THE MOVEMENT of shadows inside the front room and flicked the lighter on. In his other hand, he held a water bottle that he'd emptied, then refilled, half with gasoline, half with motor oil. A wick, in the form of a strip of dust cloth that was soaked with gasoline, was stuffed tightly into its neck, waiting for the flame. Two other identical projectiles were ready and willing by his feet.

The rock had drawn the guys from the Chrysler into the room, in time to receive the gas can he'd cut holes into. He knew he had to move fast and hit them before they understood what was going on. He lit the rag and lobbed the bottle in. The petrol bomb arced through the cool night air and flew into the room through the broken window. A flash of light lit up behind the shutters, followed almost instantly by a bigger fireball as the flames caught the fuel from the gas can. He heard a panicked scream, lit a second bottle, hurled it in through the same opening, grabbed the third bottle, and sprinted around to the back of the house.

◄◉►

THE LEAD GUY SHRIEKED as his arms and legs caught fire. He twisted around furiously, trying to bat the flames down with his bare hands, the second guy sidestepping around him in a panic, unsure about what to do to help. The flames were stubborn, more stubborn and stickier than expected—and hotter. The gasoline was easier to smother and kill off. The motor oil was a different story. It stuck like tar and burned stronger and harder. There was no way to get it off his clothes or off the skin on his hands, and it was growing, hungrily consuming everything it touched. Flames had also grabbed hold of the floor and were spreading across the wood.

"Get it off me," he yelled demonically as he dropped to the ground and rolled on himself, trying to suffocate the flames, unaware of the futility of his moves. Shards of glass were now cutting into his exposed, burning skin, which made the pain intolerable. The second guy took off his jacket and crab-stepped around him, looking for an opening to dive in and wrap it around him. Gray smoke was choking the room, thick with the stink of charred skin and hair and burned motor oil. The third guy, the one who'd been stationed by the stairs, was also in the room, watching his burning partner in horror. He looked around frantically, trying to find something to use to smother the flames, but the room was bare. No carpets, no curtains, no throws over sofas.

"What the fuck's going on?" the fourth guy shouted from the back of the house.

"The kitchen," the second guy ordered the third guy. "Cover the back."

But it was too late.

◄◦►

THE FOURTH GUY WAS ALONE in the kitchen. He had edged right up to the door, by the hall, trying to see what was happening while not wanting to move away from covering the house's back entrance. He could hear the screams and see the flames and the smoke and smell the stink billowing out through the living room's door and getting pushed through the house by the air coming in from the broken window, and it panicked him. It panicked him enough to snag his attention away from the back door and move him away from it enough to make Matt's move feasible.

Matt was hugging the back wall of the house and peering in through the kitchen window. He recognized the man as one of the two guys who'd escorted Rebecca Rydell off the plane, and it gave him a boost of confidence that she might be there. He registered the man's position and decided it would do. He lit the last bottle, took three steps back to give his Molotov cocktail enough momentum to break through the glass, and hurled it with all his strength. The bottle punched its way into the kitchen and exploded against the wall inches away from the guy. He bolted sideways as flames fanned out angrily, looking for fuel. That split second of diversion was all Matt needed. He kicked the door in right after the throw and caught the guy flat-footed. The guy was still swinging his gun hand around when Matt put him down with two rounds to the chest.

He pushed through the house without hesitating, scanning around for a locked door, sweeping the area with his P14. It felt weird being in there. He wondered if Danny had ever been held captive there. The feeling made him angrier. He stowed it for now and focused on finding Rebecca Rydell. His guess was they'd be keeping her in the basement, and sure enough, the door that led down, by the stairs, was shut. Not only shut, but locked, as someone was desperately hammering against it from the inside and tugging against its handle and yelling. A girl's voice, confirming Matt's thinking.

He didn't veer off to help her. There were at least four of them, and two potentially out of action still left at least two goons to deal with. Matt was easing past the stairs when another guy slipped out of the living room, on his way to help his now-dead colleague in the kitchen. Matt had a flash of recognition from the airfield. He didn't stop to ponder it. He just lunged sideways and down as the guy from the plane loosed off a couple of rounds that crunched into the walls just as Matt let the big handgun rip. A round caught the guy in the thigh, and he jerked backward momentarily; then his leg buckled and he collapsed on top of it. The shooter raised his gun, hoping for another shot. The strength had drained out of him and he looked like he was trying to lift a lead brick. Matt was on bent knees, down low against the wall, in a two-handed stance, and squeezed off two more rounds that took the guy out.

Matt stayed there for a beat. He glanced up the stairs, dismissed the idea that anyone would still be up there, and just stayed where he was and waited, arms outstretched, covering the door, watching the smoke and the flames wafting out from the living room, the screaming and the stomping echoing in his ears. He knew the fourth guy had to come back out if he didn't want to get barbecued alive. And there was only one way out of that room.

And then he heard them. The sirens, low and grating squawks, distant but closing in. Just when he needed them. He'd told Jabba to call 911 the instant the first petrol bomb exploded, figuring he'd have enough time to storm through the house before the fire engines got there, and thinking they could come in handy if things hadn't gone according to plan. The sirens grew louder, and he crouched lower, arms tensing up, expecting that the guy inside had heard them and would be needing to make a desperate, Butch-and-Sundance-like breakout. And then he heard something else: glass, shattering furiously, a loud crashing noise, and he understood. The guy had decided to bail through what was left of the bay window.

A stab of panic cut into Matt as he thought about Jabba, out there on his own without a weapon, but they'd parked a couple of houses back and he imagined neighbors were probably stepping out of their houses by now and converging outside the house, alerted by the flames and the gunshots, which would give Jabba some cover.

He waited a beat longer, straining to listen to any telltale noise that contradicted what he thought had happened, then scrambled back to the closed door. Rebecca

Rydell—it had to be her—was still banging her fists against the door and shouting.

"Hey! What's going on? Get me out of here!"

Matt tried the handle, but it was locked. "Step back from the door," he yelled back. "I need to shoot the lock off."

He waited a couple of seconds, then shouted, "You back?"

She said, "Yes," and he fired—once, twice. It more than did the trick. The locks were old and basic, the doorframe soft with age. He kicked the door in. Wooden treads led down to a basement where an attractive, tanned girl was cowering against the wall, her face riven with terror.

He extended his arm down toward her, waving her up. "Come on, we've got to go," he hollered over the increasing crackle of the flames. She hesitated for a second, then nodded nervously and rose to her feet.

They stormed out of the house, past the startled faces of a few neighbors, past a fire truck that was swinging into the driveway. Matt peered through the darkness, scanning for the Bonneville, and a stab of dread cut into him as he saw that it was no longer there. A scream of horror confirmed his worst fears and he ran faster, his heart fighting its way out of his rib cage, imagining the worst. As he drew nearer, he spotted Jabba's silhouette, flat on his back on the curb outside a nearby house.

He wasn't moving.

A couple of onlookers were huddled beside him, the man checking him out hesitantly, the woman staring down, riveted with fear, her hands cupping her mouth.

"Jabba," Matt yelled as he slid to the ground beside him.

In the darkness, it was hard to see where the wound was, but a pool of blood was spreading out from under him. He was having a hard time keeping his eyes open, but he caught sight of Matt and tried to say something, but coughed and was having trouble forming the words.

"Did we get her?" he sputtered.

Matt nodded and said, "She's right here," turning around to give Jabba a glimpse of Rebecca Rydell, who inched forward, her face flooded with sadness. "Don't talk," Matt told him, gripping his hand, tight. "Just hang on, okay? Hang on. You're going to be fine." He turned to the couple looming over him. "Call nine one one," he shouted. "Call them now."

The woman raced into the house. Matt just stayed there, hanging on to Jabba—hoping to avoid the worst, cursing himself for having dragged him along—for what felt like hours but was actually less than ten minutes until an ambulance finally showed up.

Matt stayed with him as the paramedics fussed over him before bundling him onto their stretcher with breathtaking efficiency.

Matt kept asking, "Is he going to be okay?" but he couldn't get a straight answer out of them. With a devastating sense of loss choking him, he watched as they wheeled Jabba into the back of the ambulance, shut the doors, and stormed off.

He heard another siren—a police cruiser this time—and glanced at Rebecca Rydell. She was huddled on the lawn, still shivering.

"Come on," he said as, mouthing a silent prayer for the life of his new friend, he took her hand and led her away from the horror-struck crowd that had gathered around the blazing house.

Chapter 64

Houston, Texas

"Where are they now?" Buscema asked the preacher.

Reverend Darby was in his study. It was late, but he didn't mind Buscema's call. He owed him for giving him the heads-up on Father Jerome's predicament. He also didn't mind the ego boost he got from talking about it with virtually the only other person in the country outside his organization who knew what he was doing.

"They should be landing in Shannon, Ireland, about an hour and a half from now," he told Buscema. "It shouldn't take more than a couple of hours to refuel the jet." Darby sounded even more pumped than during his sermons.

"So what time will they get here?"

"I make it around six a.m., Houston time."

Buscema went silent. Then he said, "You might want to delay their arrival a bit."

"Why?"

"Well, I suppose it depends," Buscema thought out loud. "You could sneak him in under the radar. Might be safer to play it that way."

"Or we could turn his arrival into a major event," Darby said, completing Buscema's train of thought. He pondered it for a moment, then said, "I was wondering about that. You're right. He deserves to make a big entrance. We shouldn't be sneaking him in like some petty criminal. The man's God's emissary, for crying out loud. We're not like those savages. We're going to welcome him with open arms. Let's show the country and the world where America's moral center really is."

"I can help leak it," Buscema told him. "Just give me as much of a heads-up as you can."

Darby played it out in his mind's eye. He saw it as something big. Momentous. He flashed to news footage he'd watched a year earlier, of the pope arriving at Andrews Air Force Base. The red carpet, the military dress uniforms. The president and the First Lady greeting him as he stepped off the plane. His mind went back to older footage he'd seen several times. Grainy, black-and-white footage of the Beatles, arriving at Kennedy Airport, back in 1964. That was more like it. The frenzied mob, heaving against barricades. The continuous earsplitting screams. Flashbulbs popping, women wailing. Sheer adulation. That's what this would be like. That was what it should be like. With him at the center of it.

The thought put a smile on his face. It would be a defining moment. For the country and, more significantly, for him.

I'll be upstaging the president, he thought triumphantly. *And that's only the beginning.*

"I'll give you enough time," Darby said.

"You're going to need some serious crowd control," Buscema opined.

"Not a problem. The governor is part of my flock."

"What about beyond that? Any progress on your Christmas offering?"

"The stadium's booked," the preacher confided. "It'll be a rush, but we'll make it happen. We're bringing in some performers. Big names. You mark my words, Roy. I'm going to give the people of this country a Christmas they'll never forget."

Buscema went quiet. The kind of quiet he knew Darby would pick up on.

Sure enough, the pastor said, "What is it?"

"I'm just a bit concerned about sending out the right message."

"Meaning?" Darby didn't sound thrilled.

Buscema let out a ragged sigh, as if this were a tough call. "I'm hearing grumblings. From other pastors and church leaders."

"I know," Darby fumed. "We've been swamped with calls since the news got out. Every preacher from here to California's been on the line. Even the governor wants in."

"Wouldn't be a bad idea to share that platform, Reverend. Get the word out more widely. Turn this into a much bigger and broader event. The country could use it right now."

"I'm the guy flying him in, Roy," Darby noted calmly. "I got him out of there."

"And you'll be the one greeting him when he steps off that plane," Buscema reassured him. "You. No one else."

"The governor's also pushing to be there. I'm finding it hard to keep ducking him."

"Doesn't matter, Reverend. There won't be any other pastors at the airport. Just you. It'll be your moment. That's the image people will remember when they first see him. But after that, I'd say it's in your interest to show as much generosity as you can handle and invite as many other church leaders to join you on the big day. You've got to think big. You can take the lead on this. America doesn't have a pope. It doesn't have a spiritual leader. But the country needs one. Especially given how tough things are right now. Americans need to be inspired. To feel like they're part of something." He paused, just enough to let the words settle but not enough to give the preacher an opening to argue back. "You don't want it to look like just another service at your church. This one's for the whole country. For the whole world. You can't be alone on that stage. But you can do it on your terms. And by extending a welcoming hand, you'll only be elevating your own position as a gracious host . . . and leader."

◄○►

Tough part's over, Buscema thought after hanging up with Darby. Now he'd have to wait and see if the self-obsessed blowhard would play nice and share. He needed Darby to play nice. He needed him to share his new toy with the other kids. And that, he knew, was never easy. Not when you were dealing with a spoiled brat, let alone one with a righteousness complex.

He picked up his phone and hit another speed-dial key. The man on the other end had been waiting for the call.

Buscema just said, "We're on. Leak it," then hung up.

Chapter 65

Shannon, Ireland

The Gulfstream was parked by a service hangar, away from the small airport's terminal. Gracie was pacing around by the plane as she spoke on her cell phone. She was out in the open and wasn't really worried about being spotted. It was night, and there was no one around apart from a few dozy and uninterested maintenance guys who were refueling the jet.

It was much colder there, another shock to her system after the chill of the South Pole and the warm embrace of the Egyptian desert. The cold, though, felt good. Bracing. Numbing. Which was helpful, given that she was on the phone with the abbot and reliving Finch's death in all its grisly detail.

He was on his way back from Cairo. He told her they'd delivered Finch's body to the American embassy there. It hadn't been easy getting there. He told her that fierce clashes had erupted among the hordes outside the monastery once news of Father Jerome's departure had been made public. Jeep-loads of internal security men had stormed across the plain and contained the outburst, and were now clearing away the last troublemakers, but the situation had repeated itself in Cairo and in Alexandria and in other cities across the region.

Gracie saw Dalton coming toward her, waving his BlackBerry, indicating there was a call for her. She was thanking the abbot when he remembered something and said, "I'm also very sorry about your friend's glasses. One of my brothers broke them by accident. We put the frame in the pocket of his jacket."

Dalton was right up with her and mouthed "Ogilvy" to her. Seemed like it was pretty urgent. Gracie raised a pausing index finger at him, her foggy mind trying to make sense of what the abbot was talking about.

"I'm sorry. Finch's glasses?"

"Yes," the abbot said. "One of my brothers stepped on them by accident. He didn't see them." ·

"That's all right," she said, nodding to Dalton like she was done. "I didn't notice them either," she added.

"No, you wouldn't have," he corrected. "They weren't outside. They were in the keep, and as you know, it's quite dark in there. Anyway, I'm really sorry. I know it's the kind of personal belonging that matters to loved ones at times like these. Would you please apologize to his wife on my behalf?"

"Of course," Gracie said, still distracted by Dalton. "Thanks for everything, Father. I'll call you from America." She clicked off and took the other phone from Dalton.

It was Ogilvy. His news pushed any thought of Finch to the sidelines.

"It's out," he told her, his tone urgent. "The word's out that Father Jerome's on his way here."

"What do you mean? It's been leaked?" Gracie asked. "How?"

"I don't know. It came up on Drudge half an hour ago and it's everywhere now."

She scanned around with her eyes, suddenly paranoid.

A vision of converging mobs flashed before her, then evaporated. "Do they know we're here?"

"No, they didn't mention that. All they know is that Father Jerome is out of Egypt and on his way here, to Houston. It doesn't even mention Darby."

Gracie frowned. This wasn't good. She pictured the media circus and the chaos that would be greeting them.

"We've got to change destinations. Fly in somewhere else. Somewhere quiet."

"Why?" Ogilvy asked.

"'Cause people are going to go nuts when they see him. We'll get mobbed."

"I called Darby. He told me he's got the cops lined up to help. They're gonna cordon off the tarmac, provide a rolling escort. It'll be fine."

"You're not serious?"

"Are you kidding me?" Ogilvy asked. "This is still our story. *Your* story. Every reporter in America would give both arms to be in your shoes. Think about it. Every single TV set in the country is going to be watching you as you walk off that plane right alongside Father Jerome, with Dalton's camera giving us a live inside track. And Darby wants you and Dalton to stick around. He's going to put you up with them. I'm flying out too. So just relax and get some rest and get ready for it. We've got a show to do, and you're about to get the biggest scoop of your life."

Chapter 66

"**D**ad?"

Rydell couldn't believe his ears. His pulse raced ahead with equal doses of fear and hope. He could feel it pounding against his cell phone. "Where are you? Are you okay?"

"I'm fine," she said. "They got me out. I'm fine."

Rydell's heart cartwheeled. Her voice had a quaver in it, but she didn't sound afraid.

"Hang on," she said.

He heard some shuffling as the handset evidently changed hands; then he heard the last voice he was expecting.

"Are you alone?"

He recognized Matt's voice. A sudden panic seized him. "Where are you? What have you done?"

Matt ignored his question. "She's safe. Can you get out without the escorts?"

"I don't know." Rydell faltered. "I . . . I can try."

"Do it," Matt ordered. "Do it right now. And meet us outside the place you took Rebecca for her eighteenth birthday."

The line went dead.

Rydell didn't know what to think. Was she Matt's hostage now? Was that his plan? He wasn't sure what he preferred—knowing she was in his hands, or in Maddox's.

He wasn't sure either way. What he was sure of was that now that Rebecca was out, Drucker didn't have any hold over him. Unless he tried to grab him and substitute him for Rebecca.

He had to get out.

Now.

He picked up the hotel phone and hit the RECEPTION button. Got an answer on the first ring.

"This is Rydell. I need security up here. Right now. As many guys as you can send. My bodyguards are up to something; I need protection right now. From them." His tone left no room for doubt as to the urgency involved.

The flustered voice on the other end was still fumbling through a reply when Rydell hung up. He darted to the bedroom, found his wallet and his coat, and pulled his shoes on; darted back to the door of his suite and eased against it for a peek through the peephole. He could see the two bodyguards, Maddox's men, standing outside his door. Looking bored, killing time. He waited. About ten seconds later, he heard the whine of the elevator's motor and the clunk of the doors sliding open. Four men rushed out and stormed over to the suite's door. Rydell saw the bodyguards step toward the security guys, arms raised in a halting what's-going-on gesture.

Rydell grabbed his chance. He swung the door open and stormed out, sprinting past the surprised bodyguards and through the wall of security guys, waving a panicked finger back toward his bodyguards and shouting, "Stop them. They're trying to kidnap me. Help me get out of here."

The security guys flinched with confusion, as did the

bodyguards, who were caught flat-footed by Rydell's rushed exit. Maddox's men stepped forward forcefully, one of them reaching for his holstered handgun, but the security guys weren't cowed. Two of them were beefy bouncer types, and they just stood their ground and closed in on each other, creating a barrier across the corridor. One of them, the biggest one of the lot, held up a stern warning finger and had his handgun out too, a mocking you-really-don't-want-to-do-this grimace across his face. Rydell didn't wait to watch the outcome. He slipped into the elevator, jabbed the DOWN button repeatedly until the doors rumbled shut, and rode down to the lobby, his nerves on fire. The short ride felt like forever. He raced out the second the door opened, flew out of the lobby, and hurtled into a lone, waiting cab. He ordered the guy to just go, and craned his head back as the cab drove off, to make sure they weren't being followed. He made the driver take a few rudderless lefts and rights. When he was satisfied that they were on their own, he told him where to go.

◄◦►

IT WAS A SHORT HOP around the Common and past Faneuil Hall to get to the Garden. That late at night, the traffic was light, despite the holiday rush. As the cab turned to pull into the arena's parking lot, Rydell spotted Matt across the street, leaning against a dark sedan. Rydell got the cabbie to drop him off at the gate, waited for him to drive well clear, and crossed the road to join them. He was halfway across when the rear door swung open and his daughter clambered out of the car and ran over to him.

He hugged her tight. He still couldn't quite believe it. He looked over her shoulder. Matt was just standing there, leaning back against the car, his arms crossed, an angry look on his face. Rydell kept a firm grip on Rebecca's hand as he went up to him.

"You did this." Rydell said. More like a statement than a question.

"My friend's in the hospital," Matt told him crisply. "He's been shot. Bad. I need you to make a call and make sure they give him everything he needs."

Rydell nodded and reached for his phone. "Of course."

"He's also going to need protection," Matt added. "Is there anyone you can call?"

"I've got the number of the detective who came out to the house," he said. "I can call him."

"Do it," Matt said.

Rydell kept hold of Rebecca as he made the calls. It didn't take long. His name usually helped speed things up.

They told him Jabba was in surgery, and that the prognosis was uncertain. He hung up and informed Matt.

"He's in good hands," Rydell told him. "He'll get the best of care."

"I damn well hope so."

Rydell studied him, unsure about where they stood. "I'm sorry about your friend. I just . . . I can't thank you enough for doing this," he said, hesitantly.

"I just don't like your friends," Matt replied tersely. "They have this habit of locking people up."

Rebecca turned to meet Rydell's guilty look.

"And . . . ?" Rydell braced himself for more. Were they now both his prisoners?

"And nothing. My friend's been shot and your buddies still have my brother." Matt stared at him, hard. "I thought you might want to help me make things right."

Rydell brought his hand up and massaged his temple. He looked at Matt, then slid his eyes over to Rebecca.

She was eyeing him with a mixture of confusion, fear, and accusation.

He didn't know what to do. But he had no one left to protect.

"They're bringing him back," he finally said.

"Who?" Matt asked.

"The priest. Father Jerome. He's left Egypt. He's on his way here."

"Where here?"

"They're saying Houston," Rydell said. "It's only just hitting the wires. Wherever it is, they're bound to put a sign up over him, and the odds are, that's where you'll find Danny." He paused, collecting his thoughts. "You were right," he finally conceded. "They're planning something. Something they needed me around for. I don't know what it is, but what I thought the plan was, what they insisted was still their plan . . . it's not it. It's something else. It's all about the priest now."

"Who would know?" Matt asked him, fixing him squarely.

"The others."

"I need names."

Rydell held his gaze, then said, "You only need one name. Keenan Drucker. It's pretty much his show. He'll know."

"Where do I find him?"

"D.C. The Center for American Freedom. It's a think tank." Just then, Rydell's BlackBerry trilled. He fished it out of his pocket, checked its screen. And frowned at Matt.

Matt looked a question at him.

Rydell nodded. It was Drucker.

He hit the ANSWER key.

"What are you doing? Where the hell are you?" Drucker asked sharply.

"Working late, Keenan?" He looked pointedly at Matt, holding up his free hand in a stay-put gesture.

"What are you doing, Larry?"

"Getting my daughter back." Rydell let that one sink in for a beat. Drucker went mute. Then Rydell added, "Then I thought I might head down to the *New York Times* and have a little chat with them."

"Why would you want to do that?"

"'Cause I don't know what you're up to, but I'm pretty sure it has nothing to do with what we set out to achieve," Rydell shot back fiercely.

Drucker let out a rueful hiss. "Look, I made a mistake, all right? Taking Rebecca was way out of line. I know that. And I'm sorry. But you didn't leave me any choice. And we're in this together. We want the same thing."

"You're not doing this to save the planet, Keenan. We both know that."

Drucker's voice remained even. "We want the same thing, Larry. Believe me."

"And what is that?"

Drucker went silent for a moment, then said, "Let's meet somewhere. Anywhere you want. Hear me out. I'll tell you what I'm thinking. After that, you decide if you still want to bring this whole thing down on top of us."

Rydell swung his gaze around to Matt and Rebecca. Let Drucker sweat it out for a beat. He knew he needed to hear him out. Too much—his whole life, everything he'd achieved, everything he could still achieve—was at stake. "I'll think about it," he replied flatly, then hung up.

"What did he want?" Matt asked.

"To talk. To convince me to play ball."

Matt nodded, then pointed at Rydell's BlackBerry. "They might have a lock on you."

Rydell held up the device, a curious expression on his face. "What, this?"

"They were tracking us. Through my friend's phone. Even though we've been careful. We only had it on for short bursts."

Rydell didn't seem the least bit concerned. "We can do it in the time it takes your phone to send out a text message."

Matt didn't get it.

"It's one of ours," Rydell assured him. "A piece of spyware we developed for the NSA. But there's nothing to worry about here. We're fine. My phone's vaccinated against it."

Matt shrugged, looked away, then swung his gaze back at Rydell. "What are you gonna do?"

Rydell pondered his question. "I don't know." He hadn't had any time to think and strategize. Not that he felt overwhelmed with options. Everything felt like it was crashing down around him. But Rebecca's call had changed all that.

He gazed at his daughter. Her safety was paramount. "We can't stay here," he told Matt. "Not in Boston. Not after your little visit. There's nowhere to lay low, not in this town. Anywhere we go will get flagged to the press—and to Maddox."

Matt nodded, mulled it over for a moment, then said, "Don't you want to see it?"

"What?"

"Your handiwork. In all its glory."

Rydell thought about it for a beat, then said, "Why the hell not? Let's get out of here."

Chapter 67

Houston, Texas

The crowds were visible from the sky.

Gracie didn't spot them at first. The jet was banking around the small airport, coming in on a low-altitude, looped approach. From a height of around a thousand feet, all she noticed was a solid mass, a dark blot staining the pale wintry scrub that surrounded the acres of gray concrete. The traffic jams gave it away. All the small roads leading to the field were clogged with cars. Vehicles were just strewn all over the place haphazardly, like Lego bricks tossed out of a box. They were all jammed up one against another on the fields on either side of the roads, and weren't going anywhere anytime soon. The traffic was backed up all the way to the Beltway, which was choked for a couple of miles in each direction. People were just abandoning their cars and making their way to the field, following those ahead of them like groupies converging on a big open-field rock concert. They were swarming in from all corners, heading for the northwestern corner of the airport, not far from the northern tip of the runway.

Gracie wasn't familiar with the airfield. Darby had explained to her that the chief of police had requested they avoid Hobby and Bush Intercontinental and use Ellington Field instead. For one thing, it wouldn't disrupt the commercial flights in and out of the city. Ellington was a small, mostly military airfield. A handful of private jet operators had FBOs there, but it wasn't used by any airlines. It didn't even have a terminal. It was no more than a couple of runways and a row of uneven hangars that were home to the Coast Guard, NASA, as well as the Texas Air National Guard, where, famously, George W. Bush had been based during the Vietnam War, ready to thwart any Vietcong attack on Houston. Crowd control would also be easier there. The airfield was used to handling public events, especially since it was home to the annual Wings Over Houston air show.

Still, Gracie was willing to bet they hadn't experienced anything like this.

The jet touched down faultlessly and veered off to the left at the end of the runway. It rolled on for a hundred yards or so before coming to a stop by a large single hangar that had its frontage wide-open. A twin-jet helicopter was parked nearby, a couple of men standing beside it. The captain throttled back and killed the Gulfstream's engines, and as they whined down, the noise from outside seeped in, an eerie wave of clapping and cheering that was loud enough to defy the air seals of the cabin and its triple-glazed windows.

Gracie looked at Father Jerome. His face was tight with anxiety and glistened with a sheen of sweat. She reached out and put her hand on his, smiling supportively.

"It's going to be fine," she said. "They're here to welcome you."

He nodded stoically, as if resigned to his new role.

His look brought back the same unease she'd felt on the roof of the keep, and she wondered why she wasn't feeling any relief at being back on safe and solid ground. She glanced over at Dalton. He was already getting his camera ready and turning on the Began to set up a live feed.

"You ready for this?" he asked her.

"No," she said with an uncertain smile.

◄◦►

NELSON DARBY WAITED by the empty tarmac and drank in the clamor rising up from the mass of onlookers. He was used to big crowds. His megachurch welcomed over ten thousand people every Sunday, and over fifteen thousand on special occasions. This was different. Normally, he was the one providing the fire. He was the catalyst. The crowd would soak up his energy and respond when prompted. He wasn't used to being a passive observer, but the crowd behind the barriers at the edge of the airfield were providing the fireworks themselves. They were clapping and whooping as if they were waiting for Bono to come out for an encore. A large group to the left were singing "I've Been Redeemed" and swaying back and forth with each line. And Father Jerome hadn't even stepped off the plane yet.

The pastor glanced over to his left, where the governor was standing stiffly by his side. He gave the silver-haired politician as genuine a smile as he could muster and swiveled his gaze over to his right. Roy Buscema met his gaze and nodded solemnly.

Darby leaned closer to him and said, "Good call, amigo," in a low voice.

Buscema just nodded again and kept his eyes fixed on the plane's cabin door as it cracked open.

The crowd roared as the door swung outward. Its retractable stairs slid down and touched the ground, and three of Darby's people rolled a red carpet out to meet it in preparation for Father Jerome's descent.

Without inviting any of his guests to join him, Rever-

end Darby strode up to the plane, turning briefly to acknowledge the crowd with a regal wave and his signature
megawatt smile. The hordes, pressed against the fences
that the police had barely managed to put up, roared
back their appreciation as the preacher positioned himself
at the base of the steps. The governor followed, mimicking Darby's nod to the crowd, but he'd missed the moment and failed to generate the same response.

◂◦▸

INSIDE THE PLANE, Father Jerome straightened his cassock
and padded to the front of the cabin. He seemed lost
and confused, a stranger in a strange land. He turned to
Gracie, the same anxious look darkening his face. Brother
Ameen stepped closer to him and took his hand, cupping
it with both of his.

"It's going to be fine," he told the older priest.

Gracie watched, anxious, waiting for him to settle
down. Father Jerome sucked in a deep breath, then
straightened up, nodding with renewed resolve.

"Is it okay if we start rolling?" she asked, pointing at
Dalton and his camera. Brother Ameen studied Father
Jerome, then turned to Gracie and gave her a nod. Gracie pressed the earpiece into place, lifted her BlackBerry
up to her mouth, and gave Roxberry a low-voiced go
signal. They were going out live, as planned—an exclusive for the network.

Father Jerome stooped slightly to pass through the
cabin door's low opening and stepped onto the landing
at the top of the retractable stairs. Gracie and Dalton
were inside the cabin, filming him from behind. The
crowd's reaction was thunderous. A tsunami of adulation
came barreling over them from all sides. Father Jerome
froze and stood there and let it roll over him, his eyes
swimming across the sea of faces spread out before him.

Gracie craned her neck to get a better look. There were people stretching back as far as she could see. Some carried banners; others had their arms raised. There were cries and wails and tears of joy, a torrent of religious fervor barely held back by the barricades. Television cameras and mobile broadcasting vans were everywhere, their oversized satellite dishes dotted around and giving the airfield the look of a SETI installation. A couple of news choppers circled overhead, their cameras rolling.

Father Jerome raised one hand, then another, an open embrace that spoke of humility, not of showmanship. The crowd went ballistic, clapping and screaming expectantly, their eyes scanning the sky anxiously, wondering if they'd be seeing the miracle for themselves. Father Jerome himself tilted his head up slightly, sliding a glance upward, also wondering if anything was going to appear, but he didn't wait for it. He glanced back at Brother Ameen and at Gracie and climbed down the stairs, straight into Reverend Darby's welcoming embrace.

Gracie and Dalton followed him down and hovered discreetly to one side.

"Are you getting this?" she asked Roxberry. He was back at the studio, anchoring the coverage.

"You bet." His voice crackled in her earpiece. "Keep it coming."

She watched as the reverend kept the priest's hand firmly cocooned inside his own cupped hands and whispered some words into his ear. The priest seemed surprised by what he was saying; then he nodded hesitantly, as if out of courtesy.

Darby turned to the audience, raised his arms, and flapped them down gently in a quieting gesture. The crowd took a moment to settle down, and when they finally quieted, the stillness was eerie. A combination of anticipation and foreboding was palpable. Then one of

Darby's assistants handed him a microphone and he raised a hand to the crowd.

"Brothers and sisters in Christ," he announced in his barrel-organ voice, "greetings in the name of Jesus Christ, our Lord, to you all, and thanks for coming out here with me to greet our very special visitor, Father Jerome." He stretched the *o* in Jerome, like a game announcer, and got a wildly raucous reply from the crowd.

"Now as you know, tomorrow is a very special day. Tomorrow is Christmas Day, a special time of celebration for us all, and yet . . . and yet, this year, a time of pause, a time when we must bow our heads humbly and think about these troubled, testing times we're in, think about what we could have done to make things better and what the future holds for us. And up until a few days ago, I was troubled. I was bothered and I was distressed. I was finding it hard to remain hopeful. And like many of you, I've been praying. I've been praying for God to spare our great nation. To spare it from the judgment we certainly deserve for our many trespasses, like the killing of millions upon millions of preborn children. I've been praying for God to be merciful with the millstone we deserve to have hung around our necks for our sins. For allowing our scientists to experiment with stem cells and colliders. For allowing our living children to be exploited by the deviant anarchists who now control public education and Hollywood. For tolerating those who would like to do away with Christmas altogether. And when a great nation like ours is going through troubled times such as these, when a great nation like ours is on its knees, the only normal and natural and spiritual thing to do is what we, as good Christians, should be doing all the time: calling upon God. Calling upon Him for guidance and for revival." He paused and let his somber words sink into the crowd, who went silent except for the scattered

"Amen" and "Bless the Lord"; then he sucked in a deep breath and beamed a kindly smile at the mob.

"Well guess what? I think God heard our prayers," he bellowed out, to a chorus of "Hallelujahs" and "Amens." "I know He heard our prayers. And I believe He's sending us a lifeline. A lifeline to help lead a nation and a world that are nearing moral collapse and perhaps even World War Three. A lifeline in the form of a pious, deeply spiritual man, a man who has devoted his entire life to the selfless pursuit of helping his fellow man. So I ask you all to please join me in welcoming the good Father Jerome to our great state of Texas," he boomed, triggering an even more tumultuous uproar.

Father Jerome cast his eye across the crowd, taking it all in silently. He glanced over at Gracie. She was standing next to Dalton, her mike poised in front of her, but she wasn't saying anything. She recognized the same confused, worried look on the priest's face, the one she'd seen on the roof of the *qasr* before the sign had appeared. He seemed clearly uneasy with everything that was happening.

Darby put his arm around the priest and oriented his attention back at the crowd. "Now I have a special request for Father Jerome, and I hope you'll all join me in this, as it's an invitation from the heart, from the heart of Texas and from the heart of the entire nation." He turned to Father Jerome, and said, "I know you're tired, and I know you've been through some heady days, but I'm here to ask you, on behalf of all these people and on behalf of the whole country—will you honor us with a special service tomorrow?"

The crowd whooped its approval in a crescendo of claps and cheers. Darby raised his hand to quiet them, then turned to Father Jerome, moving the mike right up to the priest's mouth and awaiting his answer. Father Jerome looked into his eyes for a beat, then gave him a nod and mouthed, "Of course."

"He said yes," Darby bellowed, and the crowd went nuts again. He raised his hands again to calm them, and said, "And you're all invited. Every one of you," pointing at the crowd. "Spend the day with your loved ones. Enjoy those turkeys and ring out those carols. And at six in the evening, come on down to the stadium at Reliant Park. We've got room for all of you." He beamed, and the crowd erupted into even louder cheers.

Darby waved to acknowledge his audience and put a guiding arm behind the priest for the best photo op he could have asked for, then herded him away from the crowd toward the hangar to their right.

"We're moving away from the crowd now," Gracie told Roxberry as she and Dalton followed, continuing their live transmission. "We seem to be headed for—" She heard the chopper's engines whining up and saw its blades start to spin. "We're headed for a chopper, Jack. Father Jerome is about to be choppered out of here, which is probably the only way out right now. I guess we're going to lose our connection, but we'll keep rolling the camera and get the pictures over to you as soon as we land."

They all piled into the helicopter—Darby, two of his assistants, the priest and the monk, Gracie, and Dalton. Less than a minute later, the chopper lifted off the ground, swooped around for a rousing pass over the crowd, and straightened out on a direct trajectory to the city, the two news choppers trailing in its wake.

Chapter 68

Houston, Texas

Matt was leaning forward, his eyes fixed on the wall-mounted plasma screen in the FBO's executive lounge at Hobby Airport. Rydell was also there, watching it with him. He had arranged the night flight from Boston, borrowing a jet from one of his dot-com buddies. It had dropped them off in Houston before continuing onward to Los Angeles, whisking Rebecca off to the relative safety of an old friend and a big city. At Hobby, Rydell had arranged for them to have exclusive use of the fixed base operator's facilities, figuring it made sense to hang back at the airport and figure out what their next move would be before going into the city proper and risking exposure. Then they'd sat back and watched.

The live coverage cut away from Grace Logan's feed and segued to the network's fixed camera at the edge of the airport, and the sight of the chopper taking off deflated Matt. He'd been hoping to see the sign show up over the false prophet, and to take its appearance as a sign that Danny was close by. It hadn't happened, but that didn't stop him from scrutinizing every corner of the screen, looking for anything suspicious right until the feed switched over to the aerial view from one of the trailing choppers and cut him dry.

Matt slumped back into the sofa, dropped his head back against it, and shut his eyes. "Reliant Stadium," he said. "That's where the Texans play, isn't it?"

Rydell was already on his BlackBerry. "Let's see what the weather's like tomorrow."

"Why?" Matt asked.

"The stadium's got a retractable roof. If it looks like it's not going to rain, they'll have it open—which they'll need to do if they're planning to put a sign up over him."

Matt kept his head back, staring at the ceiling. He sucked in a deep breath. "Tomorrow, then," he said.

They sat in silence for a moment, thinking ahead, trying to let some clarity back into their minds. Matt stared up at the ceiling. He felt a burgeoning optimism. He was getting closer to Danny, and he'd made it alive so far. The continuation of neither of which was a given, not by any measure.

"It's not going to be easy finding Danny," Rydell added. "The stadium's huge."

Matt frowned. He'd been thinking of something else. "Maybe we won't have to." He glanced across at Rydell. "Drucker told you he wanted to talk, right?"

"Last I heard, he was in D.C.," Rydell told him. Then something occurred to him. "Unless he's here. For all this."

"Call him. Tell him you're here if he wants to talk. And tell him to get his ass down here if he isn't here already."

Rydell weighed it. Seemed to like it, but with a slight reticence. "He'll suspect something's up."

Matt shrugged. "He'll still want to meet with you, and that's something we can control. We'll pick the place. We can be ready for him. Besides, it's not like I'm juggling ten different options here." He played it out one more time, then nodded, going for it. "Make the call."

"You sure?" Rydell asked.

"Get him down here," Matt confirmed. "I think we'd both like to hear what the bastard has to say."

Chapter 69

River Oaks, Houston, Texas

The area around Darby's house was entirely sealed off by the police. Running a perimeter four blocks out on three sides, their barricades were blocking all access except for residents. The back of the house looked out over the golf course, and access to the club was also now under strict police control. Officers and dogs patrolled the greens, on the lookout for overzealous believers and angry fanatics. The governor also had the National Guard on standby, should the need for more manpower arise.

The chopper set down in the parking lot of the country club, and its occupants were shuttled across the golf course to their host's mansion under police escort. News vans crowded the edges of the cordon, a long row of white vans and satellite dishes. Throngs of hysterical worshippers were massed against the barricades, clamoring for Father Jerome to come out and talk to them, desperate for a glimpse of the Lord's envoy. A couple of whackos had infiltrated their ranks and were blathering away with incoherent speeches about the imminent end of the world, but more common were the scattered choruses of hymns and carols that could be heard across the neighborhood.

Gracie and Dalton were shown to a room on the ground floor of a guest house that abutted the main building. Brother Ameen was in an adjacent room. Father Jerome was given a cosseted guest suite on the second floor. The plan was for them all to remain at the mansion until the big sermon at the stadium the following evening.

Ogilvy, who was in town, had asked for continual updates live from inside the Darby estate. Gracie and Dalton had given the network's viewers a tour of the compound, but hadn't managed to get a word from Father Jerome, who was resting in his suite and had asked not to be disturbed.

After Gracie signed off, Dalton checked his watch and said, "I'm off to the airport to get the skycam and the rest of our stuff. I might pick up some fresh clothes if the mall isn't mobbed. You need anything?"

Gracie chortled. "An alternate reality?"

"I'm not sure Gap sells those, but I'll see what I can do." He smiled.

He wandered off and left her. She went back to the room, where she collapsed on the bed. It had been a brutal few days, and there was no end in sight. She managed to tune out for all of three minutes before the phone rang.

She fished out her BlackBerry, but it wasn't the one that was ringing. She burrowed deeper into her bag, saw the soft blue glow of another screen, and pulled it out. It was Finch's phone.

She eyed it curiously. The caller's ID was flashing up. It said Gareth Willoughby. It wasn't a name she recognized at first—then it clicked. He was the producer of the BBC documentary.

She took the call.

Willoughby didn't know Finch had died. The news

took him by complete surprise. He told Gracie he didn't know Finch and said he was just returning his call.

There was an uncomfortable silence for a moment; then Gracie said, "I guess you must be glad they finally agreed to let you go up there and talk to Father Jerome, huh?"

Willoughby sounded confused. "What do you mean?"

"I mean if they hadn't said yes, or if you hadn't kept on insisting . . . who knows what would have happened. I know we probably wouldn't have flown out to Egypt."

Willoughby wasn't getting it. "What are you talking about? They came to us."

His statement pricked Gracie like a dart. She straightened up. "What?"

"They came to us. I mean, yes, we were there. Making the documentary and all that. But we didn't go looking for him. We had no idea Father Jerome was even there."

Gracie was having trouble reconciling this with everything she'd assumed. "So how'd you end up meeting him?"

"Well, it was just one of those serendipitous breaks, I suppose," Willoughby said. "We were filming there before heading out to Saint Catherine's in the Sinai. That was our original intention. Not the Syrians' monastery. We were at Bishoi at the time, you know, the other monastery near there?"

"I know the one," she told him.

"Well, Bishoi's story, the whole thing about him chaining his hair to the ceiling so he wouldn't fall asleep. It's the kind of rather wonderfully creepy detail that adds a bit of spice to this kind of show. And while we were there, we were buying supplies from this small shop and we bumped into this monk from the monastery of the Syrians. We got chatting, and he told us Father Jerome was up there in one of their caves. Acting rather bizarrely. As if he were possessed, only in a good way. Which was really timely for us."

"Hang on a second," Gracie blurted, trying to make sense of his words. "I thought everyone knew Father Jerome was there."

"No one knew."

"We looked it up," Gracie objected. "It was there."

"Of course it was—*after* we filmed our program," Willoughby corrected her. "That's when it hit the wires. Nobody knew he was in Egypt before we got there and wrapped our piece. He was on his 'sabbatical,' remember? They wouldn't say where he was. We thought he'd died at one point. And if you think about it, it was all rather fortuitous, in more ways than one."

"What do you mean?"

"Well, we wouldn't have met that monk in the first place if it hadn't been for our commissioning editor at the BBC. That's what I'm really grateful for."

"What, that they gave you the green light?"

"No, that they handed us the assignment in the first place," Willoughby said cheerfully. "It was their idea. They came up with it."

Gracie felt a buildup of pressure in her temples. "Whoa. Back up. You're saying you were sent there? This wasn't your idea?"

"No."

"So exactly how did this show come about? Give me the whole backstory."

"You know how it is," the Englishman related. "We pitch ideas. Programs we'd like to do. We keep pitching until something sticks. We agree on a budget and a timetable, and off we go. This one wasn't like that though. We were bouncing around different ideas. I was more interested in doing a piece on the odd and rather sadistic appeal of End of Times preachings in your country. You know, the lunatics who are rooting for the whole world to blow up. But then the commissioning editor came back and proposed a three-parter that they had American partners lined up for and we ended up doing that in-stead. Comparing Eastern and Western approaches to spirituality. It was different, but it was still very apropos and they were laying out a decent budget for it." He paused, taking stock of the conversation, and asked, "If I may ask, Miss Logan, why all the questions?"

Gracie instinctively put up a defensive wall. Despite the discomfort she felt at what she was hearing, a small voice inside her was telling her to protect what she was uncovering. "Nothing, really," she lied. "I'm just . . . I guess I'm just trying to better understand what got us all out there. Why Finch died." The second it came out of her mouth, she felt horrible at using his death in that way, and hoped Finch would have forgiven her for it. "Tell me something," she asked Willoughby. "The monk who told you about Father Jerome. Do you remember his name?"

"Yes, of course," Willoughby said. "He was a rather interesting chap. Lived through a lot of bad times, you know? He was from Croatia. His name was Ameen. Brother Ameen."

◄o►

GRACIE FELT like she was sinking. She felt like she'd fallen into a great whirlpool of doubt that was sucking her into its dark vortex. A vortex lined with Willoughby's words and with previous sound bites her memory was now dredging up.

She tried to order them up in a nonthreatening way, in a way that defused the most sinister thoughts that were pulling her down, but she couldn't. There was no way to gloss over it.

They'd been lied to.

She focused back on that conversation they'd had in the car after they'd been picked up at Cairo Airport. She closed her eyes and visualized the monk, Brother Ameen, telling them how the filmmakers had badgered them for access to Father Jerome and how the abbot had finally relented.

A clear lie.

The question was, why?

Her darkest instincts were going off in all kinds of directions, and none of them was good. And from that cobweb of conflicting thoughts and suspicions, another worrying sound bite rose up. It freed itself, shot up, and latched onto her consciousness.

She found her phone, pulled up her call log, and rang the number the abbot had called her from. It took a few seconds for the call to bounce its way halfway across the world. Yusuf, the driver, answered on the third ring. It was his cell phone. It was evening there, but not too late. He didn't sound like she'd woken him up.

"Yusuf," she said, her tone ringing with urgency. "When the abbot called, when you were driving back from Cairo, he said something. Something about where the glasses of my friend were found. You remember?"

"Yes," Yusuf said, sounding unsure about what she was getting at.

"He said it was dark inside. That's why whoever it was stepped on them. They didn't see them. They were inside? Inside the keep?"

Yusuf paused for a moment, as if thinking, then said, "Yes. They were in a passageway on the top floor. Near the roof hatch. They must have fallen from your friend's pocket on his way up to the roof."

"You're sure of that?"

"Yes, absolutely," Yusuf confirmed. "The abbot told me about it."

Gracie felt a cold stab in the pit of her stomach.

Finch couldn't see without them. And hard as she tried, she couldn't see how he could have climbed up there, much less how he could have found his BlackBerry on that roof, if he hadn't been wearing them.

She hung up and caught herself eyeing the door to her room as if it were a gateway to hell. Something was wrong. Something was very, very wrong. She had to do something. Her first instinct was to speed-dial Ogilvy.

"I need to see you," she said, her body stiff, her eyes still locked on the door. "Something's not right."

Chapter 70

Houston, Texas

Matt swept his gaze across the hotel's lobby with caution and walked through its elegant halls slowly. He glanced around casually, checking for security guards, cameras, escape routes, and vantage points. He traversed as far as he could, then doubled back on himself and made his way over to the café that fronted the hotel, the one that overlooked the street. He noted its layout, made a mental list of the ways in and out, took stock of the kind of clientele and their number. Then he went back out to check the service entrance at the back of the hotel.

He was there early. The meeting between Rydell and Drucker wasn't planned for another two hours. Drucker wouldn't even have landed in Houston yet, and besides, the plan was for Rydell to keep from telling him where they'd be meeting until Drucker was actually in the city. Still, Matt felt he needed to check the place out long before any of Drucker's men had a chance to get there. He knew Drucker wouldn't be coming alone. With a bit of luck, Maddox might even be with him. And even though he knew the odds were that he'd be outnumbered, Matt had something going for him that they didn't. He didn't need to be discreet. He wasn't worried about appearances or about causing a panic. He didn't care who saw him whip out a big gun and put it to Drucker's head, right there, in the café. He didn't have anything to lose. The one thing he needed to achieve was to get the muzzle of his gun pressed right against Drucker and walk out of there with him. It didn't matter who saw him do that. It didn't matter how freaked out the hotel's guests got. Only the end result mattered. He would just sit there, bide his time, wait until Rydell got the information he needed out of Drucker, and then he'd move in.

It was easier said than done, and yet, oddly, Matt was actually looking forward to it.

◄o►

SIX BLOCKS WEST OF THERE, Gracie stood with Ogilvy in Sam Houston Park. Her mind was being pulled in all kinds of directions, none of which was heartening.

They were by the Neuhaus Fountain, an installation that featured three bronze sculptures of coyotes stalking the wild frontier. A few people were ambling by, stopping to experience the peaceful setting before moving on. Gracie wasn't feeling any of that. In fact, she couldn't stand still. She was rippling with nervous energy as she took the network's head of news through what Willoughby and Yusuf had told her.

Ogilvy didn't seem to share her concern. A slick-looking man with an aquiline nose and swept-back hair, he was studying Gracie patiently through rimless spectacles.

"These guys are humble, Gracie," he remarked with an insouciant shrug. "So this Brother Ameen character didn't admit he actually pimped Father Jerome out. He was probably hoping to get some screen time himself.

Someone in his position would be the last person to admit he found the idea of a little publicity too hard to resist."

"Come on, Hal. He wasn't the least bit nervous when he was lying about it. He didn't look embarrassed or rattled at all. It wasn't like we caught him out. And what about Finch's glasses?"

"It might explain why he fell. If he couldn't see properly."

"They should have been down on the ground, somewhere next to him," she objected. "Or on the roof, and even that's a stretch. But inside the keep? One floor down from the roof? How'd he even make it up there without them?"

"What if he dropped them and broke them himself—before he got there?"

"So he just leaves them there? I don't buy that. You step on glasses, you maybe break one lens. Not both. You can still wear them for some kind of clear vision. You don't just leave them there."

Ogilvy glanced away and heaved out a ragged sigh. He looked like he was losing patience. "So what are you saying?"

"I'm saying we've got two lies that need checking out. Something's up, Hal. This is starting to stink."

"Because of a monk who couldn't admit he got a hard-on when he saw a TV camera and another who's looking for some excuse to explain his clumsiness?"

Gracie was stunned by his dismissal. "We need to look into this. We need to find a way to talk to the abbot directly, confirm where the glasses were. And get some background on this Brother Ameen. He's from Croatia, right? Where did he come from? How long has he been at that monastery? The guy's been pivotal to getting us to buy into this story and we don't know anything about him."

Ogilvy paused and looked at her like she was saying she'd been abducted by aliens. "What are you doing?"

"What?" she protested.

"You've got the inside track on the scoop of the century. This is a huge, huge story. For us and for you. We have unparalleled access. You start poking your nose around and getting Jerome and Ameen all riled up and they could shut us out. Which wouldn't go down well. Not well at all. You can't afford to mess this up right now, Gracie. It's too important. So how about you focus on that instead and put the conspiracy paranoia on hold for a while."

Gracie looked at him as if he were the one who'd been spouting abductee tales.

"Hal, I'm telling you, something's not right. The whole thing, it's been one 'lucky' break after another," she said, making quotes with her fingers. "Right from the beginning." Her mind was running ahead of her now, and she was thinking aloud. "I mean, think about it. We happen to be there when the shelf breaks off. We happen to be filming nearby. Hell, we wouldn't even have been down there if you hadn't suggested it when we were planning the whole show."

And then it happened. Her mind plucked out the disparate thoughts that were tumbling around inside her and lined them up so they all fit. Like the sides of a Rubik's Cube falling into place. She saw a connection that was there all along and made a realization that suddenly seemed so obvious to her she couldn't imagine it not to be true.

Almost without thinking, she said, "Oh my God. You're in on it too."

And in that briefest of moments between her saying it and his responding, in the nanosecond of his looking at her before he opened his mouth, she saw it. The tell. The tiniest, hardly noticeable hesitation. The one her most basal instincts enabled her to see. The one they wouldn't let her ignore. A visceral pull-focus moment that made her feel like her very soul had been yanked right out of her.

"Gracie, you're being ridiculous," he said dismissively, his tone even.

She wasn't listening to his words. She was reading through them, reading the creases around his eyes, the dilation of his pupils. And she was now even more irretrievably, horribly sure of it. "You're in on it too, aren't you?" she insisted. "Say it, goddammit," she flared. "Say it before I shout it out loud to everyone here."

"Gracie—"

"It's fake, isn't it?" she blurted. "The whole damn thing. It's a setup."

Ogilvy took a step forward and raised a calming hand out to her. "People are starting to stare. Don't make a fool of yourself."

She shoved his hand away from her and stepped back. Her mind was racing away. "You played me. You played me all along. This whole assignment. The trip to Antarctica. All that support, all that enthusiasm. It was all bullshit." She glared at him, questions burning out of her. "What are you doing? What the hell's going on?" Her mind was racing ahead, drawing on all its processing reserves. "You're faking this? You're faking a Second Coming? For what? You're setting up a new Messiah? Is that what this is? You want to convert the world?"

Ogilvy's eyes were flicking left and right now. The tell was confirmed beyond a doubt. "You think I'd want that?" he hissed, trying to remain calm. "You know me better than that. It's the last thing I'd want."

"Well then why?" she insisted. "Don't tell me this is about saving the planet?"

Something in Ogilvy shifted too. He seemed to give up the pretense and framed her with a fervent glare. "Maybe. But first and foremost, it's about saving our country," he stated firmly.

And right then, another realization burst out of the mire, like a diver on his last breath breaking surface and gasping for air. "Was Finch's death an accident?"

Ogilvy didn't answer fast enough. Something tore inside her.

"Goddammit, Hal," she shouted, the horror of it making her inch back another step now. "Tell me Finch's death was an accident. Say it."

"Of course it was," he assured her, opening his hands out defensively.

But her gut was telling her otherwise, and his eyes and the lines around them were confirming it. "I don't believe you." Her heart thumping wildly, she took another step back, suddenly hyperaware of her immediate surroundings. She didn't see any innocent-looking strollers or joggers. All she could register were two stone-faced guys with short haircuts, dark suits, and no ties, one at each entrance to the fountain area. Their body language wasn't casual.

Her eyes shot back to Ogilvy. He acknowledged the men with a barely perceptible nod. They started toward her with a threatening gait. Closing in. Blocking any escape route.

She looked at Ogilvy in disbelief, still backing away from him. "Jesus, Hal. What are you doing?"

"Only what's necessary," he replied, somewhat apologetically.

Gracie couldn't just stand there. She spun on her heels and sprinted off, heading straight for one of the heavies coming at her, screaming her lungs out, calling for help. She tried to fake him out and veered left before swinging right, hoping to slip past him, but his arm whipped out and caught her and pulled her in. The other suit was on them a couple of seconds later. The first guy spun her around and pinned her arms behind her back, immobilizing her. She twisted around, trying to free herself, but couldn't resist his viselike grip. Instead, she lashed out with her right foot, kicking the suit facing her in the shin, catching it head-on. It must have hurt, as he jerked back and winced hard, but he came back with a backslap across the face that snapped her head sideways and rattled her teeth. She felt groggy and raised her eyes in time to see the suit facing her bring his hand up to her mouth. He pressed something against her nose, a kind of gauze patch. The smell from it was strong and sour. Almost instantly, she felt all the strength in her body seep away. Her eyes jerked sideways and she caught a glimpse of one of the coyotes that suddenly seemed far more threatening than she'd realized; then her head lolled down, her chin thudding against her chest. She saw a few of the flagstones under her feet fall away before everything drifted off into a silent and hollow darkness.

Chapter 71

They met in the five-star downtown hotel, as per Rydell's instructions. Located just off the lobby, the Grove Café seemed like a good spot. It was an open, public area with other people around. Rydell felt he'd be safe there.

Drucker was already there when he arrived. He was seated at a low table by a wall of glass that looked out onto the street. It was late afternoon under clear skies, and a few pedestrians were promenading by on the wide pavement outside. Drucker motioned for Rydell to join him.

As Rydell sat, Drucker reached down and pulled out a small box from his briefcase. He placed it squarely on the table, to one side. It was black and heavy and the size of a paperback novel, and had a couple of small LED lights on its side.

"You don't mind, do you?" he asked Rydell, "just in case you were planning on taping any of this." He didn't really wait for an answer and discreetly nudged a small button on the box. The LEDs lit up. Rydell shrugged and glanced around to see its effect. A couple of people in the room who'd been talking on their cell phones were now examining them curiously and pressing random buttons to try to get a signal back. Rydell knew they wouldn't be able to. Not until Drucker was done and had switched off his jammer.

Drucker gave Rydell a knowing smile and covered the jammer with his napkin. A waitress came over to ask what they wanted, but Rydell sent her away with a stern shake of his head. They weren't here for an afternoon tea.

"I'm surprised you're down here," Drucker said. "Couldn't resist seeing its effect with your own eyes?" He cracked a slight smile, but it didn't hide the fact that he seemed to be fishing for something.

Rydell ignored the question. "What are you up to, Keenan?" he asked evenly.

Drucker sat back and exhaled slowly. He studied Rydell like a principal wondering what to do about a wayward student. After a moment, he said, "Do you love this country?"

Rydell didn't get the question's relevance. "Excuse me?"

"Do you love this country?" Drucker repeated firmly.

"What kind of a question is that?"

Drucker opened his palms. "Indulge me."

Rydell frowned. "Of course, I love my country. What does that have to do with anything?"

Drucker nodded, as if that was the right answer. "I love it too, Larry. I've devoted my whole life to serving it. And this used to be a great country. A world leader. The Japanese, the Chinese . . . they weren't even a speck in our rearview mirror. We put a man on the moon forty years ago. Forty years ago. We used to be the standard-bearers of modernity. We were the ones showing the rest of the world how it's done, how science and technology and new ideas can help us live better lives. We were the ones exploring new visions of what a twenty-first-century society should look like. And where are we now? What have we become?"

"A lot poorer," Rydell lamented.

"Poorer, meaner, fatter . . . and dumber. We're moving backward. Everyone else is charging ahead and we're backpedaling to the point where we've become a joke. We've lost our standing in the world. And you know why? Leadership," he said, jabbing an angry finger at Rydell. "It's all about leadership. We used to elect presidents who blew us away with their intelligence. With their knowledge of the world and their sharp wit and their dignity. Guys who used to inspire us, guys the rest of the world respected, guys who made us proud. Guys who had vision."

"We have one of those now," Rydell interjected.

"And you think we're out of the woods?" Drucker shot back. "You think, hey presto, the country's safe now? Think again. We just had eight years of an oil wildcatter I wouldn't even hire to run a car wash, eight years of a guy who thought his instincts were manifestations of God's will, eight years of criminal incompetence and unbridled arrogance that brought our country to its knees, and did we learn anything? Clearly not. Hell, it took the economic meltdown of the century to just barely manage to scrape through this victory. This was no landslide, Larry. Damn near half the country voted for more of the same—or worse. We actually came this close to putting someone who thinks *The Flintstones* is based on fact, someone who only got a passport a year before the election and who wouldn't take an interview for a month while she was whisked away to be quietly educated about what's happening in the real world, someone who actually thinks she's going to see Jesus Christ again on this earth during her lifetime and who thinks our boys in Iraq are out there doing God's work," he raged, slamming his palm against the table. "We actually came this close to putting someone as risibly, absurdly unqualified as that within a seventy-two-year-old cancer-weakened heartbeat of the presidency. As ridiculous and insane as that sounds, it actually almost happened, Larry, and it could still happen. That's how blinded we've become when it comes to choosing our leaders. And do you know why it almost happened? You know why they almost got away with it?"

Rydell thought about Father Jerome and started to see what Drucker was getting at. "Because God is on their side," he said.

"Because God is on their side," Drucker repeated solemnly.

"Or so they claim," Rydell added with a slight, mocking shrug.

"That's all it takes. We'll elect any bumbling fool, any champion of mediocrity to the highest office in the land as long as they have God as their running mate. We'll hand them responsibility for everything—the food we eat, the homes we live in, the air we breathe—we'll give them the power to nuke other countries and destroy the planet, even when they can't pronounce the world 'nuclear' properly. And we'll do that proudly and with no hesitation at all just as long as they say the magic words: that they believe. That they have Jesus in their heart. That they seek the guidance of a higher father. That they can look into the heart of a Russian president instead of talking to the experts. We've got presidents making policy decisions based on faith, not reason. And I'm not talking about Iran here. I'm not talking about Saudi Arabia or the Taliban. I'm talking about us. I'm talking about America and this evangelical revival that's sweeping the country. We've got presidents making political decisions based on the Book of Revelation, Larry. The Book of Revelation."

He settled back to catch his breath and watched Rydell for a reaction before pressing on. "We were a great country once. A rich country the rest of the world envied. Then they put a guy in there who thought Russia was an evil empire and thought we were living through the prophecies of Armageddon. They got us a guy who found Jesus but can't read a balance sheet, and they're out there running the country down to the ground and waging wars in the name of God and getting our boys blown to bits, and half the country's still marching into church every Sunday and coming out with a big smile and waving the flag of their redeemer nation—"

"I know you're angry about Jackson," Rydell interrupted, the face of Drucker's deceased son suddenly flashing up in his mind and making him aware of what was really fueling this, "but—"

"Angry?" Drucker growled. "Oh, I'm not just angry, Larry. I'm fucking furious. And don't get me wrong. I'm not one to mollycoddle our troops. A soldier's job is to put his life on the line for his country. Jackson knew that when he signed up. But our country was not at risk here. This is a war that never should have happened. Never," he bellowed. "And the only reason it did was that we had an incompetent fool with daddy issues and a Messiah complex running the show. And that can't be allowed to happen again."

Rydell leaned in closer. He knew how much Drucker had loved his son, knew of all the grand plans he'd had for him. He had to tread carefully. "I'm with you on this, Keenan. We're on the same page here. But what you're doing is—"

Drucker headed him off with a quieting hand and nodded like he knew what Rydell was about to say. "We can't allow this to go on, Larry. They've got it so politicians can't get elected these days if they say they believe in Darwin. They've turned a college degree into a stigma and 'elitist' into a dirty word." His eyes narrowed. "In the America of the twenty-first century, faith trumps competence. Faith trumps reason. Faith trumps knowledge and research and open debate and careful consideration. Faith trumps everything. And we need to turn that whole mind-set on its head. We need to bring back a respect for fact. For knowledge. For science and education and intelligence and reason. But you can't reason with these people. We both know that. You can't have a political debate with someone who thinks you're an agent of Satan. They won't compromise, because to them, compromising means compromising with the devil, and no God-fearing Christian would want to do that. No, the only way to put an end to this is to make it embarrassing for people and for politicians to flaunt their faith. We've got to take that tool away from the guys who're using it to win elections and advance whatever agendas they have. We need to make it as embarrassing to say you're a creationist as it would be if you said you still support slavery in this day and age. We need to sweep religion into the dustbin of political discourse, just like we did for slavery. And we have to do it now. The country's caught in a voodoo trance, Larry. You've seen the numbers. Sixty percent of the country believes the story of Noah's Ark is literally true. Sixty percent. There are seventy million Evangelicals out there—a quarter of the population, attending a couple of hundred thousand evangelical churches, most of which are run by pastors who belong to conservative political organizations, and these guys are telling them which way to vote. And the people are listening, and they're not voting for the guy whose policies make sense. They're not voting for the guy with the brains or the vision. They're voting for whoever will help them improve their standing when they get to the pearly gates. And it's getting worse. This delusion is spreading. There's a new megachurch opening every other day. Literally every other day."

Drucker fixed Rydell with blazing intent. "You think global warming is around the corner? This threat's already here. We may have dodged the bullet with this election, but they're still out there, they'll be back, and they'll fight twice as dirty. They look at it as a war. A war against secularism. A crusade to reclaim the kingdom of God from the nonbelievers and save us all from gay marriage and abortion and stem-cell research. And the way things are going, they're going to make it. At some point, these prayer warriors are going to put a televangelist in the Oval Office. And then we'll have a bunch of whack jobs running Capitol Hill and another bunch of nutcases facing off against them in the Middle East, each of them thinking God wants them to show the other the error of their ways, and guess what? It's going to get ugly. They'll be lobbing nukes at each other before it's over. And I'm not going to let that happen."

Rydell wasn't following. "And you're going to do that by giving them a prophet to fire them up even more?"

Drucker just stared at him enigmatically. "Yes."

"I don't get it." Rydell pressed on. "You're giving them something real, a real miracle man to worship and rally around. A Second Coming to unite them all."

"Yes," Drucker repeated, leading him.

Rydell tried to follow his train of thought. "You're getting all the church leaders to embrace him and hitch their wagons to his train."

"Yes." This time, a hint of satisfaction cracked across Drucker's face.

Rydell's brow furrowed. "And then you'll get him to change his message?"

Drucker shook his head. "No," he stated. "I'll just pull the rug out from under him."

Rydell stared at him questioningly—then his eyes shot wide. "You're going to expose him as a fake?"

"Exactly." Drucker's hard stare burned into him. "We'll let it run for a while. Weeks. Months. Just let it build. Let every pastor in the country accept him and endorse him as God's messenger. Let them spread the word to their flocks," he added, spitting out the word mockingly. "And when it's all sunk in and settled, when it's deeply embedded and they're all on the hook—we'll show him for what he really is. We'll show them what the sign really is."

"And you'll show them how gullible they are." Rydell had a faraway look on his face as he imagined the outcome in his mind's eye.

"The preachers will have so much egg on their faces they'll have a hard time stepping behind those pulpits and facing their people. The churchgoers will feel like they've been had—and maybe they'll start questioning the rest of the crap they hear in those halls. It'll open up a whole new discussion, a whole new questioning frame of mind. 'If it was so easy to fool us today, with everything we know . . . how easy was it to fool people two thousand years ago? What do we really know about that?' It'll put everything about religion on the table. And it'll make people think twice about who they're willing to follow blindly."

Rydell felt heady. He himself had been ready to try to convert the world to his cause, but this . . . this went much further. He let out a weary hiss and shook his head. "You'll make a lot of them even more fanatical than they already are," he warned.

"Probably," Drucker agreed casually.

"And you could also start a civil war," Rydell added, "if not a world war."

Drucker scoffed. "Oh, I very much doubt that."

"Are you kidding me?" Rydell flared. "You're going to have a whole bunch of really angry people out there. And they'll be looking to take it out on someone. Who's going to shoulder the blame? You can't exactly stand up and tell them, 'Hey, we did it for your own good.' The country's already split right down the middle on this. You'll polarize them even more. The blowback will be horrendous. There'll be blood in the streets. And that's before you get the blowback from the rest of the world. You've seen what's starting to happen in Pakistan, in Egypt, in Israel and Indonesia. It's not just Christians who are buying into your little scam. Muslims, Jews, Hindus . . . they're fighting among each other over whether or not he's the real deal. And they're going to be seriously pissed off when they discover it's got Uncle Sam's fingerprints all over it. People don't take kindly to having others mess around with their beliefs, Keenan. They get real angry about that. And it's Americans who are going to pay for it with their blood. You're gonna end up triggering a war you're trying to stop."

"Well, if they're so closed-minded, if they don't see the danger of their ways and insist on marching down that path to destruction, then they're beyond saving." Drucker seethed. "We had a war over slavery. Maybe we do need a war over this." He gave a haughty shrug. "If it's going to happen sooner or later, might as well just get it over with. And then maybe we can build something more sane from its ashes."

Rydell felt as if someone had reached in and yanked his lungs out with pliers. "You're insane," he told Drucker. "You've lost all sense of perspective."

"Not at all."

"You can't do this, Keenan," Rydell insisted.

"No. Not without a fall guy," Drucker conceded.

Rydell stared at him, the words colliding with his tangled thoughts, and instantly got it. "Me. That's what you need me for."

Drucker nodded stoically. "I needed a fall guy. Someone with a completely different motive, one that wasn't in any way related to the politics of this country. Because this can't be seen as a political act—you're absolutely right about that. The only way to do this is to paint it as the desperate act of a visionary genius with no political motive other than trying to save the planet. And who knows? It may well end up giving people more awareness of the global warming problem."

"But you couldn't care less either way," Rydell said sardonically.

"Not true, Larry. I care. But I'm not even sure what, if anything, we can realistically do about it. And bringing reason back into politics—that's going to help the polar bears more than pushing Hummer into bankruptcy, don't you think?"

"This isn't about saving the polar bears or the rain forests, Keenan," Rydell said angrily. "It's about social justice. For everyone on the planet."

"Social justice is about freeing people from the clutches of witch doctors and superstition," Drucker fired back.

Rydell rubbed his brow, letting Drucker's words sink in. The room was suddenly feeling much hotter and tighter. "How was it all meant to end for me? 'Suicide'?"

Drucker nodded. "Once the hoax is exposed. A tragic end to a heroic attempt." He sighed and leaned forward. "I'm sorry, Larry. But I hope you can see the sense in what I'm trying to do here. The urgency. And that, at some level, you agree that it had to be done."

Rydell sat back and shrugged. "I hope you won't be disappointed if I tell you I won't play along."

Drucker gave him a negative, dismissing wave of his hand. "Please, Larry. Give me some credit."

Larry looked at him, waiting for more—and suddenly froze at Drucker's composure.

"You're going to have a stroke," Drucker told him, casually. "A bad one. In fact it's going to happen sooner than you think. Maybe right here in this restaurant. In front of all these people. You'll end up in a coma. One we can manage. And during that time, we'll"—he paused, choosing his words—"massage your personality. You know, like we did with the priest. We'll put the right answers in your mind. Make you more amenable to our plans. And when the time comes, we'll help you take your own life, after leaving behind a detailed, contrite, and moving explanation of why you did what you did." Drucker studied his face, as if intrigued by Rydell's reaction to his words. "It's the stuff of legends, Larry. No one will ever forget your name, if that's any consolation."

Rydell felt a surge of sheer terror—and just then, he noticed something behind Drucker. A man in a dark suit, one of his drones. He swung his head around toward the entrance of the café. Two more men appeared there. His mind tripped over his only option—to make a loud, visible run for it and hope the commotion screwed up their plans—and he was about to push himself out of his chair when he spotted something else. To his side. Out, on the street. A white van that had been parked there all along. Its side door, sliding open. Two silhouettes, standing inside, on either side of something big and round and mounted on a stand, something that looked like a projector lamp. His hands slipped off the chair's arms as he tried to push himself to his feet, but he never made it past a couple of inches off the seat cushion. The blast of noise was horrific. It assaulted his senses like a hammer blow that came from inside his skull, overwhelming every nerve ending in his head with an unbearably loud and shrill noise that wouldn't stop. His eyes burst into tears and he yelled out, the force of the caustic sound blasting him out of his chair in front of a stunned roomful of hotel guests. His hands shot up to protect his ears, but it was too late as his legs crumpled under him and he fell to the ground, retching and coughing and sputtering with convulsions.

Drucker's men rushed to his side. They helped him up and instantly bundled him out of the room, avoiding any brusque moves, and displaying the well-trained, expert moves of caring, efficient bodyguards. One of them even called out for a doctor. Within seconds, they'd hustled him out of the café and into a waiting elevator.

Its doors slid shut with a silent hiss, and it glided down to the hotel's underground parking lot.

Chapter 72

Matt's pulse thundered ahead as he saw Rydell get blasted out of his seat by an unseen force. There was no noise, no physical disturbance. It was as if he'd been punched backward by a huge invisible fist. Then he was there, bent down on the ground, writhing in agony, the contents of his belly spewing out onto the café's richly textured carpet.

He'd been ready to make his move. Waiting in a corner booth, behind the grand piano by the bar, away from the main seating area, biding his time at a staging point he'd chosen carefully. His fingers were wrapped around the Para-Ordnance's wide grip, ready to yank it out and shove it up against Drucker's ribs. But they'd moved first. Whatever they did to Rydell had sent Matt's plans to the shredder.

He rose and charged toward the café's entrance. He caught sight of Drucker heading out of the room, flanked by two of his men. He was turning right, headed for the hotel's front doors, whereas Rydell had been taken left, to the elevators. Matt hurtled across the café. He skidded to a stop at its entrance. Drucker was leaving the hotel with his escorts. There were a lot of people around him. Hotel guests, bellboys, valets. No way he could get to him. He'd missed his chance. He spun his gaze in the opposite direction. The lights over the elevator Rydell was in scrolled down to indicate he was being taken to the hotel's parking lot.

Matt chose to go after him instead. If Drucker had him again, Matt would be left with no leverage. Leverage he needed if he was going to see his brother again.

He bolted across the lobby, past some shocked guests and through the door to the hotel's internal stairwell. Flew down the stairs, three at a time, gripping the banister at the turns and flinging himself around them like an out-of-control bobsled. Six flights later, he was at the parking level. He burst onto its smoothly painted concrete floor in time to see a dark gray van squealing away and turning onto the exit ramp. His eyes traveled across the garage. He heard a door click open to his left, spun his gaze that way, and rushed toward the noise. A valet was getting out of a car. A big Lincoln Navigator SUV, silver. Matt didn't flinch. He sprinted right up to him, yanked the car keys from his grasp, and shoved him away before climbing in and spurring the big V-8 to life. He slammed the selector into drive and cannoned out of the parking spot and onto the exit ramp.

He emerged into the golden-orange glow of dusk and threw a quick glance in each direction. The city center was an orthogonal grid of alternating one-way avenues, some of them five lanes wide. This one went east-west, and the van was pulling away to the right, heading west. He nudged the gas pedal. The Navigator slid out from under the garage entrance's canopy and accelerated onto the avenue. The van was cruising away, three hundred yards down the road.

Matt threaded the big SUV through a rolling chicane of slower vehicles and caught up with the van in no time. He held back, keeping a car between them. The road was straight and wide, the traffic sparse. The intersections were vast and generous, concrete plains outlined by patterned stone infills that gave them the feel of a Beverly Hills piazza. Two blocks on, a big green sign appeared overhead, announcing the on-ramp to the interstate and, beyond, to I-90. Matt knew he had to do something before they hit the highway. Once they were on it, all kinds of unknowns would come into play. He risked being spotted. He risked losing them. He risked them getting to wherever it was they were going, and having them end up with the home advantage.

He had to make his move.

The road was as wide as a runway and didn't have any cars parked on either side. The block they were coming up to was lined with a row of thin trees to the left, and some kind of granite colonnade on the right. It wouldn't do. Too brutal. Matt edged the Navigator right and peered ahead. The next block looked more promising. The left side was edged by a bunkerlike parking garage and wouldn't do. The sidewalk on the right, on the other hand, led to a rise of a dozen or so wide, low steps that climbed up to a raised open area outside an imposing stone-clad office building.

Matt settled on it and mashed the pedal.

The V-8 growled as the Navigator surged out from behind the buffering sedan and overtook it from the left. Matt went out wide to the left, then veered right and aimed the Navigator's nose at the van's left front corner. He didn't lift off. The Navigator homed in on the van like a guided missile. A split second before it slammed into it, Matt jerked the wheel to the left and righted the SUV. It hit the van at a tangent, catching its driver unawares, its momentum flinging the van off its trajectory and sending it shooting off to the right. Matt flung the wheel back to the right, bringing the Navigator right up against the van's left side, hugging it tight and nursing it along its diagonal trajectory; then he swerved right even more to close the deal. The van had nowhere to go, and its driver knew it. He must have stood on the brakes, as the van lurched forward on its front wheels, lighting them up in a cloud of rubber, but he was still going too fast. The van bounced heavily up the stairs before slamming against one of the building's massive square pillars.

Matt ramped the Navigator over the curb and flew out of it just as the van hit the column. He stormed up the steps, the stainless-steel handgun out and ready to draw blood, eyes peeled for any movement.

The van had hit hard. Its radiator was smoking and its front end curled around the column. Matt didn't know what state he'd find Rydell in. One thing he knew, though, was that the guys in the front wouldn't be at their healthiest. The van had a steep front rake and little if no hood to protect the engine in case of a frontal collision. Plus, he knew, the guys weren't expecting the hit.

Passersby and people who worked in the building were edging forward to check out the crash, only to reel away at the sight of Matt and his handgun. He ignored them and rounded the side of the van, knees bent in a wide, low stance, eyeing the van's doors and windows cautiously, looking for any sign of life. The front was badly mashed up, and Matt was pretty sure he wouldn't be getting any grief from there. He side-stepped away to the back of the van, extended an arm across one of its back doors, and rapped on it with his gun. He pulled his hand back quickly, anticipating a few rounds through the bodywork. None came. He reached over and pulled the door open, then swung across, looking down the gun-sight of the P14.

Rydell was in there, writhing on the floor, shaken up but alive. His hands were held by nylon cuffs. He saw one of the guys he recognized from the hotel, his head bloodied, trying to straighten himself up. The guy glanced up, saw Matt, blinked twice, and fumbled for a gun. Matt squeezed off a round and saw a red splatter burst out from the guy's chest.

"Come on," he yelled at Rydell, who nodded vaguely like someone who'd been in a solitary confinement sweatbox for a month. As Matt reached in to him, he saw something else. Another body, lying facedown behind Rydell. A woman. Her hands were tied behind her back, same nylon cuffs. Matt climbed in and, carefully, turned her over. She had a fat piece of duct tape covering her mouth. He peeled it off and recognized her instantly. Gracie Logan, the news anchor who'd been covering the sign's appearances. He reached in farther and put his fingers to her neck, looking for a pulse. She was alive.

She stirred at his touch, then flinched, her eyes wide with shock.

"Where are . . . ? Who . . . ?" she mouthed incoherently.

"Give me your hand," Matt told her as he tucked the P14 under his belt. He helped her up and slung her arm over his shoulders.

"Come on," he told Rydell. He half-carried Gracie as he cut past a gaggle of dumbstruck onlookers, down the steps to the waiting Navigator. He set her down in the backseat, got in behind the wheel with Rydell beside him, and powered away.

In the rearview mirror, Matt saw Gracie straighten up. She was slowly coming out of it. Her eyes swept across her surroundings before settling on Matt's face.

"You okay?" he asked her.

She stared at him blankly. She looked like she had the mother of all hangovers. Then things must have come flooding back, as her face tightened up with a worried frown.

"Dalton," Gracie blurted. "I've got to get Dalton out of there."

"Who?"

Her hands were rummaging around, looking for something. "My phone. Where's my phone? I have to call Dalton. It isn't safe." She turned to Matt. "I have to warn him."

Matt looked down the street, saw a bank of phone booths, and pulled over. He helped Gracie out. "Where are we going? Where shall I tell him to go?" she asked.

"Who are you talking about?"

"Dalton. My cameraman. They'll be going after him too."

Matt tried to fill in the blanks. "Where is he?"

"At Darby's mansion," she said, her expression vague, as if she wasn't exactly sure.

"The preacher?"

"Yes." She concentrated hard. "No. Wait. I'm not sure." She shook her head. "He went to the airport," she added after a beat. "Yeah, I'm pretty sure of that. Either way, he's on his cell." She picked up the handset. "What'll I tell him?"

Matt gave it a quick thought. "Just tell him to get somewhere safe. If he's still out, tell him to stay away from the preacher's place. We'll call him back and tell him where to meet us."

She started to dial, then paused and studied him curiously, her eyes still foggy, and asked, "Who the hell are you?"

"Just make the call," he told her. "We'll get to that later."

Chapter 73

They were all scattered around the motel room, a motley crew of haggard escapees: Matt, Gracie, Dalton, and Rydell. A week earlier, apart from Gracie and Dalton, none of them had met. They hadn't even come close. They had roamed completely separate spheres, lived disparate lives, had different ambitions and concerns. And then everything had changed, their lives had been upended, and here they were, crammed into the small room, wondering how to stay alive.

Dalton had joined them at the motel, arriving not long after they had. They'd spent the next couple of hours filling one another in on how they'd ended up in that room, each contributing his or her part of the story. The conversation had been urgent and intense as the different pieces had fallen into place, the string of troubling news only brightening up when Rydell had gotten through to the doctor treating Jabba back in Boston. The surgery had been successful. Jabba had lost a lot of blood, but he was stable, and his prognosis was cautiously optimistic.

"What do we do now?" Dalton asked. He still looked spooked, having only just found out that Finch had been murdered, and that the likely suspect was a monk they'd been palling around with.

"I keep thinking of Father Jerome," Gracie remarked, shaking her head. "He knew something was wrong. I could see it in his face." She turned to Rydell. "You don't know what they've done to him?"

"I don't know the grim details," Rydell admitted. "I didn't want to hear about it when they brought it up. They mentioned stuff. About using drugs. Electroshock therapy. Implanting memories and adjusting character. To make him more accepting of his new status, I guess."

"Nice," Dalton said with an uneasy wince.

"He said he heard voices. Up on the mountain. He thought God was talking to him," Gracie mentioned.

Rydell nodded thoughtfully. "They would have used an LRAD on him. A long-range acoustical device," he speculated. He slid a glance at Matt. "Same thing they used on me at the hotel. It can also send sound accurately over long distances. Like a sniper rifle, only for noise—or voices," he explained. "They were talking to him through it."

A pensive silence smothered the room.

After a brief moment, Gracie glanced over to Rydell. "You really thought you could get away with this?" she asked him. Her voice was flat. She was still in shock at Ogilvy's betrayal. At the thought of how she'd been played. At the idea of Finch having been killed because of this.

"I had to do something," he said with a tired shrug. "People aren't listening. They're too passive. Too lazy. They don't listen to reason until it's too late. They don't want to listen to politicians. They certainly don't want some tree-hugger in Birkenstocks telling them how to live. They won't take the time to read or to listen to the experts. Look at the financial meltdown. Experts have been warning about it for years. Buffett called derivatives 'financial weapons of mass destruction.' No one listened. Then it all fell apart overnight." He looked around the room, as if looking for a hint of understanding, if not empathy. "I couldn't just sit back. This isn't about your 401(k) losing half its value. It isn't about losing your home. It's about the planet losing its ability to sustain life."

"It's like Finch said. It's all in the branding," Dalton remarked, throwing a glance at Gracie. "'Global warming' sounds way too nice and cozy. They should have called it global boiling."

"It's geocide," Rydell said before leaning back into the darkness.

A couple of nods sent the tired room back into silence. Gracie finally broke through the weary haze again and asked Rydell, "If you weren't going to be the fall guy . . . do you agree with what Drucker said? With what they're trying to do?"

Rydell thought about it for a moment and gave a pained shake of his head. "I agree with what he thinks is wrong with our country. History's shown us, time and again, that mixing religion and politics only brings destruction. And I have no doubt that it's a real danger, maybe more dangerous than anything Homeland Security is worried about. But I don't agree with his solution. And I certainly don't agree with his methods." He looked around the room. "No one was supposed to get hurt. Drucker's just out of control. And he's not done. Who knows what message he'll choose to put into Father Jerome's mouth before he's through. He could make him say or do anything he likes. And the whole world's listening."

"We've got to stop him," Gracie put in. "We've got to go live with what we know."

"No," Matt said flatly from the corner of the room.

Gracie turned to him. "What are you talking about? We've got to go public."

Matt shook his head. "We can't break the story. Not yet. If we do that now, they'll kill Danny. I need to get him out first, make sure he's safe. After that, you can slap it on the front page of *The New York Times* or wherever you want. It's all yours."

"You heard what they're planning, Matt," Gracie argued. "The show's tomorrow. It's going to be huge—and it'll be watched across the planet. And you've seen what's going on out there. People are buying into it, fighting over it. Every hour we wait, this thing's sinking in deeper. If we wait until after the show to blow the lid off this thing, it might be too late to undo the damage it'll have caused."

"Once that happens, we'll be kind of doing their work for them if we expose it, won't we?" Dalton asked. "I mean, that's their plan, right?"

"We don't have a choice," Gracie pointed out. "It's not ideal, but we have to do it and we have to do it now."

"They can't expose it," Matt countered. "Not yet. Not as long as they don't have you," he said as he chucked a nod at Rydell. "They don't have their fall guy, right? So who are they going to blame it on? They've got to blame it on someone—someone without a political axe to grind. Plus as long as they don't have you locked up"—he aimed his words at Rydell again—"they'd be running the risk of you coming out with your side of the story. They'd be screwed. They've got some figuring out to do before they tell the world it's a setup."

"Which they will, sooner or later—there's no doubt about that," Gracie interjected. "No way they'd let this run indefinitely. They'd be handing the Christian Right the keys to the kingdom. And we can't let that happen either."

Matt paused at the thought. There didn't seem to be a way out, and although all he could think about was getting his brother back safely, he suddenly realized there were bigger considerations he couldn't shy away from.

He chewed over it for a moment, then said, "We've got a small window before they figure out their fallback position, right?" He glanced over to Rydell. "They might even be wondering if you'll keep quiet. As a trade-off for getting your green message out there."

"They'd be wrong," Rydell confirmed without hesitation.

"Either way, they won't do anything yet. Not until they come up with another endgame that doesn't leave them holding the bag. Which gives me a bit of time to try and get Danny back. Even if it means letting them put Father Jerome up on that stage. You can't ask me to give up on him. Not when I'm so close."

He looked around the room. The others glanced at one another, weighing his words.

He looked at Gracie. She held his gaze, then nodded warmly.

"The country's already well on its way to buying it," she finally said. "Tomorrow night will make it harder to come back from, sure, but . . . we can hold off till then. Besides, it seems to me that none of us would still be around if it wasn't for Matt. We owe him that much."

She glanced around, judging the others' reactions. Rydell and Dalton each nodded their agreement. Her eyes ended up settling on Matt.

He smiled and gave her a small nod of appreciation.

"Okay, so how do we do it?" Gracie asked him.

"How do we do what?"

"Find your brother." She caught his confused look and flashed him a slight grin. "What, did you think we were going to bail on you now?"

Matt glanced around the room again. Saw beaming support from everyone around him. Nodded to himself, accepting it. "We've got to assume they're going to put a sign up over Father Jerome tomorrow, right?"

Gracie nodded. "No doubt about that."

"Then that's how we'll do it."

◄○►

THEY STAYED UP most of the night, studying maps, plans, and photographs of the stadium pulled from the Internet, examining its layout and the spread of the surrounding area, trying to anticipate where Danny and the launch team were likely to be positioned.

By dawn, they felt they'd reached a consensus on how Drucker's guys might try to stage it. They'd pretty much followed Rydell's lead. Having the guy who'd been in charge of the sign's technology gave them a nice head start, but there were still a lot of unknowns. Then as the first glints of sunlight broke through the darkness, the TV started showing cars and people already setting out on their pilgrimage, and they knew they had to get going too.

They loaded up the little gear they had into the back of the Lincoln. After they were done, Matt saw Gracie standing alone, down the walkway from their room, at the edge of the porch, staring out at the brightening sky. He ambled over and joined her.

"You okay?"

She studied him, then nodded. "Yeah." She studied him for another beat, then looked away again. "It's so weird. To think of how divided the country's become. To think that people need to resort to . . ." She shook her head. "When did we become so hateful? So intolerant?"

"Probably around the same time some power-crazed

douche bags decided it would help them win elections," he quipped.

She smiled and let out a slight chuckle. "Now why doesn't Brian Williams ever put it in those terms?"

Her expression darkened as an eclipse crossed over her face.

"What are you thinking about?" Matt asked.

"Father Jerome. He's . . . You couldn't ask for a more decent human being. To think of the hell they must have put him through . . ."

Matt nodded thoughtfully. "It's not going to be easy for him. When this thing breaks."

Gracie stared at him, and her face flooded with concern. "His whole belief system's going to get wiped out."

"I think it's more than his belief system you need to worry about," Matt said. "You're going to need to get him into some kind of protective custody. They'll rip him to shreds."

Gracie shrank back, winded by the thought. "We're damned if we do and damned if we don't, aren't we?"

Matt shrugged. "We don't really have a choice. We have to do this."

"You're right." Gracie relented, although it was clear from her haunted look that it wouldn't be that simple.

Matt let a moment pass, then said, "I want to thank you. For backing me up in there. And for not bailing on me."

She waved it away. "After everything you've been through? I owe you my life."

"Still, I know it wasn't easy," he insisted. "Putting the scoop of a lifetime on hold. I mean, there's no doubt you'd be the biggest face on television right now if you walked into any newsroom and just told them what you know."

"Just how shallow do you think I am?" She smirked.

"Not shallow, just . . . realistically ambitious."

Gracie smiled and looked wistfully into the distance. "My Woodward and Bernstein moment," she chortled, self-mockingly. She laughed inwardly. "It's like, all your life, you wait for a big moment like this, you hope for it and you work hard to make it happen, you imagine it and picture yourself basking in its glory . . . then when it actually happens . . ."

"When it comes out, it'll change everything for you, you know," he told her. "And not necessarily for the better."

She glanced over at him. "I know." Her eyes had lost their disarming sparkle. For something every reporter dreamed about, it was starting to feel more like a nightmare.

He nodded, not really wanting to explore the darker side of what lay ahead. He pushed out a slight, comforting smile. "Come on. Let's see how the rest of the day turns out first. And take it from there."

Chapter 74

The roads were already jammed by early morning. Miles of cars, streaming in from every direction, choking the Loop and the South Freeway and all the approach roads leading to the stadium at Reliant Park. It was unlike anything the city had seen before. Unlike anything any city had seen before: an antlike procession of packed cars squatting over every square inch of available asphalt for miles around and converging on the biggest sports, entertainment, and convention complex in the country.

It was a clear, perfect day, and by noon, the temperature was in the high seventies and all the parking lots were filled. More than half a dozen of them, scattered around the stadium, the Astrodome, the arena, and the exhibition center. Over twenty-six thousand parking spots, every single one of them taken. The four-wheeled invasion didn't stop there. It spilled over into the vast, empty lot that used to house the Six Flags AstroWorld before it was torn down in 2006. Seventy-five acres of flat, bare earth that nestled against the south side of the Loop, soil that was once the proud home of Greezed Lightnin' and the Ultra Twister, now shuddering under the rumble of an unstoppable flood of cars, trucks, and vans.

They came by car, by foot, by any means possible.

MetroRail was running extra trains to try to cope with the crush, their cabins struggling to retain the heaving mass of flesh pressed against their walls. Helicopters were ferrying in news crews and reporters, all of whom were busy setting up their satellite dishes and hustling to get the best vantage points to cover the event. Police choppers circled overhead, keeping an eye on the teeming chaos below. The gates of the stadium itself were closed shortly after twelve. Seventy-three thousand people had already filed in by then, after spending hours in long lines, waiting to be frisked for weapons and cleared, the last of them pushing and shoving and fighting their way through in a desperate attempt to make it inside. A few angry, hysterical worshippers wouldn't take no for an answer and were creating scattered spots of trouble. Isolated brawls also broke out in the parking lots as cars jostled for position. Surprisingly, though, most of those who had made the journey were calm and well behaved. The police were doing a commendable job in marshaling the pilgrims around and keeping things civil. Darby's people had also brought in a small army of volunteers to manage the flows on the outside and to help those inside get settled. They were distributing free bottles of water and pamphlets promoting Darby's evangelical empire. The crowds in the parking lots, the ones who didn't make it into the stadium, weren't brooding over missing out. They'd come prepared and were already settling into a festive mood. The lots were brimming with tailgate parties. Turkey, eggnog, and carols were on offer everywhere. Whole families, young and old, people of all shapes and sizes and colors, were joined in one seamless celebration as a rolling wave of Christmas music wafted across the fields of multicolored sheet metal.

◄○►

THEY LEFT EARLY, only pulling in briefly at a gas station to pick up some baseball caps and cheap sunglasses to shield their faces, and they still hit the jams. They passed a weathered billboard that said, "Let's meet on Sunday at my house before the game.—God," and shortly after, the stadium appeared in the distance.

That first glimpse of it, all the way from the freeway, cut through Matt's weariness and gave his spirits a boost. Even at that distance, it was clear that the roof was open. It was the NFL's first retractable-roof stadium, a staggering 500-foot-long and 385-foot-wide sunroof. The big trusses that held it up were far apart, with one side resting over each end zone. Seeing them spread open like that sent a quickening rush through his veins. If they were open, it meant there was a strong chance the sign would be making an appearance. He felt he was getting closer to Danny. He was daring to hope that he might actually see his brother alive again. It felt good to think about that, especially after everything he'd been through over the last few days.

The cars weren't moving. Matt and Gracie left Rydell and Dalton in the big silver SUV and walked the rest of the way. As they approached the center, Matt cast his eyes across the huge complex and tried to fit Rydell's read of the situation onto it: having the launchers outside the stadium and the transmitter inside. The reasons Rydell had drawn that conclusion were simple. It was hardly likely that the compressed-air launchers would be placed anywhere near the crowds inside the stadium, or within its walls. In such close proximity, someone was bound to notice the large canisters shooting up into the sky, no matter how silent they were. On the other hand, the laser transmitter that gave life to the motes and controlled the sign's appearance had to be inside the stadium. In imagining how Drucker and his people would stage the event, they were certain that, at some point, the sign would appear within the stadium's envelope. And if that were the case, a beam from anywhere outside the stadium wouldn't be able to reach inside. This wasn't great news. It meant they had to have a look inside—without any weapons, given the security searches at the gates. Of some solace was the fact that it was likely the plotters would want the sign to appear over the stadium as well. That helped narrow down the possibilities. There weren't too many positions inside the stadium from which a transmitter would have a sight line that would allow it to track something as huge as the sign upward through the roof and out into the sky overhead.

The question was, would Danny and his master board be with the transmitter, or the launchers? Or, equally possible, somewhere else altogether?

That third possibility wasn't worth thinking about. As for the first two, they knew it was going to be difficult to cover both angles. They didn't have the manpower, and their limited efforts would be slowed down significantly by the crush of people. As far as the launchers were concerned, the good news was that there weren't that many places they could be. The stadium was surrounded by acres of parking lots on all sides, which were surely too visible to launch from. The bad news was, the few possible spots where they might be were so far apart that covering all of them in the short window of time they had to do it in would be impossible.

That was why they planned to split up. Matt and Gracie would comb the stadium for the transmitter, while Rydell and Dalton would scour the area outside for the launchers.

They braved the onslaught and stood patiently in line and finally made it into the stadium shortly before the gates came down. Nearby, Rydell and Dalton were worm-

ing their way to the parking lots and maneuvering the
SUV to the east end of the red zone, by Reliant Center.
They ended up tucking it into a slot at the far end of the
lot, by the fence, somewhere they hoped they'd be less
noticed.

Once inside, Matt and Gracie advanced with caution.
The noise and the energy inside the stadium overwhelmed them the minute they stepped in. The building
itself was staggeringly large, a monumental glass-and-
steel coliseum for the twenty-first century. With its roof
wide-open and the clear sky overhead, it was simply
breathtaking. What greeted them within its cavernous
embrace was unlike anything Matt or Gracie had experienced. Every single seat was occupied. Tens of thousands
of people, talking and laughing and singing and waiting.
A hodgepodge cross-section of Americana, all of them
united by a common yearning. Ducktailed older men
standing side by side with teenage mall rats. Middle-aged
couples, holding hands or carrying young clones on their
shoulders. Yuppies in chinos and polo shirts alongside
plumbers in stained overalls. Well-coiffed Texas matrons
with elegant European scarves next to big-haired strip-
pers in sequined cowboy hats. Whites, blacks, and Lati-
nos of all shapes and sizes, all of them punch-drunk with
anticipation, giddy at the idea of being in the presence of
a new Messiah, cheerful and fired up, hugging and kiss-
ing and waving and chatting and singing along to the
sounds of Casting Crowns and Bethany Dillon that
blared overhead.

Looking down at the stadium floor spread out below
them, it was clear to Matt that their initial read of the
layout was correct. A large stage had been erected in its
center. The area around it was off-limits to the public. A
knot of TV news crews, reporters, and photographers
were busy setting up around the stage. TV programming

across the country, if not the world, was likely to be pre-empted when Father Jerome got onstage. Matt glanced up at an overhead clock. It was one o'clock. According to Darby's impromptu invitation, the festivities were due to start at five. That gave him and Gracie four hours to do their sweep. It sounded like a lot of time, but it wasn't. The place was enormous. And although the sheer size of the crowd was working in their favor as far as giving them some kind of cover, it wasn't making their task any easier. Getting across the main concourse had taken forever due to the human obstacle course they had to get through. It was like swimming in molasses. The density of the crowd was also masking what lay beyond the bobbing heads and jousting bellies, even for someone of Matt's six-foot-four stature.

Matt's eyes circled around, taking in the tiers of seating that soared about him, looking for a transmitter so small you could hide it in an overhead baggage compartment.

"Where do we start?" Gracie asked.

Matt shrugged. It was a daunting task. He needed to narrow down the search area if they were going to stand a chance. He thought back to the assumptions they'd made. The stadium was a pretty standard shape, a fat rectangle with the long sides arcing outward. It had several levels of seating: five tiers of raked arena seating, intercut by three banks of suites that ran along the sidelines on the second, fourth, and top levels. Matt looked around, trying to picture the invisible cone of the laser signal that would be animating the smart dust. He tried to visualize the sign appearing inside and overhead, and worked back from there to suss out where the best vantage point would be for the transmitter. The banks of suites caught his eye. They provided both the right coverage and privacy. Matt discounted the ones on the highest level. They were tucked away under the sides of the roof. It didn't seem to him that they'd allow enough of an angle to control the sign if the plan was to have it over the stadium. That left the two lower levels of suites to check out, on levels four and two, and the club suites on level three. One bank along each sideline. Six banks of suites in total.

"Up there," he said, pointing at the upper suites. They'd start up there and work their way down.

Gracie nodded, and followed him out of the seating blocks and back onto the main concourse and the stair-wells.

◄○►

IN A FAR CORNER of the parking lot, Dalton clicked the Draganflyer's black carbon fiber rotor blades into place and tightened the harness around the airborne camera. He'd recharged its lithium battery overnight, and it was all set to go. He had it laid out on the back deck of the Navigator, away from curious eyes. As he got it ready, he kept looking out, glancing around suspiciously, wary of any danger. He couldn't help it. The idea that Finch had been murdered so ruthlessly and effortlessly was still gnawing at him. Militias and angry mobs in Middle East-ern or African countries he could deal with. Silent, anon-ymous killers in black robes who snuck up behind you and threw you off roofs—the thought made him shud-der.

He checked the remote-control unit again. Felt satis-fied that he hadn't missed any connections, then set it aside and checked his watch. Less than three hours to go. Even though it would have been really useful to scan the surrounding areas, they'd decided not to use the skycam before the sign came up. It was too risky. They didn't want some overexcited pilgrim or the cops—or Drucker's men for that matter—to blast it out of the sky. Instead, he and Rydell were going to recon the area around the stadium on foot, doing opposite sweeps from the edge of the parking lots, until it got dark.

He looked around. It wouldn't be easy. The lot was heaving with cars and people, huddled against the soaring wall of the stadium. Dalton shrugged, tried to get the image of Finch being shoved off the roof out of his mind, and set out to begin his search.

KEENAN DRUCKER GLANCED at his watch. Two hours to go. He frowned. Things weren't going well. Not well at all.

Losing Rydell was a huge blow. Drucker hated being in that position. Right now, he couldn't read the man's state of mind. There had been too many upheavals. Rydell had to be unhinged, and unhinged meant unpredictable or, worse, irrational. Would he act impulsively and bring the whole thing down on them all, even if it destroyed him in the process? Or would he retreat and regroup and try to come up with a way out that kept him in the clear?

Drucker wasn't sure. He hoped it would be the latter. That would also give him time to regroup. Time to come up with an alternative. Because right now, he needed one.

He frowned, his eyes burning into the framed portrait of his son that stared back at him from the edge of his desk. He felt like he was failing him. Failing his memory, failing to make up for his pointless death.

I won't fail you this time, he insisted inwardly, his fists clenching tightly, choking the blood out of them and turning them a deathly shade of white.

"We might need to bring our plans forward," Maddox's voice prompted him from his speakerphone. The soldier sounded bleak, defeated. Not a tone of voice he was used to hearing from him.

"We can't do that," Drucker grumbled. "Not with Rydell running around out there. Any sign of his daughter?"

"No," Maddox said. "The plane dropped her off in L.A. She's not using her cell or her credit cards. She's out of play for the time being."

Drucker sighed. "They'll go for the brother. That's all Sherwood cares about. Are you all set for that?"

Maddox just said, "We're ready."

"Then finish it," Drucker ordered him, and hung up.

Chapter 75

Afternoon turned to evening as the sky overhead went from bright blue to a soft pink and the clocks skipped past five o'clock. Matt and Gracie still hadn't found anything. They'd worked their way down from the top of the stadium without success. The show was about to start, and they still had a lot of ground to cover.

Checking out the suites wasn't easy. For this unscheduled event, all the seating in the stadium was free—except for the suites. Matt and Gracie quickly found out that most of those had been allocated to Darby's personal guests, some to the media, and the remainder to the guests of the other preachers that Darby had invited to share the stage with him. Access to the suites sections was restricted and tightly controlled by beefy security guys in black sweatshirts who knew all the scams. Still, Gracie managed to get into both banks of suites on the fourth and club levels by charming some bona fide invitees and tagging along with them, dragging Matt with her. They swept through them, all forty-five suites in each bank, on the lookout for any high-tech gear or for men who didn't look like they were there for a spiritual experience. They didn't find either.

They had just cleared the first bank of suites on the club level when the music faded down and the lights dimmed. Everyone pushed forward for a closer view. Matt and Gracie edged closer. A chorus of voices rose on the overhead speakers and the reverend's hundred-member choir filed onto the stage, taking up their positions solemnly as they sang "Let There Be Light." The crowd erupted wildly, clapping and cheering before joining in. The effect was remarkable. Seventy thousand voices, all singing together, soon accompanied by the countless thousands of others outside the stadium's walls, a chorus of worship echoing across the Houston twilight.

Matt frowned. Father Jerome's appearance was drawing near, and they still hadn't found any trace of Danny or of the guys who were holding him. Matt had to make some decisions. He had to go for the likeliest spots and forget about the rest. There wasn't enough time. He scanned the dark stadium, and settled on two target areas beyond the bank of suites they were still checking out: the two banks of suites on level two. Each bank had thirty-nine suites in it, which would take time to vet. They'd have to forgo the main seating tiers and hope for the best.

The singing ended and Darby strolled out onto the stage, basking in the wild applause. Massive overhead video screens beamed a close-up of his face across the stadium.

"Greetings in Christ," he boomed, drawing the same words back from the excited masses.

Matt and Gracie weren't going to stick around for his speech. They slipped back through the suite and pressed on with their sweep.

They advanced slowly, checking out the rest of the floor. Half an hour later, they'd come up empty-handed. Two other megapastors had come onstage in the meantime, delivering rousing sermons to tumultuous cheers. In between their speeches, the choir sang backup to some of the biggest names in Christian rock. Matt and Gracie descended to the level three concourse and were on their way to level two when Gracie suddenly gasped and spun around and ducked into the cover of Matt's bulk.

"What?" he asked.

She peered out, then slipped out of view behind him again. "Ogilvy," she said. "He's right there."

Matt's fists clenched. "Which one?"

"Slick guy, by the concession stand. Graying hair, rimless glasses. He's in a light-colored suit."

Matt scanned the crowd. The concourse was filled with wall-to-wall people. A couple of heads parted and he caught a glimpse of someone fitting Gracie's description. "Come on," he said in a low voice as he took Gracie's hand and cut through the crowd behind Ogilvy. He lost him, then saw him appear again, about fifteen yards ahead, heading for the suites. The fact that Ogilvy was about five-six wasn't helping. Matt tried to press ahead, but the crush of people was like quicksand. He saw a small opening in the crowd and nosed into it, only to slam into a couple of tall rancher types who were cutting across him on their way back from the concession stands. One of them spilled his beer all over his shirt and shoved Matt back angrily.

"Watch your step, doofus," the man snapped. "What's your rush?"

Matt's arm tightened and his eyes narrowed and he was about to pounce, but Gracie held him back and subdued him with a forced smile.

"Easy, big guy." She turned to the angry rancher and cranked her flirt look up to eleven. "No damage done, boys. What do you say we just forgive and forget and go back to enjoying the sermons. It *is* Christmas, right?"

Matt held back and waited for the other guy to nod. The rancher scowled, thinking about it, then grudgingly gave him a tiny bob of the head. Matt nodded back, took Gracie's hand, and pulled her into the throng of people, but he couldn't see Ogilvy anywhere. He craned his neck and hoisted himself on the tips of his toes and scanned around intently.

There was no sign of him.

◄◦►

OUT AT THE EDGE of the red lot, Rydell and Dalton watched with awe as the crowd rose into song and settled down again. Some of them had brought small 12-volt-powered TV sets with them, and clusters of people were massed around each set, listening to the sermons and responding with the occasional "Amen."

Rydell cast his gaze across the plain of cars, then looked up at the sky. The last glints of daylight had dipped down behind the horizon. "Let's send it up," he said. "We can't wait much longer."

Dalton brought the Draganflyer out of the Lincoln and set it down on the ground. He checked the light and flicked the HD video camera under its belly to night-vision mode. He then switched the Draganflyer's engines on, glanced around, and guided it up. It rose quickly with the silent whirr of a high-powered household cooling fan and disappeared in the night sky.

Rydell studied the area around them, trying to divine where he would put the launchers. To their right were some low-lying structures, on the other side of Kirby Drive. "Let's send it out over those buildings over there," he said, pointing in that direction. Then he seemed to have second thoughts. He shifted his gaze over to the stadium. Something about its north-south axis was tugging at his mind. His eyes narrowed a touch, and he said,

"Actually, send it up there," pointing behind them, north of the stadium. He checked the image the skycam was sending back onto Dalton's laptop. It had that ghostly, pale-green night-vision look, but the high-definition processor was doing its job and the detail was surprisingly clear. "And keep your eyes on that screen."

◄◦►

"DAMMIT," Matt hissed. "We've lost him."

His eyes scoured the concourse around him. Ogilvy had vanished into the crowd.

"The network," Gracie blurted. "Maybe they wrangled a suite here. Maybe that's how they brought the transmitter in."

"Makes sense. But how do we find out where it is? I didn't see any guest lists. It's all a big mess in here."

They also had another problem. There were two banks of suites on level two, but they were at opposite ends of the stadium. One was to the east, facing the Astrodome. The other faced west. Getting across from one to the other meant they'd have to get through another human swamp.

"We won't have time to check both banks," Gracie said.

Just then, the music changed into a deep, heraldic burst of brass and the lights across the stadium dimmed again. The crowd hushed to a bone-chilling silence. The air was thick with nervous expectation. And Darby reappeared onstage, welcomed by a thunderous uproar. He milked it for almost a minute before raising a calming hand and asking the crowd, "Are you ready?"

The answer was a thunderous "Yes."

"My fellow children of Christ, please give a warm Houston welcome and open your hearts to our special guest, Father Jerome." Every single person in the stadium was standing up, clapping and cheering rapturously as the slight figure of Father Jerome appeared. He looked unimaginably small on the huge stage, shuffling forward slowly, looking around at the crowd in awe, dwarfed by his own image on the overhead video displays. A blinding fusillade of flashbulbs accompanied him as he padded across to the center of the stage and gave Darby a small, courteous bow. Darby ushered him over to a microphone stand and waved him on before retreating a few steps into the shadows.

Matt and Gracie stood there, rooted to the floor, transfixed by the crowd's reaction. The entire stadium reverberated with an air of majesty. Gracie watched the close-up of Father Jerome's face on the screens. He was looking up, taking in the scene, clearly overwhelmed by the sheer scale of it all. Droplets of sweat were sliding down his forehead. He didn't seem to know what to say. The whole crowd was on its feet and just stood there, silent, hanging on what God's messenger would proclaim. He cleared his throat with a small cough, looking around slightly fearfully—and then his expression changed, as if he'd been mildly startled by something. He cocked his head a little and his eyes blinked; then he swallowed and said, "Thank you all for being here and for welcoming me here tonight."

The crowd responded exuberantly with "Amens" and applause.

As Father Jerome embarked on his sermon down below, an idea burst through the chaos in Matt's mind. "I need to call Rydell," he told Gracie. "Quick."

Gracie had Dalton's cell phone with her. Rydell still had his. She speed-dialed him and passed the phone to Matt.

◄◦►

RYDELL PICKED UP on the first ring.

"Do you have the skycam up?" Matt asked, his tone urgent.

Rydell was eyeing the screen on Dalton's laptop closely. "It's over the medical center, just north of here," he informed him. "Nothing so far."

"What happens to its video downlink if it crosses into the transmitter's signal?" Matt asked breathlessly.

"It would interrupt it, for sure," Rydell speculated.

"It wouldn't mess it up so it couldn't fly, would it?"

Rydell thought about it for a beat, then said, "It might. The laser signal could override the signal from the skycam's remote controller. We could lose control of it while it's in the beam's path. Might fry it altogether."

Dalton flashed him a concerned look.

Matt's voice shot back. "We've got to risk it. Send it over to us, inside the stadium. It's the only way we're going to find out where their signal's coming from."

"Okay," Rydell said, spinning a finger horizontally in the air to Dalton and gesturing at the stadium. "Let's just hope it gets there in one piece." He turned to Dalton, and told him, "We're going in."

Dalton used the screen to guide him and fingered the joysticks to turn the black skycam around. Rydell was huddled behind him, his attention riveted to the screen. As Dalton banked the Draganflyer around, he flinched and exclaimed, "Did you see that?" He jabbed a finger at the screen, but the Draganflyer was zooming back and whatever he was pointing at was gone.

"What?" Dalton asked.

"There was something, back there." He pointed at the top left-hand corner of the screen. "On the roof. Can you flip the camera around so it's pointing backward?"

Dalton's face was tight with concentration as his fingers made microadjustments to the joysticks. "Can't do a full one-eighty. It's just a forward sweep. I can spin it around and fly it backward, but it's gonna reach the stadium any second now and I don't want to risk it and fly blind."

Rydell frowned and nodded. "Okay, keep going. We'll come back to it."

"If it's still flying by then," Dalton worried.

◄◊►

MATT AND GRACIE scanned the rectangular opening of black sky and waited as Father Jerome finished his sermon.

"Matt, he's doing it," she told him, pointing at the stage.

Matt looked down, the cell phone still on his ear. "Come on, guys."

"It's almost there," Rydell said, clearly tense.

Down on the stage, Father Jerome tilted his head back and slowly raised his arms outward from his sides until they were slightly above the horizontal, as if he were about to catch a massive beach ball. The crowd shuddered and all eyes turned to the empty air under the stadium's open roof.

"Pray with me," Father Jerome beseeched his followers. "Pray with me that God gives us a sign and guides our thoughts and helps us do his will."

Murmurs rose and lips quivered across the stadium as the crowd started to pray. And then a gasp reverberated throughout the giant hall as a ball of light appeared over Father Jerome. It was small, perhaps eight or ten feet in diameter, a swirling, cloudy sphere of light. An upwelling of flashbulbs lit up the tiers as the apparition just floated there for a few seconds, then started to rise. It reached the halfway point between Father Jerome's head and the stadium's full height and held there for a moment, blazing to a twinkling backdrop of thousands of flashbulbs; then it flared out and expanded into the now-familiar, massive sphere of brilliance.

The crowd was cowed into a nervous silence as the sign rotated before them. Then, like a breaking wave, euphoria rolled across the arena and the crowd erupted into a mighty roar, bigger than anything any touchdown at the stadium had ever generated. Amid wailing "Amens" and "Hallelujahs," the massed faithful waved their arms and hugged their cheeks in adulation and awe. People were crossing themselves. Some people fainted; others wailed hysterically. Most just stared in disbelief while tears of joy ran down their faces.

Matt's skin tingled. It was the first time he'd seen it live, and its power blew him away. He had to keep reminding himself that it wasn't supernatural. That it was Danny's work. That his brother had played a crucial role in making it possible.

He could sense his presence. More than ever, he had to find him.

He looked up and hissed into the cell phone, "Where is it?"

"It's in," Rydell announced. "It just dropped in from the north face of the opening."

Chapter 76

Matt stared up intently, straining to find the tiny black machine—then he spotted it. It was barely visible, its stealthy matte finish blending into the night sky, but it was there. He kept his eyes glued to it and sized up its position relative to the banks of suites. He decided to go for the east bank first.

"Okay, bring it down so it's by the lower end of the sign and take it around the stadium counterclockwise," he told Rydell. "And let me know the second you get any interference."

"Got it," Rydell acknowledged.

—◦—

Out in the red lot, Rydell and Dalton watched the laptop's screen breathlessly as the Draganflyer dived into the stadium and circled the sign. All around them, clusters of people were huddled around those who'd brought portable TVs with them, watching the sign in breathless awe.

"Here we go," Dalton mumbled, nervousness catching in his throat.

—◦—

MATT STRUGGLED to keep the tiny contraption in view as it began its wide circular sweep around the inside of the stadium. The cell phone was glued to his ear and he could feel his pulse thumping against his cheek. Gracie was on alert too, scanning the entrance behind them, still wary of Ogilvy, uncomfortable with his presence there.

Across the stadium, the crowd was still enthralled by the sight before them. The sign was just hovering there, a gargantuan ball of shimmering energy. Matt's gaze kept getting drawn to it. It was incredibly hard to resist staring at it, and as soon as his eyes strayed over to it, he'd pull them away, back to the Draganflyer's last position, trying to stay focused on the tiny black dot.

The skycam had almost reached the southern tip of the east bank of suites when Rydell's voice shot into his ear.

"We've got something. Shit, we're losing it," he shouted.

Matt's neck flinched forward, as if the extra couple of inches would make a difference. He saw the skycam go into a wobble; then it just arced down violently, as if it had suddenly lost all power or been smacked down by a big invisible swatter, and dropped like a rock.

Matt's heart skipped a beat as he saw it plummet, but his eyes raced back up and lasered in on the suites that faced its last stable position. They were the very last ones, at the southeast corner of the stadium.

"Come on," he yelled to Gracie, grabbing her hand and bolting back onto the concourse, racing for the escalators.

◄◦►

"SHIT," Dalton yelled as he lost control of the Draganflyer, his heart pounding, his face clenched in panic, his

THE SIGN ◄○► 485

fingers desperately playing the joysticks in search of a re-action.

The image on the laptop's screen fizzled out and was replaced by gray static, its accompanying hiss just making things worse.

"It's gonna fucking kill someone," he blurted—then the image on the screen suddenly flickered back to life. It was unnerving—a plunging point-of-view from the camera as it dived at a rapidly growing crowd.

"Pull it up," Rydell yelled.

"I'm trying," Dalton fired back. The people in the camera's sights grew bigger, their eyes shot wide as they spotted the alien device hurtling toward them and their faces went taut with alarm—and then it came back to life and swooped away just over their heads, avoiding them and pulling up until it just hovered in place by the stadium's roof.

Dalton let out a huge breath of relief and darted a look of sheer delight at Rydell. "Whose brilliant idea was that?" he asked, his voice shaky.

Rydell gave him a big pat on the shoulder. "Great job, man. Great job. Now get it out of there and let's check out that building."

A crescendo of excitement erupted around them. Rydell and Dalton moved back from the SUV's trunk and stared up at the top of the stadium as a wave of gasps rolled across the parking lot.

The sign was now rising slowly into the night sky, a curved sliver of light peeking out above the stadium's roof.

◄○►

MATT LEAPT OFF the escalator onto level two and raced across the landing area that led to the entrance of the suites. Gracie was trailing close behind. The crowds were gone; there was no one around. Everyone was watching the miracle taking place in the arena. The bouncers were also gone, probably watching alongside the guests in one of the suites.

They were coming in from the north side, and the target suite was all the way down the concourse that ran behind the suites, at the south end of the bank. As Matt charged down the curving concourse, two things happened: He thought something must have changed in the arena as a chorus of *ooh*s and *aah*s rippled through the suites' doors. And he saw a man walking his way, heading out of the suites area just as Gracie yelled out, "Matt," from behind him.

The guy had graying hair, rimless glasses, a light-colored suit, and looked slick. The recognition was mutual as Ogilvy flinched with surprise, but he didn't have time to do much else before Matt just slammed right into him without slowing down, grabbing him by the arms and spinning him and shoving him up hard against the concourse wall. Ogilvy let out a pained gasp as Matt's weight crashed into his back and winded him. Matt felt his wound light up with a spike of pain, but ignored it and belted Ogilvy with a punch to the kidneys. The man buckled forward under the pain. Matt was in overdrive. He didn't let up for a second. He just grabbed Ogilvy's right arm, yanked it way up high behind him until it almost snapped, then shoved him forward and led him down the concourse at a half jog.

"Which one are they in?" he rasped.

Ogilvy's head was lolling left and right, like a boxer with cut eyes, teetering on his last legs.

"Which one?" Matt asked again, still rushing ahead. He knew the suite he wanted was one of the last ones in the row and didn't really need Ogilvy to answer. He figured the target suite wouldn't be like all the others. They all had their doors wide-open, the clusters of people inside them all crowding the front barlike counter. Maddox's boys wouldn't be as welcoming, and their suite would have its door shut. Maybe even someone outside, on guard. Within seconds, they'd rounded the concourse. Sure enough, the last suite had its door closed. Matt pushed Ogilvy up against the door and rapped on it firmly while twisting Ogilvy's arm right up so his shoulder blade was about to pop out.

"Get them to open up, nice and friendly," Matt hissed into his ear.

"Yeah?" came a low grunt from inside.

Ogilvy swallowed hard, then blurted, "It's Ogilvy," trying to sound unruffled but not quite pulling it off.

The guy behind the door must have hesitated, as he didn't open immediately; then the door cracked open. Matt lifted Ogilvy off his feet the second he heard the lock jangle, ripping his shoulder tendons in the process, and shoved him against the door like a vertical battering ram. The door slammed backward, hitting the guy standing behind it in the face. The doors to the suites were rock-solid and soundproof. The impact sounded like the guy had been pounded with a baseball bat. It knocked him off his feet and sent his gun flying out of his hand and tumbling heavily to the ground. Matt stormed in, keeping Ogilvy in front of him like a shield. His eyes registered two other guys in there, in addition to the guy on the ground. They were waiting for him and had silenced handguns trained on the door. Matt didn't slow down. He kept charging forward, holding Ogilvy in front of him, flying across the room in five long strides. Ogilvy jerked and flailed as several rounds cut into him, but the shooters didn't have that much time to fire before Matt was right on top of them. He launched Ogilvy at the one dead ahead of him and leapt across at the other shooter, catching his firing arm with his hands and pushing his gun away while landing a heavy elbow across his jaw. He heard it snap as he spun around, still gripping the guy's gun wrist with both hands and tracking it around through ninety degrees until it was facing the other shooter, who was busy pushing Ogilvy's bloodied body off of him. The two silenced handguns pirouetted around in unison to face each other, only the one under Matt's control got there a split second earlier and he squeezed hard against the guy's trigger finger. The handgun belched a round that caught the opposing shooter squarely in the neck. The guy recoiled as a burst of blood geysered between his shoulder blades, just as he let off a round of his own that whizzed by Matt and buried itself somewhere in the wall behind him.

Matt felt the shooter behind him squirm. He slammed his elbow back into him, mashing his throat. He felt the shooter's body go rigid as the man convulsed in a pained gurgle—then Gracie yelled, "Matt," again. He spun his gaze back toward the entrance to the suite and to the guy who'd taken the door in the face. Half his face was glowing an angry purply red. It had to hurt. He was on his knees, straightening up, looking across at Matt. He'd just recovered his gun when Gracie screamed and just hurled herself at him, tackling him from the side. The shooter reacted fast—he just whipped up his arm and deflected her, sending her crashing against the wall behind him, but it bought Matt the precious seconds he needed to play puppet master again and raise the arm of the shooter behind him and fire off a couple of rounds into purple-face.

He took a second to catch his breath and let his heartbeat go back to something that vaguely resembled normal, then wrenched the handgun out of the shooter's hand, kicked him aside, and pushed himself to his feet.

Gracie stood up, her face locked in shock, and stepped over to join him.

He cast his eyes around the suite, and a grim realization hit him. There was no transmitter in the room. No control master board. And no Danny either. He thought back to Ogilvy wandering around the stadium, to the shooters' position when he'd come through the door. It had been a trap. They were waiting for him, using Ogilvy to draw him in. The transmitter had to be nearby—the signal had come from that general area—but it didn't matter anymore. He was sure they wouldn't have risked having Danny inside the stadium. He had to be outside somewhere. That was, if he wasn't controlling the transmitter from across the state, or the whole country, for that matter.

Matt's heart sank. He frowned as Gracie took a couple of steps and looked out through the suite's floor-to-ceiling glass pane, into the heart of the arena. He edged over and joined her. The sign had risen through the open roof. Its bottom edge was just beyond the tangent to the roofline, dipping into the cube of empty air over the stadium floor. Father Jerome was still on the stage, his arms outstretched, mumbling a prayer. And every single person in the stadium was still standing.

A warble snapped his attention. It was Dalton's cell phone. Rydell was calling.

He picked it up.

"We think we've got them," Rydell blurted out breathlessly. "Get your ass out here. They're here."

Chapter 77

"Where? What's going on?" Matt asked, his voice racing.

"There's a tall building that backs up against the entrance of the red lot on the north side," Rydell said. "Might be a hotel. I'm not sure. It's got a pool on one side and a parking lot all around it. There are four guys on the roof. They've got the launchers."

The words were like an afterburner to his senses. He glanced out the glass wall. The sign was hovering over the stadium now. His mind rocketed back to Rydell telling him it could stay up around fifteen minutes before it burned out. He knew it wasn't long before it would vanish, and once that happened, the crew with the launchers would also be gone. Taking Danny—if he was there—with them.

"Where are you?" Matt asked.

"At the east end of the lot, by the Center."

Matt was recalling the park's layout from the Web site they'd studied the night before. "So if I come out the north gate—"

Rydell jumped in. "Just head straight up across the lot and you'll hit it. It's about five hundred yards away."

"I'm on my way. Keep this line open and keep me

posted." He turned to Gracie, his face alight with hope. "They've got a fix on the launchers. I'm going after them." He stepped over to the downed shooters, retrieved two of their handguns, and stuffed them under his belt. He pulled his shirt out and let it hang down to cover them. "Come on. You get back to the car and wait with the guys."

"You can't go after them alone," she protested.

"Don't really have a choice," he told her. "We've got to go."

◄◦►

OUT IN THE RED LOT, Rydell and Dalton stood transfixed before the laptop's screen. The Draganflyer was in a holding pattern about two hundred and fifty feet over the target, its night-vision lens on full zoom. They were probably the only people for miles not to be staring at the blazing sign that had now cleared the stadium's roof and was hovering in the night sky above it. It was a mesmerizing, awesome sight, visible for miles around. The thousands of onlookers in the parking lots and on the jammed freeways were just rooted in place, utterly enthralled by the otherworldly apparition.

Rydell checked his watch. He knew what was coming, and sure enough, it happened almost on cue. The sign pulsed slightly, like a beating heart, then just faded out like a snuffed-out candle. The crowd reacted with an audible collective intake of breath and scattered cries of "Praise the Lord" and "Amen."

He glanced at the screen. The guys on the roof were moving fast now, packing their gear. He knew how efficient they'd be. They didn't surprise him. Within a minute, they'd stowed the launch tubes and the rest of their gear and disappeared into the building.

"Come on," he mumbled, almost to himself, and

craned his neck, angling to get a better view of the stadium's north entrance, as if he could spot Matt, but the entrance was too far and his sight line was blocked by all kinds of tall vehicles. He glanced across at the north end of the lot and the big building that loomed over it, behind a row of trees. He shook his head ruefully, and made a quick decision.

"The guns are in the glove compartment, right?" he asked Dalton.

Before Dalton could answer, he'd already scurried over and pulled out the Para-Ordnance.

"What are you doing?" Dalton felt a stab of fear at the sight of Rydell holding the silver handgun.

Rydell flicked his eyes across at the stadium, then up at the building, then back at Dalton. He handed him his phone. "I've got to help Matt. Stay with the car." And before he could object, Rydell was gone.

◄◦►

MATT EXPLODED out of the stadium's north entrance and just plowed on, with Gracie close behind. He reached the lot and stopped, shot a quick glance across the cars to get his bearings, and pointed Gracie in the direction Rydell had said the big SUV was parked.

"They should be around there somewhere, at the back."

She nodded, and he was gone.

He sprinted through the rows of cars, SUVs, and pickup trucks, cutting around the clusters of revellers, twisting and ducking and weaving like a wide receiver charging the end zone and looking for his own Hail Mary pass. One and a half minutes later, he saw the last row of cars and the low perimeter fence of the lot. He threaded his way through a couple of camper vans and reached the fence, then stopped in his tracks at the sight of Rydell, waiting for him, breathing heavily. He joined him, catching his breath, nodding a question.

"Figured you could use some help," Rydell said, lifting his jacket to expose the handgun he had tucked under his belt.

Matt tugged his shirttail up to give Rydell a glance of his own arsenal and gave him a slight grin. He held the phone up to his ear.

"Anything?" he asked.

Dalton's voice came back. "No movement, but the lot on the south side of the building is crawling with people. They've got to have their car on the other—hang on." He stumbled. "Okay, we've got one, two, three—four guys, coming out of the east face of the building and heading for what looks like—it's a van, by the trees in the northeast corner of the lot."

Matt snapped the phone shut and stuffed it in his back pocket. "You know how to use it?" he asked, pointing at Rydell's silver handgun.

Rydell nodded easily. "I'll manage."

Matt flicked him an okay nod and took off for the trees.

They hurdled the low fence bordering the parking lot and cut across the scrub and the thicket of trees that led to the building. A neon sign informed Matt that it was a Holiday Inn. He led Rydell to the right, past the pool area and its terrace café. It was teeming with people, hotel guests who were now discussing the sign's appearance animatedly. They kept going, rounding the hotel and reaching its front parking lot.

Matt hugged the side of the building and looked out. The lot was wide and had poor lighting, and its far reaches were bathed in near darkness. There was a row of cars, then a lane, then two rows of cars, another lane, and one last row of cars. He could make out the roof of the van all the way down, on the far right. It was parked facing the hotel, with its loading bay backing up against another thicket of trees that separated the hotel from the next property. He looked a question at Rydell. Rydell nodded his confirmation that it was the right van. Matt saw movement around it, figures silhouetted in the night. Saw one of them lifting a big tube and handing it to someone out of sight. He looked to Rydell again for confirmation. Rydell nodded. They were Maddox's men. Loading up.

Matt felt a tightening in his gut. Danny could be right there. Less than fifty yards away.

He pulled out his guns and handed one to Rydell.

"This one will be quieter than that cannon you've got there. Go wide that way," he whispered, gesturing for Rydell to move in from the left. "I'll cut across from the right. And stay low."

Rydell confirmed with a slight nod and slipped away in a low crouch.

Matt crept closer to the van. He hugged the cars, slithering through the narrow gaps between them, his eyes locked on the target. It was a Chevy work van. The big, long-wheelbase model. White and anonymous. He heard one of its doors clang shut and saw one of the men stepping toward the back of the van. The others were out of sight behind it. Matt moved in closer, sucked in a deep breath, and rose just enough to clear the roof of the car in front of him, gripping his handgun in a two-handed stance, ready to pump a couple of silenced bullets into Maddox's men—but there was no one there. They were gone. His nerves bristled as he swept his gun left and right, his eyes and ears at Defcon one—then he heard a rustle off to the right, in the trees beyond the van, and saw a shooter emerge, pulling Rydell along with him, a silenced handgun pressed against the billionnaire's temple.

Matt flinched, unsure about what to do—just as something hard nudged him in the back.

"Drop it," the voice said. "Nice and slow."

Matt's heart cratered. They'd been expected. For a split second, the notion of making a move sparked in his mind, but the guy behind him cut it short with a sudden, hard punch to Matt's ear that sent him down to his knees. He dropped his gun, and his vision went blurry. He stayed down for a moment, waiting for it to settle, and through his bleary veil, he glimpsed the vague outline of someone climbing out of the back of the van. It was Maddox, and—he wasn't alone. He was dragging someone out of the van with him, yanking him by the neck, a handgun pressed against it.

Matt squinted, straining to cut through the fog in his head, but even before it lifted, the recognition was instant.

It was Danny.

He was there. He was actually there.

And very much alive.

Matt's insides cartwheeled. He pushed himself to his feet, and the adrenaline boost coursing through him brought Danny's face racing into focus. He gave Matt a pained smile. Matt nodded back and couldn't suppress a broad smile, even though things weren't looking too promising for them.

Maddox acknowledged Matt's presence with a shrug, but his eyes registered genuine surprise when he saw Rydell.

"Well, what do you know?" he quipped, clearly pleased with the unexpected presence of the tycoon. "And people say there is no Santa."

◄○►

GRACIE FLARED. "What are they doing?"

The image on the laptop's screen showed the two figures they knew to be Rydell and Matt putting their guns down and stepping back from the van in defeat. Seconds later, two other figures appeared from the van, tightly bunched, one behind the other.

"Is that a gun?" she asked, fear catching in her throat.

"Hang on," Dalton said. He fingered the joysticks expertly and brought the Draganflyer down slightly closer for a better look.

The top view of Maddox's extended arm grew bigger on the screen. And there was no mistaking the gun that was staring Matt and Rydell in the face.

◄○►

DANNY GRUNTED against Maddox's tight hold. "I'm sorry, bro," he told Matt. "I couldn't warn you."

"Don't worry about it." He saw that Danny's hands were tied together with plastic flex-cuffs.

Danny glared at Rydell. "What's he doing here?" he asked Matt.

"His penance," Matt replied flatly.

Danny shook his head sardonically. His stare burned into Rydell. "Too little, too late, don't you think? Or do you also have the power to raise the dead?"

Rydell kept quiet.

Maddox swung his right arm straight out, flicking his handgun in a horizontal arc from Matt to Rydell and back.

"Sorry to have to cut this happy reunion short, boys," he said tersely, "but we've got to get going. So how about you say good-bye to your pain-in-the-ass brother one last time, Danny boy." He settled his gun sight on Matt and gave him a curious, almost respectful nod. "It's been good knowing you, kid. You did really well."

"Not well enough," Matt retorted gruffly.

"No, believe me, you did real well," he insisted.

Maddox raised the gun a couple of inches for a head shot, no emotion whatsoever registering on his face. Matt's heart stopped at the thought of a bullet shredding into him—then Maddox whipped back as something slammed into him from out of nowhere, something big and black that rocketed out of the night sky with a stealthy whoosh and batted his arm off savagely to one side. His gun went flying off as Maddox howled, the chopper's carbon fiber blades slicing through skin and muscle, and he fell to the ground in a burst of dark blood.

Matt was already moving as the Draganflyer crashed heavily into the van's open door—he rammed his elbow back into the shooter behind him, yelling, "Go," to Rydell as he spun around and pushed the man's gun hand away while battering him with a cross that ripped his jaw out of its sockets and sent him tumbling to the ground. Matt went down with him, fighting for the gun, but the man's hand was like a vise around his automatic and he wouldn't let go—they wrestled for it like starved, rabid dogs fighting over a bone, until the gun spat out a shot that caught the shooter in the gut and he flinched back in agony.

Rydell wasn't as quick or as effective—he was grappling with his shooter, his hands clasped around the man's wrist, struggling for the gun. The shooter pulled him in and suckered him into a head butt that caught Rydell flat across the bridge of his nose. Rydell's legs caved in and he rag-dolled. Matt rose in time to see the shooter spin around, his gun rising to align itself on Matt—

—then the shooter jerked back to the tune of a couple of silenced coughs. Matt blinked. It took him a second to realize what had happened; then he saw Danny gripping Maddox's gun tightly, a thin tendril of smoke spiraling out of the muzzle of its silencer. Danny stared at the shooter's inert body for a beat, then turned to Matt, his face locked in disbelief at what he'd done—

Danny opened his mouth to say something—

Matt's eyes went wide—

"Watch out," he blurted, but—

It was too late—Maddox had already sprung to his feet behind Danny. He crashed into him as Matt dived for the gun that had fallen from his shooter. Matt managed to grab it before Maddox made it to the gun Danny had dropped—only Danny was blocking a clear shot. Maddox's eyes met Matt's for a nanosecond before he shoved Danny toward Matt and scurried back away from them, and disappeared behind the van.

"Move," Matt yelled to Danny, pushing him away, bolting after Maddox—he charged around the van and into the thicket of trees that edged the parking lot, but the darkness had swallowed his quarry up. Matt fired a couple of rounds out of frustration, but he knew he wasn't going to score a hit. Maddox was gone.

The lot went eerily quiet. Matt turned, scanned the area, then stepped around Rydell and his fallen shooter and joined Danny. He embraced him with a big bear hug. Pulled him back and ruffled his hair.

"Merry Christmas," he told him.

"Best one ever," Danny replied, his face all lit up with nervous relief. Rydell got up and joined them. Danny faced him for a beat, a hard, angry glare simmering in his eyes. Then he balled his fists and whipped up his still-tied arms in a big, curving swing that caught Rydell on the cheek and knocked him to the ground. Rydell spat out some blood, but stayed down for a moment. Then looked up at Danny, who was just looming over him.

Matt looked on curiously. "I couldn't have made it here without his help, bro," Matt told Danny.

Danny eyed Rydell a couple of more seconds, then turned away and shrugged dubiously. "It's a start," he grunted.

"Can we get out of here now?" Matt asked, stepping across to help Rydell up.

Rydell looked toward Danny. "I'm sorry," he said, his words laced with genuine regret.

"Like I said," Danny said as he walked away, "it's a start."

Less than a minute later, they were in the van, pulling away from the hotel's parking lot and easing past the long rows of parked cars that lined the roads on both sides.

Chapter 78

They'd changed motels for safety, moving to a different side of town, just in case—although with Maddox badly hurt and a lot of his men dead, they were starting to feel like maybe the crosshairs had lifted off them a little.

Danny and Matt were in their own world. They had a lot of catching up to do and took turns filling each other in on their tortured journeys.

"I've got to call Mom and Dad, let them know I'm okay," Danny said enthusiastically, still fired up by his escape.

Matt had skirted around mentioning them, but he couldn't duck it any longer. He held Danny's gaze as he tried to find the words to tell him what had happened, but Danny read his expression before he'd eked out a single word.

"Who? . . . Mom?" he asked.

Matt nodded, but his pained look held more portent than just one parent.

"Not . . . *both*?" Danny mouthed the words in total disbelief.

Matt nodded again.

Danny's face tightened, drowning with confusion.

Then it just crumpled with profound grief. Matt had already told him about Bellinger's murder. The triple whammy hit him real hard. He sank to the floor and gripped his head in his hands, feeling as if his veins were flooding with lava.

A more somber mood enshrouded them as Danny told Matt of his despair during those two years. How he'd tried to sneak an e-mail out to him and been caught. How he'd contemplated suicide. How they'd threatened him and drugged him after that.

"You're here now," Matt finally told him. "You're out and you're safe." Matt smiled. "And that's way more than either of us had a couple of days ago."

"Tell me more. About Mom and Dad. About how it all happened," Danny asked him.

◄◦►

IN AN ADJACENT ROOM, Rydell stewed alone. He'd found it as uncomfortable to be around Danny as Danny found it to be around him. He also had a lot on his mind.

It was over—that much was clear. Once Gracie returned, the story would blow wide-open. And then, whichever way you looked at it, his life was over too. His role in it would be part of the story. A big part of it. There was no way anyone was going to shield him from it. Not Gracie, not Matt or Danny, not Drucker. And even if they'd wanted to, there was no way they'd be able to do it. Not in this blog-rich age. And he wasn't prepared to run either. It wasn't his style. Besides, there was nowhere for him to run to. No, he'd be there to face up to what he'd been a part of.

The hardest part of it all was thinking about what it would do to Rebecca. It would be nothing short of devastating. It would follow her for the rest of her life. His mind kept churning it, desperate to find a way to mitigate that, to keep her out of it, but there was nothing he could think of that could do that.

◄◦►

BY THE TIME GRACIE and Dalton finally joined them a couple of hours later, the reunion was a bittersweet, subdued celebration. Yes, they were all safe. Yes, Danny was alive—and free. And Gracie and Dalton were about to become superstars. But there was a downside to the forthcoming media feeding frenzy too. A downside well beyond Rydell's very public downfall. One that looked far more daunting the more they talked about it.

In the background, a TV was switched on, replaying the evening's events in an almost continuous loop, with all kinds of talking heads coming in and out to comment on it.

"What's this going to do to all those people who were out there celebrating tonight?" Gracie asked, pointing at the screen, her voice edgy with concern. "And not just them, but everyone around the country who was tuning in. Everyone around the planet who's been buying into Drucker's scam, for that matter. What's going to happen to them? How are they going to take it?"

"What's the alternative?" Dalton countered. "We can't let the lie run. We'd just be digging all those people a deeper hole for Drucker to push them into. The sooner we end this, the better."

"I know." Gracie nodded. "It still feels wrong. It's lose-lose." She rubbed the bridge of her nose, then spread her fingers out and massaged her forehead. "I hate this," she groaned.

"Finch was murdered because of it," Dalton reminded her.

"Vince too," Danny added. "And Reece. And many others."

Gracie heaved a ponderous sigh. "They were killed to keep it quiet until Drucker was ready to pull the cover off. And now we're going to do it for him."

"We have to do this," Danny chimed in. "The longer it runs, the more painful it will be when the truth comes out."

Gracie nodded grudgingly, then said to Rydell, "I'll need you to go on the record. We'll need the evidence."

Rydell nodded somberly. "What choice do I have?"

She shifted her gaze across the room. "Danny?"

He nodded. "Hell, yes."

Gracie acknowledged it, then slumped back in her seat, a frustrated, haunted pallor to her face.

Rydell turned to Danny. "How were they planning on doing this? Do you know? How were they going to expose him?"

"They made me design a debunking software. They were going to run it over him once they were ready to out him."

Rydell pressed. "What does it do?"

"It simulates a breakdown in the technology. Like if you're watching TV and the signal breaks up. It makes it go all jumpy with static; then it just crashes. It's designed to be minimally counterintuitive. What you'd expect to see if the sign was a fake. It'll conjure up a broadcast that's going haywire." Danny gave him an uncomfortable smile. "It was either that or a huge Coca-Cola sign."

"What if we don't do this and it never comes out?" Gracie threw in, thinking aloud. "I mean, what if there was a way to get Drucker and his guys to keep their mouths shut?"

"The evangelicals would get to keep their new Messiah, and Darby and his friends on the far right would get to choose our next few presidents," Rydell observed gloomily.

"Well, by breaking the story and letting people know who was really behind it and what their agenda was, it'll be even worse," Gracie countered. "Either way, Darby and all his pals are going to come out of this stronger. Once you and Drucker are exposed, all the heathens and depraved liberals across the country are going to be demonized. We'll be giving the hard-core right their biggest rallying cry since the fall of the evil empire. Branding people as 'anti-American' will get a whole new lease on life. They'll run away with the next ten elections and turn the country into a Christian theocracy."

"Hang on, we're talking about a handful of guys who put this stunt in play, not an entire political party," Danny protested.

"It doesn't matter," Gracie argued back. "What matters is how they'll spin it. How they'll use it to split the country even further. They'll tar everyone with the same brush and make it look like everyone on Drucker's side of the aisle was in cahoots with him. That's what they do. And they're damn good at it too. Just imagine what someone like Karl Rove could do with it."

"Hey, maybe we could draft him and the other scumbags who sold us the war in Iraq and have them pin this thing on Iran," Dalton joked.

The others all turned to him with deeply unamused eyes.

"What? I'm kidding," he protested, his palms turned out.

A dreary silence smothered the room. On the TV, the anchor was back on briefly before the image cut away to footage of violent riots in Islamabad and in Jerusalem. Across the screen, people were clashing furiously as cars blazed behind them. Police officers and soldiers were in the thick of it, trying to stop the carnage.

Gracie sat up. "Turn it up," she told Dalton, who was closest to the TV.

". . . religious leaders have urged their followers to show restraint while the questions surrounding Father Jerome are answered, but the violence here shows no sign of abating," an off-camera reporter was saying.

An anchor came back on, and a banner at the bottom of the screen said, "President to make statement on Houston events."

"Following the unprecedented events in Houston earlier this evening," he announced, "a White House spokeswoman indicated that the president would be making a statement tomorrow."

Gracie and the others didn't need to hear the rest.

Drucker's web was spinning out of control.

"Even the president's getting suckered into this," Rydell said.

"We can't let that happen," Gracie insisted. She let out a dejected sigh and sagged back in her seat. "This is just going to sink us all." The room went silent. After a moment, Dalton asked, "So what do we do? 'Cause it seems to me like we need to do this pronto, but we're screwed either way, whether we expose it or not."

Rydell sat up. "We can expose it," he stated. "We have to. But only if I take the fall for it. Alone."

That got everyone's attention.

He pressed on. "It's the only way." His voice was quivering slightly, a tremble of nerves that was alien to Larry Rydell. "My plan didn't call for a fall guy. It was never intended to empower or undermine any religion. It was just meant to get people to listen. But now . . . after what they've done, the way they've turned it . . . We're all agreed that we can't let this lie go on. But Drucker's right. We need a fall guy with no political motive if we're going to avoid tearing this country apart. And that fall guy's got to be me." He sighed, then looked around at them with renewed determination. "There's no other way out of this. If anyone here has a better idea, I'm all ears, but . . . I don't see it happening any other way."

"Great," Gracie grumbled. "So Drucker wins."

"Don't worry about Drucker," Rydell assured her quietly. "I'll make sure he pays."

Gracie nodded stoically. No one knew where to look. Rydell was right, and they knew it. But the thought of doing what Drucker was going to do anyway, albeit long before he was planning to, was swirling inside them like a tuna melt that was a month past its sell-by date.

Gracie turned to Matt. He hadn't said a word throughout.

"You got somewhere else you got to be, cowboy?" Gracie said, a slightly provoking grin bringing a quantum of light back to her eyes.

"We're forgetting someone in all this," he said. "Remember?"

Gracie saw it even before he'd finished saying it. "Father Jerome."

"Damn," Dalton groaned.

"Can you imagine what's going to happen to him if this thing breaks?" Matt asked.

"They'll rip him to shreds," Rydell said.

"But he wasn't in on it," Dalton noted. "You'll make that clear, right?" he asked him.

"It doesn't matter," Matt frowned.

"They'll protect him," Dalton argued. "We can make sure they do. Get him somewhere safe before we go live."

"And after that?" Gracie asked, her voice thick with emotion. "Where's he going to go? His life will be over, and it'll be our doing." She glanced at Matt. "We can't do this," she argued, resolve hardening her voice. "Not without letting him know what's about to happen to him. He needs to be part of this decision. We can't just have it all hit him unprepared." She shifted her focus back to Matt. "I have to see him. Talk to him—before anything happens."

"You saw the news. They flew him back to Darby's place," Rydell reminded her. "You walk in there, Drucker'll make sure you don't come out."

"What if you say you want to interview him, one-on-one?" Danny offered.

"Too dangerous," Rydell grumbled. "Besides, he's got to be the most heavily protected guy on the planet right now."

Gracie glanced over at Matt. He seemed to be processing something. "What?" she asked him.

He turned to Danny. "How much gear is there in that van?" he asked him, hooking a thumb toward the motel's lot.

"What do you mean?"

"I mean, how much of their gear is in there?"

"The full kit," Danny said.

"What about the laser transmitter? It was inside the stadium, wasn't it?"

"One was. We had another with us. For when the sign was all the way out over the roof. It took over then."

Matt nodded. Visibly putting something through its motions in his mind's eye. "And how much smart dust do you have left in there?" He caught Gracie's expression and noticed her posture straightening up.

"I'm not sure. Why?"

"Because we're going to need it. We can't feed Father Jerome to the wolves." Matt glanced around the room. "He was dragged into this, like Danny. And he's a good man, right? As decent as they come—isn't that what you said?" he asked Gracie. "We can't let Drucker ruin his life. Not until he's had his say on the matter." He paused to gauge the others' reaction, then turned to Gracie. "What does Darby's place look like?"

Chapter 79

River Oaks, Houston, Texas

The chaotic scene outside the entrance to Darby's gated community was hardly normal, but at least it was quiet. It was almost five o'clock in the morning, and the gathered masses were down for the night. They slept in their cars, in sleeping bags by the side of the road, anywhere they could. Others were still awake, huddled around makeshift campfires, chatting, milling around expectantly. A small, tireless contingent was still crowding the entrance gatehouse, waiting for their Messiah to make an appearance. Some wailed in pained desperation while others sang spiritual chants of varying origin. A few diehards goaded the wall of security guards and cops who manned the perimeter barricades. The news crews sheltered quietly by their vans and their satellite dishes, taking turns on watch, afraid to miss out on something. All across the neighborhood, whispered prayers wafted through the evergreen trees that lined the drives, mingling with a thin predawn mist that gave the lushly forested area a portentous, expectant feel.

The sign's appearance changed all that.

It took them all by surprise, lighting up the night sky, blazing out of the stygian darkness, pulsating with mysterious, unexplained life as it hovered in place just above the treetops.

It was right there, up close and huge.

And it was right over Darby's house.

The crowd snapped to attention. The believers, the reporters, the cops, the security guards. Even the dogs went manic. Within seconds, everyone was up, on edge, pointing and shouting excitedly. The worshippers were pressing against the barricades, desperate to get closer to it. The cops were scrambling to contain the sudden swell of people. The news cameras were rolling, the field reporters rubbing the tiredness from their eyes and rambling on into their mikes.

Then it started to move.

Drifting, slowly, silently. Floating sideways, away from Darby's house. Gliding over the trees, heading east, over a neighboring house, toward the country club.

And opening a floodgate of pandemonium.

The crowd broke out and went after it. The sudden shift in their momentum caught the cops by surprise and outflanked them. The barricades toppled over, breached by a wave of hysterical believers who streamed through the trees, chasing the shimmering apparition. Police radios crackled sharply and footfalls crunched heavily as the cops and the security guards raced off to try to control the invading horde.

◄◊►

THE COPS PATROLLING THE EDGE of the fairways on the estate's western perimeter saw it too. Their radios squawked to life seconds later. Incoherent bursts of chatter were flying across the airwaves. The six of them, who had been making the rounds in twos, converged by Darby's tennis court to try to make sense of what was going on. They could hear the chaos, an eerie upwelling of noise that subverted the stillness of the night. It was heading away from the house. The rear of the estate, where they were—the part that backed up against the golf course—was calm.

Then one of them saw something. A hint of movement, slipping across the trees at the edge of the fairway. He focused his gaze in that direction and nudged the others to attention. It was hard to see anything in the darkness. The light was coming from behind them, from the porch lights around Darby's garden and pool and, farther away, the sign in the sky. They fanned out a few yards from one another, muscles tensing up slightly, hands resting on their handguns' grips, eyes scanning on high alert. Then another one of them saw something. Looked like two figures, creeping along the far edge of the tennis court, heading toward the house.

"Over there," he hissed, pulling out his handgun and pointing it through tense fingers—then it hit him. It hit them all. A blast of unbearable static, a hissing shriek from hell. It overwhelmed their senses, an anvil punch to their eardrums that shocked them into unconsciousness. A couple of them wet their pants before they even hit the ground.

◄◦►

MATT GLANCED into the darkness behind him. He couldn't see them, but he was grateful that Danny, Dalton, and Rydell were there, manning the LRAD, hiding in the trees by the seventh green, covering their backs. So far, the diversion was working. But it wouldn't last long. They had to be in and out in fifteen minutes or so.

He waited for a couple of seconds to make sure the guards were staying down, then nodded to Gracie and gave her a let's-go gesture, knowing that she wouldn't hear him through the wax plugs shielding her eardrums.

They struck out over the lawn and crept up to the rear façade of the house. Matt spotted two guards walking past the guesthouse and motioned for Gracie to hold position. They both crouched in silence and waited for them to pass, then slipped across to a set of wide French doors. Matt pulled his earplugs out. Gracie followed suit.

"This it?" he asked her in a whisper.

She nodded her confirmation. "Stairway's off to the right. His bedroom's upstairs, first door on the left."

"And the monk's on the ground floor, beyond the stairs?"

Gracie nodded.

He acknowledged it with a tight nod of his own and pulled out his handgun. He'd brought one of the silenced automatics with him, even though he wasn't planning on using it unless things got really desperate. Defending himself against Maddox's goons was one thing. He didn't really have a problem with that. This was different. Gracie had told him that the guys babysitting Father Jerome were cops and private security guards from the estate. They were just doing their job, and he wasn't about to cause them any damage beyond the reparable.

He tried the handle. It was open. He slipped inside. Gracie followed. They waited in a low crouch, by the French doors, listening hard. There was no sound coming from the house. Matt glanced around. They were in the guesthouse's spacious living room. It was lined with bookcases and featured an oversized sofa that faced a big, stone fireplace. It was dark except for a pale glint of light that bounced in from the hallway.

They crossed the room on tenterhooks and slithered up the stairs. Found the first door on the left. Matt tried the handle. It was unlocked. He cracked the door open and slipped through, with Gracie on his heels. Let her in and feathered the door shut behind them. His palm sensed the locking button on its handle, and he pressed it in.

They crossed over to the bed. Father Jerome was fast asleep, breathing in with a slight wheeze. Gracie bent down beside him, glanced hesitantly at Matt, then nudged Father Jerome's shoulder softly. He stirred awake. He turned over, his eyes blinking open. He saw her, inhaled sharply, and pushed himself up.

"What . . . ? Miss Logan . . . ?" He glanced across the room and saw Matt standing by the window, peering out from behind the curtains. "What's going on?"

She flicked on the small lamp by the bed. "We have to be quick. You need to come with us. Your life's in danger," she said, maintaining an even but urgent tone.

"Danger? From what?"

"Please, Father. There's no time. Trust me on this. We have to go now."

He stared at her, his tired face wrinkled with uncertainty. Held her gaze for a brief moment, then nodded and got out of bed. He was wearing dark pajamas.

"I have to get dressed," he told her.

"There's no time. Just put your shoes on," she insisted.

He nodded, and slipped on his socks and lace-up shoes. Matt came over. He put a friendly hand on the old man's shoulder. "My name's Matt Sherwood, Father. Everything's going to be fine. Just stay close to Gracie and try not to make any noise, okay?"

The old priest nodded his readiness, the deepening creases in his forehead betraying his unease. Matt glanced at Gracie. They exchanged tight nods; then Matt opened the door and stepped out.

He didn't see it coming. The strike came flying out from the right, his attacker hugging the wall closely. It nailed him just behind his right ear, a downward blow that had a hard leading edge to it, as if the fist had been balled around a hard stump. It lit up the inside of his skull. Matt thudded heavily to the floor as Gracie screamed at the sight of Brother Ameen moving swiftly out of the shadows and landing a heavy kick on Matt's midsection.

Matt grunted heavily as the kick lifted him off the cool tiles of the hallway. He slammed back against the wall, unsure of where the next blow was coming from, his vision blurred. He sucked in a sharp breath and pushed himself onto his hands and knees in time for another kick to explode across his ribs and send him flying back into the wall. Then the monk was right up against him, his thin, taut arms like steel cables around his neck, choking the life out of him. Matt struggled to suck in some air, but the monk's grip wasn't about to cooperate. The energy was seeping out of him fast. He tried hitting back with his elbows, but they only found air, and every thrash was draining the little strength he had left in him. He tried to fight off the encroaching dizziness and drew on his last reserves to try a rear head butt, snapping his neck back as hard as he could. The monk saw it coming and jerked his head sideways to avoid it, then tightened his hold on Matt even more. Matt felt his throat getting crushed, felt all kinds of cartilage in there popping and tearing and twisting, felt his lungs retching for air. He gasped, struggling to breathe now, his eyes feeling like they were about to pop out of their sockets—

Then he heard a loud shriek and a dull, crashing thud and felt the monk's grip slacken. He sucked in a barrel-load of air and sprung backward, shoving Ameen, and turned to see the monk spinning off him before righting himself and shaking his head back to life. Gracie was standing there, her face locked with surprise and fear, the lamp from the old priest's bedside table now upturned and tightly gripped in her hands, its shade all bent out of shape. She was holding it up like a baseball bat, ready for another swing, her body all tight and curled and hunched like a predator's about to pounce. The monk wasn't cowed and he didn't give her another chance. He swung a lightning arm out and whipped the lamp out of her hands, then brought his arm back with its knuckle out again and caught Gracie on the left temple. The blow landed with a sharp crack. It sent her flying back into the room before she hit the ground hard.

Matt shook some clarity back into his own head and leapt at the monk just as he was turning to face him again. Matt was much bigger and bulkier, but Ameen was a tight coil of hard muscle and knew where and how to hit. They wrestled and punched their way across the hallway; then the monk's fist found Matt's bullet wound. A gush of pain erupted across him, causing a momentary blackout that pulled down his defenses and opened him to a frenzy of sharp jabs. Matt recoiled, his body jerking with each blow as if bullets were drilling through him. He was at the edge of the stairs when he heard Gracie scream his name. A flash of lucidity broke through the encroaching darkness, and he saw the monk's fist racing down at his head for a final, crippling blow. He jerked sideways without thinking, tightened every muscle he could still control, and grabbed the monk's arm, twisting it savagely and spinning it around like it was a spoke on a six-foot wheel. The move caught the monk by surprise and bent him forward, lifting him off his feet as his shoulder tore out of its socket. Matt kept a tight grip on the monk's arm and fed his momentum by twisting it even higher in a circular sweep. The monk's head came down and his feet left the ground as he vaulted over the railing backward and flew into the air, before landing in a heavy, sickening crack at the bottom of the stairs.

Matt creaked his body upright, edged over, and looked down. The monk's body just lay there, slack and silent. Matt glanced back at Gracie. She stepped over to him, closely followed by a shell-shocked Father Jerome. She looked down. Frowned. Then nodded.

"Come on," Matt whispered, his voice hoarse. "We don't have much time left."

They slipped down the stairs, past the Croatian's corpse. There was no need to check for a pulse. The man's head was bent at an angle that precluded life. They threaded their way back out of the living room, past the pool and the tennis court, and skirted the edge of the fairways just as the sign faded out and plunged the neighborhood back into darkness.

By the time they got back to the Lincoln, it was loaded up and waiting for them. They all crammed into it and slipped away, a pregnant silence enshrouding the car as they wondered how the city—and the world—would react to their Christmas surprise.

Chapter 80

Houston, Texas

Maddox blocked out the pain as he watched the ER team deal with his own Christmas surprise. He'd told the admitting nurse he'd had an accident while fixing up his lawn mower. A valid credit card with a high limit had taken care of the rest. The surgeons had been working on him for over three hours, cutting and drilling and screwing and sewing away at his mangled arm while a couple of tubes snaked into him and replenished the blood he'd left among the trees by the stadium.

He'd insisted on only having local anesthesia, deciding he'd had enough unexpected surprises for one night and knowing full well that he could have even managed without it. They'd just about succeeded in saving the arm, but he wouldn't have any use of it for a long time, and even then, the doctors had told him that he'd have very limited use of it. The blades had hacked their way through muscle and tendons with abandon. When all was said and done, his arm would be little more than a decorative limb. His right arm. His good arm. In his simmering anger, he'd been tempted to get it over with and have them shear it off at the elbow, but he'd pulled back from the idea, not wanting to make his appearance even more grotesque than it already was. He'd settle for one working arm. He'd just need to train it to compensate.

Even in his weakened, half-drugged state, he registered the commotion in the hospital as news of the sign's appearance over Reverend Darby's house had spread. The news was troubling. He knew that wasn't part of the plan. Which meant someone was going off piste. He wondered if Drucker was behind it, and if so, what he was doing. He realized things were unraveling from all fronts, but he accepted it stoically and knew better than to let his mind fester on what had gone wrong. He knew he needed to focus on the way forward—on completing the task he'd set for himself and, with a bit of luck, on his own freedom and survival. He knew when the time was right to cut one's losses, when it was better to find a new boat than to keep bailing out a sinking ship. And with Rydell, the Sherwood boys, and that reporter running free, that ship wasn't just sinking; it was about to be torpedoed into smithereens.

He knew what he had to do: push forward, press on, and, worst case, live to fight another day. It was what he was trained for. He thought back to Jackson Drucker and the rest of his men, thought of their chewed-up bodies littering that Iraqi ghost town, thought about how he'd failed them all. But he'd lived and he was fighting on, and he had to keep doing that. And that didn't involve him spending any more time in that ER ward than he had to. Which was why, less than an hour after they'd finished patching him up, he was already outside the hospital and making his way to downtown Houston.

Chapter 81

They were still debriefing Father Jerome by the time dawn finally made its appearance over the western suburb of Houston, all five of them—Matt, Gracie, Rydell, Danny, and Dalton—helping one another out in the difficult task of telling the frail old man how the last twelve months of his life had been one big lie.

They told him about Rydell's original plan. About the smart dust and the launchers and the planet reaching its tipping point. About Drucker's taking hold of it and perverting it to his agenda. Then they got into the more sensitive topic of what Drucker's people had done to him. The treatments. The drugs. The LRAD talking to him up on the top of the mountain. And with every new revelation, with every additional detail, his bony shoulders sagged farther and the creases in his weathered face got deeper.

By the end of it, he looked thoroughly bewildered, but he was holding up better than Gracie had expected. She'd been worried about how he would take it, but he hadn't fallen apart. He'd seen a lot in this life, she reminded herself. Bad things. More than most people could ever imagine. For all his physical frailty, the man seemed to have a remarkable inner strength. And yet . . .

surely, it all had to be devastating, she told herself. Then she remembered his comment on the plane, and wondered what his inner voice had been telling him all along.

"The voice on the mountain," he finally said, looking vaguely into the distance. "It was amazing. Even though it didn't make sense that it could actually be happening to me, it felt so . . . real. Like it was inside my head. Like it knew what I was thinking."

"That's because they put those thoughts in your head in the first place," Gracie told him, her tone careful and soft.

Father Jerome nodded, a sanguine acceptance darkening his face. He sighed heavily, and after a moment, he lifted his gaze toward Rydell. "And you're going to say it was all your idea?"

Rydell nodded.

Father Jerome's brow furrowed with a dubious shrug.

Gracie caught it. Her eyes darted across to Matt, who seemed to catch it too; then she swung back to the priest. "What is it?"

The priest didn't answer. He seemed to be in his own world, processing everything he'd been told, weighed down by it all.

"I'm tired," he finally said in a hollow voice. "I need to rest."

◄◦►

GRACIE AND DALTON retreated to their room, Rydell to his. In the fourth room, Danny and Matt stretched out on their beds, staring at the ceiling, sharing a moment of peaceful reflection. They'd caught the early-morning news on the in-room TV. The top story was, as expected, the sign's appearance over Darby's mansion and the subsequent frenzy, but there was no mention of Father Jerome going missing. So far, they were keeping it quiet.

After a while, Danny asked, "What are you thinking about?"

"Same thing you're thinking about," Matt said.

"Drucker?"

Matt replied by way of a slight grunt.

"It just really gets my goat, you know?" Danny said. "The idea that he might weasel out of this without damage."

"Look, the guy's a dirtbag, no argument. But there's not much we can do, short of putting a bullet through his skull."

Danny didn't answer.

After a beat, Matt asked, quite matter-of-factly, "You want to go put a bullet through his skull?"

Danny tilted his head to one side, gave Matt a maybe look, then stared at the ceiling again. "Not really my style."

"Didn't think so."

"But if Rydell doesn't take care of him in a big way, I might want to reconsider."

"We could grab him and lock him up in my cellar for a couple of years as payback," Matt remarked flatly. "Just feed him dog food and toilet water."

Danny pursed his lips and nodded, mock-mulling it over. "Nice to know we've got options," he said with a smile.

Matt tilted his head over to him. "It's good to have you back, man."

Danny nodded warmly, then turned to stare at the ceiling. "It's good to be back."

◄◦►

In his room, Rydell wasn't staring at any ceiling. He was pacing around, racking his brain, trying to think of another way out. He needed to call Rebecca. He needed to hear her voice. He checked the clock on his cell phone. It was still too early on the West Coast. Especially for Rebecca. That thought brought an inkling of a smile to his face. It also released a tear that trickled down his cheek.

He wiped it off with his sleeve and sat down on the edge of the bed. What an end, he thought. Everything he'd achieved. A true master of the universe, self-made, from nothing. And it was all about to be flushed down the toilet.

He had to talk to Rebecca. He tapped an *R* into his contacts list, pulled up her number. Poised his finger on the call button. But couldn't do it. Not because of the time difference. Because he didn't know what to tell her.

He set the phone back down next to him, felt his eyes filming over, and watched his hands shiver.

◄o►

It was almost noon when Matt stepped out of his room to hit the vending machine again. Gracie was out there too, leaning against the grille of the Navigator, a cold can of Coke in her hand. He downed some coins and pulled out a can of his own. Snapped the lid open, took a long sip, and joined her.

"Can't sleep?" he asked.

"Nope." She smiled. "My body clock's so out of whack I don't even know what day it is."

"It's the day after Christmas," Matt said with a knowing smile.

"Really?" She grinned and looked around. "Not exactly a white one this year, huh?"

Matt nodded. Took another sip. Said, "You should get some rest. You're about to have the most intense few months of your life. Of anyone's life."

"What, even worse than the last few days?" she quipped.

"Oh yeah." He shrugged. "That was a cakewalk."

"Some cakewalk," she said, dreamily. She caught his glance, then looked away, staring through the scenery around them, her mind wandering off.

"What?" he prodded.

She shrugged. After a quiet moment, she said, "It seems like such a waste, don't you think?"

"What?"

"All those people, at the stadium. Around the world. Hanging on his every word. Singing. Praying. Did you ever hear anything like that in your life?"

He didn't reply.

"They were loving it. They loved believing in him. They were lifted by it. I know, it's primitive and it's cultish and it's even a bit creepy, but somehow, some part of me thought it was beautiful. For a moment there, they were all happy. They'd forgotten about their problems and their jobs and their mortgages and everything that was wrong in their lives. They were happy and they were hopeful. He gave them all hope."

"False hope," Matt corrected.

"What's wrong with that?" she asked, as much to herself as to him. "Hope isn't real by definition, is it? It's just a state of mind, right?" She shrugged, falling back to earth. "If it wasn't for all those self-serving leeches using him . . . twisting everything for their own purposes. Using something as beautiful and as inspirational as that to fill their own pockets and grab more power . . ." She looked at him forlornly. "Such a waste, you know?"

"Same old, same old." He shrugged. "It's the way of the world."

She nodded ruefully. Stood there quietly for a moment, then asked, "So what are you going to do? You're part of this story too, you know. People are going to want to hear your side of it."

He cocked his head at her with a pleased look on his face and said, "Good."

"Why?"

"I thought I might get me a ghostwriter," he mused. "Knock out a book about it. Something punchy. Like something that guy who wrote *The Perfect Storm* would write. Maybe flog the movie rights to some studio for a cool mil." He flashed her a grin.

"Yeah, well, get in line, bub," she countered.

He let out a slight chuckle. Turned to look at her. It suddenly occurred to him that she was a great-looking girl. Great-looking and, with all the rest of it, everything any man could ask for. And much as he wanted to put the whole nightmare of the last week behind him, the thought of it keeping them involved in each other's lives for a while longer had taken over as the preferred option.

But they had to get through the tough part first.

"When are you going to hit the button?" he asked her.

Her face tightened at the uncomfortable thought. "I don't know. How about we let everyone out there enjoy a few more hours of peace. Christmas was only yesterday . . ."

"Tomorrow?" he asked.

"Tomorrow." She nodded.

They dunked their empty cans in the trash and trudged back to their rooms. They were outside Father Jerome's door when it cracked open. The old priest was standing there, holding it open, a knot of concentration etched across his forehead.

"I'm sorry. Did we wake you?" Gracie said.

"No," he said. He didn't look like he'd slept at all, and seemed deeply consumed by his thoughts. He studied them for a beat, then said, "Can you get everyone together? I've been thinking about everything that's happened, and . . . We need to talk."

Chapter 82

Houston, Texas

The sky was still as balmy and clear as it had been on the big day itself. A relative calm had reasserted itself over the city, even though the air was still heavy with expectation. There hadn't been any fresh news about Father Jerome in over twenty-four hours, and the city was trying to carry on with life while awaiting the next moment of revelation.

The first people to see the ball of light pulsating over the reflecting pool were the families and couples and joggers who were out enjoying a day in the park. It was small and spherical, maybe twenty feet across, and was hovering innocuously around a couple of hundred feet up over the south end of the long, rectangular ceremonial pool, by the Pioneer Memorial obelisk, at the northern tip of Hermann Park. Curious onlookers gravitated toward it, scanning the grounds around them with wary eyes. They soon spotted the man underneath it, the one in the black cassock and the richly embroidered hood. The light was hovering over him as he walked slowly away from the obelisk.

The onlookers converged on him, calling others over, pointing him out. The park was hugely popular and was surrounded by some of Houston's most beloved attractions: the zoo, the Garden Center, the Museum of Natural Science with its cylindrical butterfly greenhouse, and the iconic Miller Outdoor Theatre. Given the weather and the holiday, there were a lot of people out there, and it didn't take long for most of them to swarm in on the frail old man who was walking innocently along the edge of the tranquil body of water. They spoke to him, greeted him, and threw hesitant questions at him, but he didn't answer or meet their eyes. He just nodded enigmatically and kept ambling quietly, seemingly lost in his thoughts. They kept a respectful distance, staying back a few yards from him. Those who breached that private zone were told off by others and made to pull back. Throughout, Father Jerome kept moving, slowly, until he made his way up the ceremonial steps to the platform that looked down over the pond.

He stopped there and turned, looking out onto the wide-open area before him, framed against the statue of Sam Houston and its monumental arch. The park police were quick to get involved; they reeled in as much backup as they could muster and soon set up a protective cordon around the platform. The news vans rushed over too. Before long, hundreds of people were spread across the grounds of the park, their eyes locked on the tiny figure with the sphere of shimmering light floating above him who just stood there and looked down on them in silence.

Once everything was in place—the crowd, the coverage, the protection—he took a step forward and raised his hands to a wide, welcoming stance. A ripple of sh-sh-sh's rolled over the crowd, and the entire park was shrouded in silence. Even the birds and the branches of the trees seemed to fall into line as any trace of noise seeped away from the ceremonial plaza and was replaced by an ominous stillness.

Father Jerome's eyes traveled slowly across the field of onlookers and back. He then tilted his head up to look at the sphere of light floating over him, nodded thoughtfully, clenched his fists with resolve, and addressed the crowd.

"Friends," he began, "something wonderful has been happening these past few days. Something amazing, something breathtaking and strange and surprising and . . . something I don't quite understand," he confessed. A murmur of surprise coursed through the crowd. "Because the honest truth is . . . I don't know what's happening. I don't know what this is," he said, pointing upward at the hovering ball of light. "I don't know why it's here. I don't know why it chose me. What I do know, though, is that its meaning hasn't been properly understood. Not by others. Certainly not by me. Not until last night. And now I think I do understand. I understand what it's trying to tell us. And I'm here to share that with you."

◄◦►

KEENAN DRUCKER STOOD in his hotel room, openmouthed, staring at the TV screen, wondering what the hell was going on.

He'd been on edge since he'd gotten news of Father Jerome's disappearance from Reverend Darby's mansion, and he'd been worriedly anticipating a quick press blowout from Rydell and his new friends. The fact that it hadn't happened threw him. He'd wondered why they hadn't gone public, what Rydell was up to. And the sight on the screen before him, of Father Jerome walking through a park with a growing horde of followers congregating around him, wasn't making things any clearer.

He heard his suite's doorbell ring, and crossed to see who was there, his mind still in thrall to the events taking place less than a mile away. He checked the peephole and stiffened at the sight that greeted him; then he composed himself and unlocked the door.

"Jesus," he said when he saw Maddox's heavily bandaged arm and his sweaty face. "You didn't tell me it was that bad."

Maddox pushed into the suite, ignoring the comment. "There's a lot of commotion in the lobby. Have you seen what's happening?" He'd barely said it when he saw the live coverage on the TV. He stepped closer to the screen, then turned to Drucker with a suspicious frown. "What are you doing?"

"It's not me," Drucker protested. "I don't know what's going on."

Maddox studied him dubiously. "It's not you?"

"I'm telling you this has nothing to do with me," Drucker insisted. "It's got to be Rydell. He's running things now. They got the priest out last night."

"The sign," Maddox realized, filling in the gaps mentally. "I thought it was something you'd planned. Then I tried Dario's phone and got some cop, and that didn't add up."

"Dario's dead," Drucker confirmed.

Maddox nodded. Things were unraveling even worse than he'd thought. He turned to the screen, his mind processing what he was seeing. "So what's he up to? What are they doing?"

"I don't know. Maybe Rydell's got the others convinced the global-warming message is too important to kill."

"But he knows you can blow it all up for him," Maddox remarked.

"He can also take me down with him," Drucker reminded Maddox, then added, "and you too, in case you forgot. He was the fall guy, remember? Without him, we're out of options." Then his face relaxed with a comforting realization. "They're not going to expose him. They can't. Not yet. Not before they figure out who they're going to pin it on." His face lit up. "Which gives us time. Time to figure out how to expose him without fingering ourselves as his puppet masters. Time to come up with another way out."

Maddox studied him for a beat, then came to a quick conclusion. If he was going to disappear—if he was going to live to fight another day—he had to make sure he didn't leave anyone behind who could ruin things for him. Like a career politician who wouldn't think twice about selling him out to save his own skin.

But what he was seeing brought back to life a far more attractive option. One he thought had been wiped off his playbook.

He pulled out an automatic before Drucker had time to blink and shoved it right up against the man's forehead. "I already have. Sit down."

He herded Drucker backward and into an armchair facing the TV; then in one swift movement, he bent down, grabbed Drucker's shaking hand with his gun hand, and arced it up so the silencer's muzzle was jammed against Drucker's mouth.

Drucker stared at him, terrified and confused.

"Thing is, right from the get-go, I never thought exposing Jerome was a good idea," Maddox told him. "He's much more useful this way. The truth is, we're not out of options here, Keenan. You are." And he pulled the trigger.

The bullet ripped out the back of Drucker's head and sent a gray and burgundy mess splattering across the wall behind him. Maddox placed the gun in Drucker's limp hand, pressed Drucker's fingers tightly against the grip and the trigger, then let it drop as it would have had Drucker been alone.

Swift, Silent, Deadly. It was one hell of a good motto.

He pulled out his cell phone and hit the well-worn speed-dial number. "I think we're back in business. How's our boy?" he asked.

"He's still put, at home," his NSA contact told him. "Watching the live coverage from the park."

"Good. Let me know if he moves. I need him to be home." He glared at the screen, then slipped out the room, already calculating the quickest route to Hermann Park.

Chapter 83

Father Jerome stared at the crowd and hesitated, and felt a shiver spread across his lips and a tremble in his fingers. His forehead went sweaty as other thoughts started rising out of the caverns of his mind, fighting for attention. His eyes strayed, darting left and right nervously, clouded with uncertainty. Then a familiar voice echoed in his ears.

"You're doing great," Gracie told him. "Just keep going. Remember everything we talked about. Think about what you really want to tell these people. Block everything else out and open up your heart to them, Father. We're right behind you."

A ghost of a smile broke across his face, and he cast his gaze over the crowd, a renewed resolve blossoming within him. He bobbed his head in a slight gesture of confirmation, and pressed on.

◄○►

CROUCHED IN THE BACK of the van, Gracie put her binoculars down and turned to address Matt across the big drum of the LRAD.

"This thing's just incredible." She grinned, patting it. "I want one."

"Why not. It *is* Christmastime, right?" Matt said with

an easy smirk. Then his expression tightened and he said, "Let them know I'm going in. And keep your eyes on Father Jerome in case he wobbles again." He popped the door open.

"Good luck." She smiled.

He smiled back and said, "I'll see you in a little while." He pushed his cell phone's earpiece into place and glanced across at Dalton, who was behind the wheel. They exchanged a tight nod; then Matt slipped out of the van and headed for the plaza.

◄o►

ACROSS THE FIELD from the plaza, tucked away behind the Miller Outdoor Theatre, Danny watched the proceedings through another set of binoculars while Rydell liaised with Gracie on the phone. The Navigator was parked nearby, tucked away in the service lot behind the theater, its rear door open. The launch tubes were huddled beside them, now freshly stacked with the last of the smart dust canisters.

"Matt's on his way," Rydell told Danny.

Danny nodded. "Launchers ready?"

"They're all set," Rydell told him. "You sure you had enough time to write the new programs?"

"They'll be fine," Danny said flatly.

Their eyes met. An unspoken anger still festered behind Danny's gaze. Rydell winced and said, "I'll make it up to you. I promise."

Danny shrugged, and said, "Let's make sure we pull this off first," then turned his attention back to Father Jerome. "Ready?"

Rydell nodded. "Ready."

"Let 'em rip."

◄o►

"WE'RE LIVING IN A FRACTURED WORLD," Father Jerome announced. "Others have come before me. Blessed with revelations, with inspirations. With wise and noble thoughts that they tried to share with those around them. To help humanity. To give us food for thought. But all it's done is turn man against man. Their wise and noble words and their selfless deeds have been misinterpreted, twisted, abused . . . hijacked by others for their own glorification. Institutions have been built in their names . . . great big temples of intolerance, each one of them claiming to be the true faith and pitting man against man. Turning their words into instruments of control. Instruments of hate. Instruments of war."

He paused, breathing in short, ragged bursts now, sensing the unease spreading among the crowd. He frowned and redoubled his concentration, pushing the conflicting thoughts back, and said, "We have to try and fix that."

Just then, the sphere of light spread out, growing outward until it dwarfed the piazza below it. The audience gasped, staring in wonderment as the sign pulsed and rippled with life before morphing into the sequence of geometric patterns it had previously displayed—only this time, it ended up settling on a different image. A cross. A large, blazing cross, burning in the sky over Hermann Park.

A loud cheer and shouts of "Praise the Lord" and "Amen" burst through the throng of onlookers as the cross just held there—but their joy was cut short when the sign started morphing again. The crowd gasped once more as the sign seemed to ripple and stretch outward and around before settling into another sign. Not a cross, this time. A star. The Star of David. The crowd flinched with surprise, roiled by the change, confused and scared and caught off-balance—but the sign wasn't done yet. It held that shape, then changed again. It didn't stop. It kept going, shape-shifting into a rotating sequence of symbols associated with other religions—Islam, Hinduism, Buddhism, Bahaism—and kept going, reaching back into history, assuming representations of all kinds of religious movements stretching back through the spider cults of Peru to the sun gods of ancient Egypt and Mesopotamia and all the way back to the very dawn of civilization.

The changes sped up, the symbol spinning from one shape to another, faster and faster, a haphazard and dizzying light show. It sped up until the symbols became almost indistinguishable, the intensity almost blinding—and then, all of a sudden, it just vanished. Just died out. In the blink of an eye, and without any sound or warning, it was just gone.

The crowd went silent, as if they were all robots and someone had hit a MUTE button. The stunned onlookers just stared around at one another, mystified, not knowing what to think—then the sign burst out in its former glory, assuming its familiar pattern, the shape that was first seen over the ice shelf, and just held it and shimmered above the priest's head.

◄◦►

"INTERESTING LIGHT SHOW YOU'RE PUTTING ON," the voice rasped from behind them.

Danny and Rydell turned and froze at the sight of Maddox approaching them from behind. He had a long, black case slung over his shoulder and held a gun in his left hand, his uninjured hand. A curious mix of anger and confusion lined his weary face.

He stepped closer until he was about ten feet away from them and stopped. He guided his gaze above their heads, at the massive sign lighting up the sky a couple of hundred yards farther away, by the monumental arch.

It hadn't been that hard for him to find them. Not for someone who knew what to look for. A vantage point, within a certain range, somewhere where they could work and watch and not be seen. There hadn't been that many options. The third spot on his sweep turned out to be the right one.

"I'm feeling all warm and cuddly inside," he chortled, gesturing for them to raise their hands. "Love and peace and goodwill to all men. Is that what you're selling them?"

"It's working," Rydell told him, glancing across at Danny as he set down his cell phone without killing the line. He raised his hands slightly. "They're listening."

"And you think that's going to make a difference?" His voice rose with his anger. "You think our enemies are going to buy into that horseshit too? Wake the fuck up, Larry. They may be listening, but it's not going to change anything."

"It could. Look, I don't know what you and Keenan have in mind, but I don't want them to stop believing in God," Rydell said, raising his voice and volleying the anger back at Maddox. "I'd just like them to use their own minds a bit more. Just listen to Father Jerome. Listen to what he's saying."

"It's an admirable thought," Maddox said mockingly. "We are the world. We are the children, right? It's great. Everything he's saying out there, it's just great—but you know what it's going to do?" He set his pack down on the ground, reached into it, and pulled out a sniper rifle. "It's going to get him killed."

◄◦►

GRACIE STIFFENED the second the words echoed through the headset of her cell phone.

Maddox was alive—and there. And by the sounds of it, he'd taken them by surprise.

An icy panic stabbed the back of her neck. She turned to Dalton in alarm and said, "I need to call Matt. We've got trouble."

Chapter 84

The crowd was thoroughly rattled and exploded with awe at the appearance of the familiar sign before Father Jerome raised his hands to calm them and his voice burst out, cutting through the confusion.

"Many of us have preached the same message, the only message that counts," he bellowed as they quieted to listen to his words. "A message of humility. And charity. And kindness and compassion. That's all that matters. And yet it hasn't worked. All these religions we've built have been around for hundreds, for thousands of years. And yet the world is angrier and more divided than ever. And we need to do something about that."

—◇—

"MATT." Gracie's voice burst through his earpiece. "It's Maddox. He's got Danny and Rydell."

Matt's feet froze for a beat—he missed one step, maybe two—then he was suddenly weaving through the crowd, hurtling toward the Miller Outdoor Theatre, a tangle of horrific images tumbling through his mind.

—◇—

MADDOX SWUNG THE RIFLE at Rydell and Danny. "As soon as he's done talking, he's going to get his head blown off. We'll make it look like some towelhead nutjob took him out. We've got a bunch of them on watch. 'Cause that's how all good prophets end up, isn't it? They have to die for their cause."

Rydell started to say something, but Maddox cut him off sharply.

He mocked him loudly. "Come on. You can't do these things half-assed. You've got to go all the way. You've got to close the deal. If you really want people to believe his words, if you really want his words to be seared into the minds of all those millions of people out there, he needs to die. He has to. To become a martyr. 'Cause martyrs . . . they're so much harder to ignore, aren't they?"

Danny studied him for a beat, then said, "And after he's dead . . ."

Maddox nodded casually. "Yep. With you both out of the picture, it'll clean things up, nice and tidy. They won't find you. They will find the Iranian whacko who shot Jerome, though. A card-carrying fanatic with a great CV, someone we've been watching for quite a while. He'll have his head blown off, of course. Self-inflicted. One for the team."

"You weren't planning to expose Father Jerome?" Rydell asked.

Maddox shook his head. "Nope."

"But Keenan . . ." Rydell got it. "He didn't know."

Maddox flashed him an icy smile. "Of course not."

"So the Iranians, the Muslim world," Danny said. "They'll get the blame?"

"Of course." Maddox smiled. "Beautiful, isn't it? The prophet who wanted to set us free, shot by an agent of intolerance."

"You'll start a war," Danny blurted. "The people who've bought into Father Jerome—they're going to be mad as hell."

"I'm counting on it," Maddox replied coolly.

Rydell took a step forward. "Think about what you're doing here, Brad—"

"I've thought about it, Larry," Maddox hissed, anger flaring across his face. "I've done nothing but think about it while I've watched us pussyfoot around and let these savages slaughter us. 'Rules of engagement,'" he spat out indignantly. "Geneva Conventions. Senate hearings the minute you try and bitch-slap the truth out of some kamikaze who doesn't think his life's worth anything anyway. We're just too weak. We don't have the balls to get things done. We're playing by the rules against an enemy who knows wars don't have rules. They're laughing at us out there; we're getting our asses handed to us and you know why? Because they get it. They know how to get things done. They know that if someone slaps you, you don't turn the other cheek. You rip their fucking arm off. And the only way we're going to win this thing is to get people really angry, so angry that they'll be baying for blood."

"You'll be dragging millions of innocent people into a war just to punish a few extremists—"

"It's not just a few extremists, Larry. It's all of them. It's the whole fucking region. You weren't out there. You haven't lived among them. You haven't seen the hatred in their eyes. Your 'we are all one' bullshit won't work. We can't live together. It's just not going to happen. There's a fundamental difference between us and them on every level. They know it. We know it. We're just too gutless to face up to it. And they're coming after us. They're not going to give up. Make no mistake—they're our enemies, plain and simple. They want to destroy us. They want to conquer us, and it's not a land grab. It's a holy war. And to win a holy war, you need a crusade. We have to go after them with everything we've got, no holds barred. Once and for all. We need to wipe them off the face of the earth. And the death of your fake prophet will make it happen. It'll be one hell of a call to arms, one that'll be heard around the world." He leveled the gun at them. "So you just keep that sign up there and settle back until he's done. Then we'll finish this."

◄◦►

FATHER JEROME FIXED his eyes fervently on the massed onlookers and jabbed a stern finger in their direction.

"We all pray to the same God," he told them. "That's all that matters. Everything else—all these institutions we've built in His name, all the rituals and public expressions of faith—we created those. We did. Humans, people like you and me. And maybe we were wrong in creating them and giving them the power they have over us. Because God doesn't care about what you eat or what you drink. He doesn't care about how often you pray to Him or what words you use or where you go to do that. He doesn't care who you vote for. He only cares about how you behave toward one another. That's all that matters. He gave you all great minds, minds that have allowed you to achieve great advances. You sent a man to the moon from this very city. That's how clever you are. You can create life in test tubes. You can wipe out the planet with the weapons you keep creating. You hold life and death in your hands, and you are all gods. And like it or not, you control your lives with everything you do, with very action you take. What you do. What you buy. Who you vote for. And you have infinite powers stored inside you. You have minds that allow you to achieve the impossible. Minds that allow you to reason. To talk to one another and debate things openly. And those same minds should be enough to tell you how you should treat one another. Every single one of you knows that. You can see that for yourselves. You know that hurting and killing one another is wrong. You know that sitting idly while others die of starvation is wrong. You know that dumping lethal chemicals in rivers is wrong. Every day, each and every one of you is faced with a choice, and it's how you choose to behave that matters. It's that simple."

◄o►

"ALMOST DONE." Maddox seethed as he watched Father Jerome from their vantage point.

Rydell watched him inch toward the Navigator and prop the rifle on the SUV's side mirror. He turned to Danny.

"Run the debunking software."

"What?" Danny asked.

"Run the damn software," Rydell yelled. "Better to expose him than get him killed and start a war."

"Don't," Maddox growled, spinning the rifle at them—

"Wait," Danny blurted, raising his hands. "Just calm the hell down, all right? I'm not doing anything."

"Danny, listen to me," Rydell urged him. "He can't kill us both. He needs the sign to stay up. Run the goddamn software."

"Don't even try it, Danny boy," Maddox warned. "It doesn't matter to me if the sign dies out right now. It's done all I needed it to do."

Rydell turned to Maddox in exasperation. "Listen to me," he pleaded. "This is good. This can change things. It can make things better for everyone. It'll achieve what you're trying to do without—"

"Enough," Maddox yelled, his voice ripping up the

air like a mortar shell. "You know what, Larry? You're no longer needed here." He raised the gun, three inches maybe, and squeezed the trigger—

—just as Matt tackled him from the side. The bullet flew wide, missing Rydell and ricocheting against the side of the theater as Maddox and Matt fell against the hard ground. Maddox spun around and lashed out with a fierce kick that caught Matt across the chest and winded him.

Matt recoiled in pain as Danny and Rydell rushed Maddox. The soldier scrambled to push himself off the ground, but he forgot his right arm was mangled as if a dingo had been at it and instinctively used it to right himself, causing a torrent of agony to flood through him. He fell back again and glared at Matt as his left hand dived under his jacket. Matt saw the grip of an automatic sticking out from behind Maddox's belt, saw the rifle he'd dropped lying a few feet away, and dived for it.

Maddox's hand had less distance to travel and came up first—but he didn't count on Danny, who was already there and threw his weight against him and shoved him to one side, hard. Maddox flew sideways and landed on his right arm again, and his scream sliced through the empty lot before Matt shut him up permanently with three high-powered rounds to the chest.

◄◊►

"You don't need anyone to tell you what to believe or who to worship," Father Jerome was telling the crowd. "You don't need to follow any set of rituals. You don't need to worry about an angry God not allowing you into heaven. You don't need to march into these great temples of intolerance and be told what is God's inerrant and infallible word, because the simple truth is that nobody really knows that. I don't. All I know is that you're not slaves and you're not part of any grand master plan. If there is a God, and I believe there is one, then you are all God's children. Each and every one of you. You create your own destiny. And you need to accept that responsibility and put aside your egocentricity and stop looking for excuses in tired old myths. You make your own fate every single day. You need to look after one another. You need to look after the land that feeds you and gives you the air you breathe. You need to assume your duty toward all of God's creation. And you need to accept the credit for the good and take the blame for the bad."

He looked across the stunned crowd and smiled. "Enjoy your lives. Look after your loved ones. Help those less fortunate. Make the world a better place for all. And allow me one last humble request. Please don't allow my words to you here today to be used and abused in the same way." He cast his gaze across the onlookers again, shut his eyes, and raised his hands. The sign held there for a moment longer—then it dropped down, slowly, until it engulfed the entire platform around Father Jerome in its dazzling light, obscuring him and his protective ring of cops and park patrolmen from view. The massed audience flinched backward, gasping in horror—then the sign split up and divided itself into smaller balls of light that shot outward, over the crowd, spreading themselves evenly all over them. A horizontal field of hundreds of smaller signs, each no more than three feet across, now hovered over the sea of onlookers, almost within reach of their outstretched hands.

It took a couple of seconds for the first gasp and the first shout to draw the crowd's attention back to the platform at the top of the steps.

The cops and the park patrolmen were looking around in puzzlement. The whole crowd looked on, also bewildered.

Father Jerome was gone.

Chapter 85

Across town, at his mansion in River Oaks, Reverend Nelson Darby glared at his massive TV. His landline was ringing.

Again.

As was his cell phone.

The preachers he'd invited onto the stage with him were clearly watching the live telecast too. And they weren't thrilled either.

He sucked in a deep, angry breath.

Grabbed the big phone unit from the limed oak coffee table in his study.

Ripped its power cord out of the wall.

And hurled it straight through his TV screen.

They all watched the endless replays of the coverage in the executive lounge of the FBO at Hobby Airport with relief. They'd pulled it off, and so far, there was no sign of any vicious reaction, not from anywhere around the world. They all knew they'd opened a huge Pandora's box, opened up a debate that would surely rage on for months and years ahead. But it was an opportunity none of them could resist.

Rydell had booked the FBO for their exclusive use. The plane bringing Rebecca from L.A. was due any minute. It would then take them all to their various destinations: D.C. for Gracie and Dalton; Boston for Rydell, Matt, and Danny. Father Jerome would be Rydell's guest until they figured out how to reintroduce him into public life—if at all.

In the well-stocked lounge, Gracie studied Father Jerome as he watched himself on the TV screen.

"No regrets?" she asked him.

He looked at her with warm, smiling eyes. "None whatsoever. We need this. We need a new level of consciousness to deal with the challenges we're now facing. And who knows? Maybe it'll work."

"You have more faith in human nature than I do, Father," Rydell commented.

"Do I? You created this." He pointed a bony finger at Rydell. "You created something wonderful. And you did it with the best intentions. It was a shame to let it all go to waste, when it could be used to do so much good. And you had to think it would work, or you wouldn't have tried it in the first place. Which tells me you also had some level of faith in mankind heeding its call and doing the right thing, no?"

Rydell smiled, and nodded. "Maybe, Father. And maybe they'll surprise me and listen and take in one tenth of what you said." He paused, then told him, "I owe you my life, Father. Anything you want, just name it."

"I can think of a few places that could use hospitals and orphanages," Father Jerome said casually.

"Just write me up a list," Rydell told him. "It'll be my pleasure."

Gracie gave Father Jerome a soft pat on the shoulder. She looked over at Dalton, who was listening intently as Danny told him all about the technology behind the sign. She wondered if Dalton would bail on her and join Danny and Rydell in geekland, then spotted Matt over by the coffee machine, walked over and joined him.

"So I guess your Hollywood blockbuster's not gonna happen, huh?"

Matt crinkled his face in mock pain. "Nah. Just as well, really. I wouldn't know how to deal with all those groupies." He paused, then added, "Your Woodward and Bernstein moment's also gone up in smoke."

"Thanks for reminding me," she groaned.

Something in her eyes told him it wasn't that much of a lighthearted retort. "You okay?" he asked her.

"I don't know. It just feels weird. Pulling off a big scam like this. It feels a bit, I don't know, condescending. Like we know better." She chortled. "I feel like Jack Nicholson on that stand, remember? Barking out, 'You can't handle the truth.'"

"You're way hotter," he ventured.

It was just the disarming comment she needed. "I sure as hell hope so," she shot back, then beamed a melting smile at him. "But thanks for noticing. Now would you please do me a favor and find something else for us to talk about?"

He studied her smile, basked in it for a moment, then said, "You like classic cars?"

Author's Note

Faith by itself has never caused evil. What causes evil is what people have faith in, how they interpret it and—most of all—a weakness within them that, all too often, makes their faith (against its very definition) waver unless it is shared by everyone around them.

Consider Christianity's beginnings: Few were around to hear Jesus's preachings, far fewer still claimed to have witnessed the Resurrection; the faith spread nevertheless. How, a few centuries later, its sublime and bighearted message would be ignored and countless people would be terrorized in its name, is baffling. What's happening in America today, the growing number of hate-filled, amped-up fanatics who claim they have a God-given right to define their nation and impose their fundamentalist vision on all of its citizens and, ultimately, on the rest of the planet, is no less baffling—or dangerous, all the more so when combined with their collective death wish regarding the supposedly approaching End of Days. The inquisitors only had torture chambers and burning stakes. Today's leaders have rather more potent weaponry at their disposal.

Religion is universal, and its central role in the lives of many as well as its wondrous effects hardly need advertising. It is part of what makes us human. But the combination of religion with that human weakness—with the illnesses of insecurity, intolerance, ignorance, hatred of life, and megalomania—is frightening, and nowhere is that evidenced more than when religion seeps into politics. If history has taught us anything, it's that mixing the two is a very bad idea. It's something the Founding Fathers understood very well. Somehow, too many of us don't seem to share their concerns.

Consider our recent past:

> *"I turn back to your prophets in the Old Testament and the signs foretelling Armageddon, and I find myself wondering if we are the generation that is going to see that come about. I don't know if you have noted any of those prophecies lately, but, believe me, they describe the times we are going through."*
>
> —President Ronald Reagan, speaking in 1983

> *"If people aren't involved in helping godly men in getting elected, then we're going to have a nation of secular laws. That's not what our founding fathers intended and that certainly isn't what God intended. . . . We need to take back this country. . . . And if we don't get involved as Christians, then how could we possibly take it back? If you are not electing Christians, tried and true, under public scrutiny and pressure, if you're not electing Christians, then in essence you are going to legislate sin."*

> *"Florida is key with regard to a shift in this nation, and no doubt these elections in Florida are key as well. That is why there is such spiritual warfare. . . . Father, once again, once again, we'll rejoice with Your son and bring this nation into alignment with*

Your government, with Your Kingdom's principles and authority."

—Katherine Harris, secretary of state of Florida, on why she chose not to allow a recount of the Florida vote despite the numerous charges of election fraud and irregularity, and with Al Gore trailing George W. Bush by only several hundred votes in the contest for Florida's electoral votes, thereby handing Bush the 2000 election

"I recall the election in 2004. Hollywood was against us. The media were against us. The universities were against us. And despite them all, the church of Jesus Christ put George W. Bush back in the White House. We're on the winning side. We are going to win because we have the truth. We have the inerrant word of God."

—Jerry Falwell

"Gog and Magog are at work in the Middle East. . . .The biblical prophecies are being fulfilled. . . . This confrontation is willed by God, who wants to use this conflict to erase his people's enemies before a New Age begins."

—President George W. Bush, in a phone call to French President Jacques Chirac in early 2003 to convince him that Iraq had to be invaded to thwart Gog and Magog, the Bible's satanic agents of the Apocalypse

"Put on the full armor of God so that when the day of evil comes, you may be able to stand your ground."

> *"It is God's will that by doing good you should silence the ignorant talk of foolish men."*
> —Biblical quotes on the March 31, 2003, and April 7, 2003, covers of the Worldwide Intelligence Update, the daily briefing document sent to President George W. Bush by the Pentagon under Donald Rumsfeld. Such quotes were featured routinely on the covers of the documents during the early years of the Iraq war

> *"Yes, I think I will see Jesus come back to earth in my lifetime."*
> —Republican vice presidential nominee Sarah Palin, when asked if she believed in the Rapturist theology of End of Days

Compare that to where we were more than two hundred years ago:

> *"Merely the ravings of a maniac, no more worthy, nor capable of explanation than the incoherences of our own nightly dreams."*
> —Thomas Jefferson, the third president of the United States, writing about the Book of Revelation

> *"The purpose of separation of church and state is to keep forever from these shores the ceaseless strife that has soaked the soil of Europe with blood for centuries."*

> *"I have no doubt that every new example will succeed, as every past one has done, in showing that religion and Government will both exist in greater purity, the less they are mixed together."*

"If Tyranny and Oppression come to this land, it will be in the guise of fighting a foreign enemy."
—James Madison, the fourth president of the United States

Would Jefferson or Madison stand a chance of getting the nomination, let alone winning the election, in the America of the twenty-first century? I wouldn't bet on it.

Acknowledgments

Writing is essentially a solitary effort, and in an effort not to end up typing "All work and no play makes Raymond a dull boy" over and over and looking for the nearest axe, I take every opportunity to pick the brains of my friends and other hapless victims whenever I can muster up a reasonable excuse to call on them. Fortunately, they happen to be a very clever and clear-thinking bunch of people who always manage to find the time to humor me, and for that I'm very grateful to them all. In no particular order, and surely forgetting one or two, my stellar posse on this book included Richard Burston, Bashar Chalabi, Carlos Heneine, Joe and Amanda McManus, Nic Ransome (sorry I couldn't work in the line "He's not the Messiah. He's just a very naughty boy!"), Michael Natan, Alex Finkelstein, Wilf Dinnick, Bruce Crowther, Gavin Hewitt, Jill McGivering, Richard Khuri, Tony Mitchell, and my parents.

Hearty thanks go to my editors Ben Sevier and Jon Wood for their advice and their patience. Your insights were, once again, invaluable to me. Big thanks too to Brian Tart, Claire Zion, Rick Willett, and everyone at Dutton and at NAL, Susan Lamb and everyone at Orion, and Renaud Bombard and Anne Michel and everyone at

Presses de la Cité, for all their hard work and their enthusiasm, and for making it possible for me to hassle all the above-mentioned people for so-called research on a continual basis.

A very special and long-overdue kudos goes to Ray Lundgren and Richard Hasselberger, who as art directors at Dutton were responsible for the iconic covers, starting with *Templar,* that have made such a powerful impact. Ray, that cross with the Manhattan skyline was pure genius. The success of my books owes a lot to the brilliance of your cover designs. Many, many thanks to you both.

Thanks, too, to Lesley Kelley and to Mona Mourad for generously donating to charities and bidding to have characters named on their behalf.

And finally, a big nod of gratitude to my fabulous consiglieres at the William Morris Agency—Eugenie Furniss, Jay Mandel, Tracy Fisher, and Raffaella De Angelis.

Read on for an excerpt
from Raymond Khoury's novel

THE TEMPLAR SALVATION

Coming soon from Dutton

Tess Chaykin's lungs hurt. So did her eyes. And her
back. In fact, there wasn't much of her that didn't
hurt.

How much longer are they going to keep me like this?

She'd lost all sense of time—all sense of anything, for
that matter. She knew her eyes were taped shut. As was her
mouth. Her wrists too, behind her back. And her knees
and ankles. A twenty-first-century mummy of shiny silver
duct tape and—something else too. A soft, thick, padded
cocoon wrapped around her. Like a sleeping bag. She felt it
with her fingers. Yes, that was what it was. A sleeping bag.
Which explained why she was drenched in sweat.

That was just about all she was sure of.

She didn't know where she was. Not exactly, anyway.
She felt like she was in a cramped space. She thought she
might be in the back of a van, or in the trunk of a car.
She wasn't sure of it, but she could hear the distorted,
muffled sounds coming in through the tape around her

ears. From outside. The sounds of a busy street. Cars, motorcycles, scooters rumbling and buzzing past. But something about the sounds jarred her. Something felt out of place, wrong—but she couldn't quite put her finger on it.

She concentrated, trying to ignore the heaviness in her head and break through the fog that was clouding her memory. Vague recollections started to take shape. She remembered being grabbed at gunpoint on the way into town from the dig in Petra, Jordan—all three of them: her, Simmons and the Iranian historian who'd sought them out. . . . What was his name? Sharafi. Behrouz Sharafi. She remembered being thrown into some grotty windowless room. Not long after that, her abductor had made her call Reilly in New York. Then she'd been drugged, injected with something. She could still feel the prick in her arm. And that was it, the last thing she remembered—how long ago was it now? She had no idea. Hours. A whole day, maybe? More?

No idea.

Tess hated being in here. It was hot and cramped and dark and hard and smelled of, well, car trunks. Not like the trunk of some scuzzy old car that had all kinds of stinky residue wafting around. This car, if it was one, was clearly new—but still unpleasant.

Her spirits sank the more she thought about her predicament. If she was in the trunk of a car, and if she could hear noises outside . . . maybe she was on a public road. A sense of panic swelled up inside her.

What if I've just been dumped here, just left to rot?

What if no one ever realizes I'm in here?

A vein in her neck started throbbing, the duct tape around her ears turning them into echo chambers. Her mind raced wildly, spurred by the maddening internal drumbeat, wondering about how much air there was in there, how long she could survive without water or food, whether the tape might make her choke. She began to picture an agonizingly slow and horrific death, shriveling up from thirst and hunger and heat, just wasting away in a dark box as if she'd been buried alive.

The fear hit her like a bucket of ice water. She had to do something. She tried twisting around to change position, maybe get some leverage to try to kick up against the lid of the trunk or whatever the hell it was she was in—but she couldn't move. Something was holding her down. She was pinned down, strapped into place by some kind of restraint that she could now feel was tugging against her shoulders and her knees.

She couldn't move at all.

She stopped fighting against the ties and settled back, heaving a ragged sigh that echoed in her ears. Tears welled up in her eyes as the notion of death solidified around her. The beaming face of her thirteen-year-old daughter, Kim, broke through her despair and drifted into her consciousness, beckoning her. She imagined Kim back in Arizona, enjoying the summer at the ranch of Tess's older sister, Hazel. Another face glided into the picture, that of her mother, Eileen, who was also there with them. Then their faces dissipated, and a cold and hollow feeling grew in her gut, the anger and remorse over leaving New York and coming out here, to the Jordanian desert, all those weeks ago. The summer dig with Simmons—a contact of her old friend Clive Edmondson and one of the leading Templar experts around—seemed like a good idea at the time, giving her the space she needed to think things through.

And now this.

Her regrets swooped across all kinds of dark territories before settling on another face: Reilly's. She felt sick with guilt, wondering what she'd led him into by making that call, wondering whether he was safe—and whether he'd ever find her. The thought triggered a spark of hope. She wanted to believe he would. But the spark died out as quickly as it appeared. She knew she was kidding herself. He was a couple of continents away. Even if he tried—and she knew he would—he'd be out of his element, a stranger in a strange land. It wasn't going to happen.

I can't believe I'm going to die like this.

A faint noise intruded—like everything else, annoyingly muffled, as if to torture her further. But she could tell that it was a siren. A police car or an ambulance. It grew louder, raising her hopes with it—then it faded away. It rattled her for another reason. It was a distinctive sound—all countries seemed to have their own signature sirens on their emergency vehicles. But something about this siren didn't feel right. She couldn't be sure of it, but she'd heard ambulance and police sirens during her spell in Jordan, and this one sounded different. Very different.

It was a sound she'd definitely heard before, but not in Jordan.

A ripple of fear swept across her.

Where the hell am I?

Vatican City

As he strode across the San Damaso courtyard, Sean Reilly cast a weary glance at the clusters of wide-eyed tourists exploring the Holy See, and wondered if he'd ever get to visit the place with their casual abandon.

This was anything but casual.

He wasn't there to admire the sublime architecture or

the exquisite works of art, nor was he there on any spiritual pilgrimage.

He was there to try to save Tess's life.

And if he was in any way wide-eyed, it was to try to keep his jet lag and his lack of sleep at bay and stay clearheaded enough to try to make sense of a frantic crisis that had been thrust upon him less than twenty-four hours earlier. A crisis he didn't fully understand—but needed to.

Reilly didn't trust the man walking alongside him—Behrouz Sharafi—but he didn't have much choice. Right now all he could do was run through yet another mental grind of the information he had, from Tess's desperate phone call to the Iranian professor's harrowing firsthand account during the cab ride in from the airport. Reilly had to make sure he wasn't missing anything—not that he had that much to go on. Some Iranian psycho was forcing Sharafi to find something for him. He'd chopped off some woman's head to show him how serious he was. And that same whack job was now holding Tess hostage to get Reilly to play ball. Reilly hated being in that position—reactive, not proactive—though as the FBI special agent in charge heading up the New York City field office's domestic terrorism unit, he had ample training and experience in reacting to crises, but they usually didn't involve someone he loved.

The cardinal's secretary was waiting for them outside the porticoed building, sweating under the heat of the August sun. He led them inside, and as they walked down the cool, stone-flagged corridors and climbed up the grand marble staircases, Reilly found it hard to chase away the uncomfortable memories of his previous visit to this hallowed ground and the disturbing sound bites of a conversation that had never left his consciousness. The memories came flooding back even more viscerally as the secretary pushed through the oversized, intricately carved oak door and brought the two visitors into the presence of Cardinal Mauro Brugnone, Reilly's Vatican connection and, it seemed, the reason behind Tess's abduction.

The cardinal—still as husky and vigorous as Reilly remembered him from his previous visit there, three years earlier—came forward to greet him with outstretched arms.

"I've been looking forward to hearing from you again, Agent Reilly," the cardinal said with a bittersweet expression clouding his face, "though I was hoping it would be under happier circumstances."

Reilly embraced him courteously. "Same here, Your Eminence. And thank you for seeing us on such short notice."

Reilly introduced the Iranian professor, and the cardinal's secretary did the same for the two other men in the room: Monsignor Francesco Bescondi, the prefect of the Vatican Secret Archives—a slight man with thinning fair hair and a tightly cropped goatee; and Gianni Delpiero, the inspector general of the *Corpo Della Gendarmeria*, the Vatican's police force—a broader, more substantial man with a solid brush of black hair and hard, angular features. Reilly tried not to show any discomfort at the fact that the Vatican cop had been asked to join them. He shook the man's hand with a cordial half smile, accepting that he should have expected it, given his urgent request for an audience—and given the agency for which he worked.

"What can we do for you, Agent Reilly?" the cardinal asked, ushering them into the plush armchairs by the fireplace. "You said you'd explain when you got here."

Reilly hadn't had much time to think about how he would play this, but the one thing he did know was that he couldn't tell them everything. Not if he wanted to make sure they'd agree to his request.

"We've got a delicate security situation," he informed

his host. "I need your help, but I also need your indulgence in not asking me for more information than I can give you at this moment. All I can tell you is that lives are at stake."

Brugnone exchanged an unsettled look with his Vatican colleagues. "Tell us what you need, Agent Reilly."

"Professor Sharafi here needs some information. Information that, he believes, he can only find in your records."

The Iranian adjusted his glasses, and nodded.

The cardinal studied Reilly, clearly discomfited by his words. "What kind of information?"

Reilly leaned forward. "We need to consult a specific fond in the archive of the Congregation for the Doctrine of the Faith."

The men shifted uncomfortably in their seats. Reilly's request for help was looking less benign by the second. Contrary to popular belief, there was nothing particularly secretive about the Vatican Secret Archives; the word "secret" was only meant in the context of it being part of the popes' personal "secretariat," his *private* papers. The archive Reilly needed access to, however, the *Archivio Congregatio pro Doctrina Fidei*—the archive of the Inquisition—was something else altogether. It held the Vatican archives' most sensitive documents, including all the files related to heresy trials and book bannings. Access to its shelves was carefully restricted, to keep scandalmongers at bay. The events its *fondi* covered—a "fond" being a body of records that dealt with a specific issue—were hardly the papacy's finest hour.

"Which fond would that be?" the cardinal asked.

"The *Fondo Scandella*," Reilly answered flatly.

His hosts seemed momentarily confused, then relaxed at the mention. Domenico Scandella was a relatively insignificant sixteenth-century miller who couldn't keep his mouth shut. His ideas about the origins of the universe were deemed heretical, and he was burned at the stake. What Reilly and his Iranian companion could want from the transcripts of his trial didn't raise any alarms. It was a harmless request.

The cardinal studied Reilly, a perplexed expression lining his face. "That's all you need?"

Reilly nodded. "That's it."

The cardinal glanced at the other two Vatican officials. They shrugged with indifference.

Reilly knew they were in.

Now came the hard part.

◄◊►

BESCONDI AND DELPIERO accompanied Reilly and his Iranian companion across the Belvedere courtyard to the entrance of the Apostolic Library, where the archives were housed.

"I have to admit," the prefect of the archives confessed with a nervous chortle, "I feared you were after something that would be more difficult to . . . *honor*."

"Like what?" Reilly asked, playing along.

Bescondi's face clouded as he searched for the least compromising answer. "Lucia Dos Santos's prophecies, for instance. You're familiar with her, yes? The seer of Fatima?"

"Actually, now that you mention it..." Reilly let the words drift, then flashed him a slight grin.

The priest let out a small chuckle and nodded with relief. "Cardinal Brugnone told me you were to be trusted. I don't know what I was worried about."

The words bounced uncomfortably inside Reilly's conscience as the men stopped at the entrance of the building. Delpiero, the inspector general, excused himself, given that he didn't seem to be needed.

"Anything I can do to help, Agent Reilly," the cop offered, "just let me know." Reilly thanked him, and Delpiero walked off.

The three halls of the library, resplendent with ornate inlaid paneling and vividly colored frescoes that depicted the donations to the Vatican by various European sovereigns, were unnervingly quiet. Scholars, priests from various nations and other academics with impeccable credentials glided across the marble floors on their way to or from the tranquillity of the reading rooms. Bescondi led the two outsiders to a grand spiral staircase that burrowed down to the basement level. They ambled past a couple junior archivists, who gave the prefect small, respectful bows, and reached an airy reception area where a Swiss Guard in a sober dark blue uniform and black beret sat behind a counter-type desk. The guard signed them in, and five taps into the security keypad later, the inner sliding door of the air lock was whishing shut behind them, and they were in the archive's inner sanctum.

"The *fondi* are arranged alphabetically," Bescondi said as he pointed out the small, elegantly scripted nameplates on the shelves and got his bearings. "Let's see. Scandella should be down this way."

Reilly and the Iranian followed him deeper into the large, low-ceilinged crypt. Apart from the sharp clicks of their heels against the stone floor, the only noise in there was the constant low hum of the air-management system that regulated the room's oxygen level and kept harmful bacteria at bay. The long rows of shelves were packed tight with scrolls and leather-bound codices interspersed with more recent books and cardboard box files. Entire rows of ancient manuscripts were suffocating under blankets of dust, as in some cases no one had touched or consulted them for decades—if not centuries.

"Here we are," their host said as he pointed out a box file on a low shelf.

Reilly glanced back, toward the archives' entrance. They were alone. He nodded his appreciation at the priest, then said, "Actually, we really to see another fond."

Bescondi blinked at him, confused. "Another fond? I don't understand."

"I'm sorry, Father, but—I couldn't risk you and the cardinal not allowing us down here. And it's imperative that we get access to the information we need."

"But," the archivist stammered, "you didn't mention this before, and . . . I'd need His Eminence to authorize showing you any other—"

"Father, please," Reilly interrupted him. "We need to see it."

Bescondi swallowed hard. "Which fond is it?"

"The Fondo Templari."

The archivist's eyes widened and did a quick dart to the left, farther down the aisle they were standing in, and back. He raised his hands in objection and stumbled back. "I'm sorry. That's not possible, not without getting His Eminence's approval—"

"Father—"

"No, it's not possible. I can't allow it, not before discussing it with—"

He took another step back and edged sideways, in the direction of the entrance.

Reilly had to act.

He reached out, blocking the priest with one arm—

"I'm sorry, Father—"

—while the other dove into his jacket's side pocket and pulled out a small canister of mouth freshener, swung it right up to the archivist's startled face and pumped a cloud of spray right at him. The man stared at Reilly with wide, terrified eyes as the mist swirled around his head—

then he coughed twice before his legs just collapsed under him. Reilly caught him as he fell and set him down gently on the hard floor.

The colorless, odorless liquid wasn't mouth freshener.

And if the archivist wasn't going to die from it, Reilly needed to do something else—fast.

He reached into another pocket and pulled out a small ceramic syringe, yanked its cap off, and plunged it into a throbbing vein in the man's forearm. He checked his pulse and waited till he was sure the opioid antagonist had done its job. Without it, the Fentanyl—a fast-acting, incapacitating opiate that was part of the bureau's small and unpublicized arsenal of nonlethal weapons—could send the prefect into a coma, or, as in the tragic case of more than a hundred hostages in a Moscow theater a few years back, it could kill him. A quick chaser of Naloxone was crucial to make sure the archivist kept breathing—which he now was.

Reilly stayed with him long enough to confirm the drug's effect, countering the caustic discomfort he felt at what he had just done to their unsuspecting host by thinking of Tess and what Sharafi had told him her abductor had done to the schoolteacher. Feeling the archivist's breathing had stabilized, he nodded. "We're clear."

The Iranian pointed down the aisle. "He looked that way when you mentioned the fond. Which fits. 'T' is the next letter."

"We've got around twenty minutes before he wakes up, maybe less," Reilly told him as he stalked down the aisle. "Let's make them count."